POKÉMON™

ADVENTURES

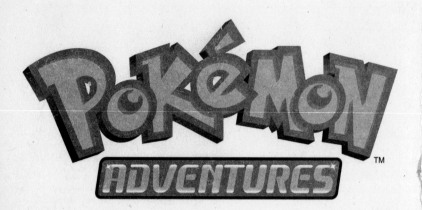

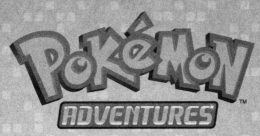

Pokémon ADVENTURES
Volume 5
Perfect Square Edition

Story by **HIDENORI KUSAKA**
Art by **MATO**

© 2010 The Pokémon Company International.
© 1995-2010 Nintendo/Creatures Inc./GAME FREAK inc.
TM, ®, and character names are trademarks of Nintendo.
POCKET MONSTERS SPECIAL Vol. 5
by Hidenori KUSAKA, MATO
© 1997 Hidenori KUSAKA, MATO
All rights reserved.
Original Japanese edition published by SHOGAKUKAN.
English translation rights in the United States of America, Canada, the
United Kingdom and Ireland arranged with SHOGAKUKAN.

English Adaptation/Gerard Jones
Translation/Kaori Inoue
Miscellaneous Text Adaptation/Ben Costa
Touch-up & Lettering/Annaliese Christman
Design/Sam Elzway
Editor, 1st Edition/William Flanagan
Editor, Perfect Square Edition/Jann Jones

Printed in the U.S.A.

Published by VIZ Media, LLC
P.O. Box 77010
San Francisco, CA 94107

11
First printing, February 2010
Eleventh printing, December 2016

  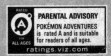

PERFECT SQUARE
www.perfectsquare.com

VIZ
MEDIA
www.viz.com

POKéMON™ ADVENTURES

5
VOLUME FIVE

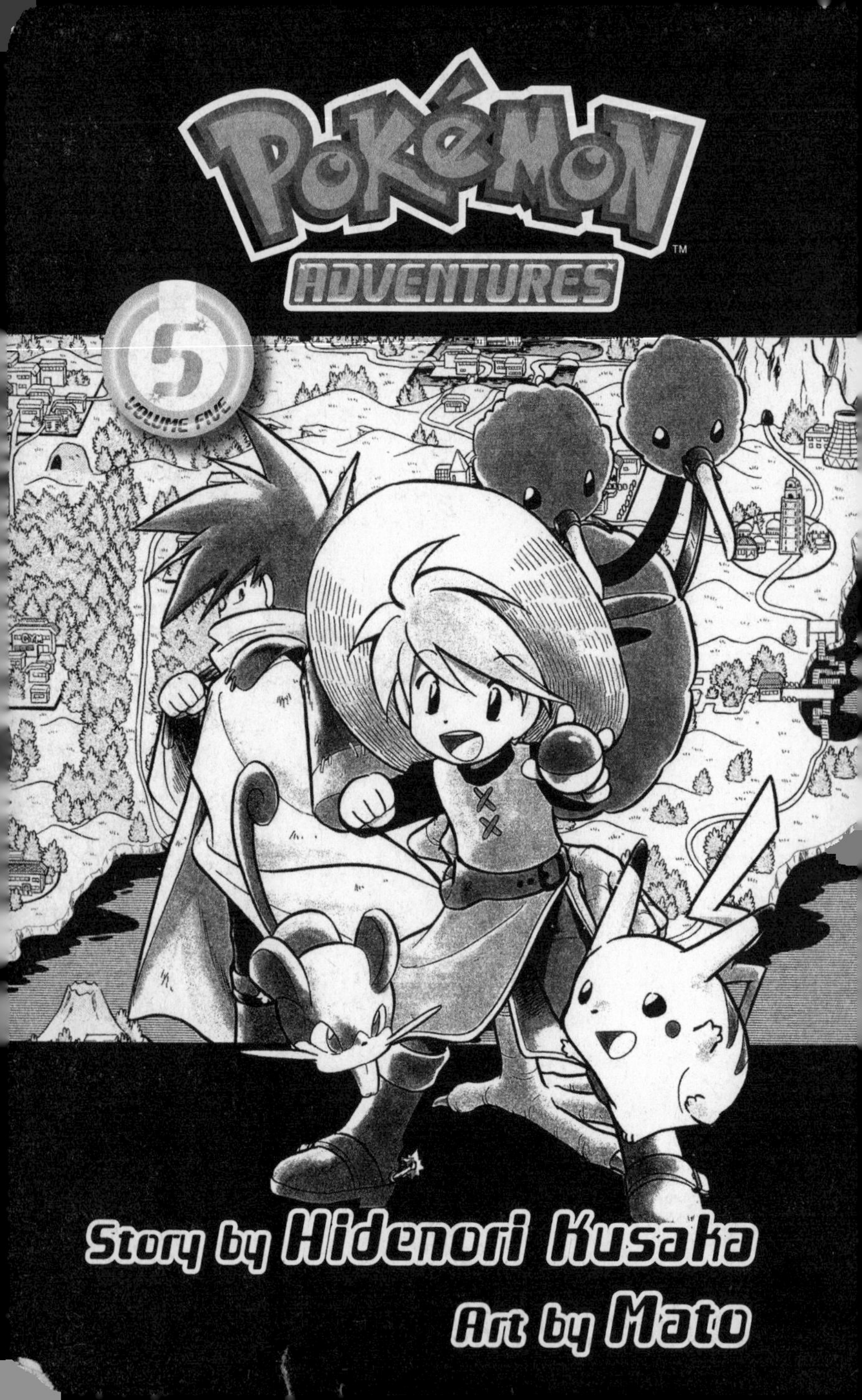

Story by Hidenori Kusaka

Art by Mato

CHARACTERS
THUS FAR...

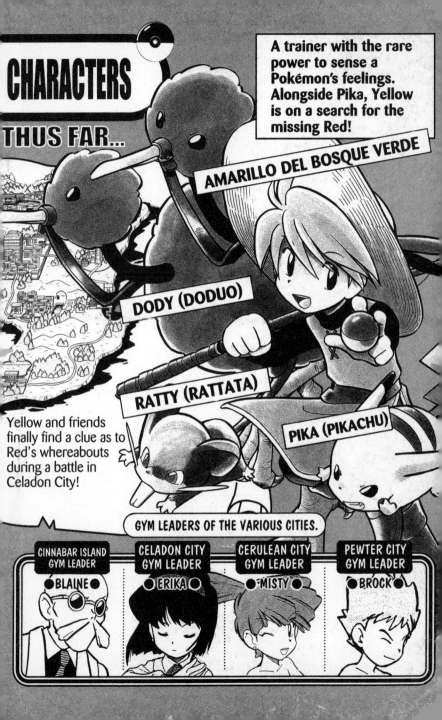

A trainer with the rare power to sense a Pokémon's feelings. Alongside Pika, Yellow is on a search for the missing Red!

AMARILLO DEL BOSQUE VERDE

DODY (DODUO)

RATTY (RATTATA)

PIKA (PIKACHU)

Yellow and friends finally find a clue as to Red's whereabouts during a battle in Celadon City!

GYM LEADERS OF THE VARIOUS CITIES.

CINNABAR ISLAND GYM LEADER	CELADON CITY GYM LEADER	CERULEAN CITY GYM LEADER	PEWTER CITY GYM LEADER
●BLAINE●	●ERIKA●	●MISTY●	●BROCK●

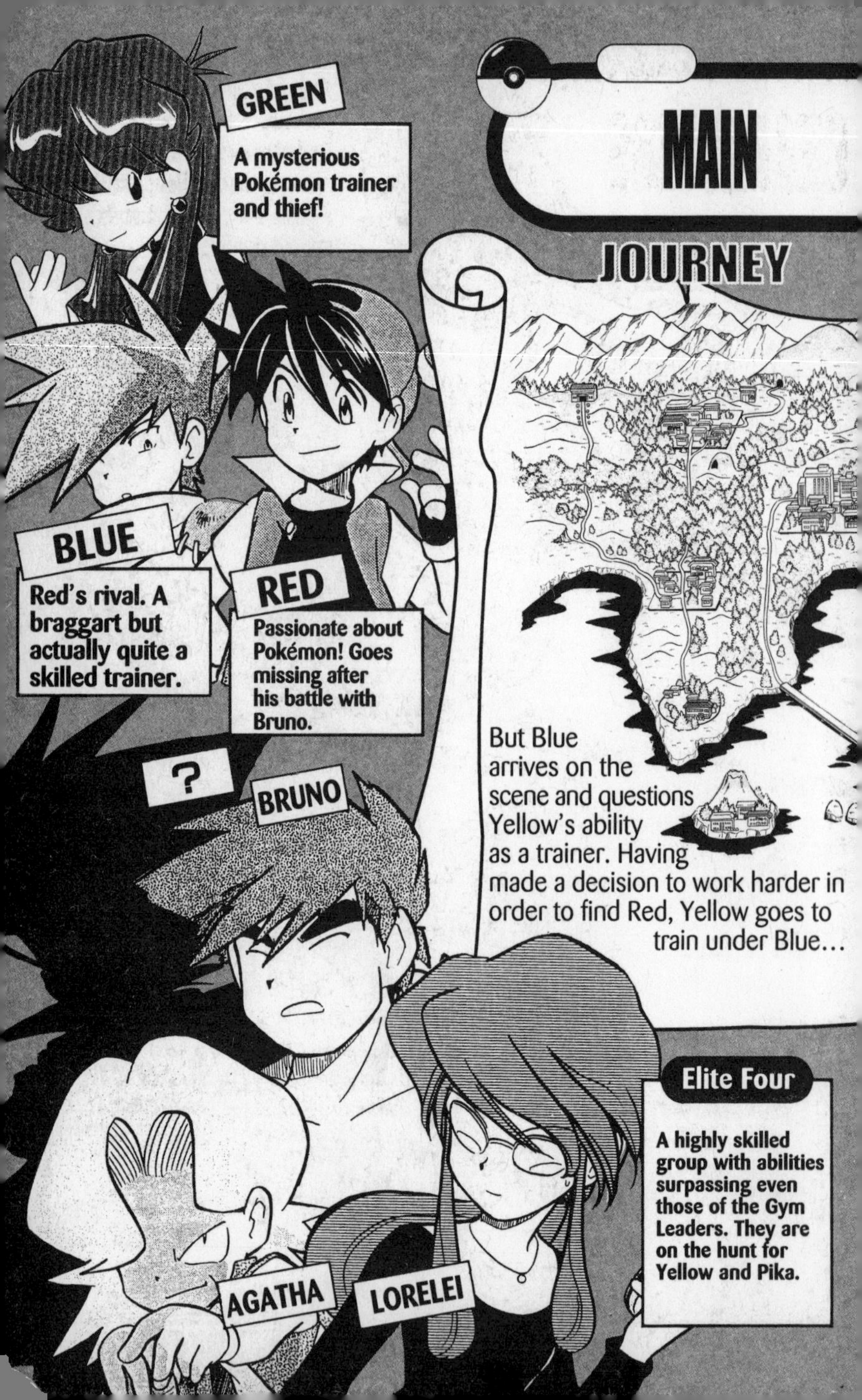
MAIN
JOURNEY
But Blue arrives on the scene and questions Yellow's ability as a trainer. Having made a decision to work harder in order to find Red, Yellow goes to train under Blue…
GREEN
A mysterious Pokémon trainer and thief!
RED
Passionate about Pokémon! Goes missing after his battle with Bruno.
BLUE
Red's rival. A braggart but actually quite a skilled trainer.
?
BRUNO
Elite Four
A highly skilled group with abilities surpassing even those of the Gym Leaders. They are on the hunt for Yellow and Pika.
LORELEI
AGATHA

CONTENTS

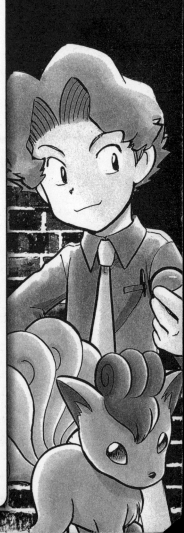

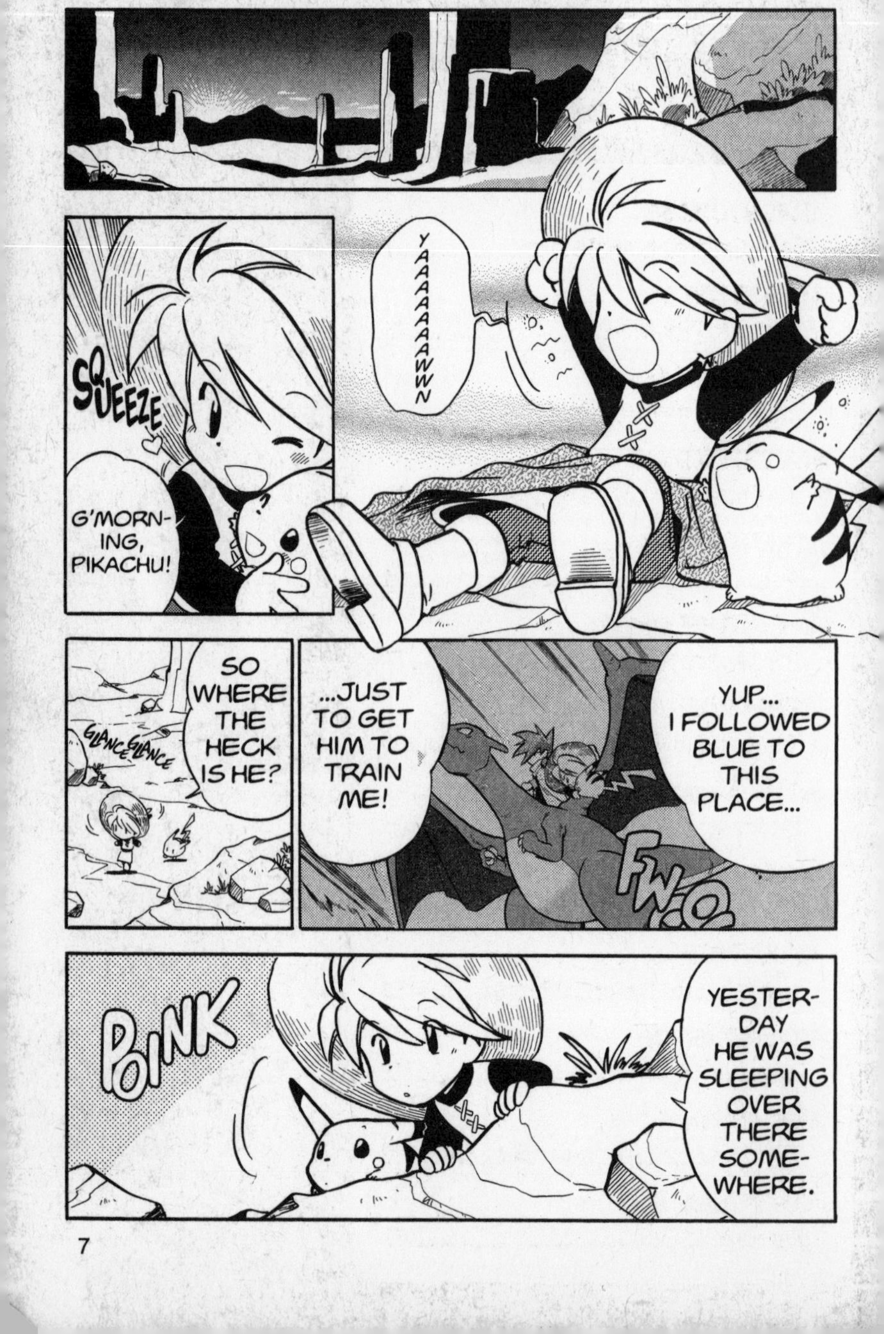
YAAAAAAAAWN
SQUEEZE
G'MORN-ING, PIKACHU!
YUP... I FOLLOWED BLUE TO THIS PLACE...
FWOO
...JUST TO GET HIM TO TRAIN ME!
SO WHERE THE HECK IS HE?
GLANCE GLANCE
YESTER-DAY HE WAS SLEEPING OVER THERE SOME-WHERE.
POINK

53 Can't Catch Caterpie!

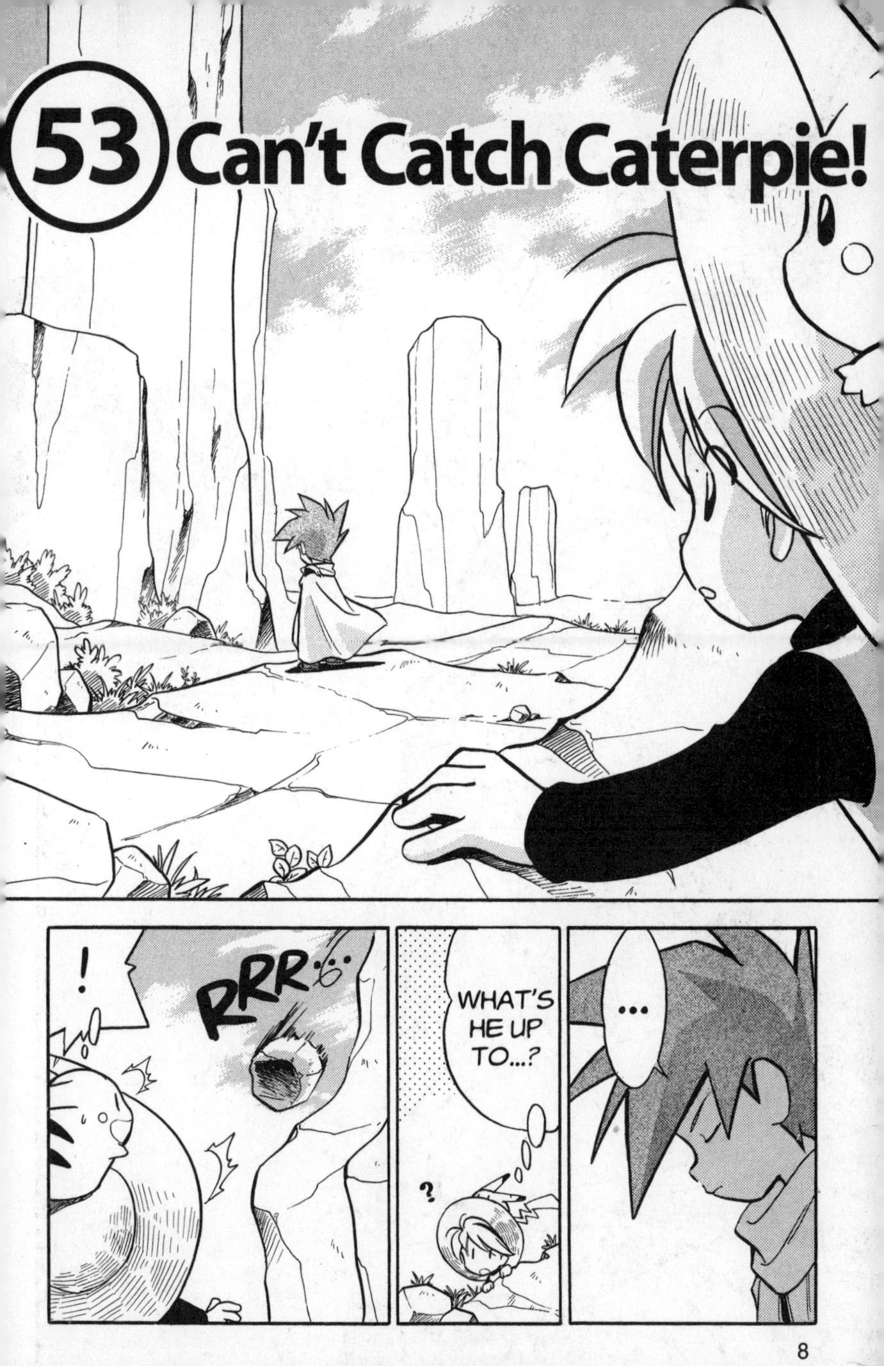

...
WHAT'S HE UP TO...?
?
!
RRR

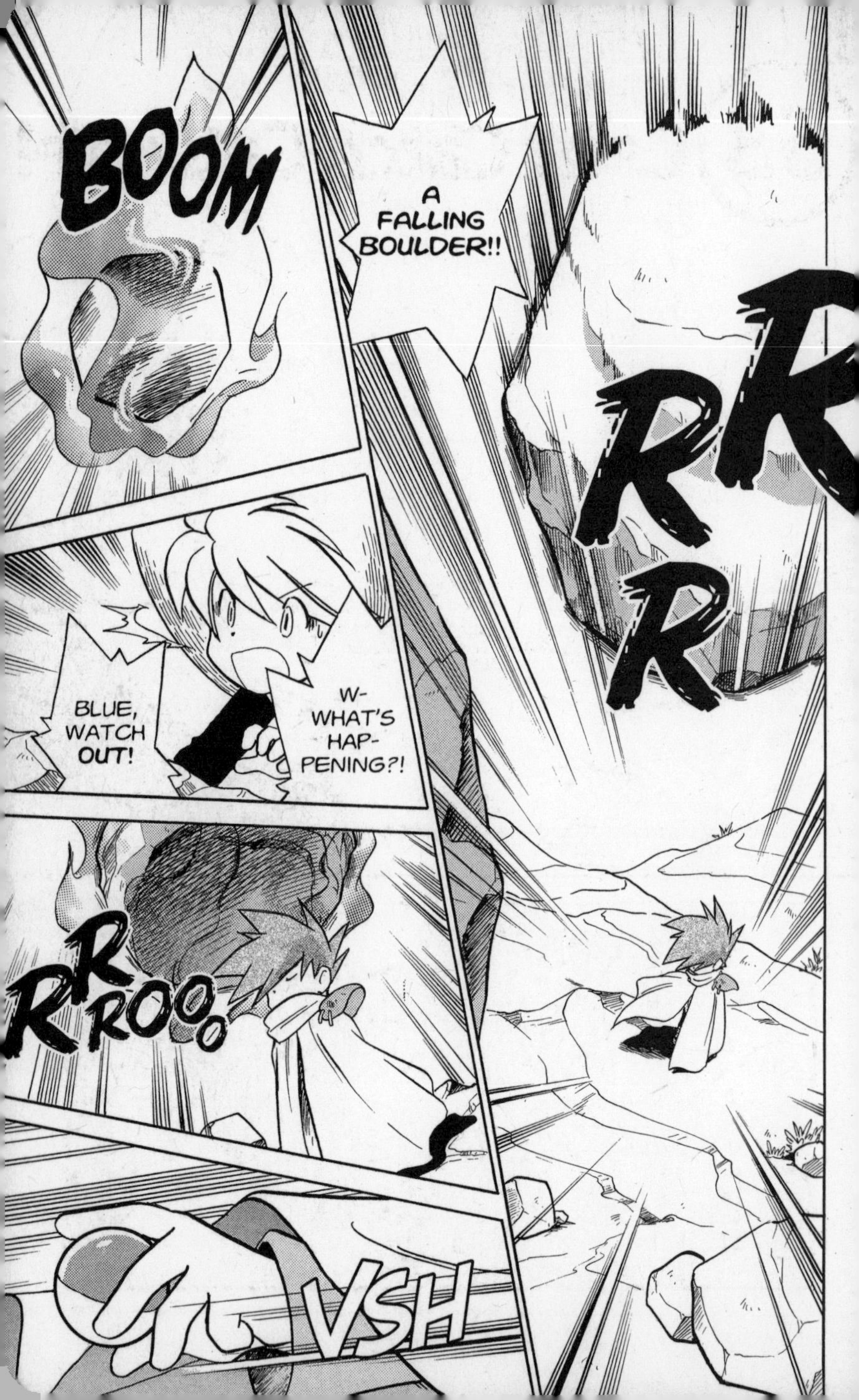
A FALLING BOULDER!!
RRR
BOOM
W-WHAT'S HAPPENING?!
BLUE, WATCH OUT!
RRRROOOO
VSH

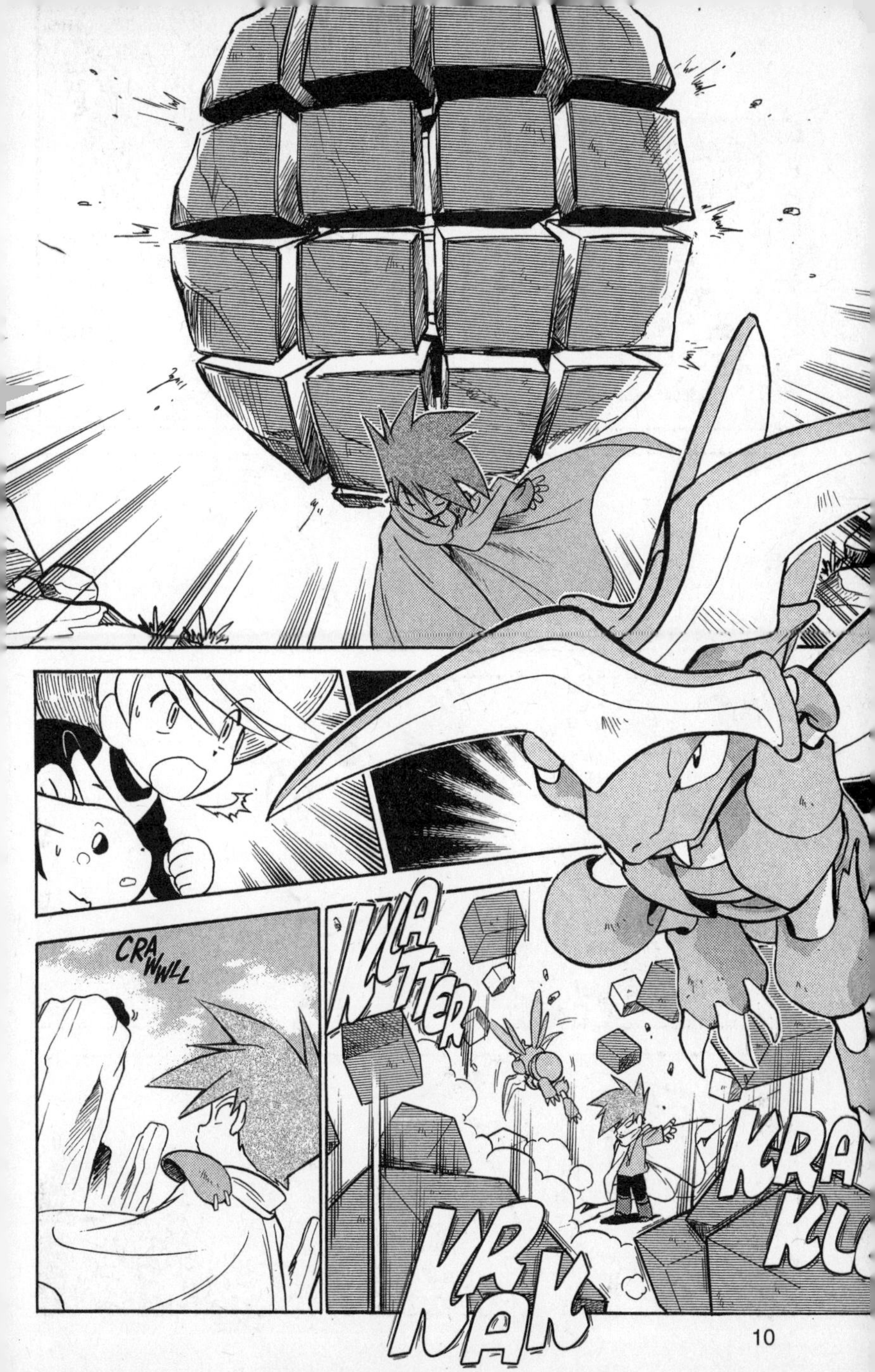
KLATTER
KRA KL
KRAK
CRAWWLL

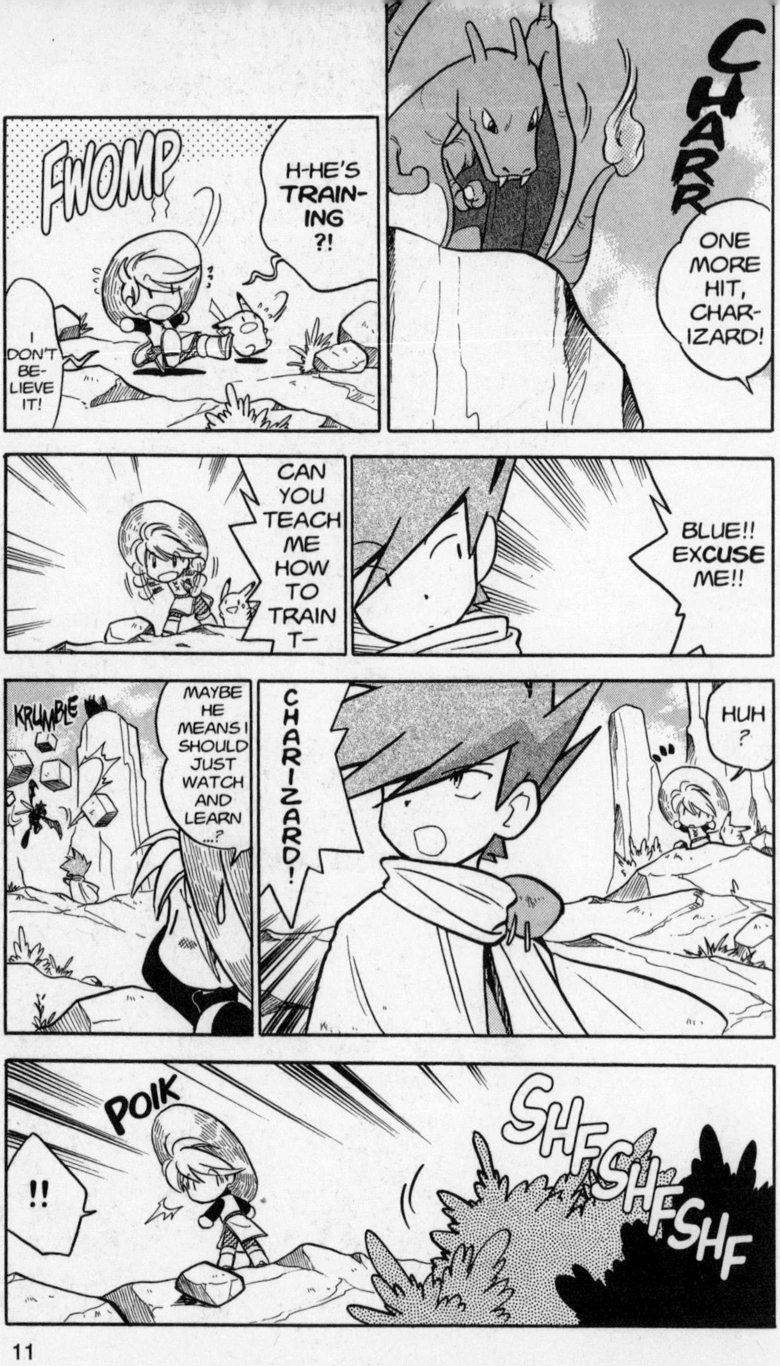
CHARR
ONE MORE HIT, CHARIZARD!
FWOMP
H-HE'S TRAINING?!
I DON'T BELIEVE IT!
BLUE!! EXCUSE ME!!
CAN YOU TEACH ME HOW TO TRAIN T—
HUH?
CHARIZARD!
MAYBE HE MEANS I SHOULD JUST WATCH AND LEARN...?
KRUMBLE
SHFSHFSHF
POIK
!!

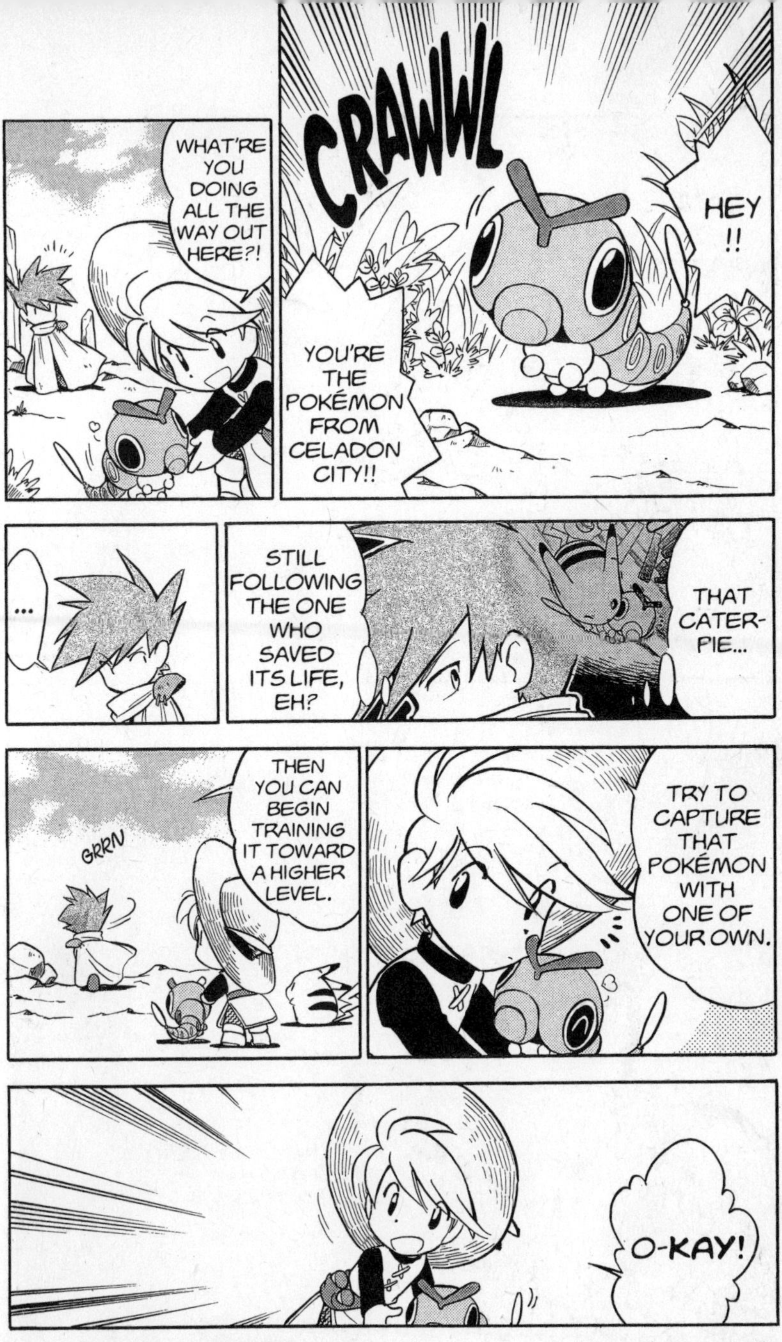

CRAWWL
HEY !!
YOU'RE THE POKÉMON FROM CELADON CITY!!
WHAT'RE YOU DOING ALL THE WAY OUT HERE?!
THAT CATERPIE...
STILL FOLLOWING THE ONE WHO SAVED ITS LIFE, EH?
...
TRY TO CAPTURE THAT POKÉMON WITH ONE OF YOUR OWN.
THEN YOU CAN BEGIN TRAINING IT TOWARD A HIGHER LEVEL.
GRRN
O-KAY!

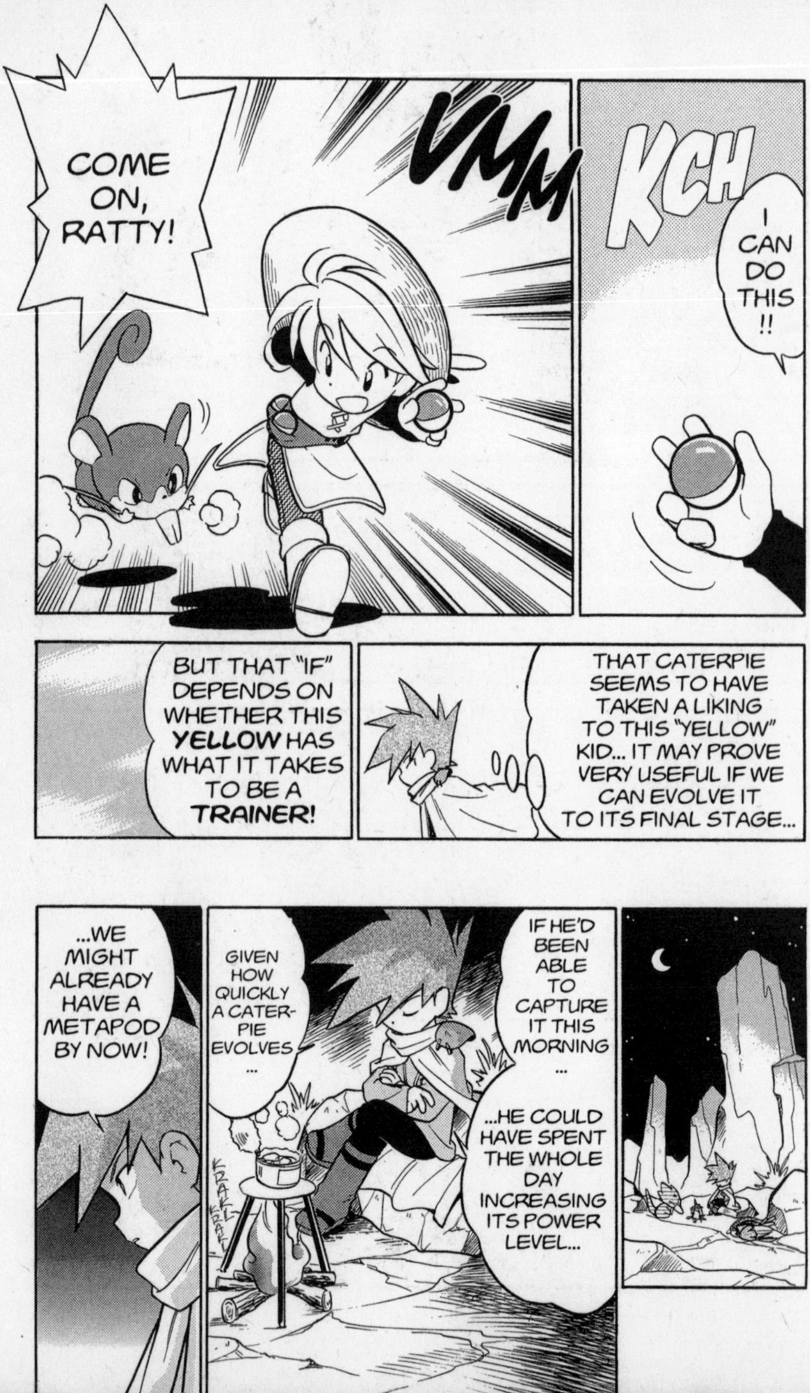
KCH
I CAN DO THIS!!
VMM
COME ON, RATTY!
THAT CATERPIE SEEMS TO HAVE TAKEN A LIKING TO THIS "YELLOW" KID... IT MAY PROVE VERY USEFUL IF WE CAN EVOLVE IT TO ITS FINAL STAGE...
BUT THAT "IF" DEPENDS ON WHETHER THIS **YELLOW** HAS WHAT IT TAKES TO BE A **TRAINER!**
IF HE'D BEEN ABLE TO CAPTURE IT THIS MORNING...
...HE COULD HAVE SPENT THE WHOLE DAY INCREASING ITS POWER LEVEL...
GIVEN HOW QUICKLY A CATERPIE EVOLVES...
KRAK KRAK
...WE MIGHT ALREADY HAVE A METAPOD BY NOW!

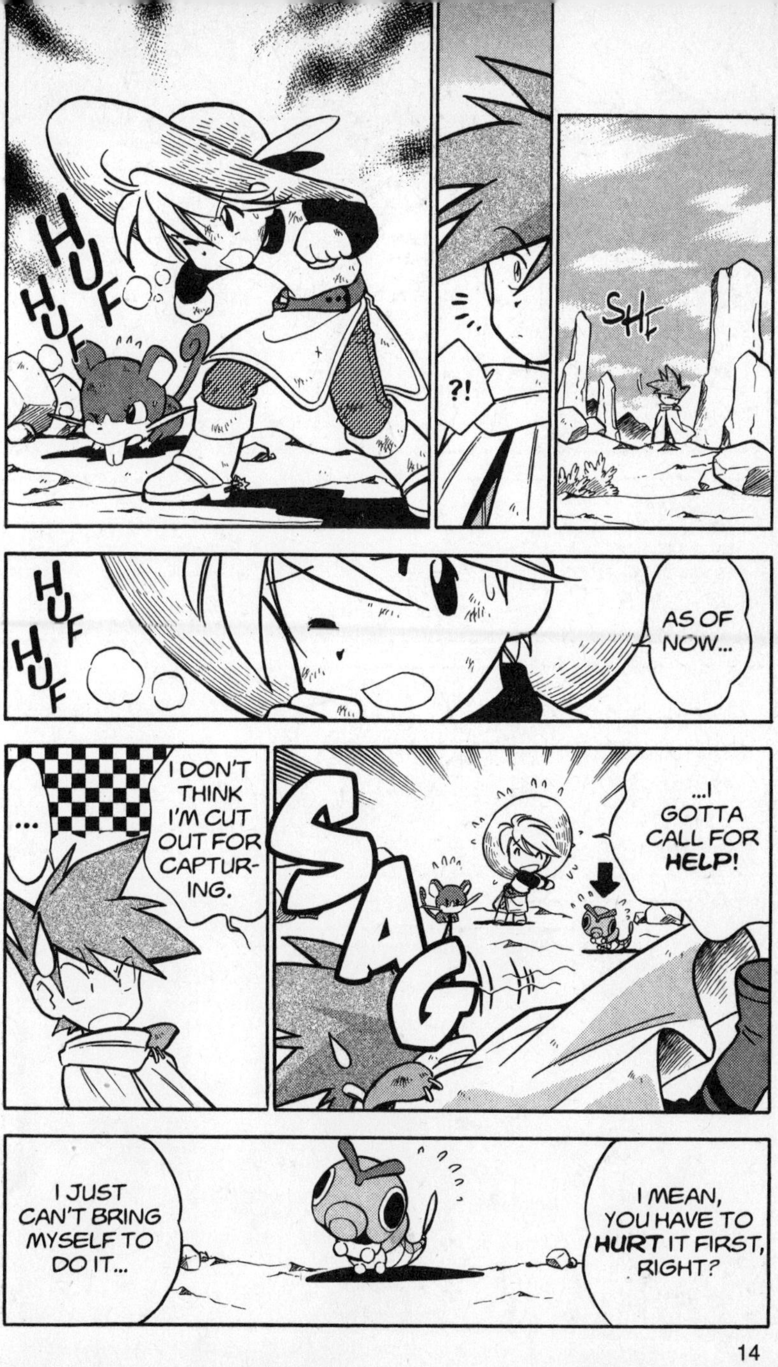
SHF
?!
HUF HUF
HUF HUF
AS OF NOW...
HUF HUF
HUF HUF
...I GOTTA CALL FOR **HELP**!
SAG
I DON'T THINK I'M CUT OUT FOR CAPTURING.
...
I MEAN, YOU HAVE TO **HURT** IT FIRST, RIGHT?
I JUST CAN'T BRING MYSELF TO DO IT...

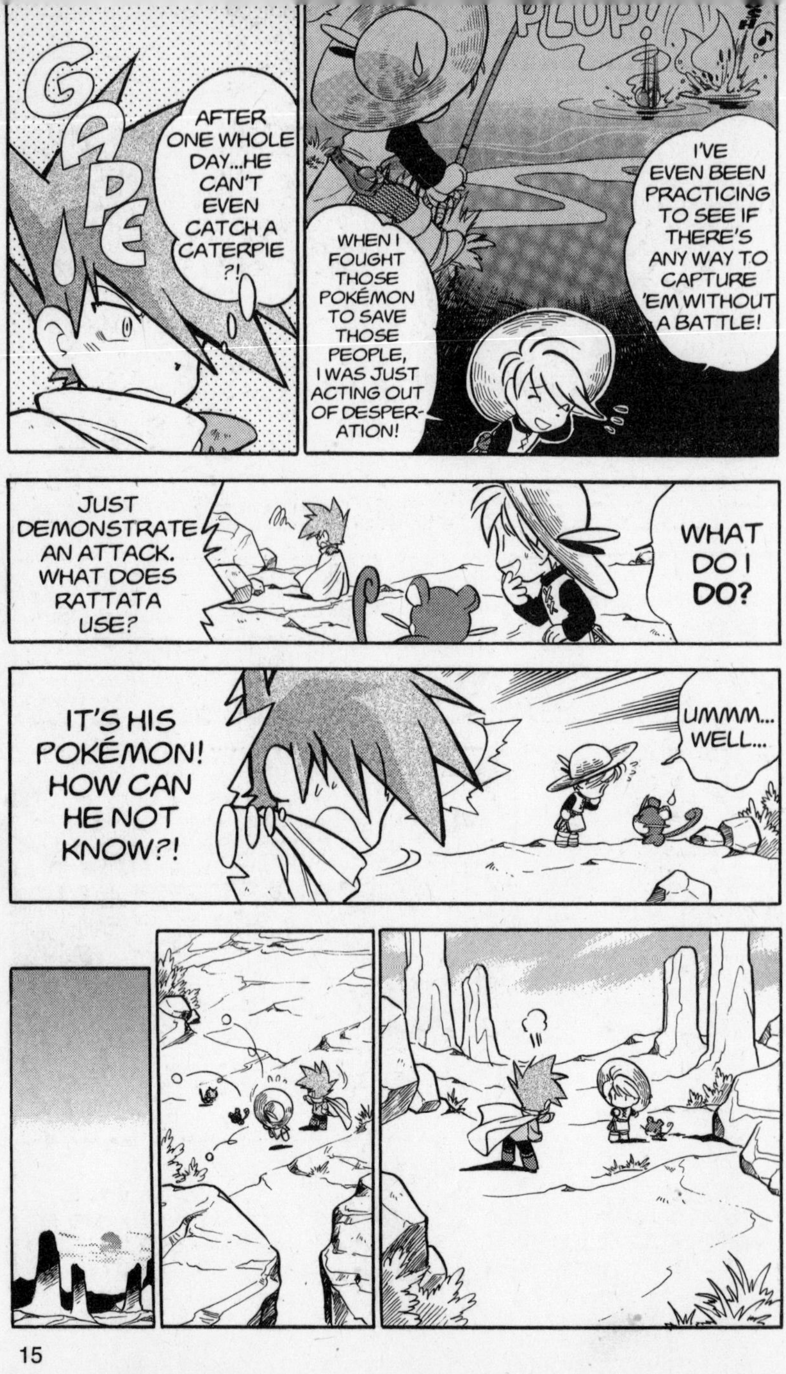
PLUP!
I'VE EVEN BEEN PRACTICING TO SEE IF THERE'S ANY WAY TO CAPTURE 'EM WITHOUT A BATTLE!
WHEN I FOUGHT THOSE POKÉMON TO SAVE THOSE PEOPLE, I WAS JUST ACTING OUT OF DESPERATION!
GAPE
AFTER ONE WHOLE DAY...HE CAN'T EVEN CATCH A CATERPIE?!
WHAT DO I DO?
JUST DEMONSTRATE AN ATTACK. WHAT DOES RATTATA USE?
UMMM... WELL...
IT'S HIS POKÉMON! HOW CAN HE NOT KNOW?!

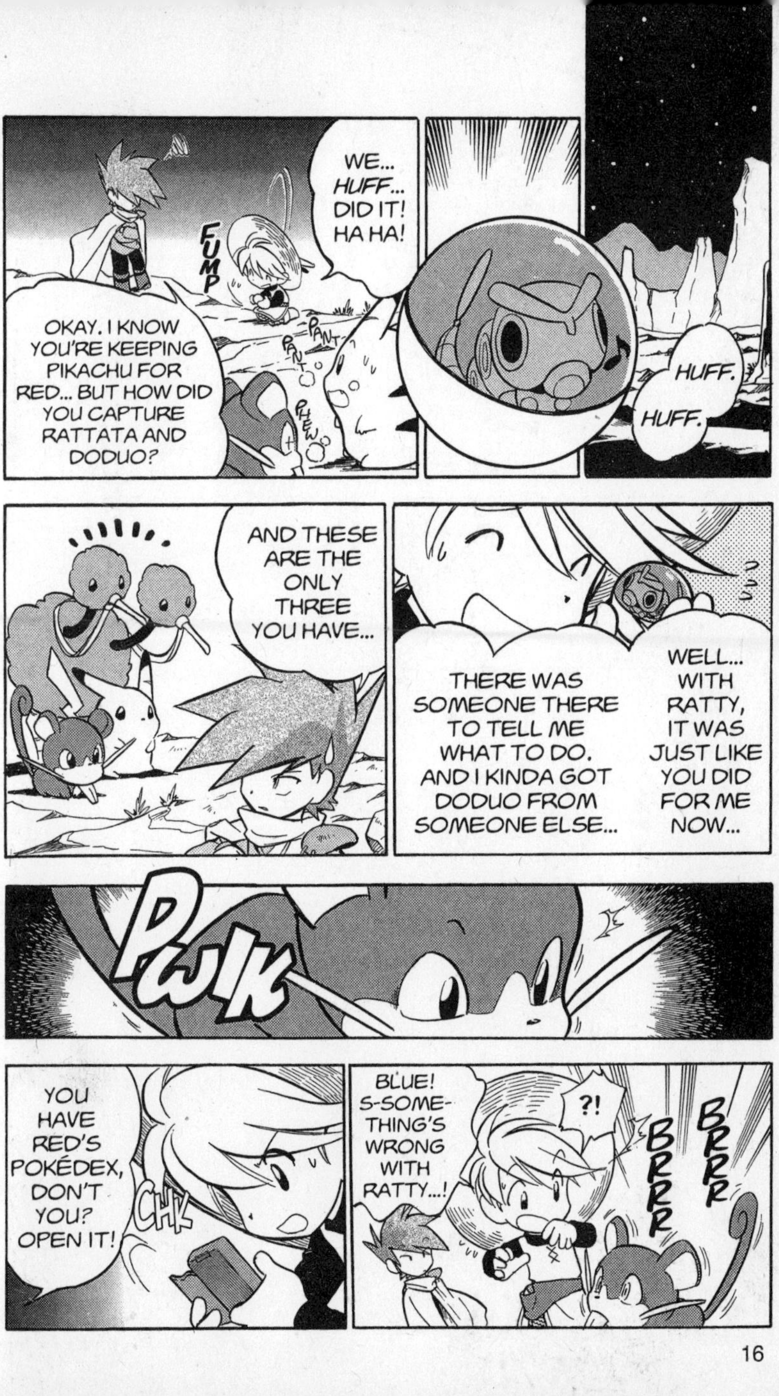
HUFF.
HUFF.
WE... HUFF... DID IT! HA HA!
FUMP
PANT PANT
PHEW
OKAY. I KNOW YOU'RE KEEPING PIKACHU FOR RED... BUT HOW DID YOU CAPTURE RATTATA AND DODUO?
WELL... WITH RATTY, IT WAS JUST LIKE YOU DID FOR ME NOW...
THERE WAS SOMEONE THERE TO TELL ME WHAT TO DO. AND I KINDA GOT DODUO FROM SOMEONE ELSE...
AND THESE ARE THE ONLY THREE YOU HAVE...
PWK
?!
BRRR
BRRR
BLUE! S-SOMETHING'S WRONG WITH RATTY...!
YOU HAVE RED'S POKÉDEX, DON'T YOU? OPEN IT!
CHK

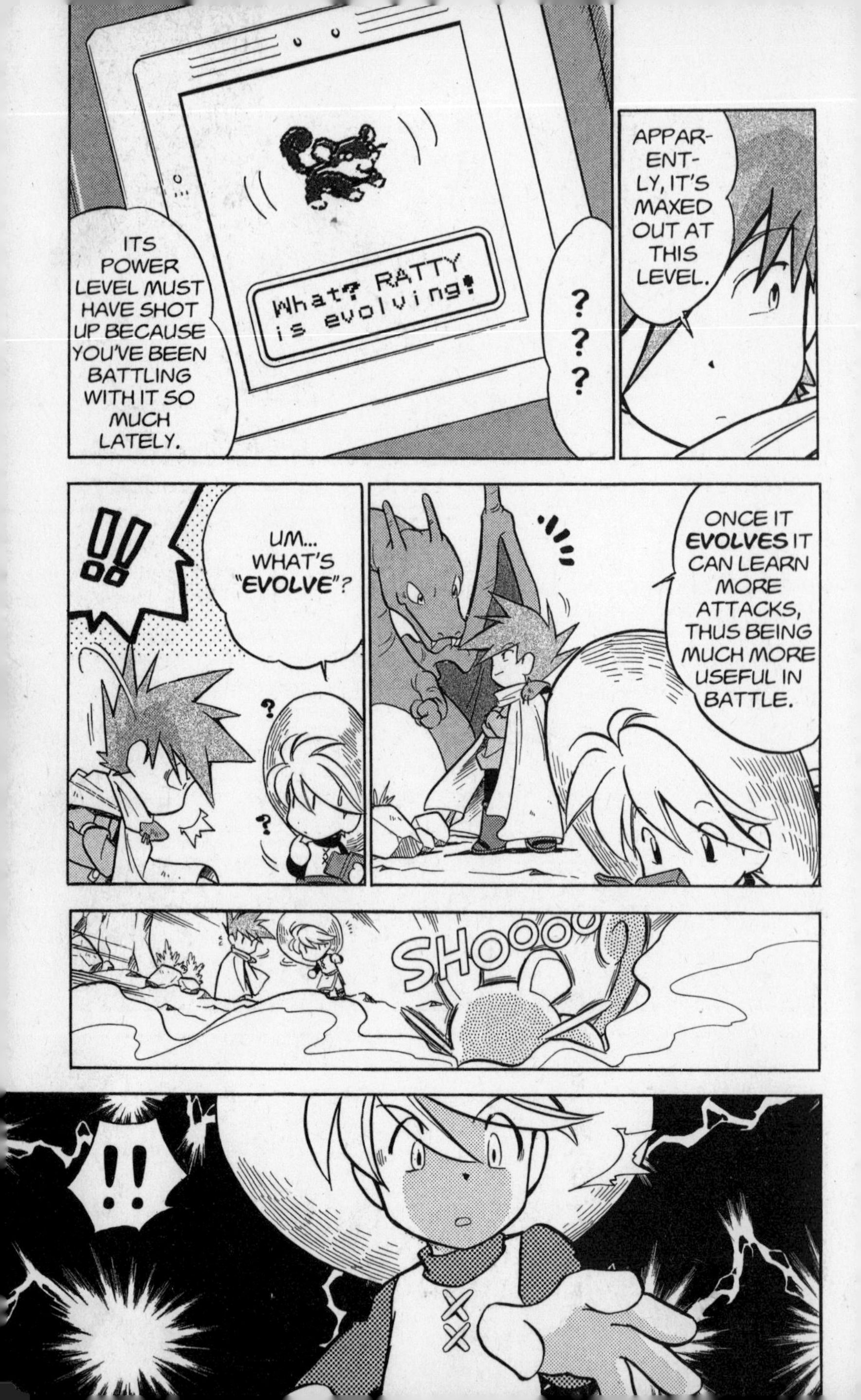
APPARENTLY, IT'S MAXED OUT AT THIS LEVEL.
???
What? RATTY is evolving!
ITS POWER LEVEL MUST HAVE SHOT UP BECAUSE YOU'VE BEEN BATTLING WITH IT SO MUCH LATELY.
ONCE IT **EVOLVES** IT CAN LEARN MORE ATTACKS, THUS BEING MUCH MORE USEFUL IN BATTLE.
UM... WHAT'S "**EVOLVE**"?
!!
SHOOOO
!!

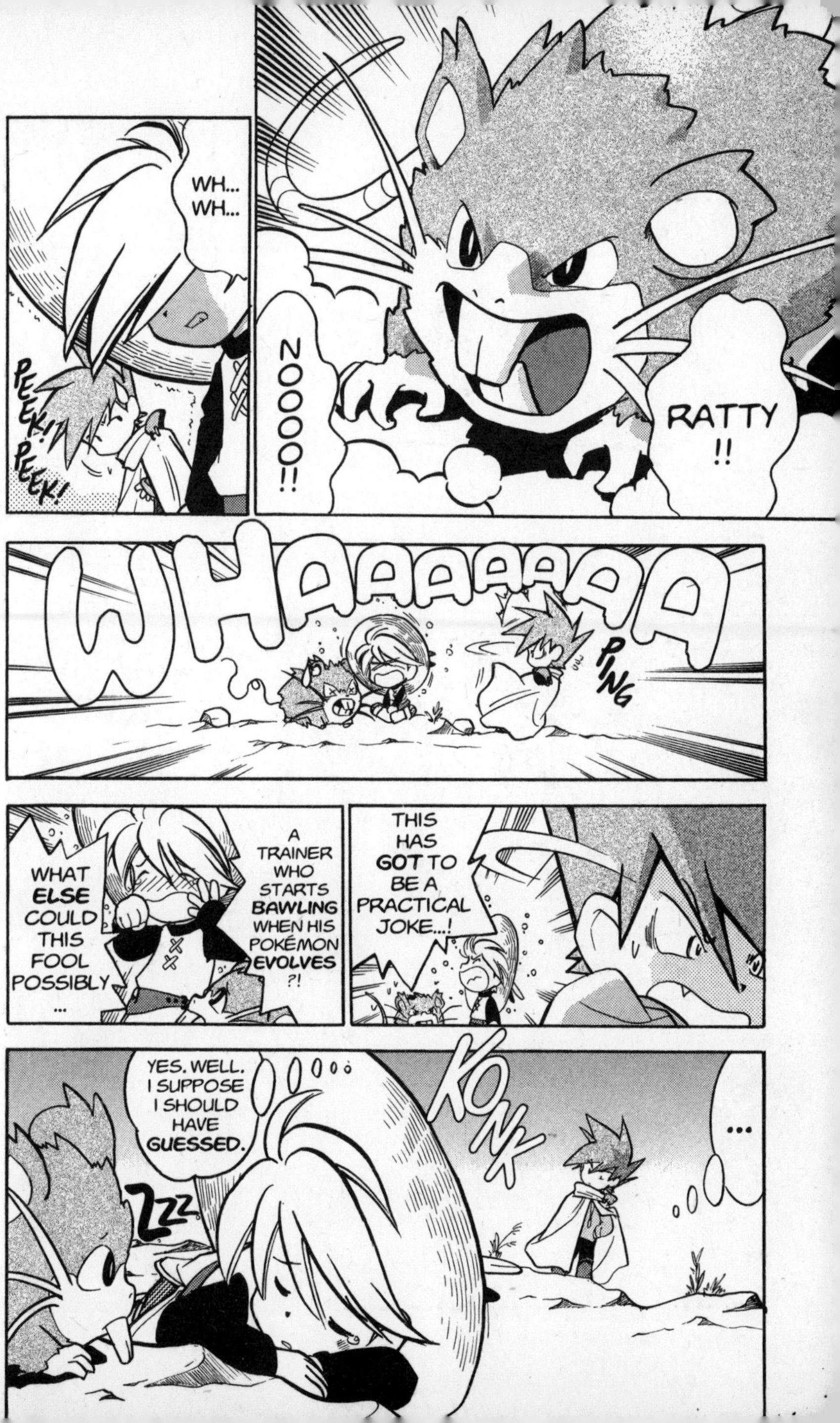
RATTY !!
NOOOOO!!
WH... WH...
PEEK! PEEK!
WHAAAAAAAA
PING
THIS HAS GOT TO BE A PRACTICAL JOKE...!
A TRAINER WHO STARTS BAWLING WHEN HIS POKÉMON EVOLVES ?!
WHAT ELSE COULD THIS FOOL POSSIBLY ...
...
KONK
YES. WELL. I SUPPOSE I SHOULD HAVE GUESSED.
ZZZ

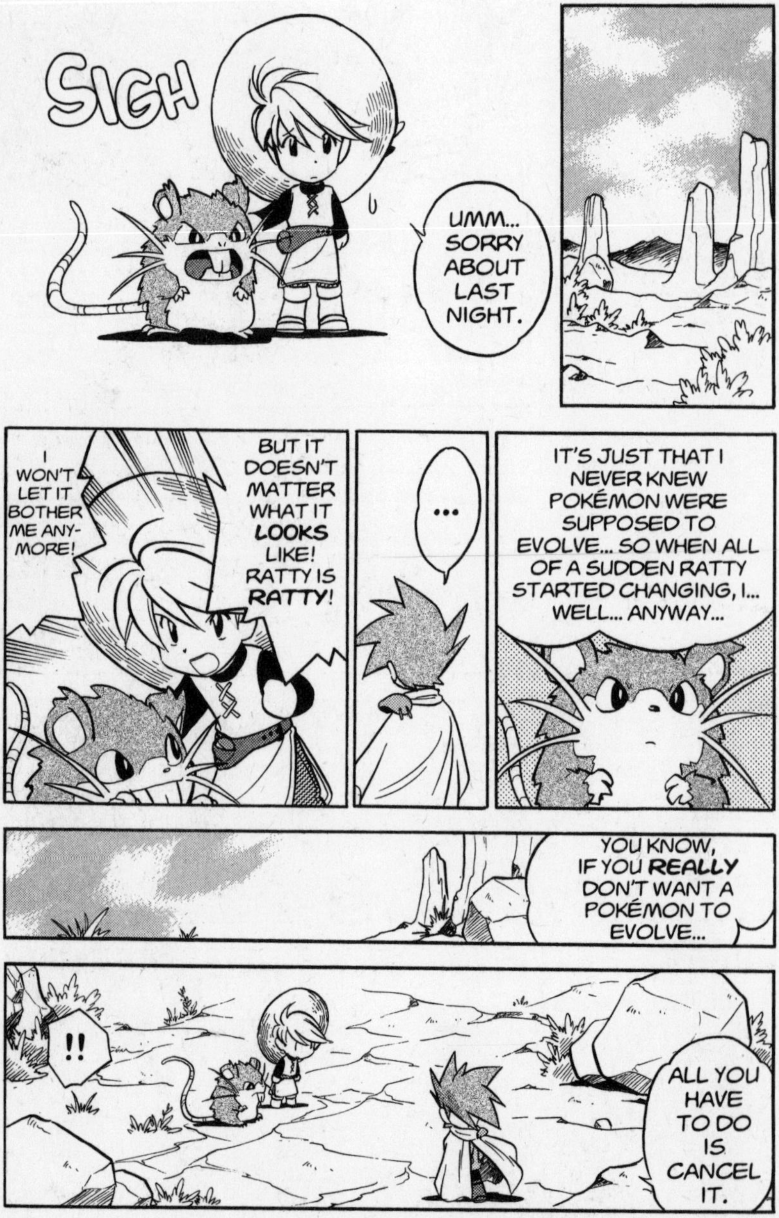
UMM... SORRY ABOUT LAST NIGHT.
SIGH
IT'S JUST THAT I NEVER KNEW POKÉMON WERE SUPPOSED TO EVOLVE... SO WHEN ALL OF A SUDDEN RATTY STARTED CHANGING, I... WELL... ANYWAY...
...
BUT IT DOESN'T MATTER WHAT IT **LOOKS** LIKE! RATTY IS **RATTY**!
I WON'T LET IT BOTHER ME ANY-MORE!
YOU KNOW, IF YOU **REALLY** DON'T WANT A POKÉMON TO EVOLVE...
ALL YOU HAVE TO DO IS CANCEL IT.
!!

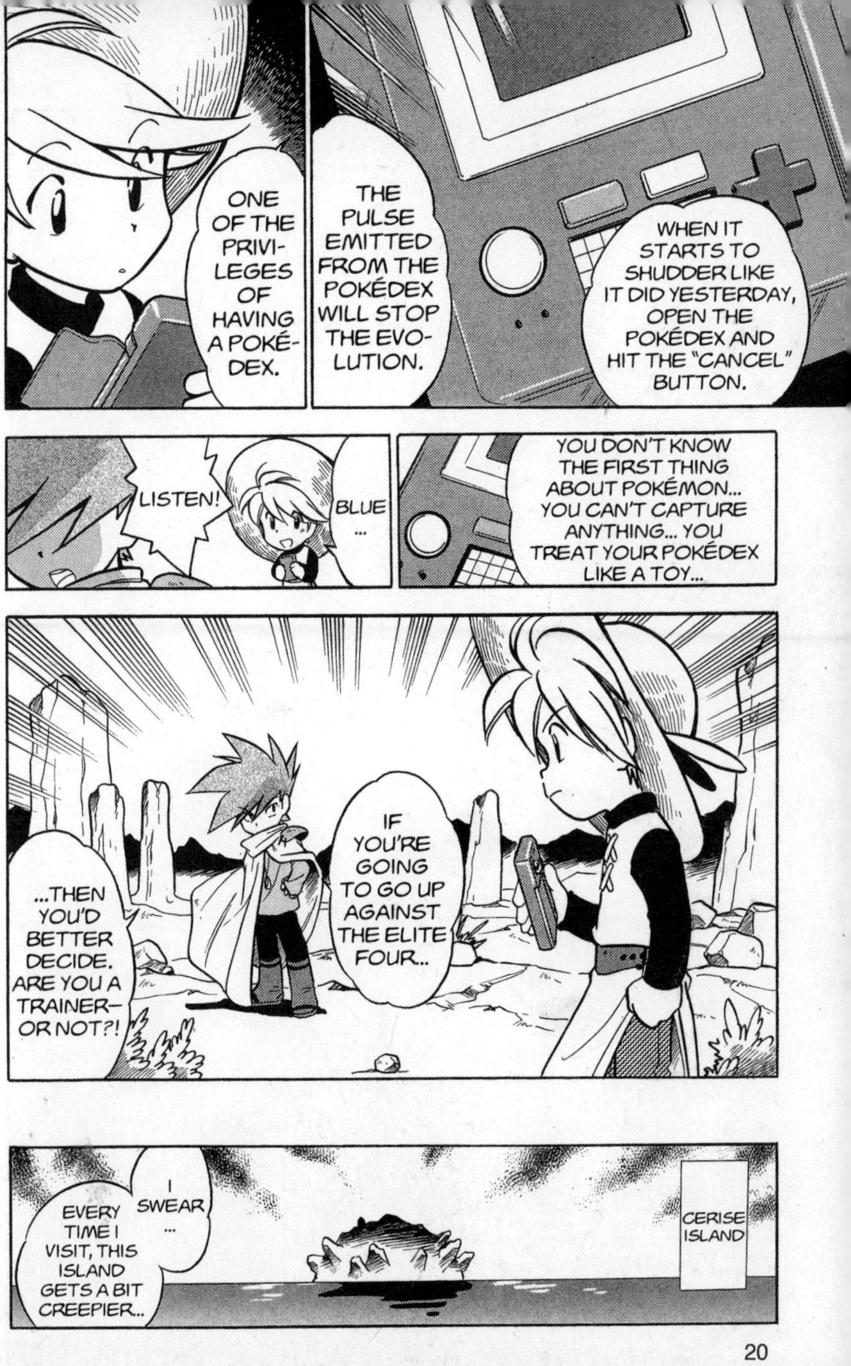

WHEN IT STARTS TO SHUDDER LIKE IT DID YESTERDAY, OPEN THE POKÉDEX AND HIT THE "CANCEL" BUTTON.
THE PULSE EMITTED FROM THE POKÉDEX WILL STOP THE EVO-LUTION.
ONE OF THE PRIVI-LEGES OF HAVING A POKÉ-DEX.
YOU DON'T KNOW THE FIRST THING ABOUT POKÉMON... YOU CAN'T CAPTURE ANYTHING... YOU TREAT YOUR POKÉDEX LIKE A TOY...
BLUE...
LISTEN!
IF YOU'RE GOING TO GO UP AGAINST THE ELITE FOUR...
...THEN YOU'D BETTER DECIDE. ARE YOU A TRAINER—OR NOT?!
CERISE ISLAND
I SWEAR...
EVERY TIME I VISIT, THIS ISLAND GETS A BIT CREEPIER...

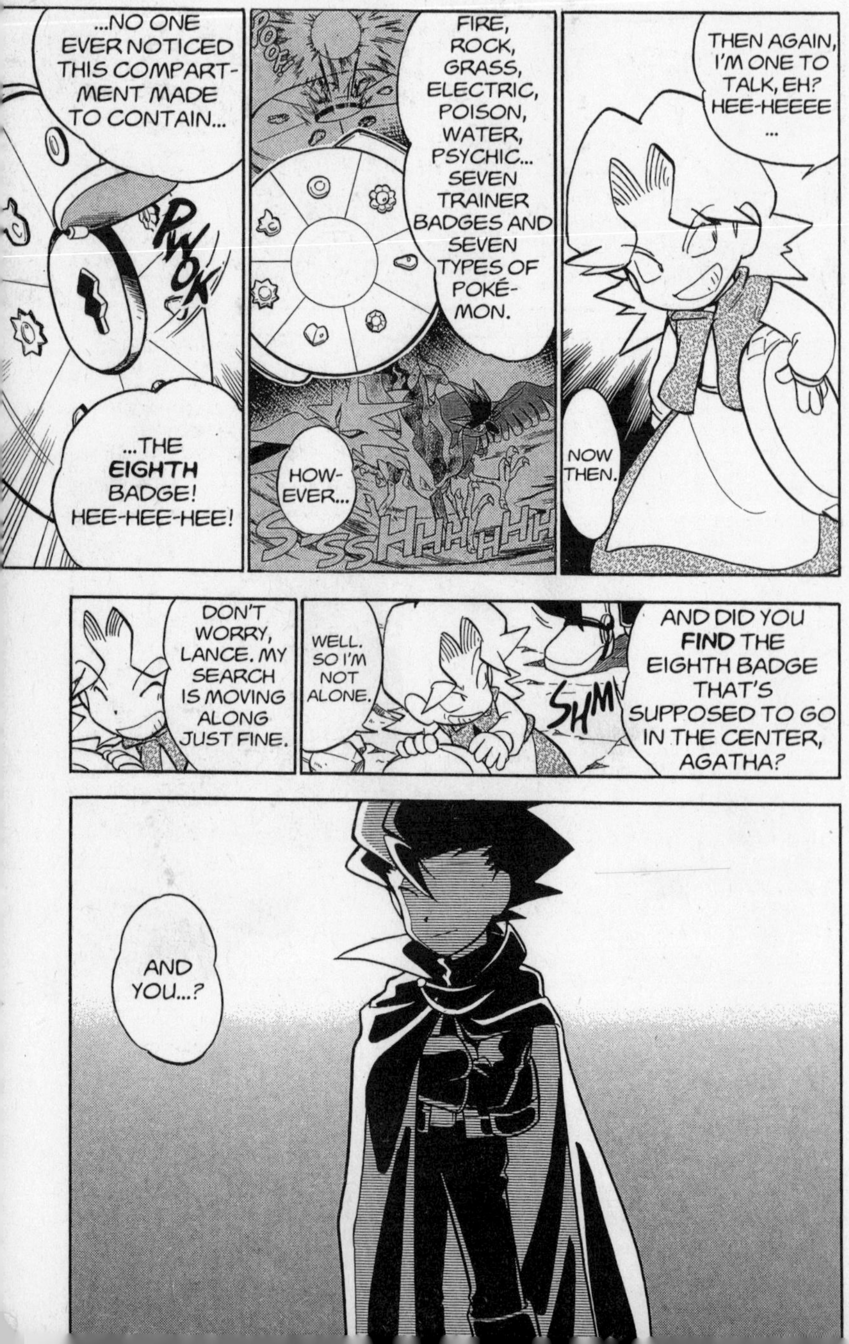
THEN AGAIN, I'M ONE TO TALK, EH? HEE-HEEEE ...
NOW THEN.
POOF
FIRE, ROCK, GRASS, ELECTRIC, POISON, WATER, PSYCHIC... SEVEN TRAINER BADGES AND SEVEN TYPES OF POKÉMON.
HOW-EVER...
SSSHHHHHH
...NO ONE EVER NOTICED THIS COMPARTMENT MADE TO CONTAIN...
PWOK
...THE **EIGHTH** BADGE! HEE-HEE-HEE!
AND DID YOU **FIND** THE EIGHTH BADGE THAT'S SUPPOSED TO GO IN THE CENTER, AGATHA?
SHM
WELL. SO I'M NOT ALONE.
DON'T WORRY, LANCE. MY SEARCH IS MOVING ALONG JUST FINE.
AND YOU...?

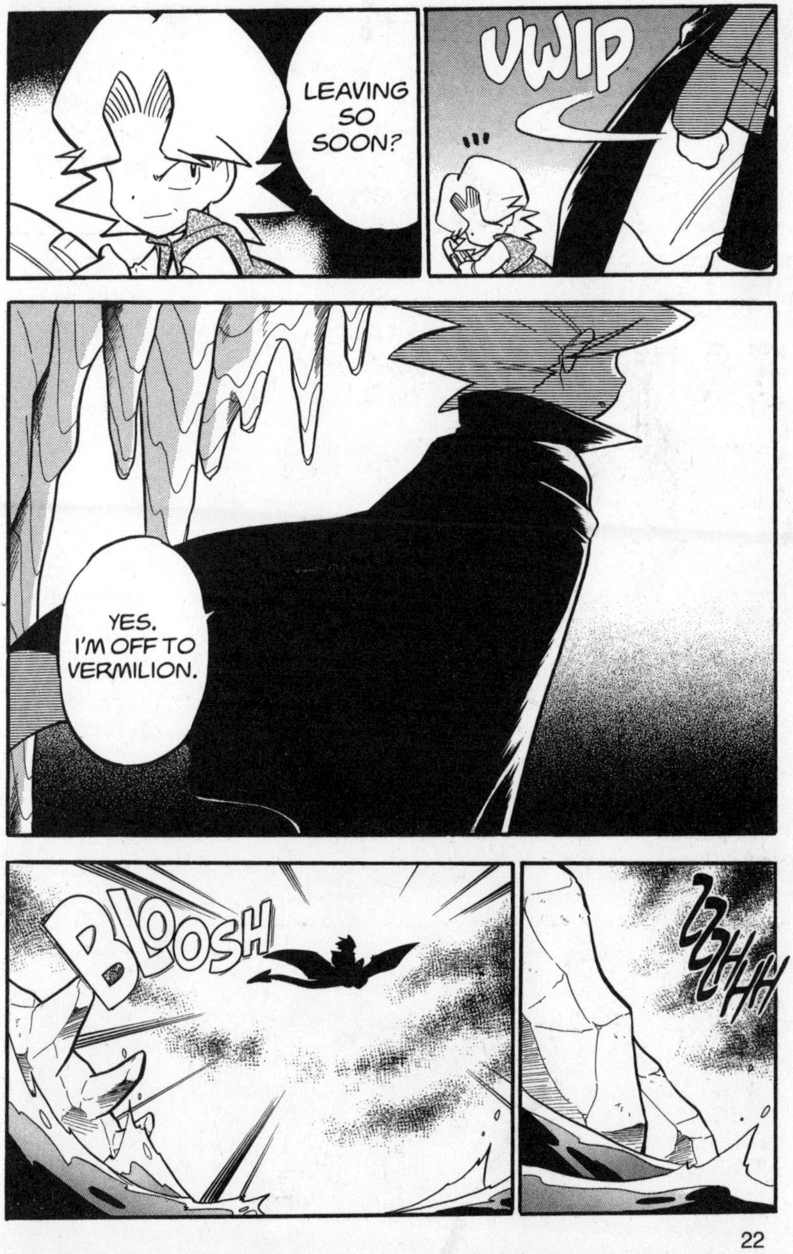
UWIP
LEAVING SO SOON?
YES. I'M OFF TO VERMILION.
ZZZHHH
BLOOSH

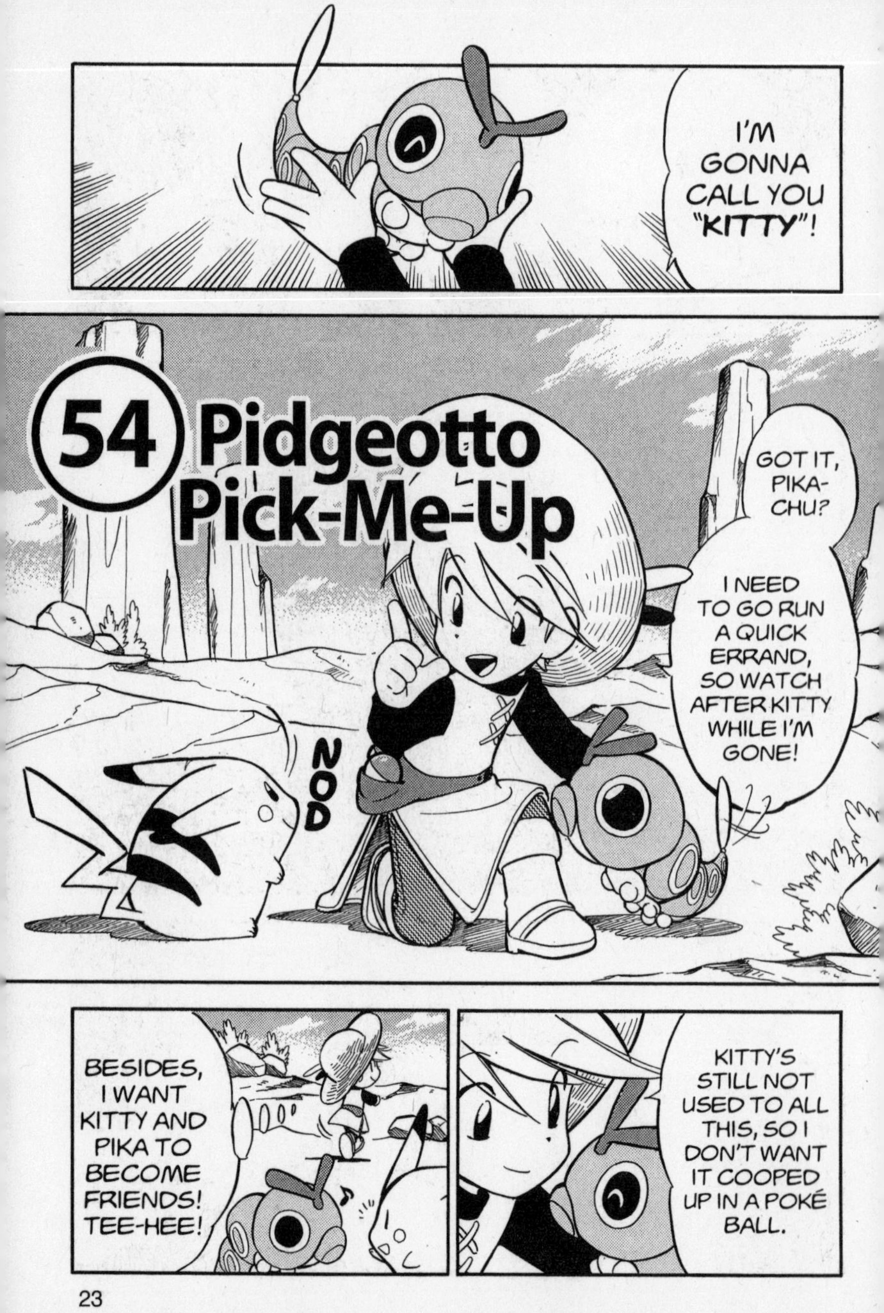
I'M GONNA CALL YOU "KITTY"!
54 Pidgeotto Pick-Me-Up
GOT IT, PIKA-CHU?
I NEED TO GO RUN A QUICK ERRAND, SO WATCH AFTER KITTY WHILE I'M GONE!
NOD
KITTY'S STILL NOT USED TO ALL THIS, SO I DON'T WANT IT COOPED UP IN A POKÉ BALL.
BESIDES, I WANT KITTY AND PIKA TO BECOME FRIENDS! TEE-HEE!

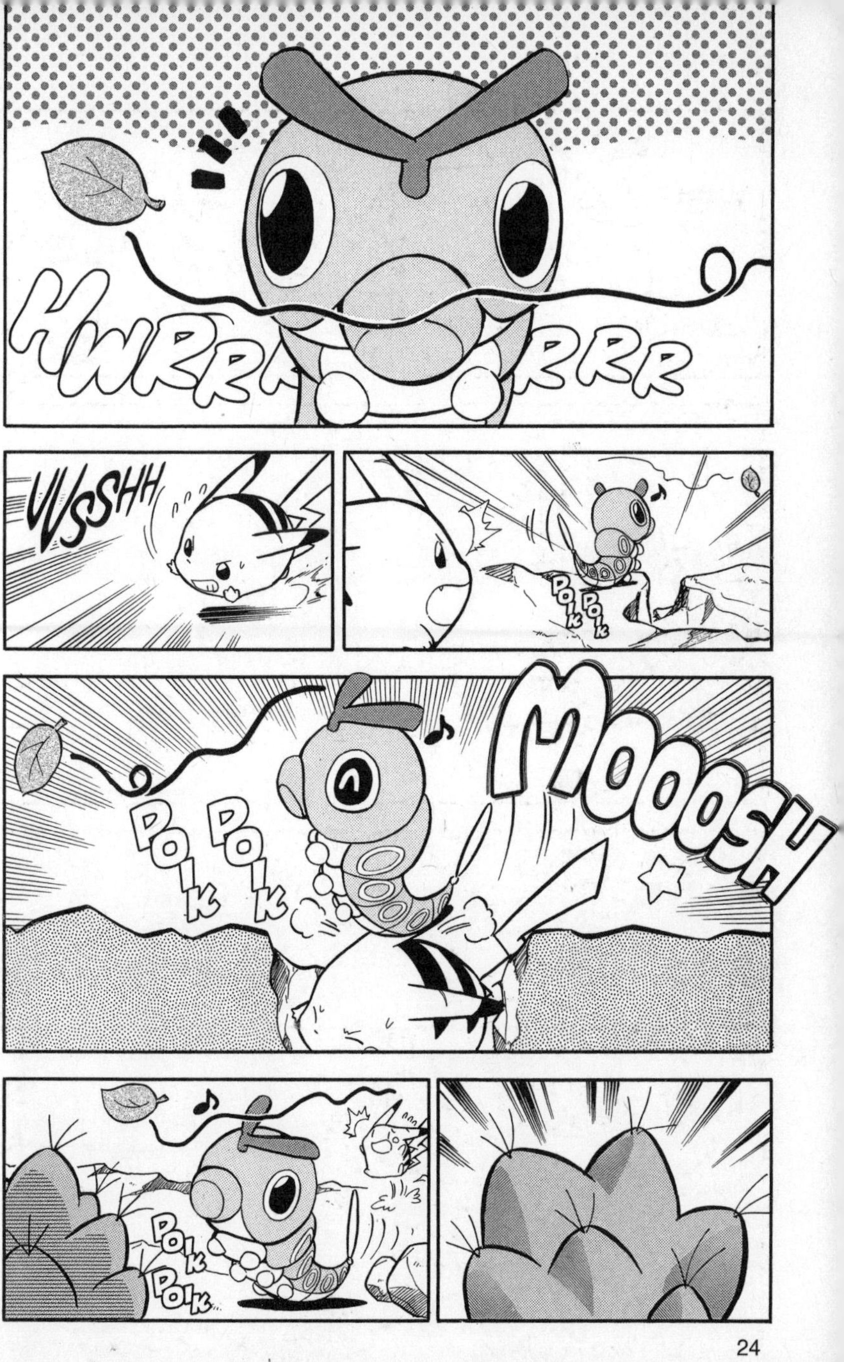
HWRR RRR
POIK POIK
VVSSHH
MOOOSH
POIK POIK
POIK POIK

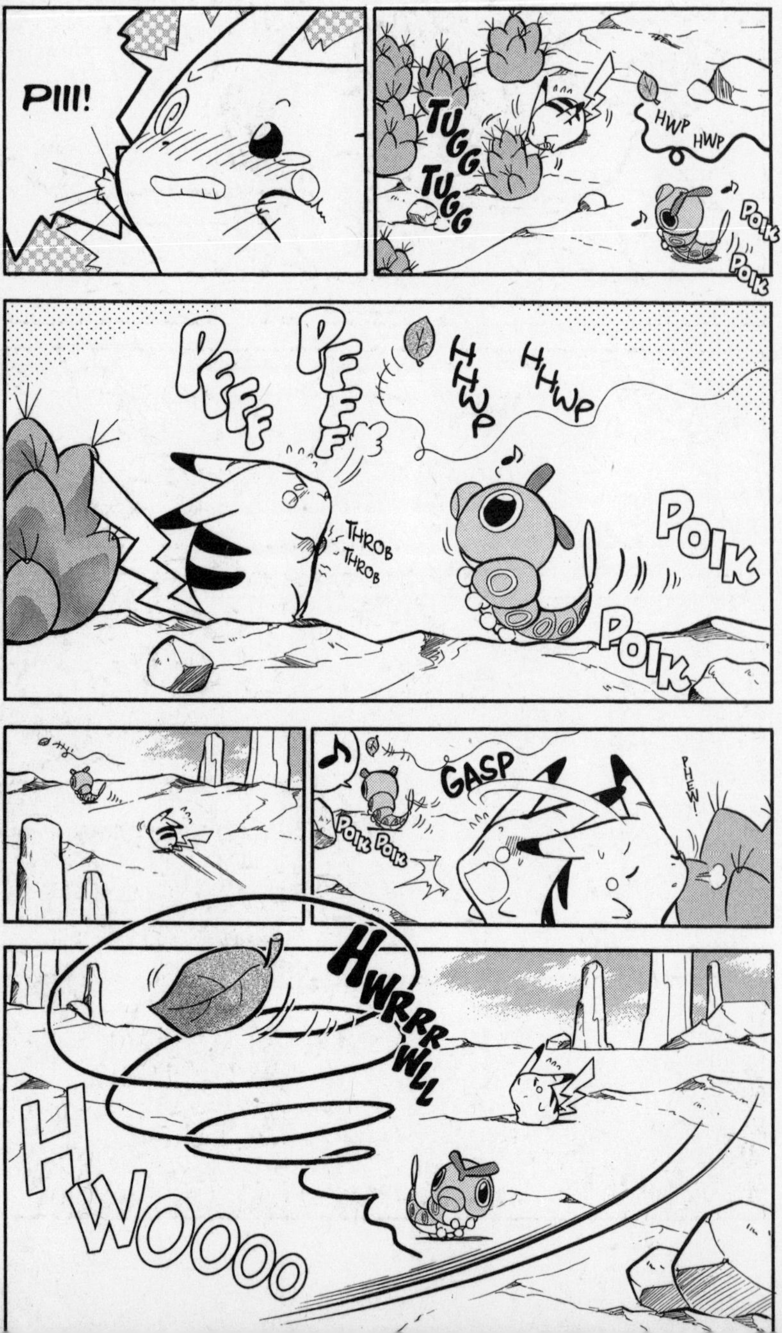
HWP HWP
TUGG TUGG
POIK POIK
PIII!
HHWP HHWP
PFFF PFFF
POIK POIK
THROB THROB
PHEW!
GASP
POIK POIK
HWRRRRWLL
HWOOOO

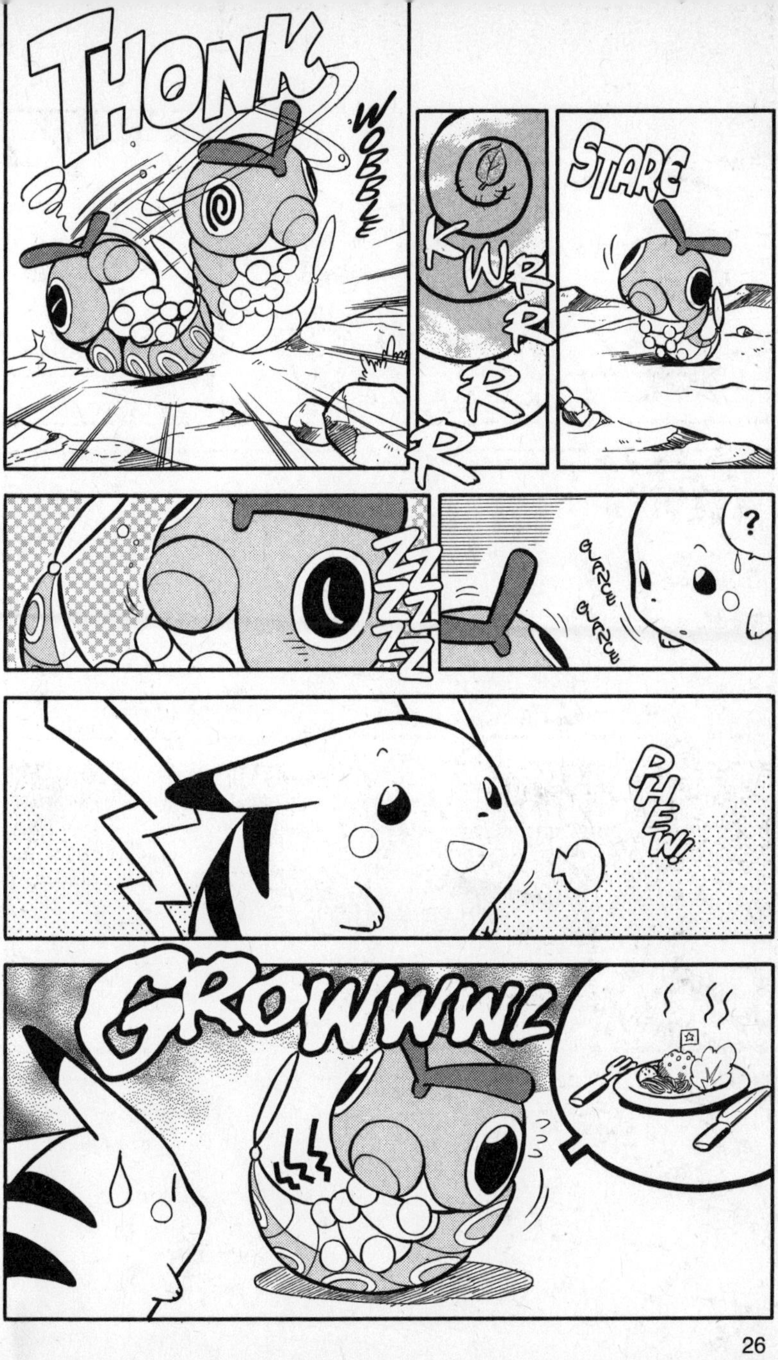
STARE
KWRRRR
THONK
WOBBLE
?
GLANCE GLANCE
ZZZZZ
PHEW!
GROWWWL

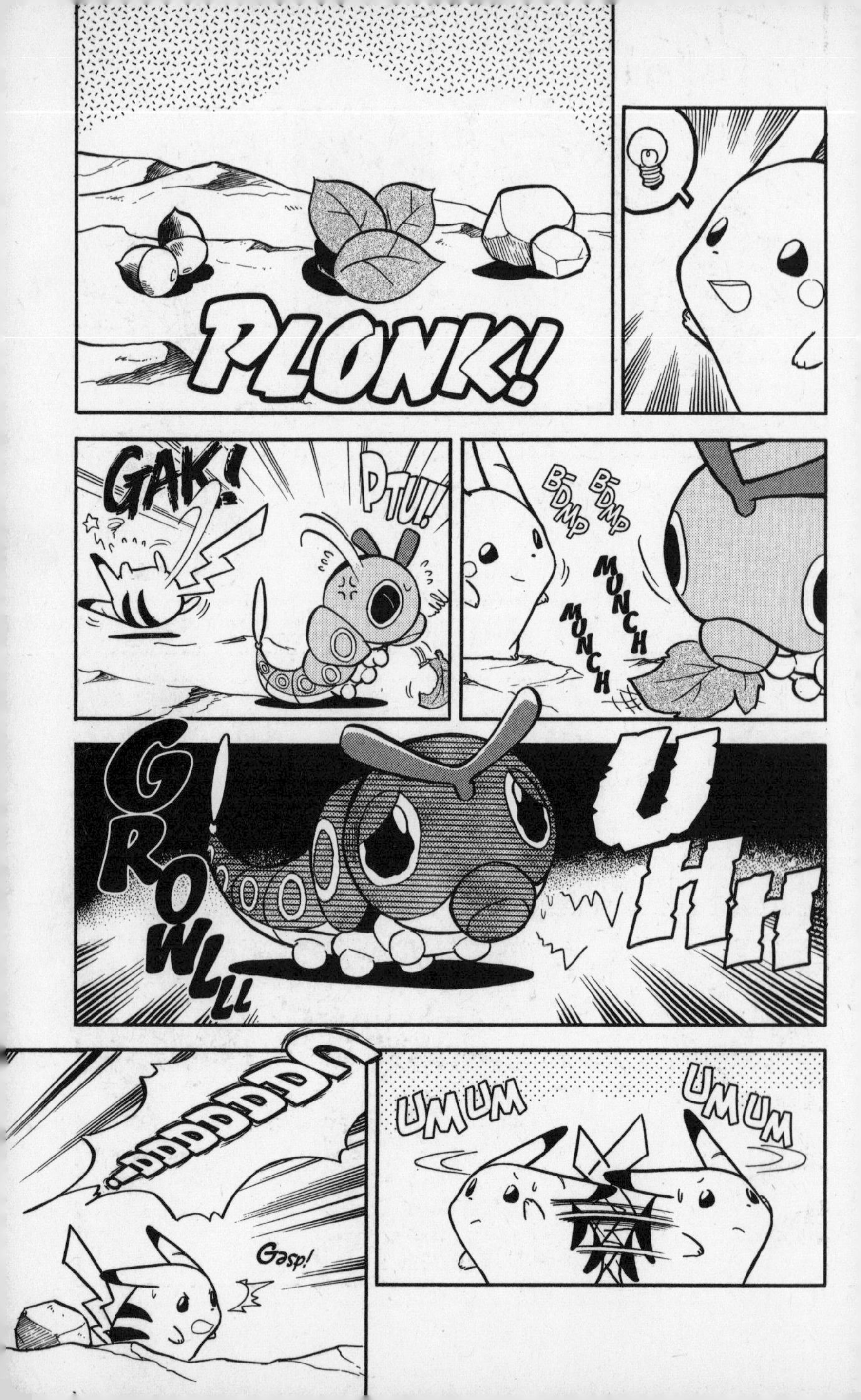
PLONK!
B-DMP B-DMP
MUNCH MUNCH
GAK!
PTU!
GROWLLL
UHH
UMUM UMUM
Ugggggg-!
Gasp!

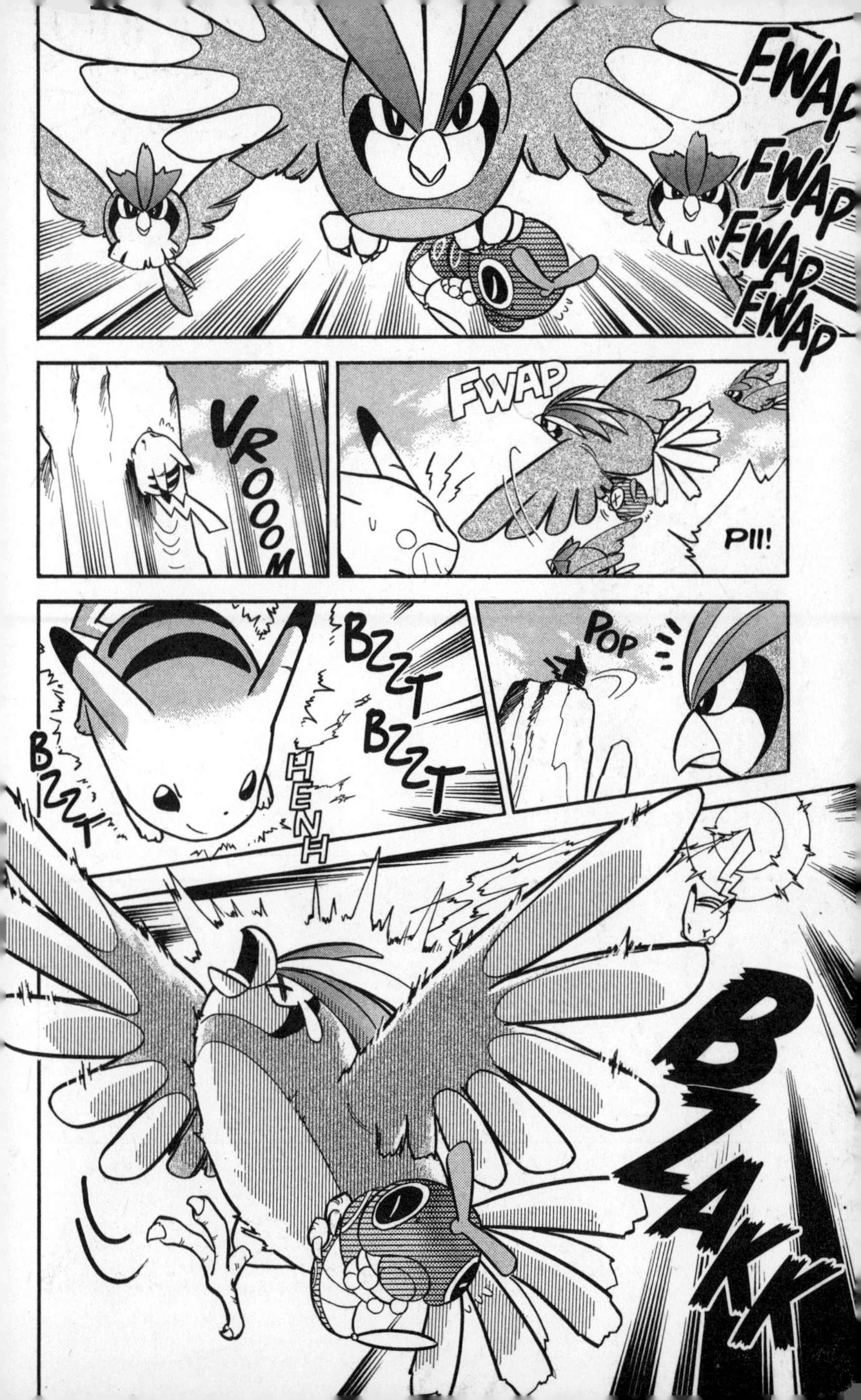
FWAP
FWAP
FWAP
FWAP
FWAP
FWAP
PII!
VROOOOM
POP
BZZZT
BZZZT
HENH
BZZZT
BZAKK

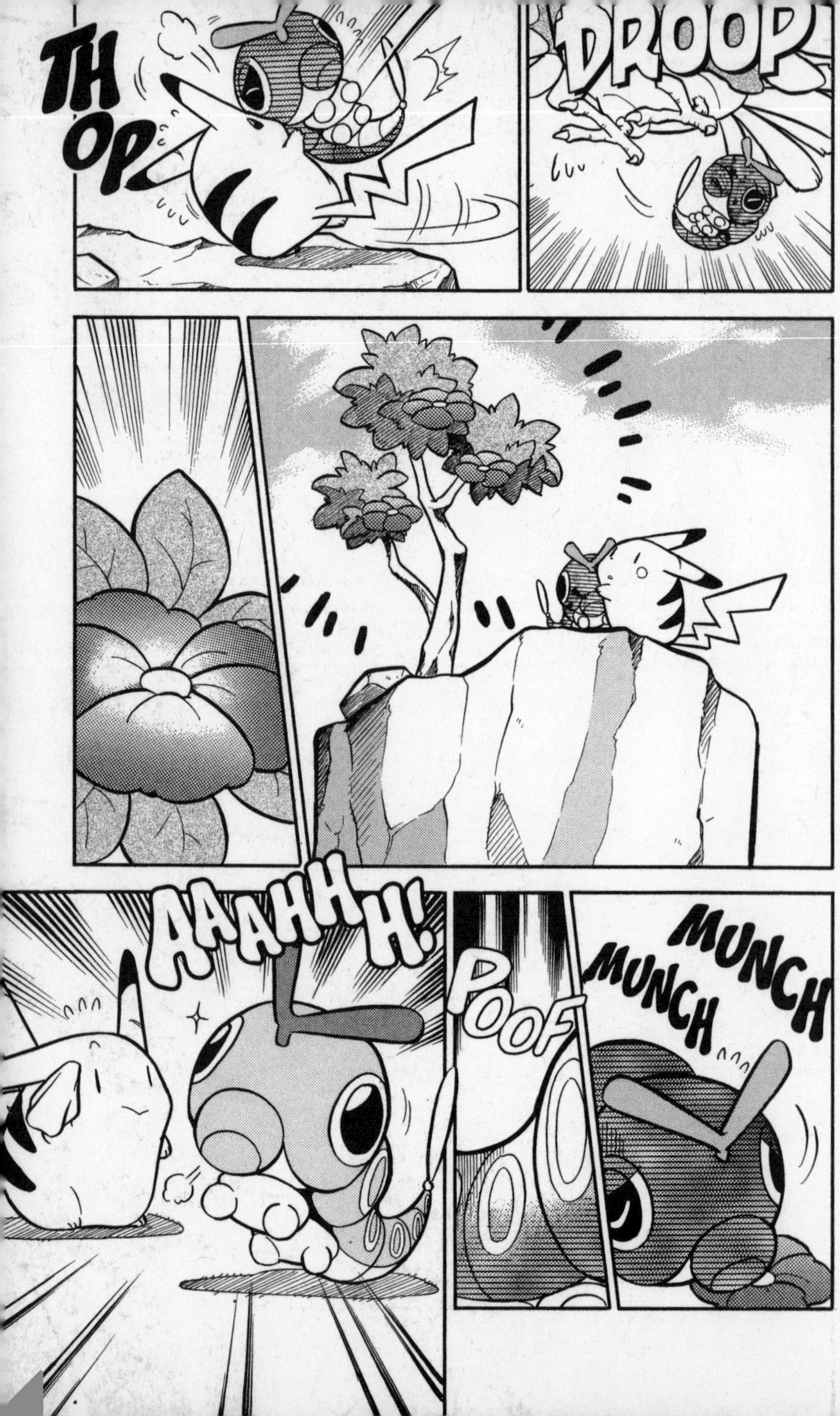
DROOP
THOP
MUNCH MUNCH
POOF
AAAHHH!

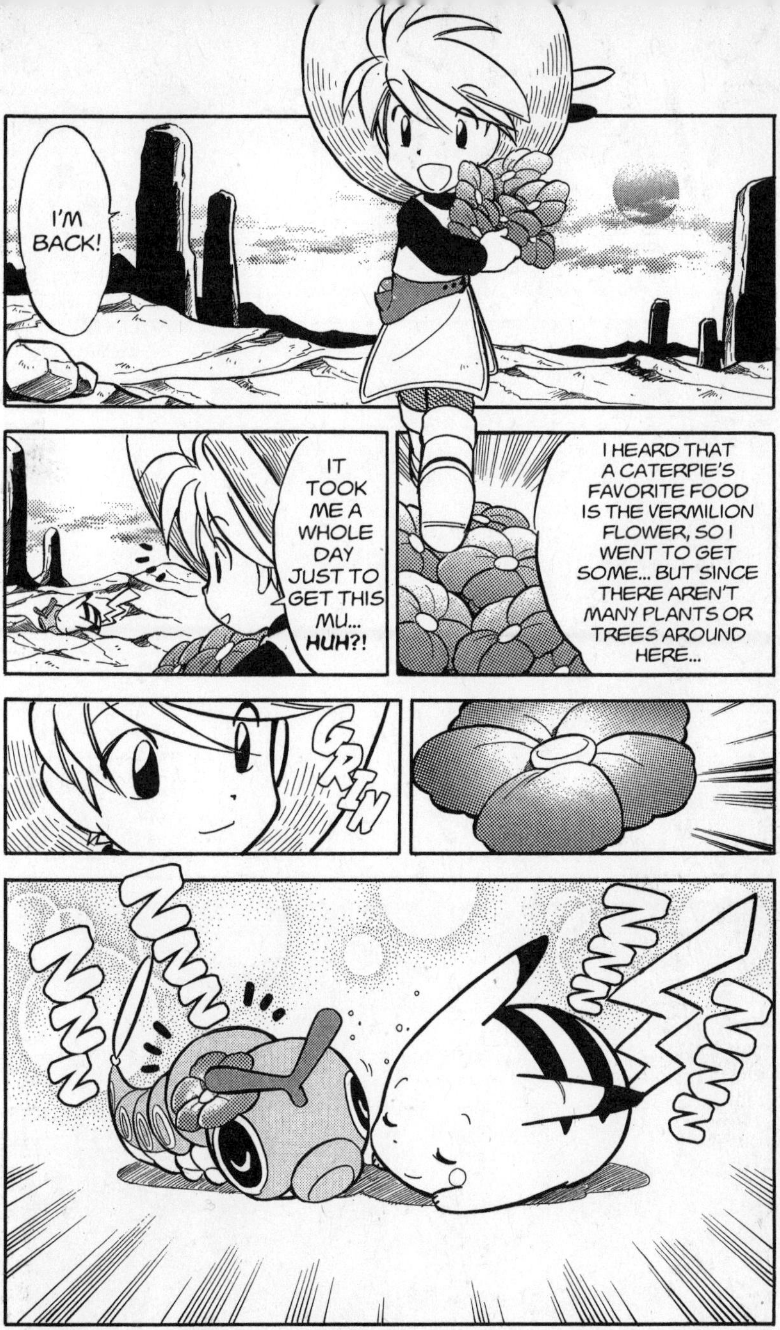
I'M BACK!
I HEARD THAT A CATERPIE'S FAVORITE FOOD IS THE VERMILION FLOWER, SO I WENT TO GET SOME... BUT SINCE THERE AREN'T MANY PLANTS OR TREES AROUND HERE...
IT TOOK ME A WHOLE DAY JUST TO GET THIS MU... **HUH?!**
GRIN
NNNN
NNNN
NNN
NNN

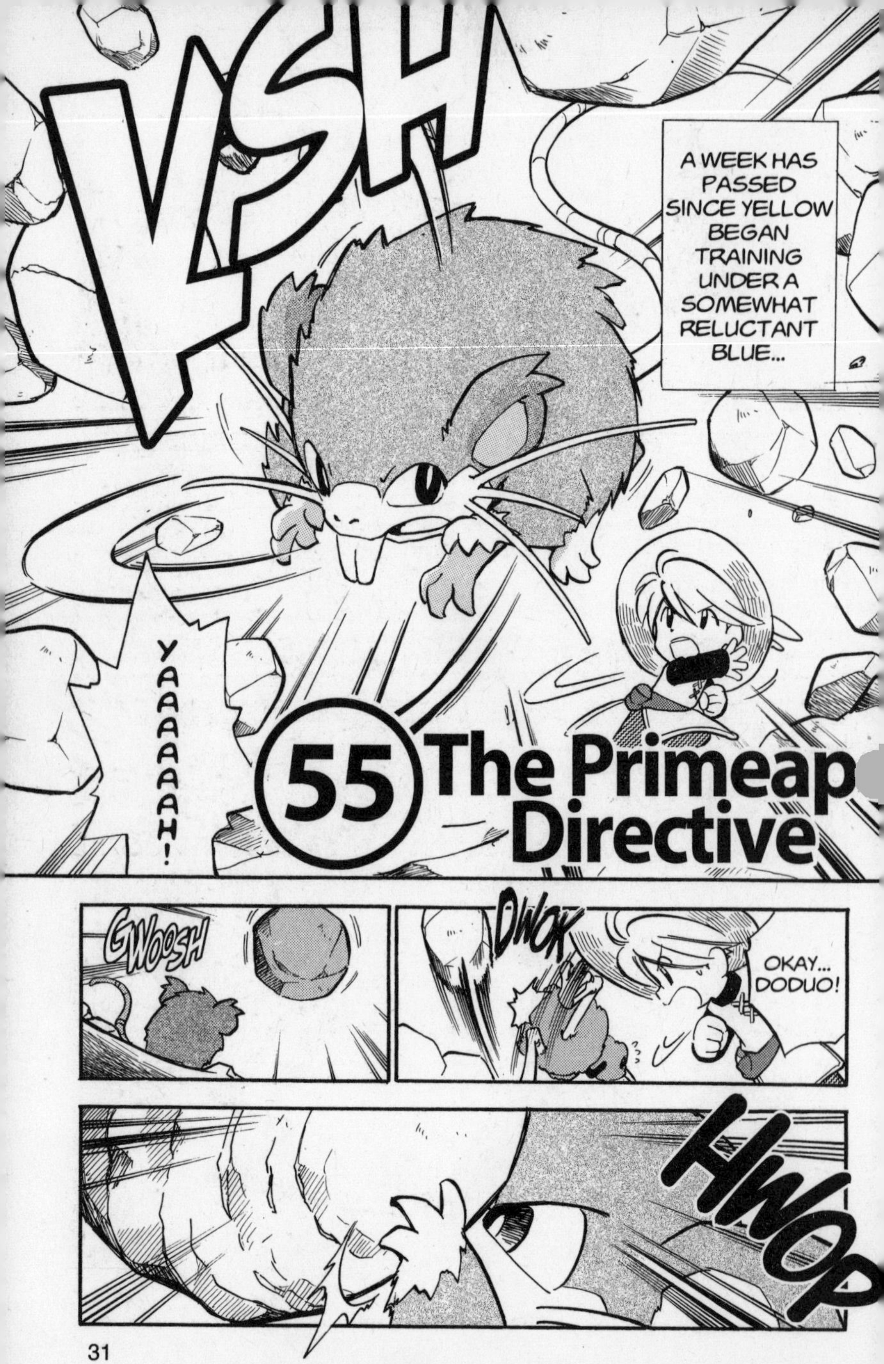
A WEEK HAS PASSED SINCE YELLOW BEGAN TRAINING UNDER A SOMEWHAT RELUCTANT BLUE...
VSH
YAAAAAAAH!
55 The Primeape Directive
DWOK
OKAY... DODUO!
GWOOSH
HWOP

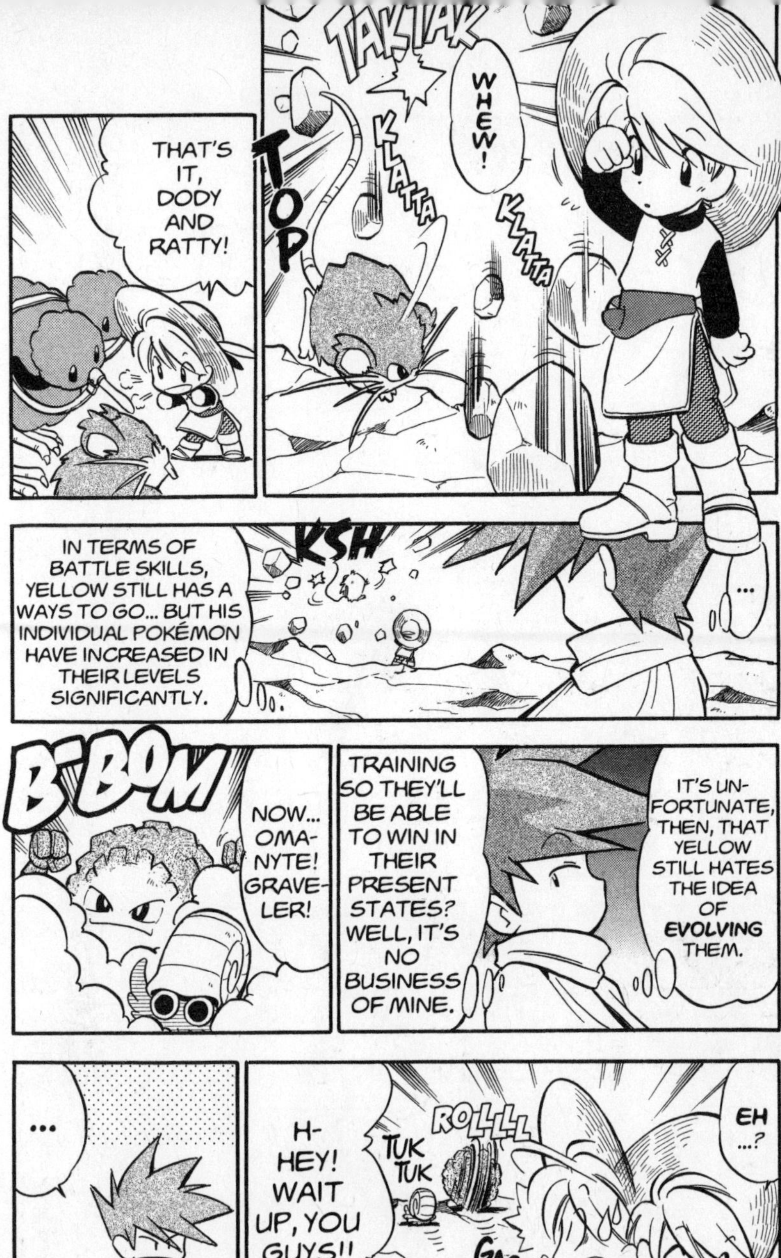
TAKTAK
WHEW!
KLATTA
KLATTA
TOP
THAT'S IT, DODY AND RATTY!
...
KSH
IN TERMS OF BATTLE SKILLS, YELLOW STILL HAS A WAYS TO GO... BUT HIS INDIVIDUAL POKÉMON HAVE INCREASED IN THEIR LEVELS SIGNIFICANTLY.
IT'S UN-FORTUNATE, THEN, THAT YELLOW STILL HATES THE IDEA OF **EVOLVING** THEM.
TRAINING SO THEY'LL BE ABLE TO WIN IN THEIR PRESENT STATES? WELL, IT'S NO BUSINESS OF MINE.
B-BOM
NOW... OMA-NYTE! GRAVE-LER!
EH ...?
GASP
ROLLLL
TUK TUK
H-HEY! WAIT UP, YOU GUYS!!
...

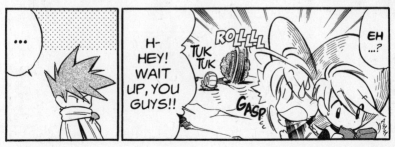

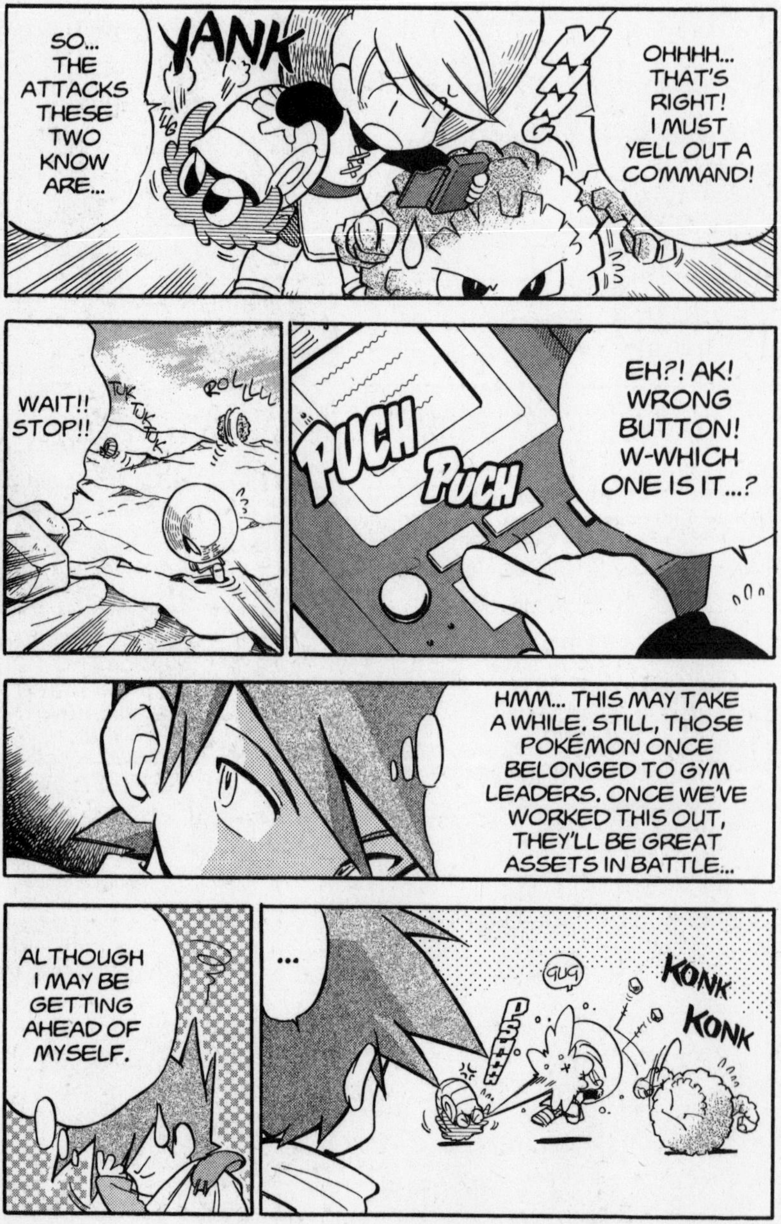
NNNG
OHHHH... THAT'S RIGHT! I MUST YELL OUT A COMMAND!
YANK
SO... THE ATTACKS THESE TWO KNOW ARE...
TUG
EH?! AK! WRONG BUTTON! W-WHICH ONE IS IT...?
PUCH
PUCH
ROLLLL
WAIT!! STOP!!
TUK TUK TOK
HMM... THIS MAY TAKE A WHILE. STILL, THOSE POKÉMON ONCE BELONGED TO GYM LEADERS. ONCE WE'VE WORKED THIS OUT, THEY'LL BE GREAT ASSETS IN BATTLE...
KONK
KONK
GUG
PSHHH
...
ALTHOUGH I MAY BE GETTING AHEAD OF MYSELF.

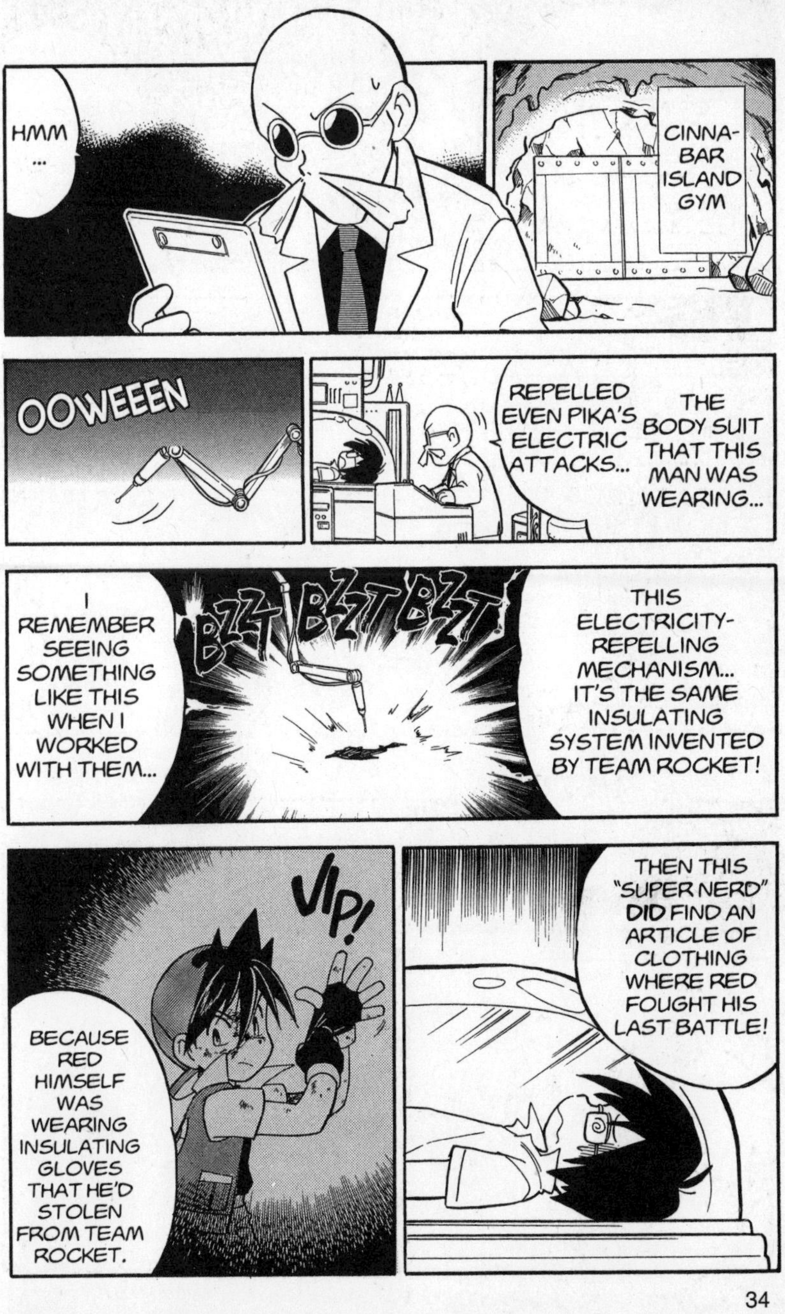
CINNA-BAR ISLAND GYM
HMM ...
THE BODY SUIT THAT THIS MAN WAS WEARING...
REPELLED EVEN PIKA'S ELECTRIC ATTACKS...
OOWEEEN
THIS ELECTRICITY-REPELLING MECHANISM... IT'S THE SAME INSULATING SYSTEM INVENTED BY TEAM ROCKET!
BZZT BZZT BZZT
I REMEMBER SEEING SOMETHING LIKE THIS WHEN I WORKED WITH THEM...
THEN THIS "SUPER NERD" **DID** FIND AN ARTICLE OF CLOTHING WHERE RED FOUGHT HIS LAST BATTLE!
JIP!
BECAUSE RED HIMSELF WAS WEARING INSULATING GLOVES THAT HE'D STOLEN FROM TEAM ROCKET.

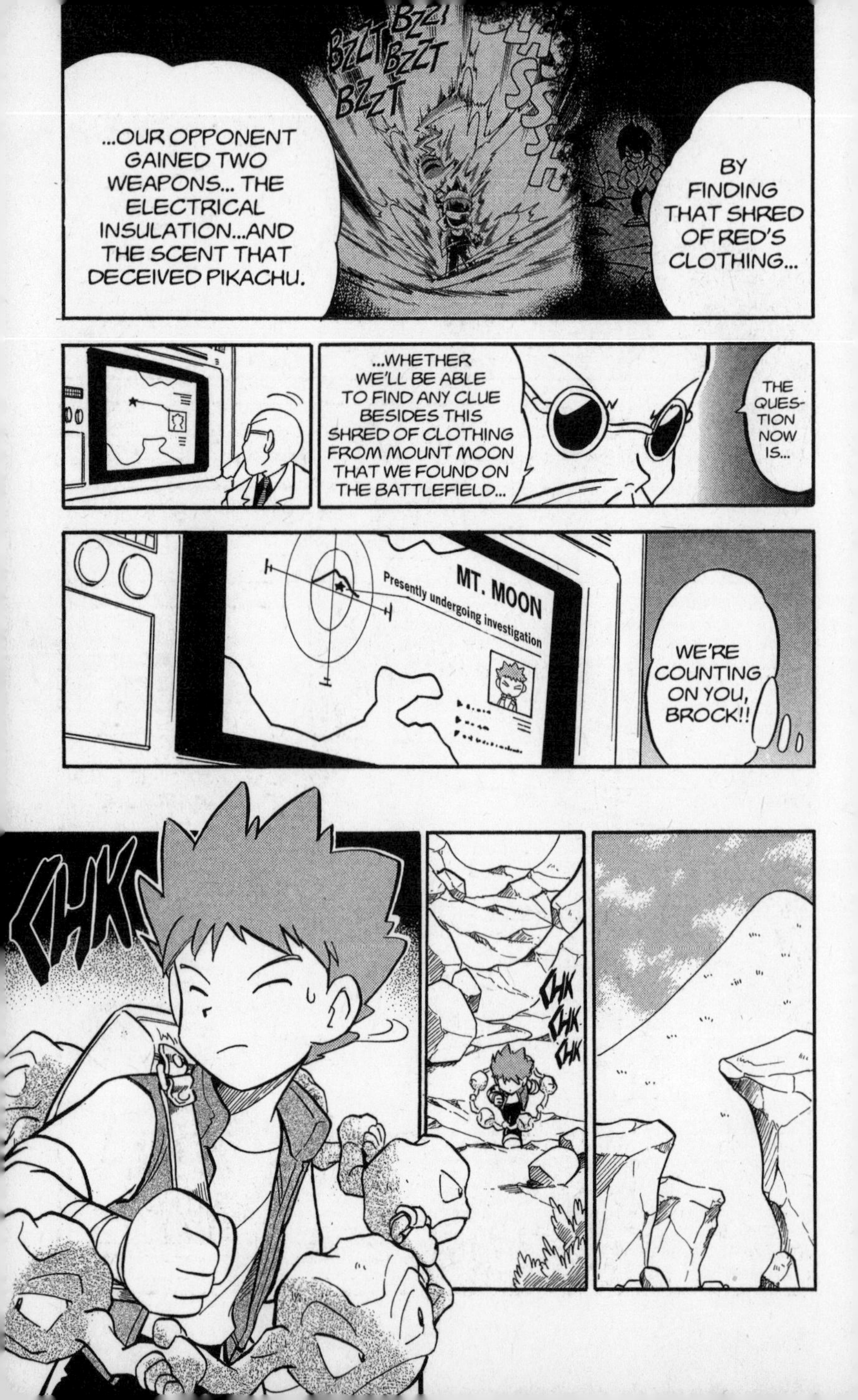
BZZT BZZT BZZT BZZT
BY FINDING THAT SHRED OF RED'S CLOTHING...
...OUR OPPONENT GAINED TWO WEAPONS... THE ELECTRICAL INSULATION...AND THE SCENT THAT DECEIVED PIKACHU.
THE QUESTION NOW IS...
...WHETHER WE'LL BE ABLE TO FIND ANY CLUE BESIDES THIS SHRED OF CLOTHING FROM MOUNT MOON THAT WE FOUND ON THE BATTLEFIELD...
MT. MOON
Presently undergoing investigation
WE'RE COUNTING ON YOU, BROCK!!
CHK CHK CHK
CHK

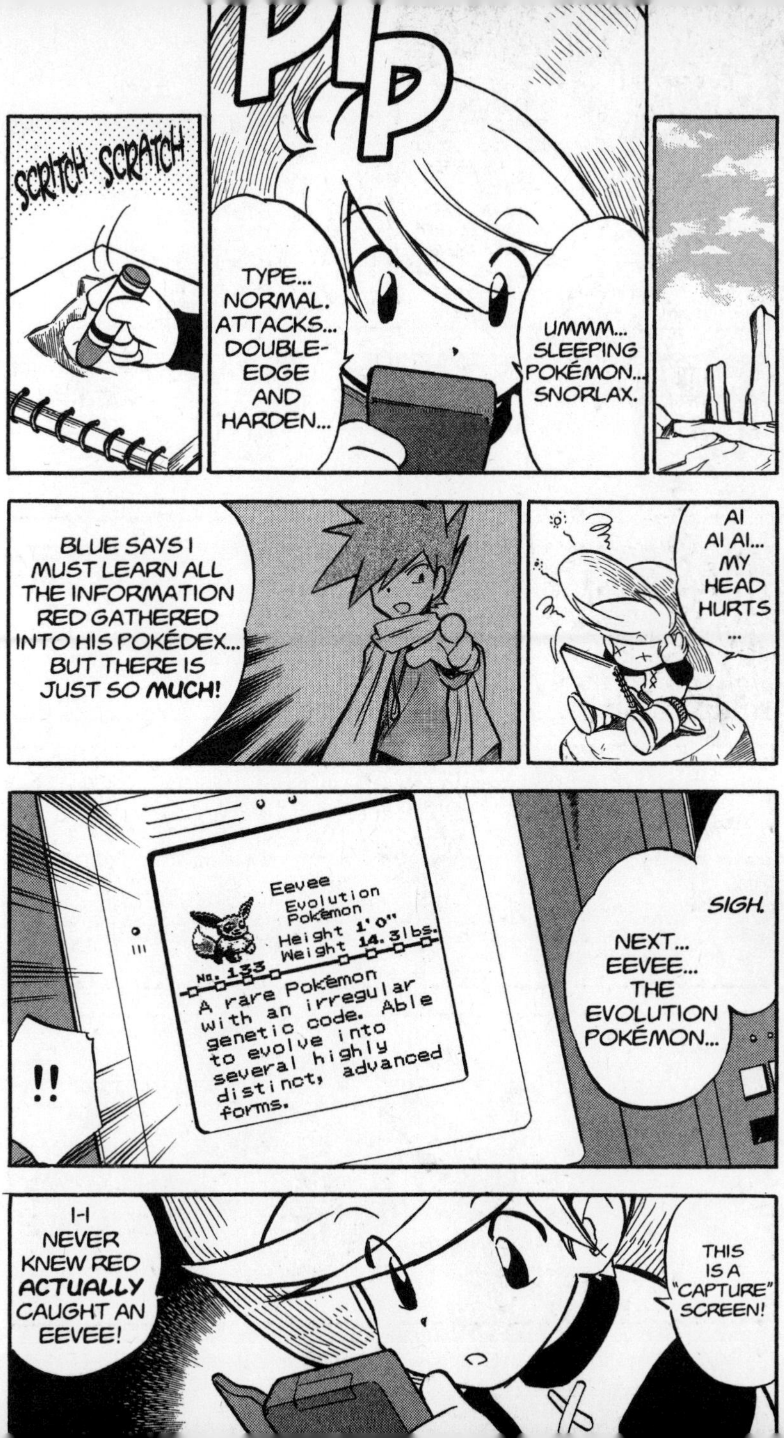
PIP
UMMM... SLEEPING POKÉMON... SNORLAX.
TYPE... NORMAL. ATTACKS... DOUBLE-EDGE AND HARDEN...
SCRITCH SCRATCH
AI AI AI... MY HEAD HURTS ...
BLUE SAYS I MUST LEARN ALL THE INFORMATION RED GATHERED INTO HIS POKÉDEX... BUT THERE IS JUST SO **MUCH**!
SIGH.
NEXT... EEVEE... THE EVOLUTION POKÉMON...
Eevee
Evolution Pokémon
Height 1'0"
Weight 14.3lbs.
No. 133
A rare Pokémon with an irregular genetic code. Able to evolve into several highly distinct, advanced forms.
!!
THIS IS A "CAPTURE" SCREEN!
I-I NEVER KNEW RED **ACTUALLY** CAUGHT AN EEVEE!

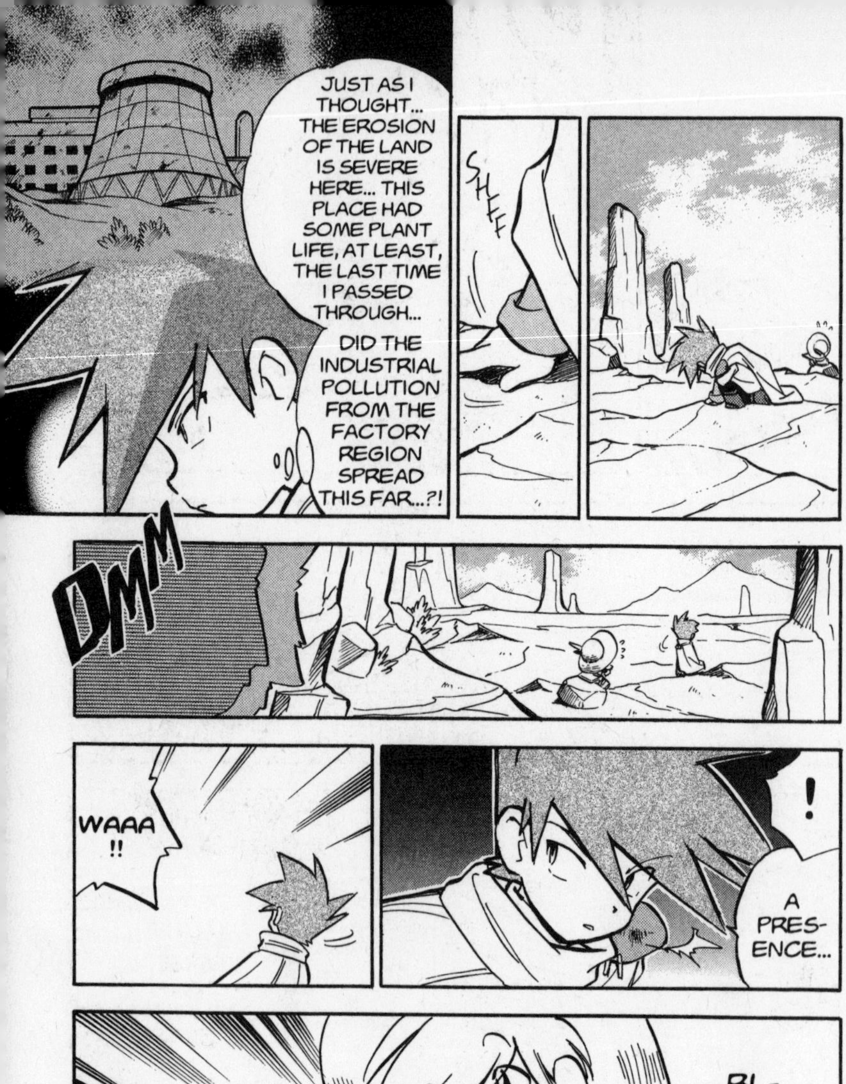
SHFF
JUST AS I THOUGHT... THE EROSION OF THE LAND IS SEVERE HERE... THIS PLACE HAD SOME PLANT LIFE, AT LEAST, THE LAST TIME I PASSED THROUGH...
DID THE INDUSTRIAL POLLUTION FROM THE FACTORY REGION SPREAD THIS FAR...?!
DMM
!
A PRES-ENCE...
WAAA!!
BL-BL-BLUE!! WE HAVE TROUBLE!!!

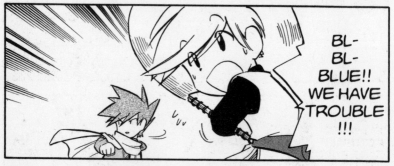

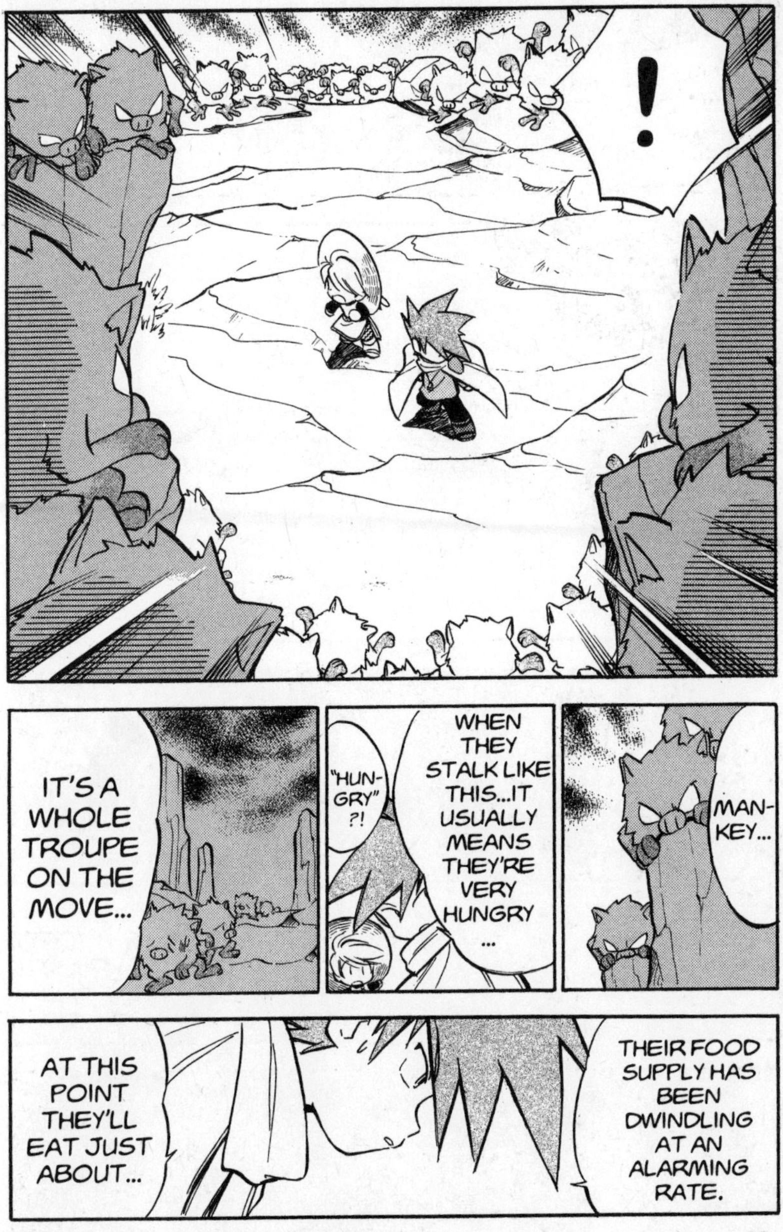
!
MAN-KEY...
WHEN THEY STALK LIKE THIS...IT USUALLY MEANS THEY'RE VERY HUNGRY...
"HUN-GRY"?!
IT'S A WHOLE TROUPE ON THE MOVE...
THEIR FOOD SUPPLY HAS BEEN DWINDLING AT AN ALARMING RATE.
AT THIS POINT THEY'LL EAT JUST ABOUT...

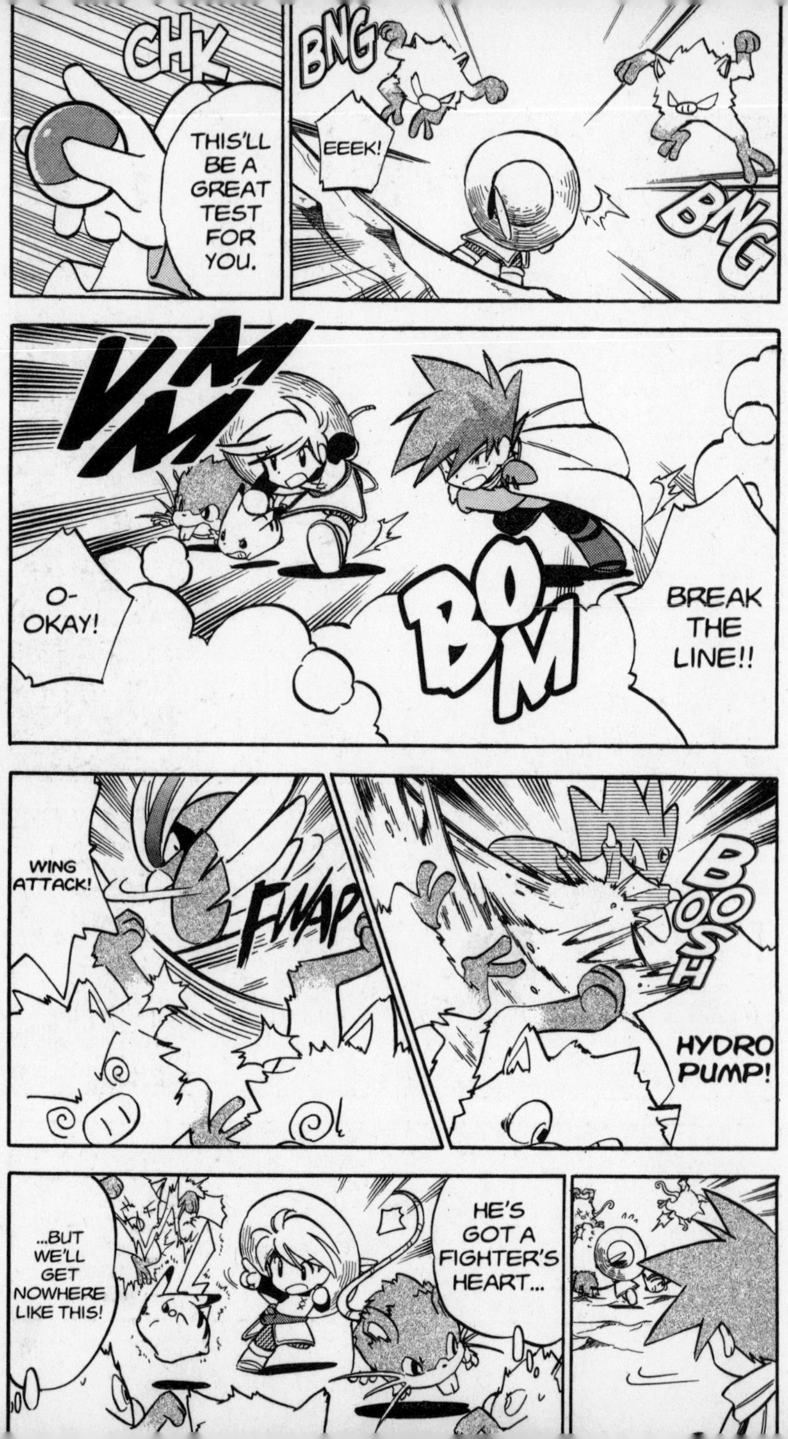
BNG
EEEK!
BNG
CHK
THIS'LL BE A GREAT TEST FOR YOU.
BREAK THE LINE!!
VM VM
BOOM
O-OKAY!
BOOSH
HYDRO PUMP!
WING ATTACK!
FWAP
HE'S GOT A FIGHTER'S HEART...
...BUT WE'LL GET NOWHERE LIKE THIS!

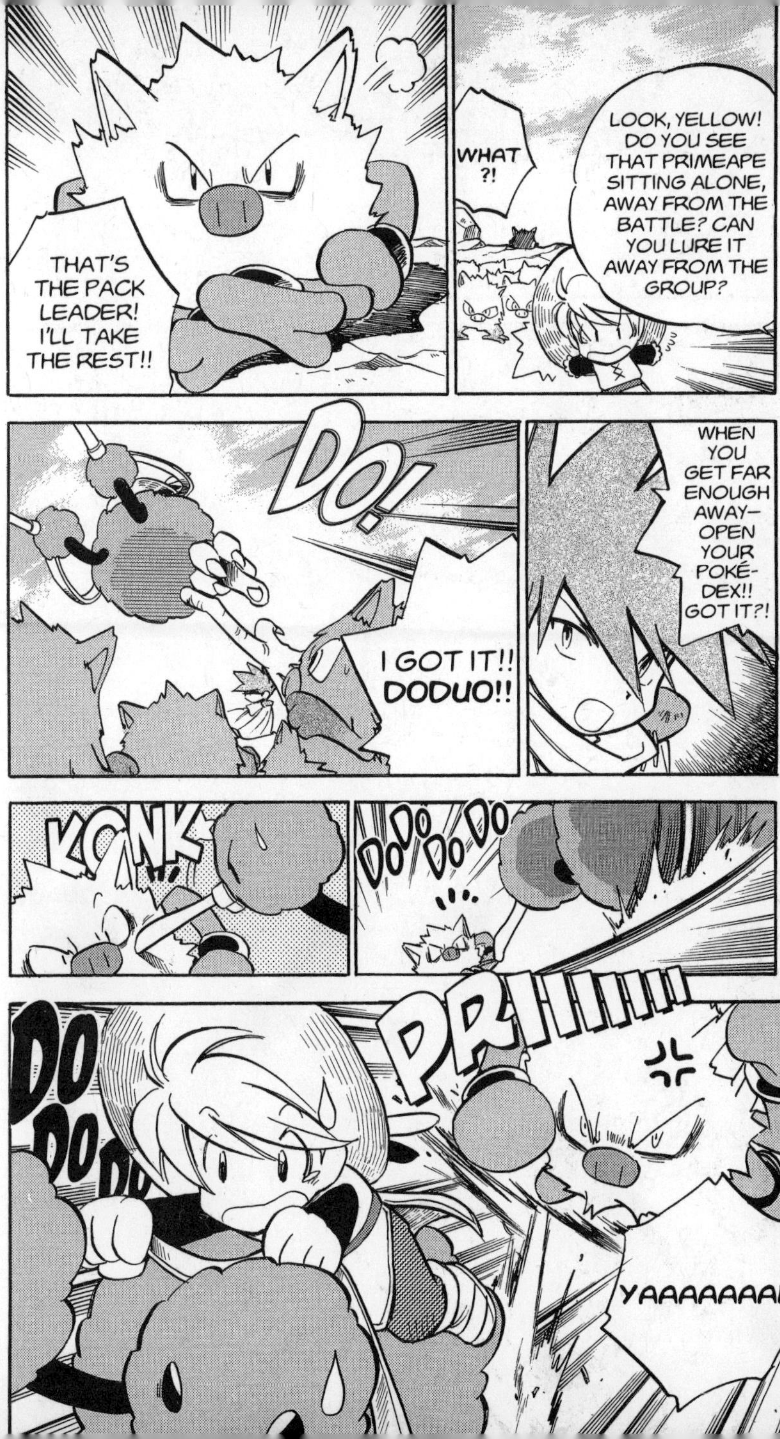
LOOK, YELLOW! DO YOU SEE THAT PRIMEAPE SITTING ALONE, AWAY FROM THE BATTLE? CAN YOU LURE IT AWAY FROM THE GROUP?
WHAT ?!
THAT'S THE PACK LEADER! I'LL TAKE THE REST!!
WHEN YOU GET FAR ENOUGH AWAY— OPEN YOUR POKÉ-DEX!! GOT IT?!
DO!
I GOT IT!! DODUO!!
DO DO DO DO DO
KONK
PRIIIIIII
DO DO DO
YAAAAAAAH!

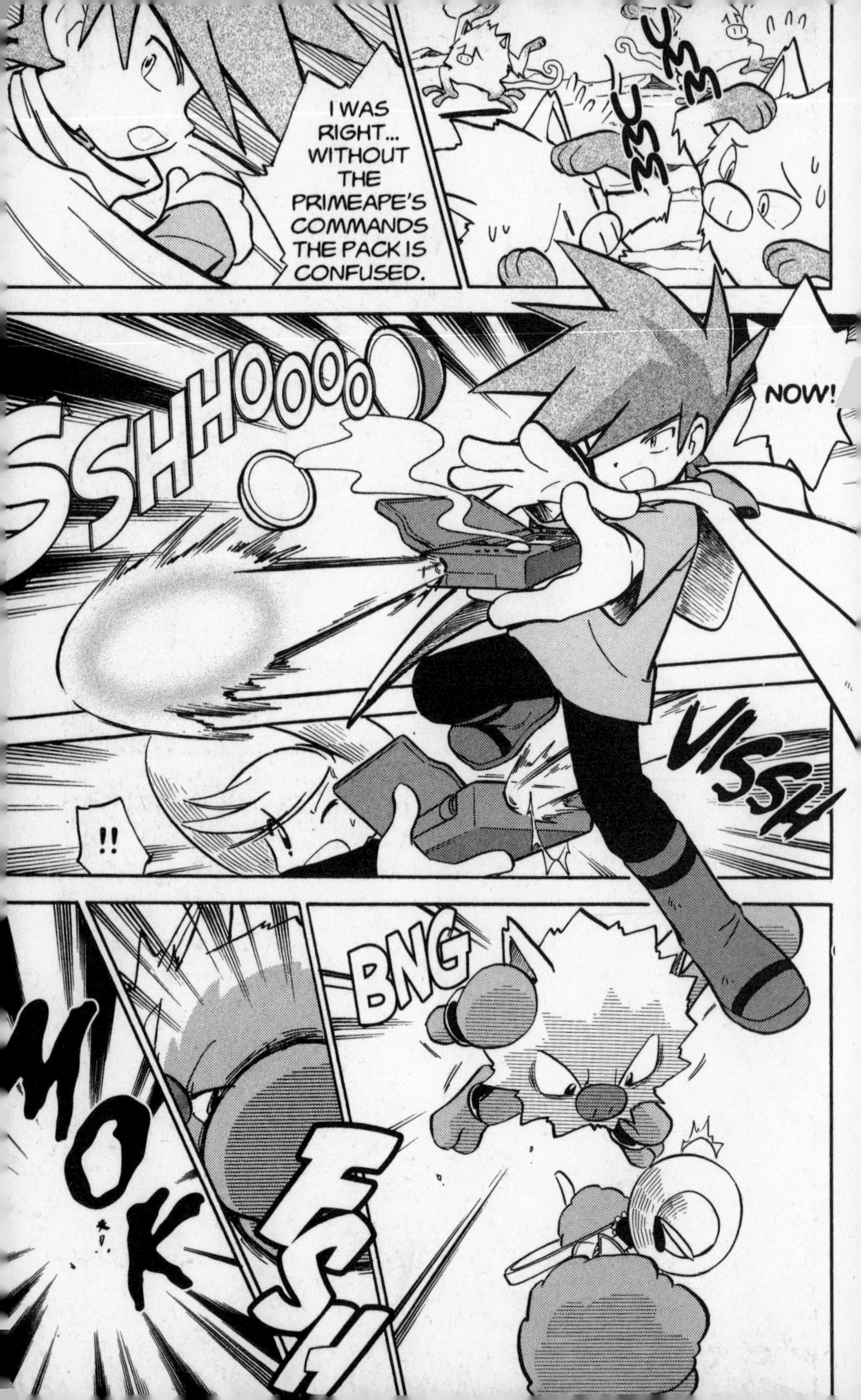
I WAS RIGHT... WITHOUT THE PRIMEAPE'S COMMANDS THE PACK IS CONFUSED.
NOW!
SHHOOOO
VISSH
!!
BNG
MOK
FSH

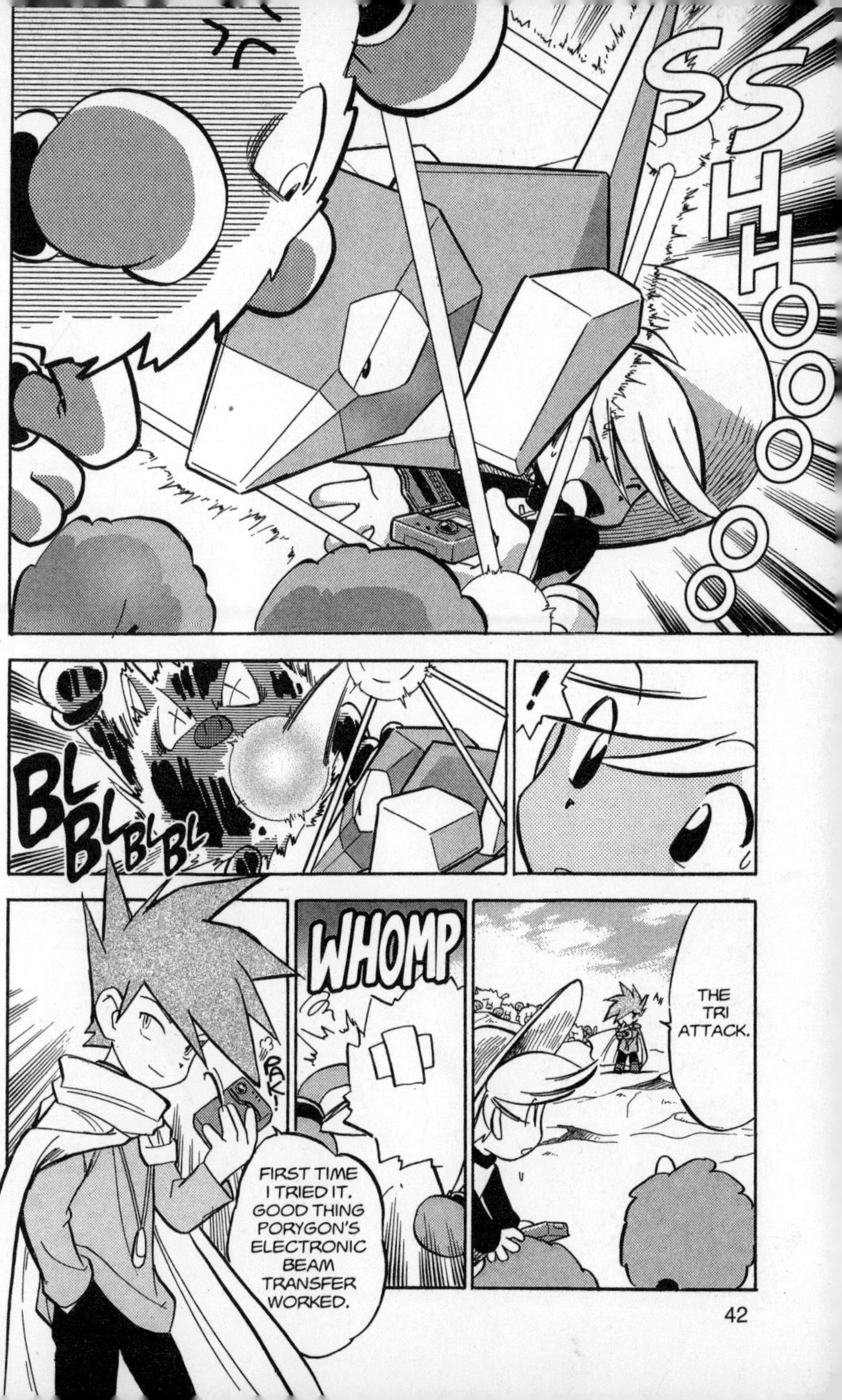
SSHHOOOOOO
!
BL BL BL BL
THE TRI ATTACK.
WHOMP
PAK!
FIRST TIME I TRIED IT. GOOD THING PORYGON'S ELECTRONIC BEAM TRANSFER WORKED.

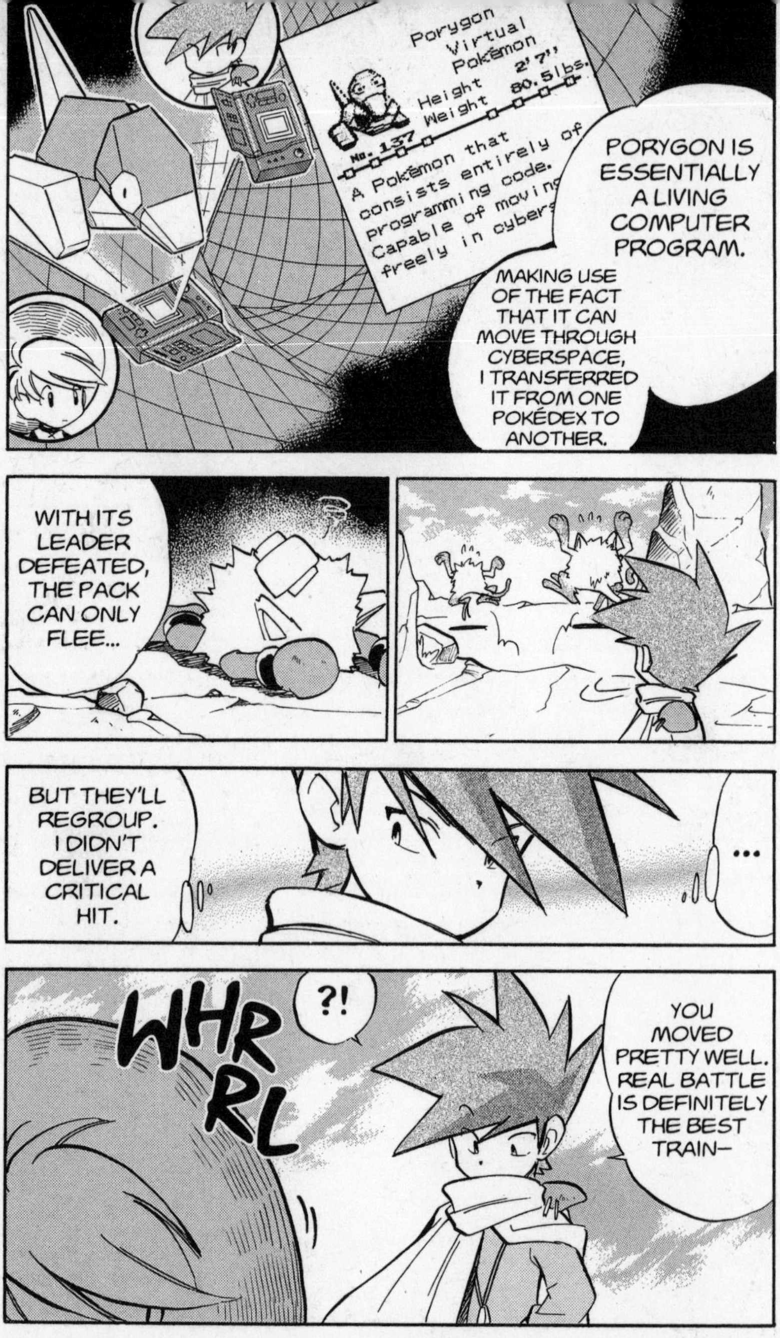
Porygon
Virtual
Pokémon
Height 2'7"
Weight 80.5lbs.
No. 137
A Pokémon that consists entirely of programming code. Capable of movin
freely in cybers
PORYGON IS ESSENTIALLY A LIVING COMPUTER PROGRAM.
MAKING USE OF THE FACT THAT IT CAN MOVE THROUGH CYBERSPACE, I TRANSFERRED IT FROM ONE POKÉDEX TO ANOTHER.
WITH ITS LEADER DEFEATED, THE PACK CAN ONLY FLEE...
...
BUT THEY'LL REGROUP. I DIDN'T DELIVER A CRITICAL HIT.
YOU MOVED PRETTY WELL. REAL BATTLE IS DEFINITELY THE BEST TRAIN—
?!
WHRRL

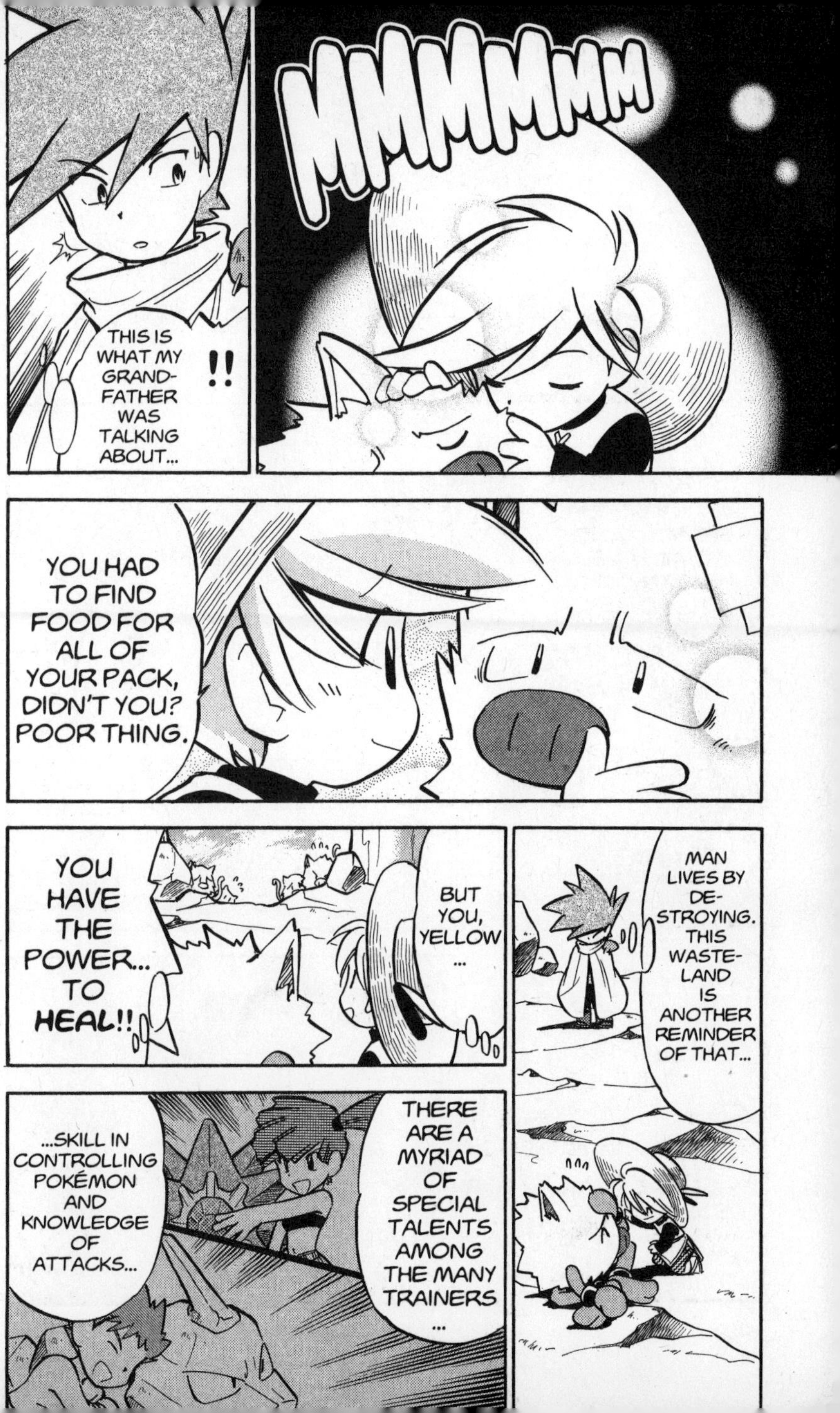
MMMMMMM
!!
THIS IS WHAT MY GRAND-FATHER WAS TALKING ABOUT...
YOU HAD TO FIND FOOD FOR ALL OF YOUR PACK, DIDN'T YOU? POOR THING.
MAN LIVES BY DE-STROYING. THIS WASTE-LAND IS ANOTHER REMINDER OF THAT...
BUT YOU, YELLOW ...
YOU HAVE THE POWER... TO **HEAL!!**
THERE ARE A MYRIAD OF SPECIAL TALENTS AMONG THE MANY TRAINERS ...
...SKILL IN CONTROLLING POKÉMON AND KNOWLEDGE OF ATTACKS...

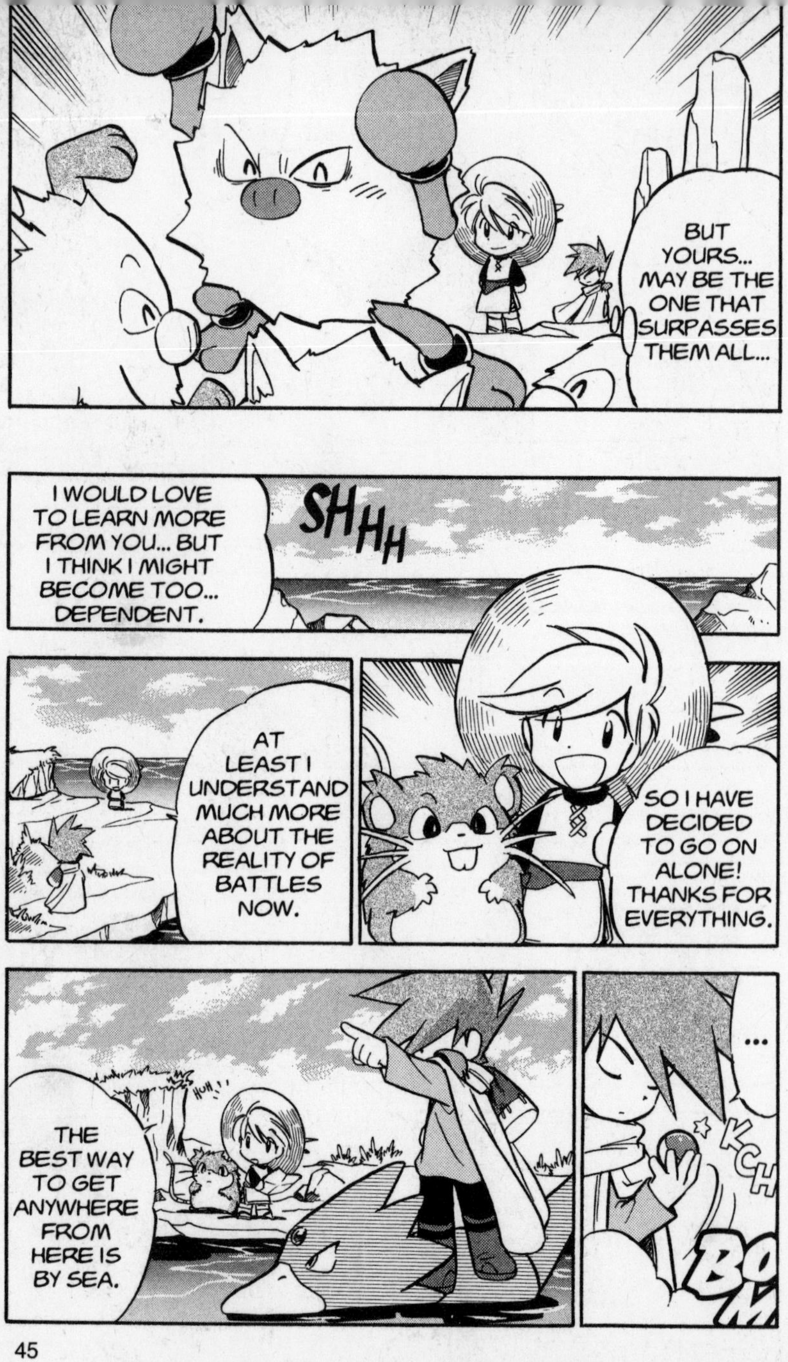
BUT YOURS... MAY BE THE ONE THAT SURPASSES THEM ALL...
SHHH
I WOULD LOVE TO LEARN MORE FROM YOU... BUT I THINK I MIGHT BECOME TOO... DEPENDENT.
SO I HAVE DECIDED TO GO ON ALONE! THANKS FOR EVERYTHING.
AT LEAST I UNDERSTAND MUCH MORE ABOUT THE REALITY OF BATTLES NOW.
...
KCH
HUH!!
THE BEST WAY TO GET ANYWHERE FROM HERE IS BY SEA.

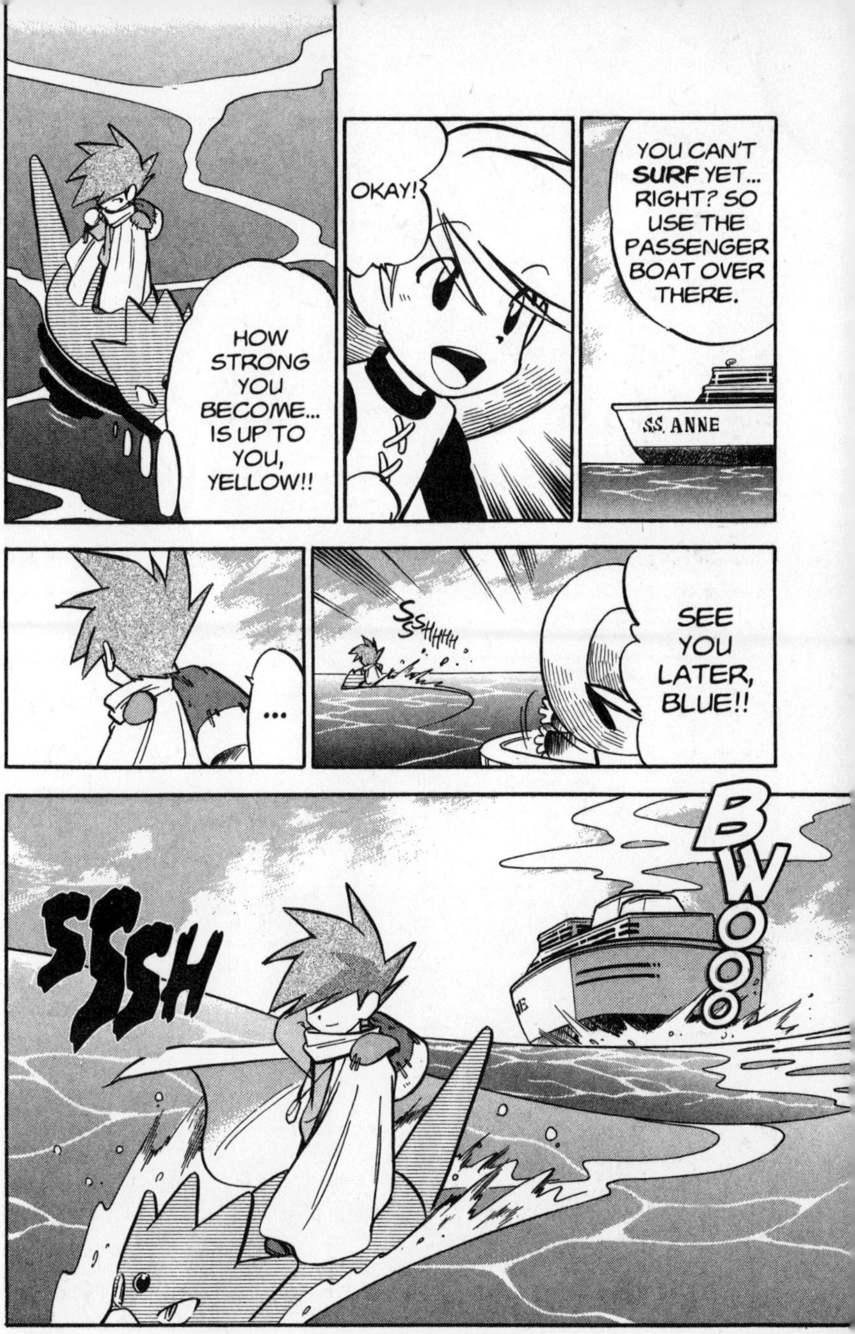
YOU CAN'T **SURF** YET... RIGHT? SO USE THE PASSENGER BOAT OVER THERE.
S.S. ANNE
OKAY!
HOW STRONG YOU BECOME... IS UP TO YOU, YELLOW!!
SEE YOU LATER, BLUE!!
SSHHHH
...
BWOOO
SSSH

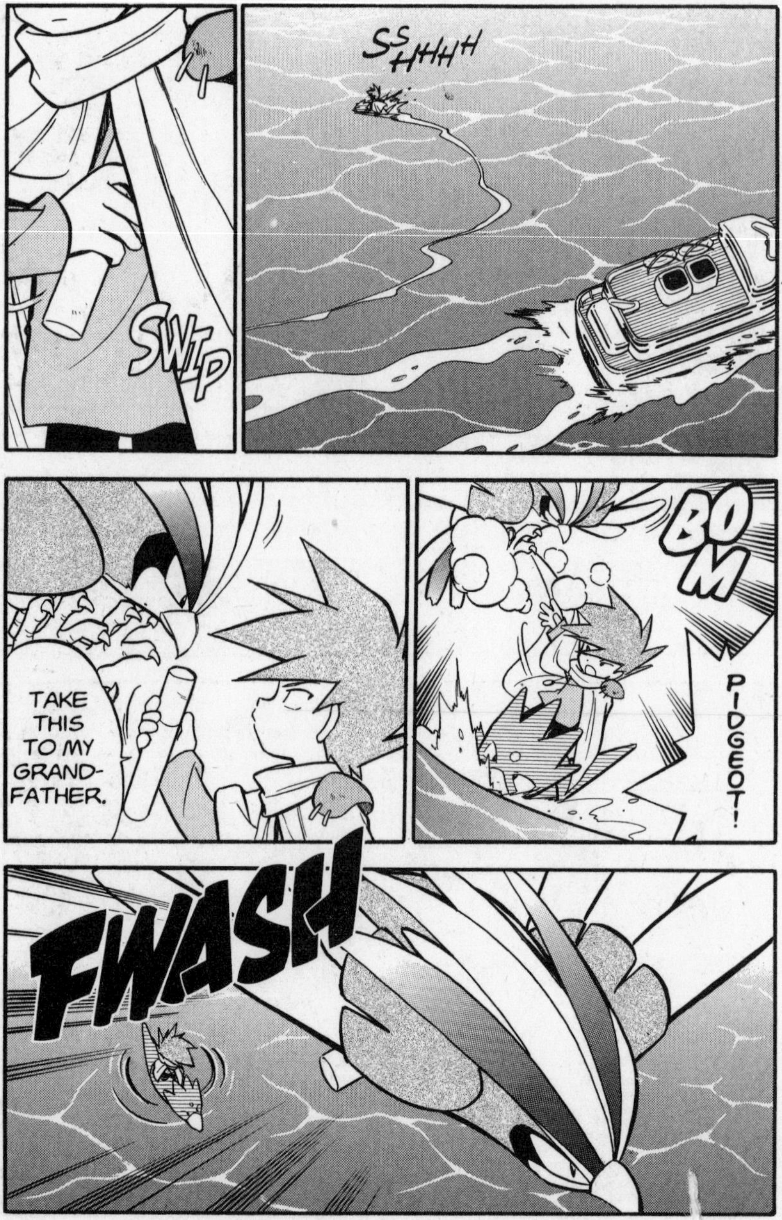
SSHHHH
SWIP
BOM
PIDGEOT!
TAKE THIS TO MY GRANDFATHER.
FWASH

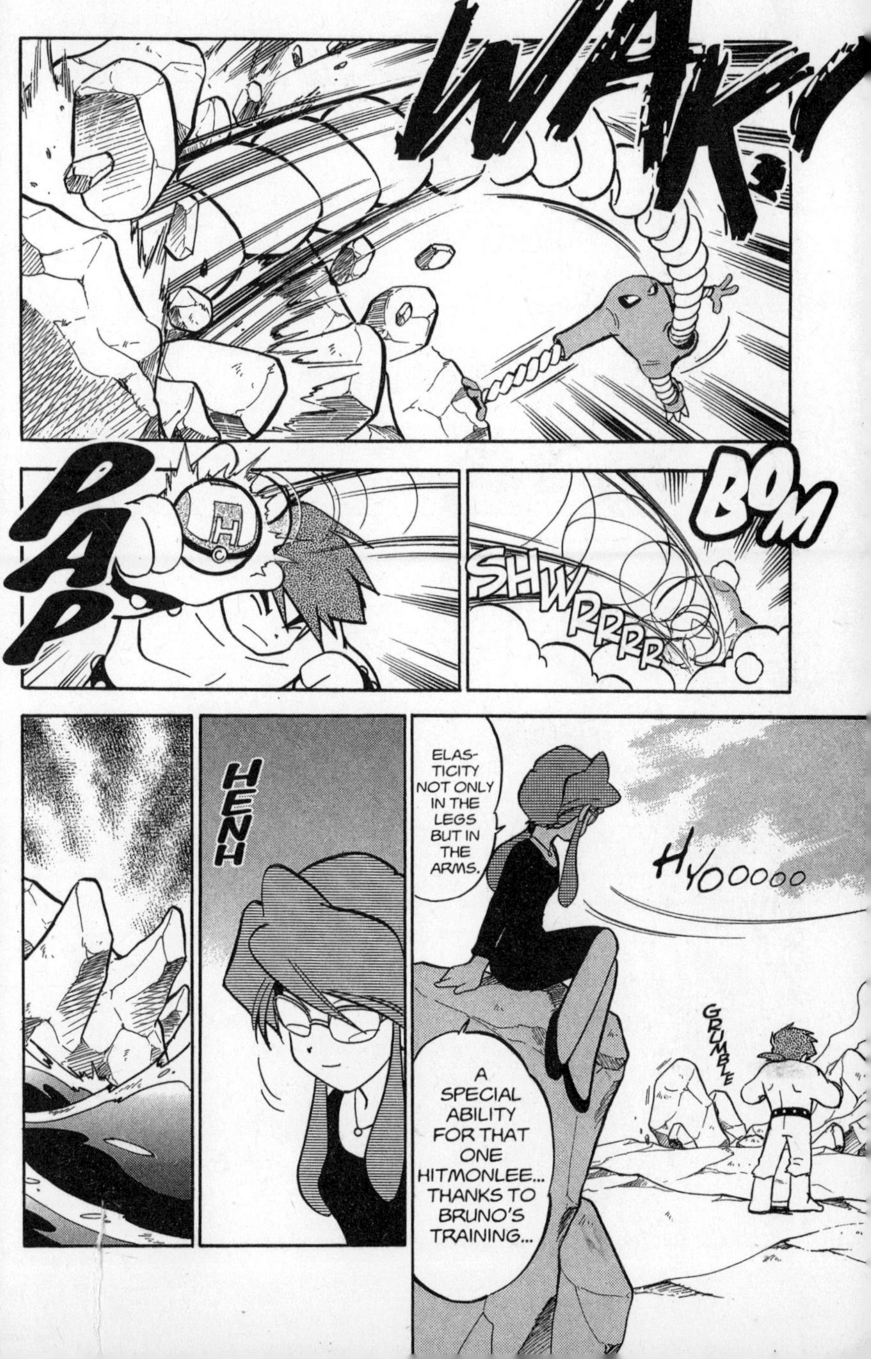
WAK!
BOM
SHWRRRR
PAP
ELAS-TICITY NOT ONLY IN THE LEGS BUT IN THE ARMS.
HYOOOOO
GRUMBLE
A SPECIAL ABILITY FOR THAT ONE HITMONLEE... THANKS TO BRUNO'S TRAINING...
HENH

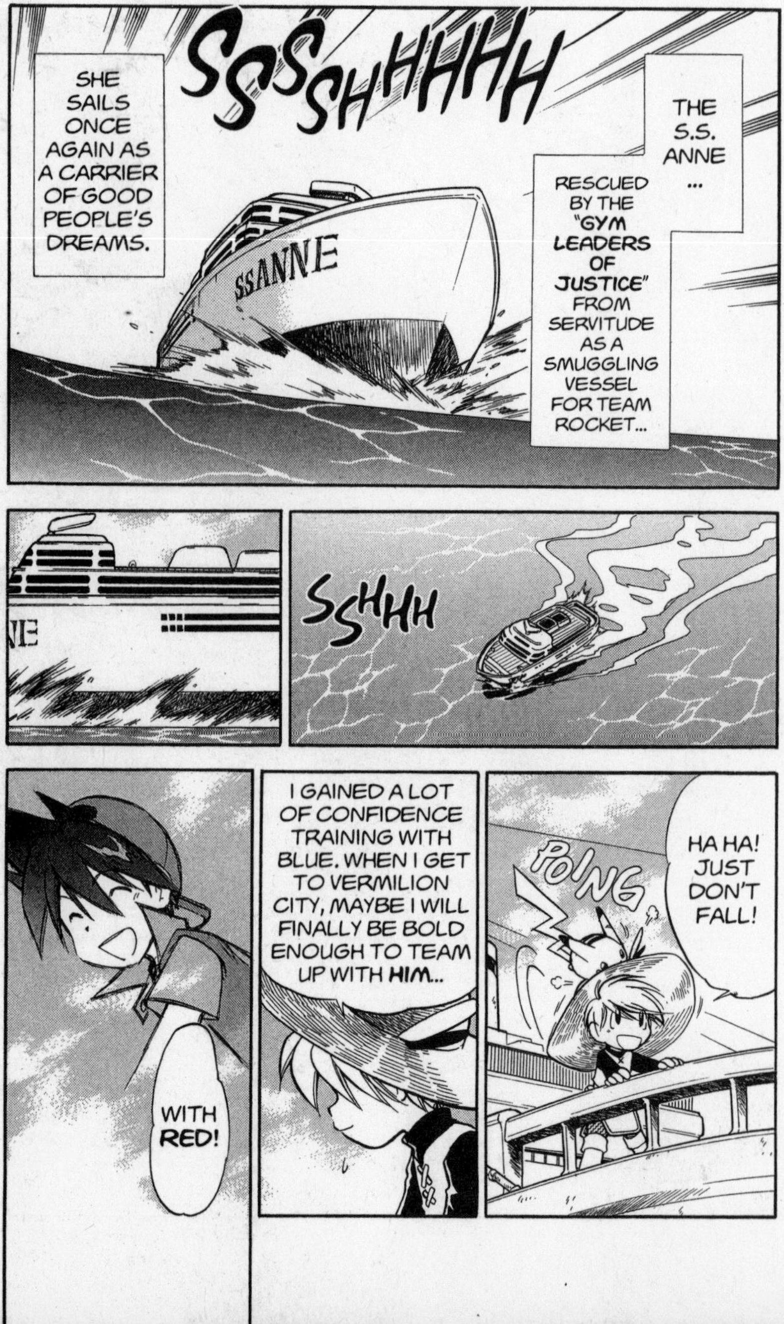
THE S.S. ANNE ...
RESCUED BY THE "GYM LEADERS OF JUSTICE" FROM SERVITUDE AS A SMUGGLING VESSEL FOR TEAM ROCKET...
SSSSHHHHHH
SHE SAILS ONCE AGAIN AS A CARRIER OF GOOD PEOPLE'S DREAMS.
SS ANNE
SSHHH
HA HA! JUST DON'T FALL!
POING
I GAINED A LOT OF CONFIDENCE TRAINING WITH BLUE. WHEN I GET TO VERMILION CITY, MAYBE I WILL FINALLY BE BOLD ENOUGH TO TEAM UP WITH HIM...
WITH RED!

56 The Coming of Slowpoke (Eventually)

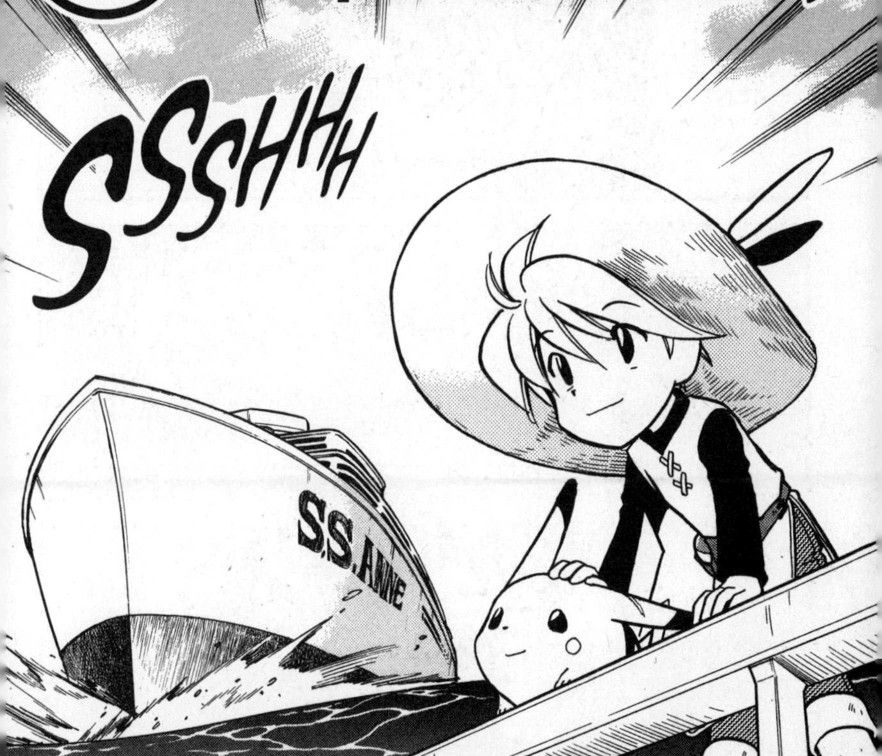
SSSHHH
S.S. ANNE

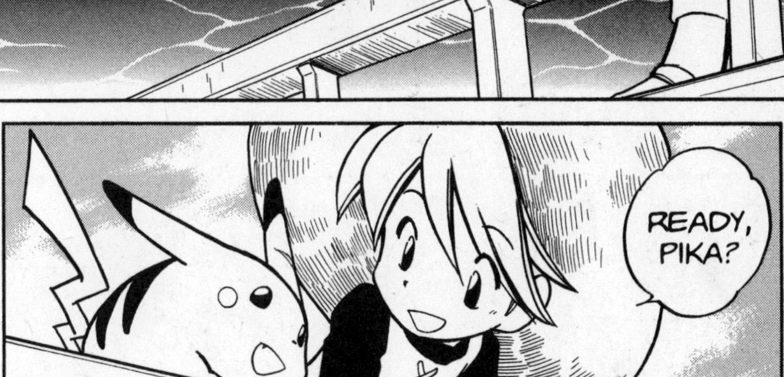
READY, PIKA?

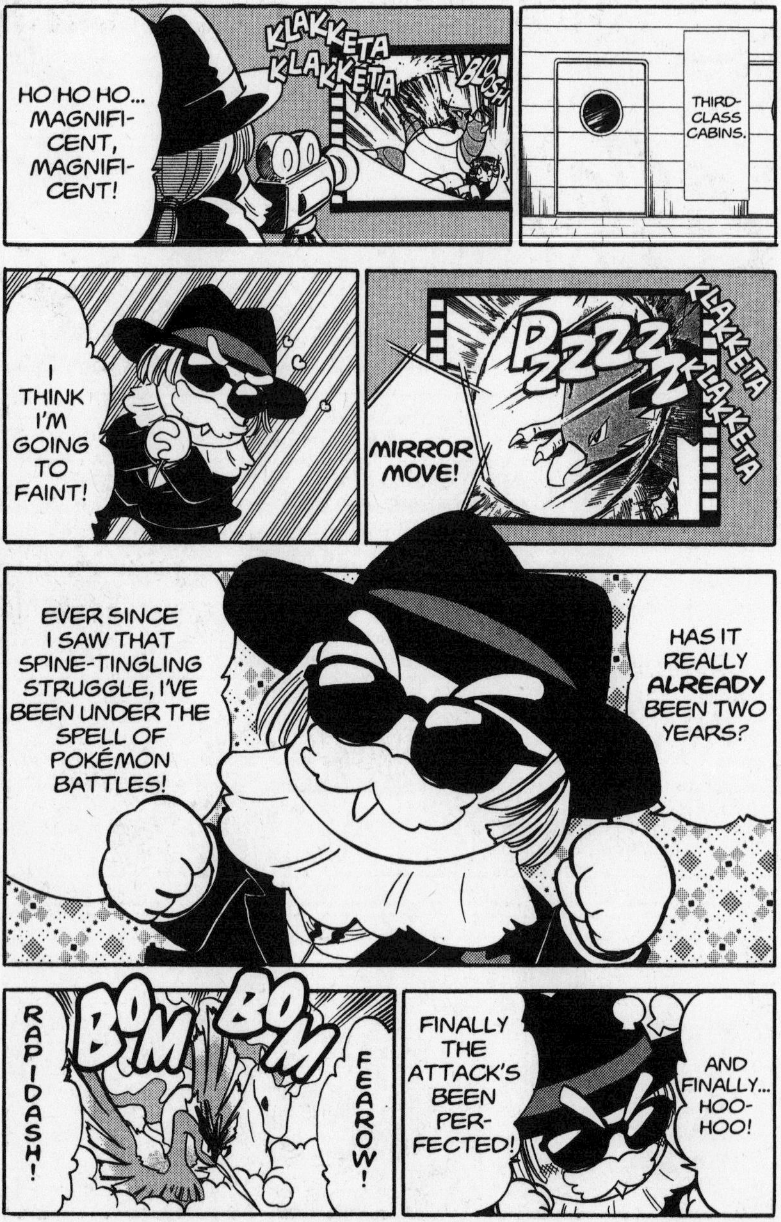
THIRD-CLASS CABINS.
KLAKKETA KLAKKETA
BLOSH
HO HO HO... MAGNIFICENT, MAGNIFICENT!
PZZZZZ
KLAKKETA KLAKKETA
MIRROR MOVE!
I THINK I'M GOING TO FAINT!
HAS IT REALLY **ALREADY** BEEN TWO YEARS?
EVER SINCE I SAW THAT SPINE-TINGLING STRUGGLE, I'VE BEEN UNDER THE SPELL OF POKÉMON BATTLES!
AND FINALLY... HOO-HOO!
FINALLY THE ATTACK'S BEEN PERFECTED!
FEAROW!
BOM
BOM
RAPIDASH!

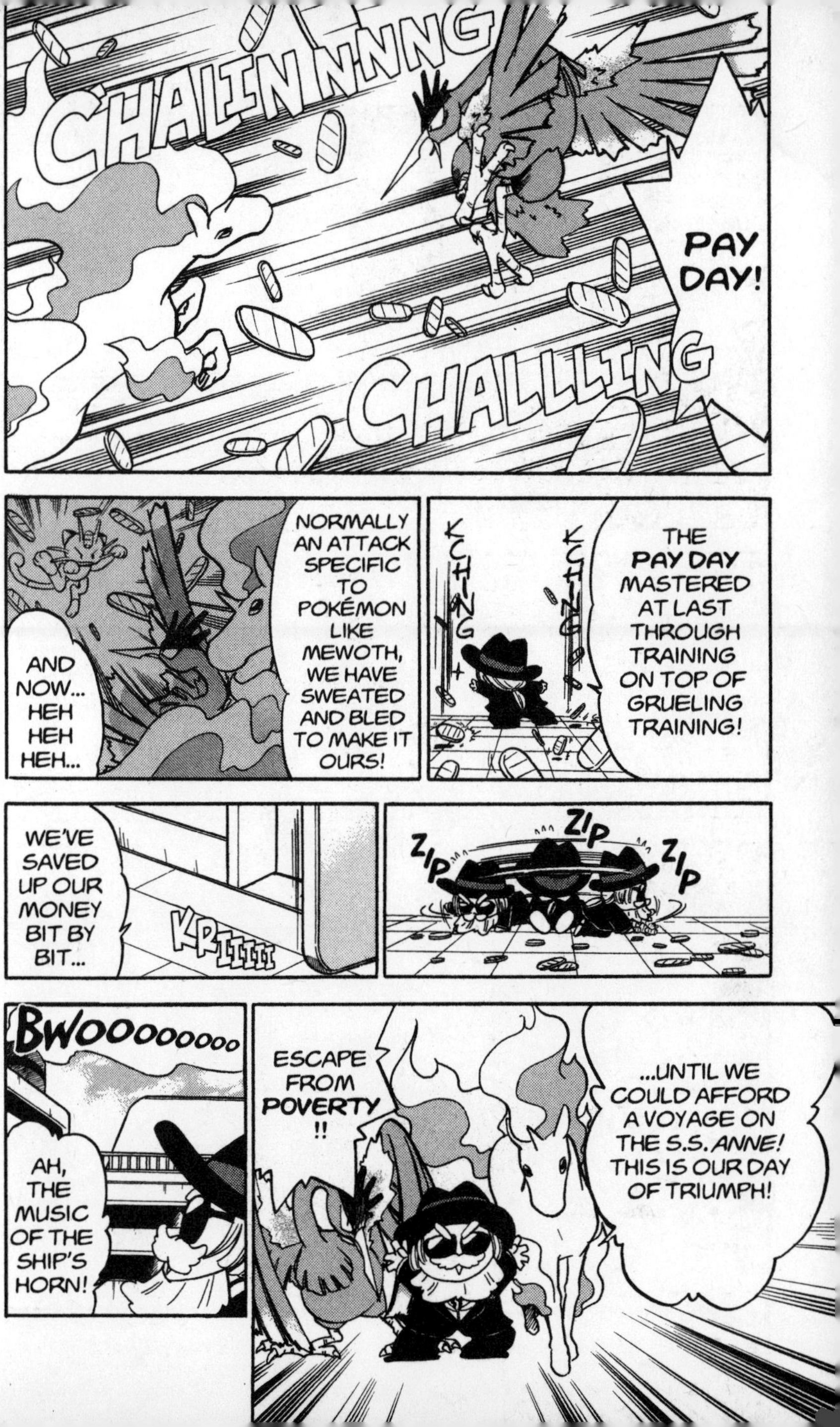
CHALINNNG
PAY DAY!
CHALLLING
KCHING
KCHING
THE PAY DAY MASTERED AT LAST THROUGH TRAINING ON TOP OF GRUELING TRAINING!
NORMALLY AN ATTACK SPECIFIC TO POKÉMON LIKE MEWOTH, WE HAVE SWEATED AND BLED TO MAKE IT OURS!
AND NOW... HEH HEH HEH...
ZIP
ZIP
ZIP
WE'VE SAVED UP OUR MONEY BIT BY BIT...
KRIIIII
...UNTIL WE COULD AFFORD A VOYAGE ON THE S.S. ANNE! THIS IS OUR DAY OF TRIUMPH!
ESCAPE FROM POVERTY !!
BWOOOOOOOO
AH, THE MUSIC OF THE SHIP'S HORN!

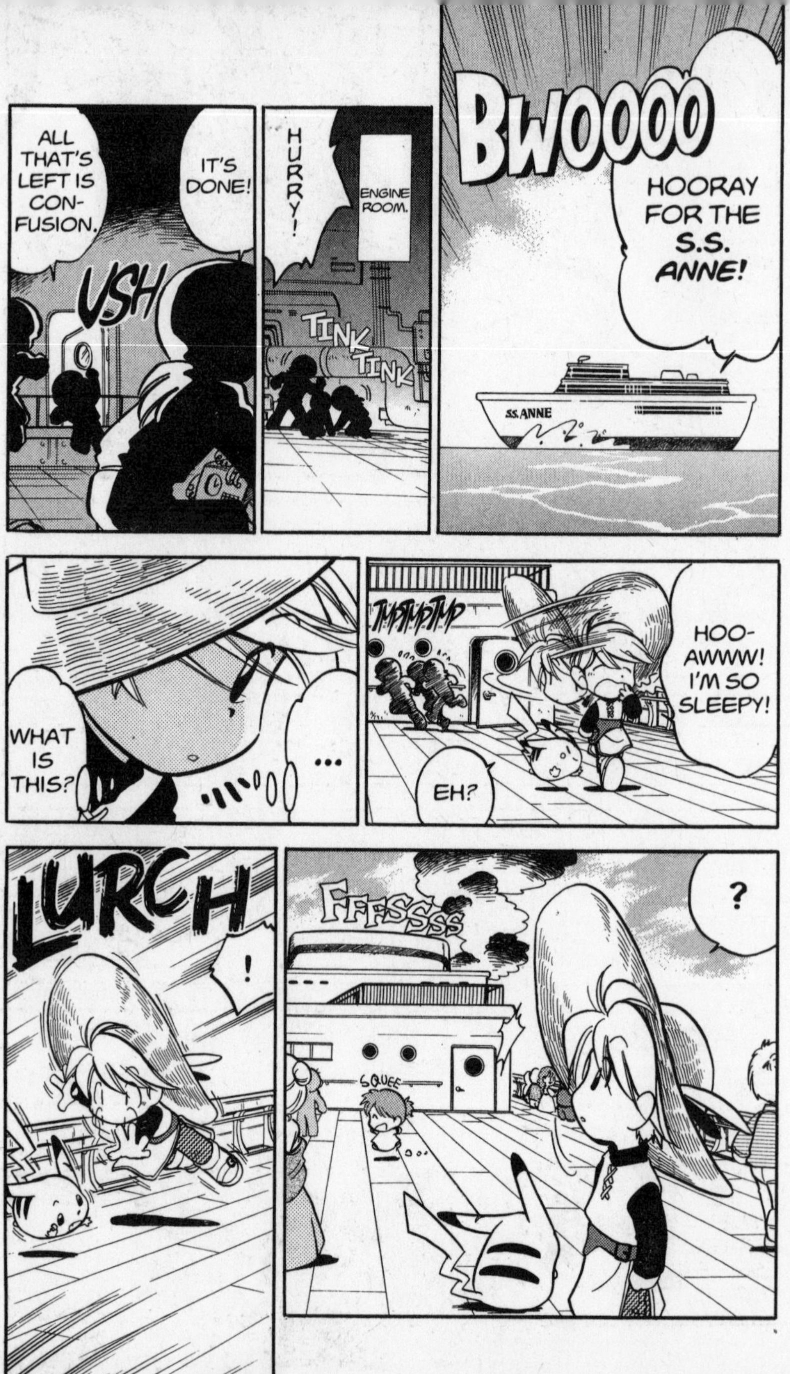
BWOOOO
HOORAY FOR THE S.S. ANNE!
S.S. ANNE
HURRY!
ENGINE ROOM.
TINK
TINK
IT'S DONE!
ALL THAT'S LEFT IS CON-FUSION.
USH
TMPTMPTMP
HOO-AWWW! I'M SO SLEEPY!
EH?
...
WHAT IS THIS?
?
FFFSSSS
SQUEE
LURCH
!

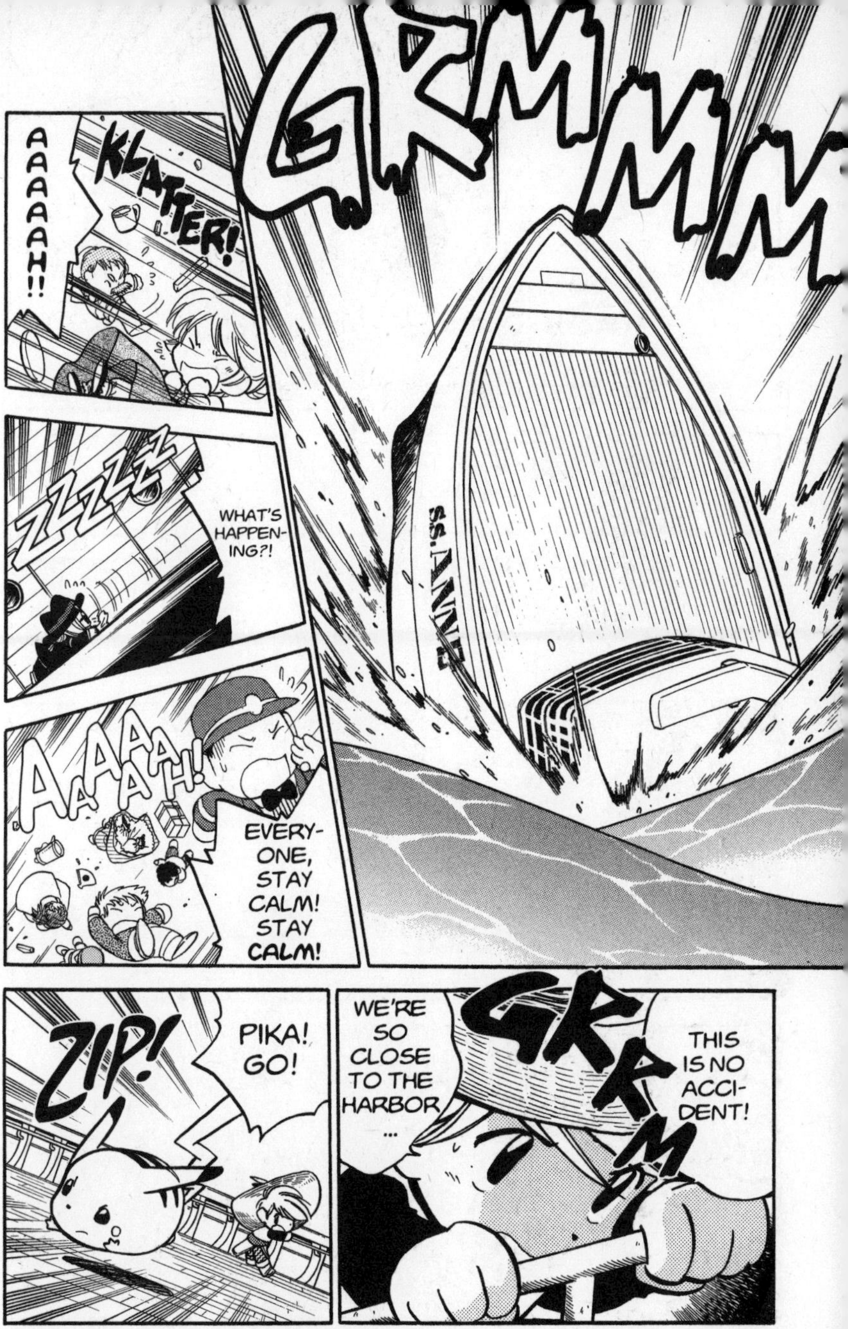
GRMMMM
S.S. ANNE
KLATTER!
AAAAAAH!!
ZZZZZZ
WHAT'S HAPPEN-ING?!
AAAAAH!
EVERY-ONE, STAY CALM! STAY CALM!
WE'RE SO CLOSE TO THE HARBOR...
GRRM
THIS IS NO ACCI-DENT!
ZIP!
PIKA! GO!

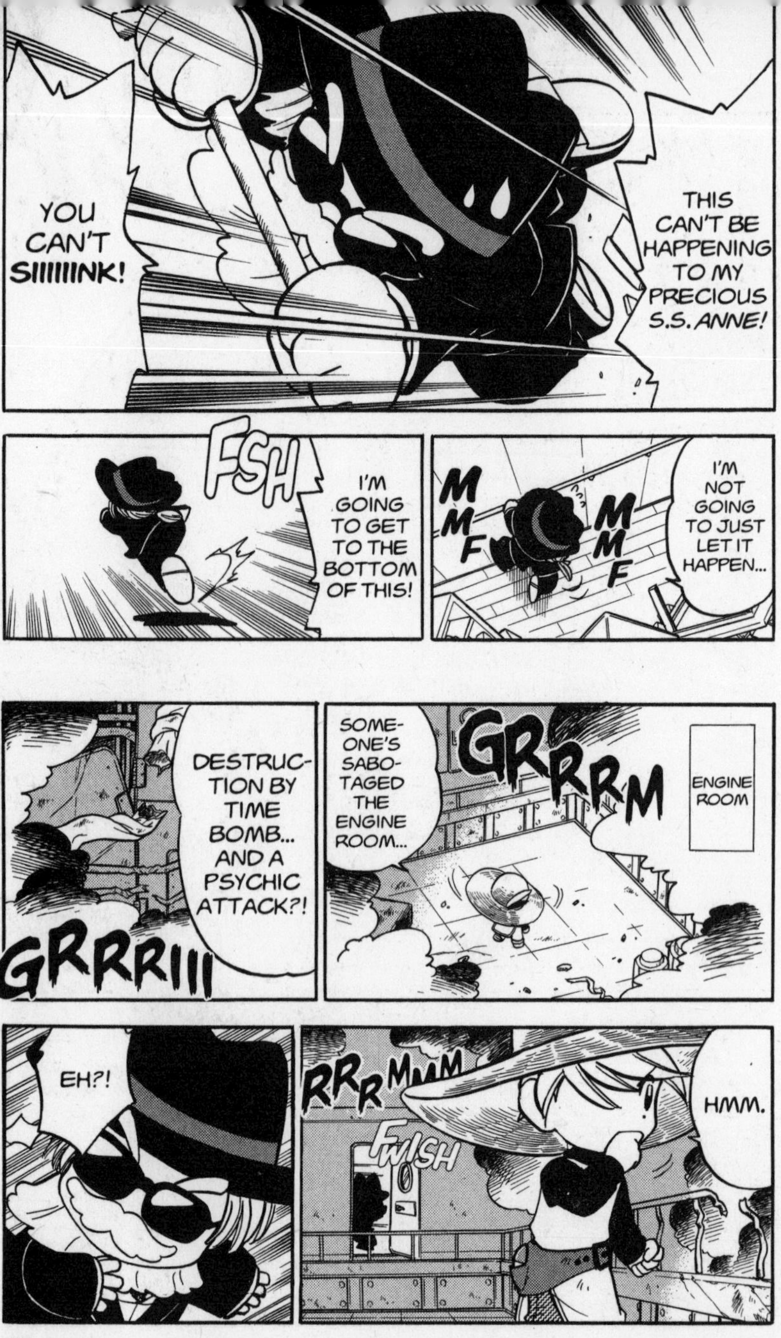
THIS CAN'T BE HAPPENING TO MY PRECIOUS S.S. ANNE!
YOU CAN'T SIIIIIINK!
I'M NOT GOING TO JUST LET IT HAPPEN...
MMF
MMF
FSH
I'M GOING TO GET TO THE BOTTOM OF THIS!
ENGINE ROOM
GRRRRM
SOME-ONE'S SABO-TAGED THE ENGINE ROOM...
DESTRUC-TION BY TIME BOMB... AND A PSYCHIC ATTACK?!
GRRRIII
HMM.
RRRMMM
FWISH
EH?!

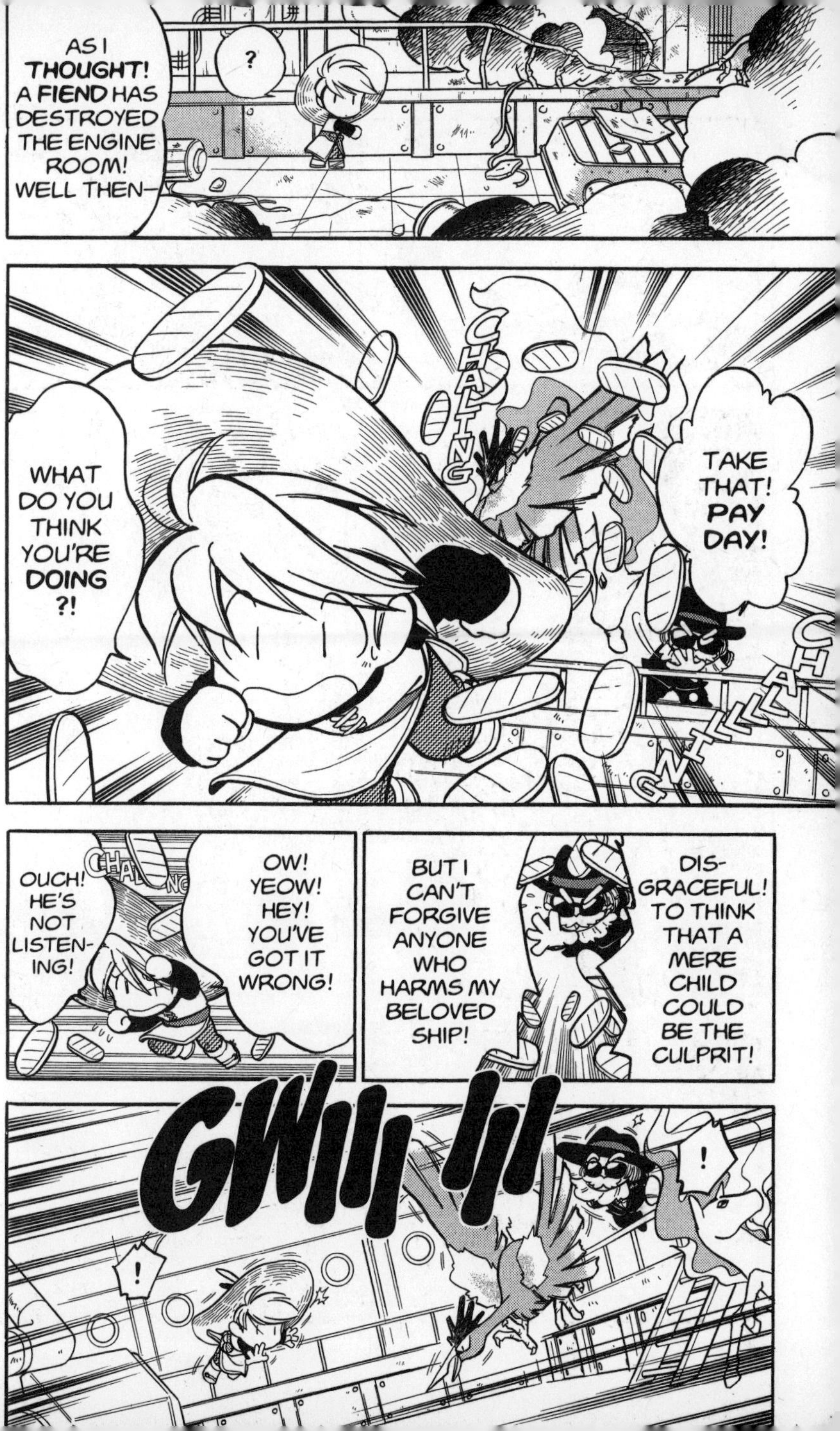
?
AS I THOUGHT! A FIEND HAS DESTROYED THE ENGINE ROOM! WELL THEN—
TAKE THAT! PAY DAY!
CHALLING
CHALING
WHAT DO YOU THINK YOU'RE DOING?!
DIS-GRACEFUL! TO THINK THAT A MERE CHILD COULD BE THE CULPRIT!
BUT I CAN'T FORGIVE ANYONE WHO HARMS MY BELOVED SHIP!
OW! YEOW! HEY! YOU'VE GOT IT WRONG!
CHALING
OUCH! HE'S NOT LISTEN-ING!
!
GWIII!!!
!

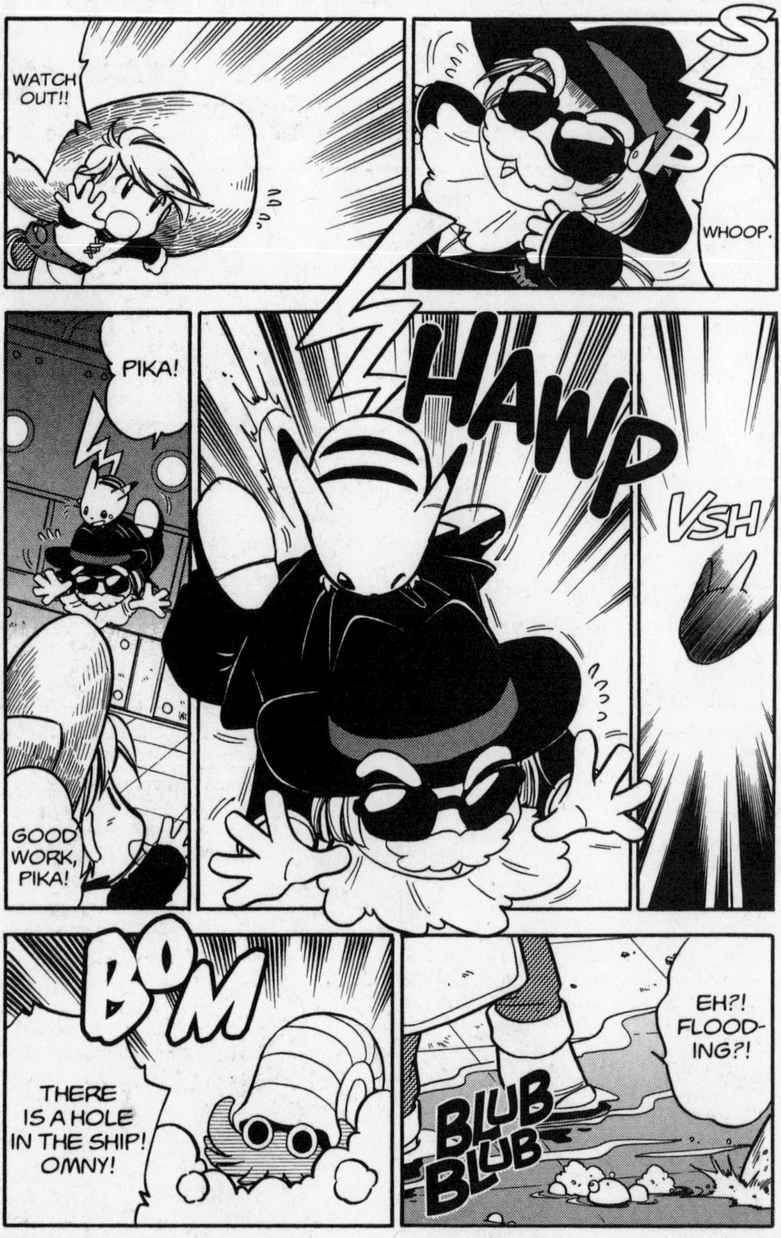
SLIP
WHOOP.
WATCH OUT!!
VSH
HAWP
PIKA!
GOOD WORK, PIKA!
EH?! FLOODING?!
BLUB BLUB
BOM
THERE IS A HOLE IN THE SHIP! OMNY!

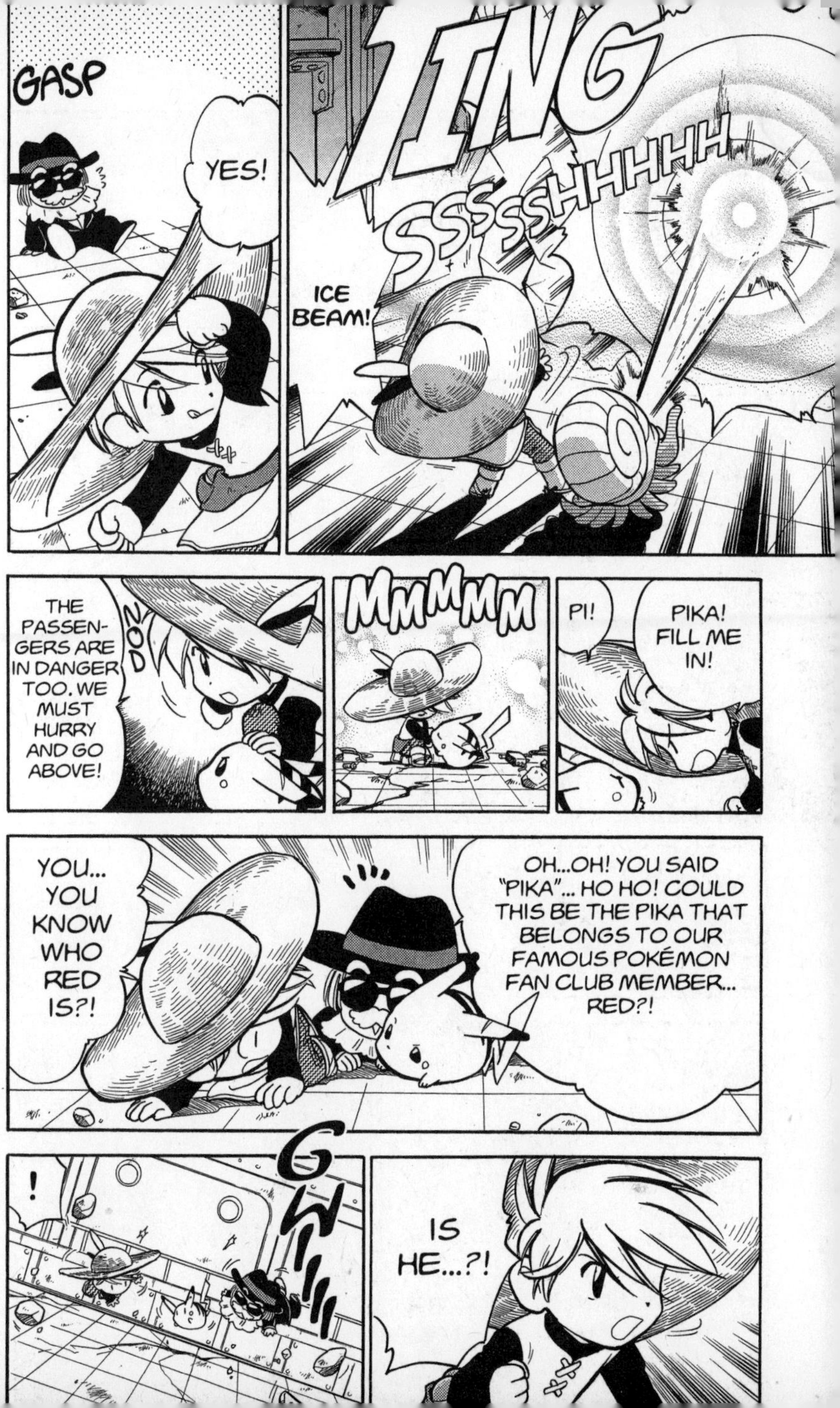
ZING
SSSSSHHHHHH
ICE BEAM!
YES!
GASP
PIKA! FILL ME IN!
PI!
MMMMMM
NOD
THE PASSENGERS ARE IN DANGER TOO. WE MUST HURRY AND GO ABOVE!
OH...OH! YOU SAID "PIKA"... HO HO! COULD THIS BE THE PIKA THAT BELONGS TO OUR FAMOUS POKÉMON FAN CLUB MEMBER... RED?!
YOU... YOU KNOW WHO RED IS?!
IS HE...?!
GW
!

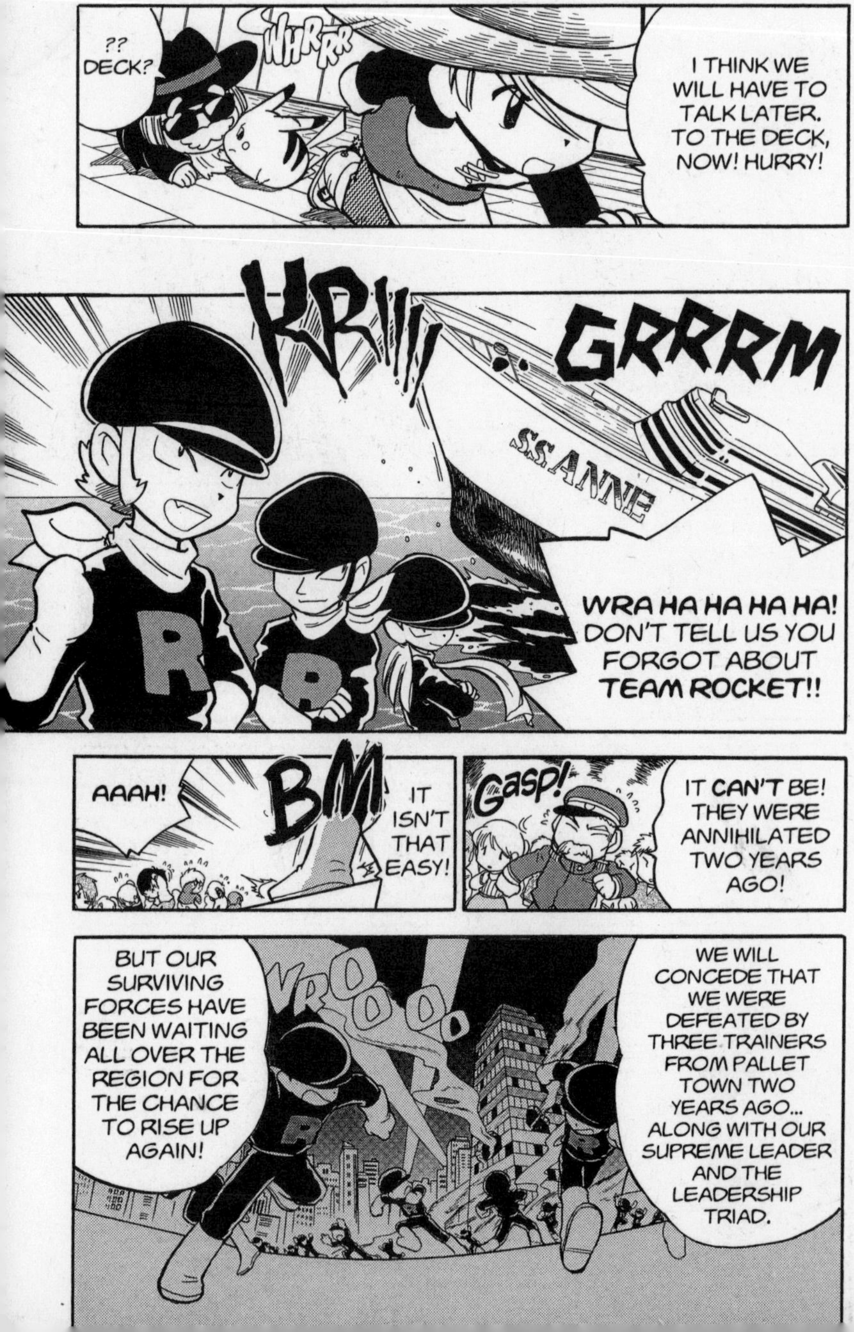
I THINK WE WILL HAVE TO TALK LATER. TO THE DECK, NOW! HURRY!
WHRRR
?? DECK?
GRRRM
KRIIII
S.S. ANNE
WRA HA HA HA HA! DON'T TELL US YOU FORGOT ABOUT TEAM ROCKET!!
IT CAN'T BE! THEY WERE ANNIHILATED TWO YEARS AGO!
Gasp!
IT ISN'T THAT EASY!
BM
AAAH!
WE WILL CONCEDE THAT WE WERE DEFEATED BY THREE TRAINERS FROM PALLET TOWN TWO YEARS AGO... ALONG WITH OUR SUPREME LEADER AND THE LEADERSHIP TRIAD.
VROOOO
BUT OUR SURVIVING FORCES HAVE BEEN WAITING ALL OVER THE REGION FOR THE CHANCE TO RISE UP AGAIN!

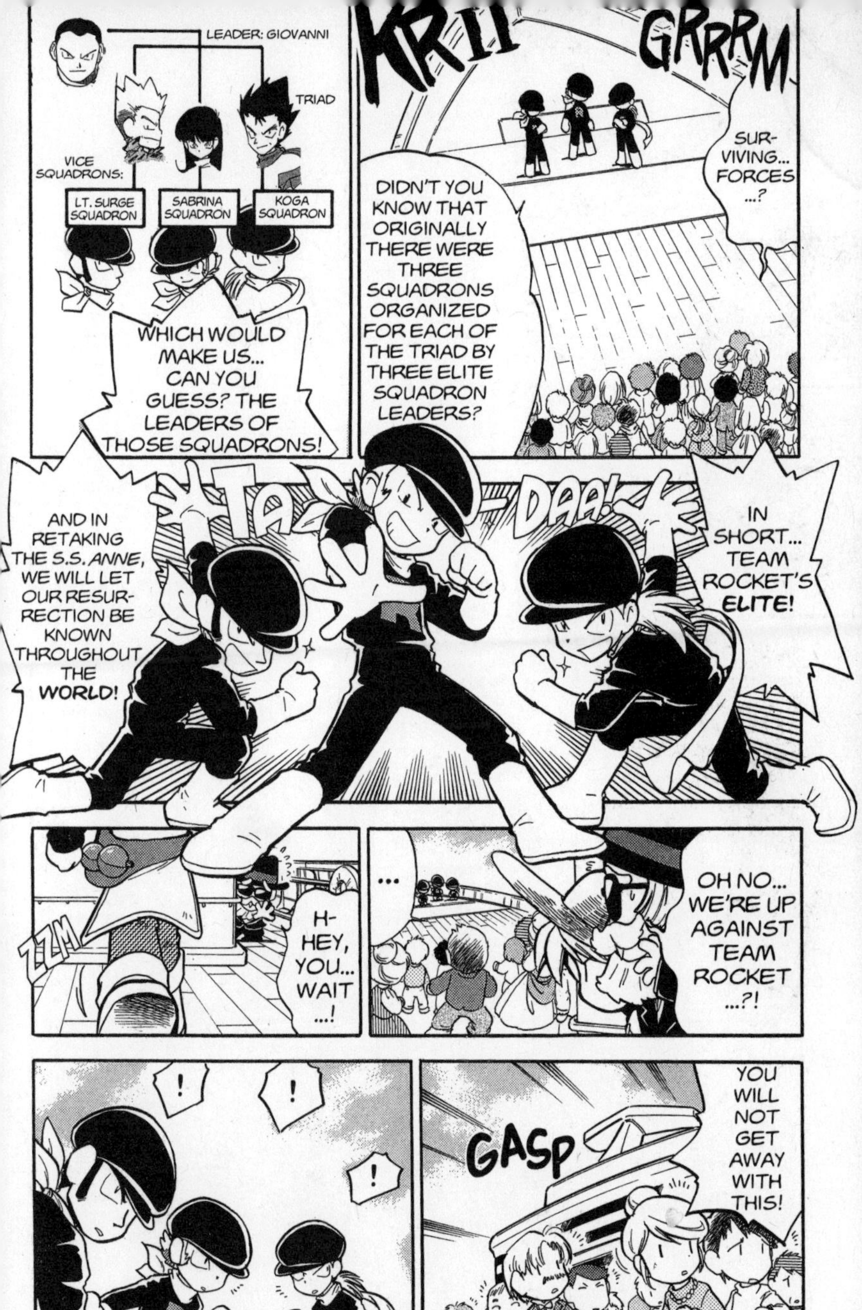
KRII
GRRRM
SURVIVING... FORCES ...?
DIDN'T YOU KNOW THAT ORIGINALLY THERE WERE THREE SQUADRONS ORGANIZED FOR EACH OF THE TRIAD BY THREE ELITE SQUADRON LEADERS?
LEADER: GIOVANNI
TRIAD
VICE SQUADRONS:
LT. SURGE SQUADRON
SABRINA SQUADRON
KOGA SQUADRON
WHICH WOULD MAKE US... CAN YOU GUESS? THE LEADERS OF THOSE SQUADRONS!
IN SHORT... TEAM ROCKET'S **ELITE!**
TA DAA!
AND IN RETAKING THE S.S. *ANNE*, WE WILL LET OUR RESURRECTION BE KNOWN THROUGHOUT THE **WORLD!**
...
OH NO... WE'RE UP AGAINST TEAM ROCKET ...?!
H-HEY, YOU... WAIT ...!
ZZM
YOU WILL NOT GET AWAY WITH THIS!
GASP
!
!
!

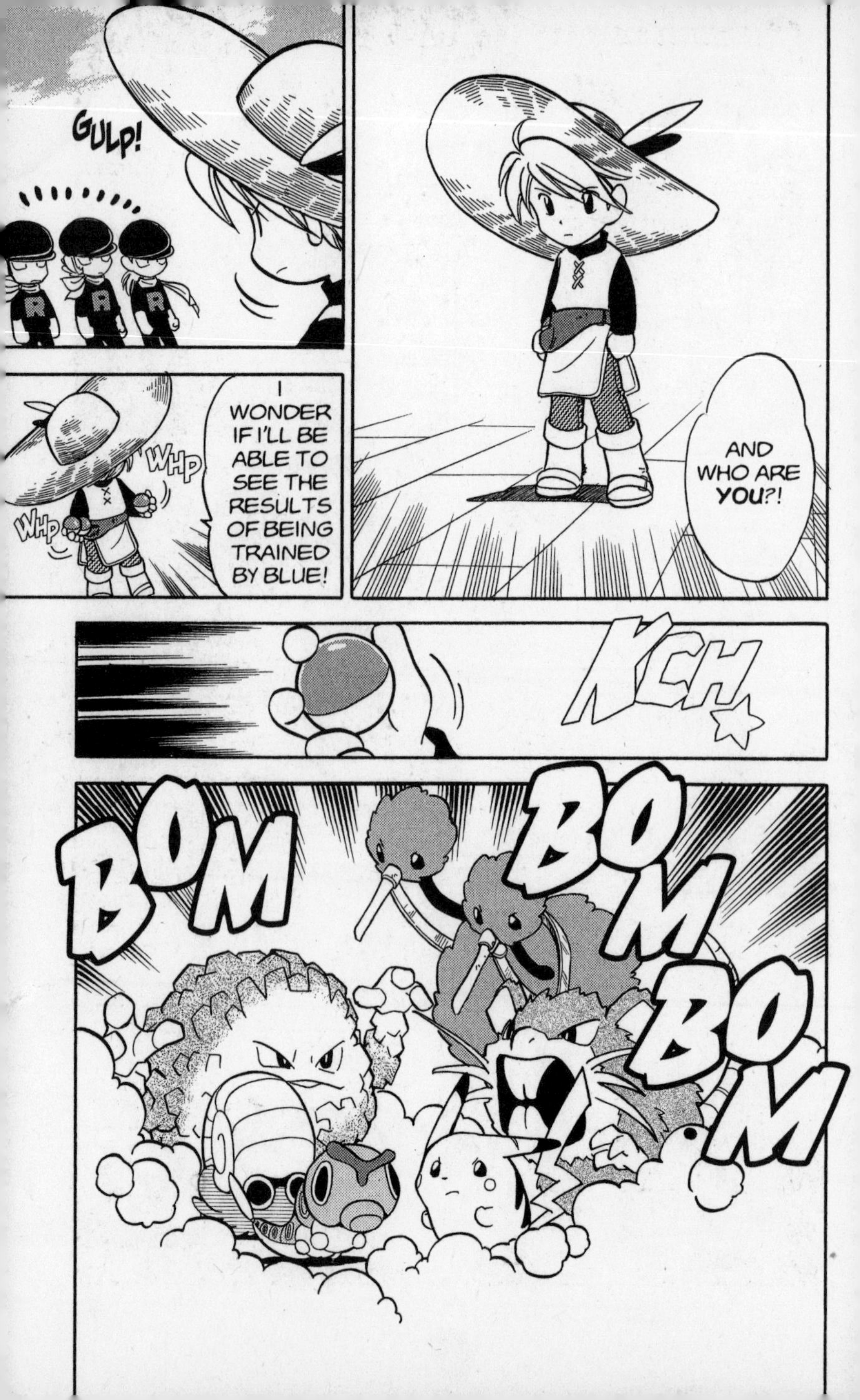
AND WHO ARE YOU?!
GULP!
I WONDER IF I'LL BE ABLE TO SEE THE RESULTS OF BEING TRAINED BY BLUE!
WHP
WHP
KCH
BOM
BOM
BOM
BOM

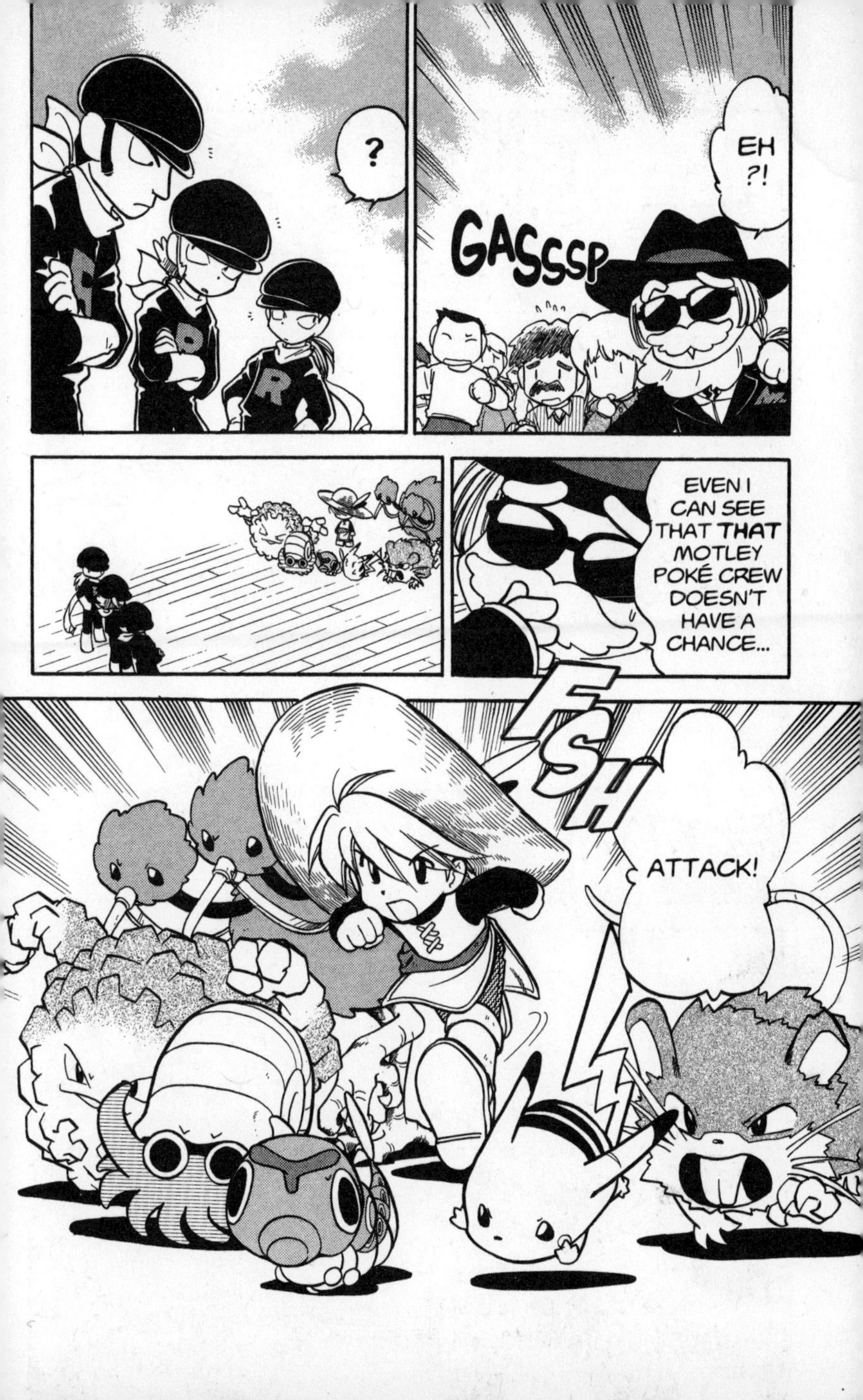
EH ?!
GASSSP
?
EVEN I CAN SEE THAT THAT MOTLEY POKÉ CREW DOESN'T HAVE A CHANCE...
FSH
ATTACK!

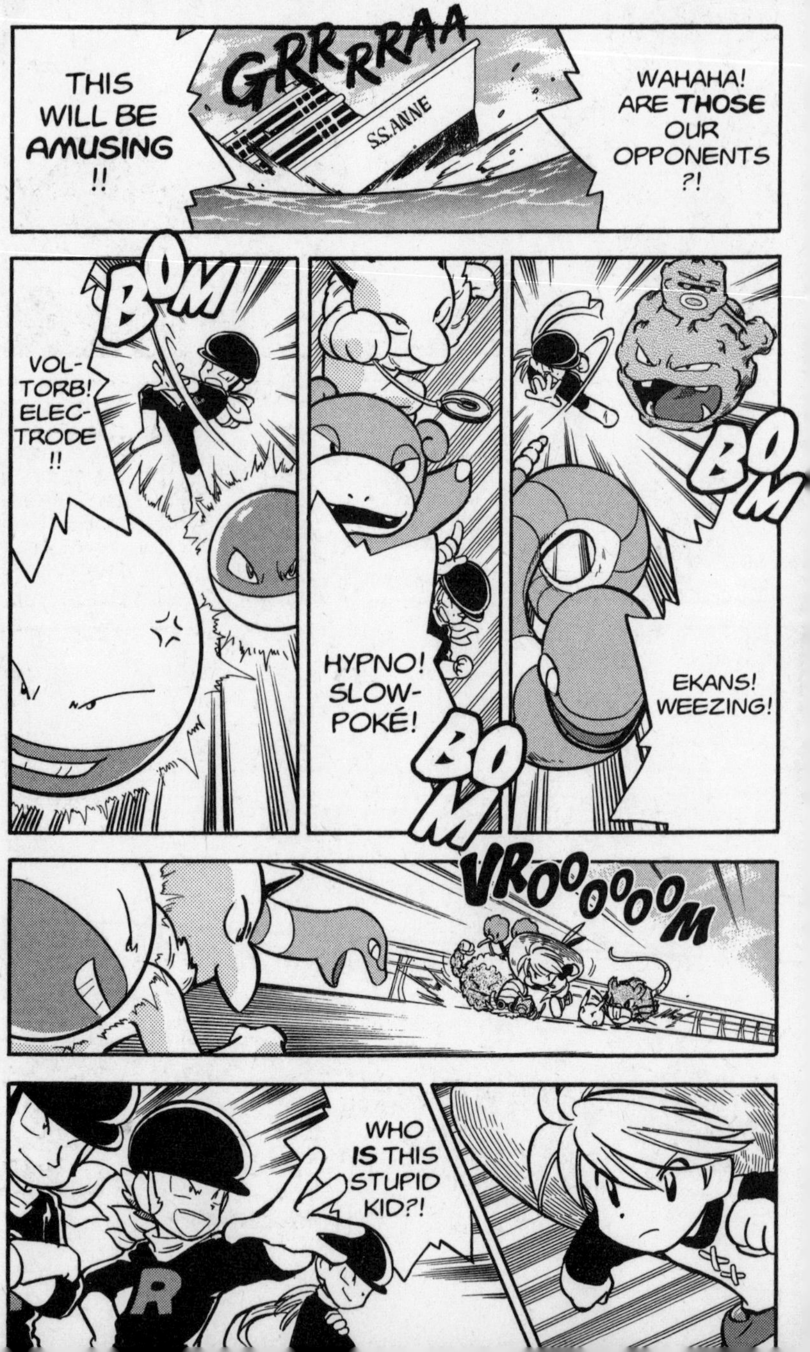
WAHAHA! ARE THOSE OUR OPPONENTS?!
GRRRRAA
S.S. ANNE
THIS WILL BE AMUSING!!
BOM
EKANS! WEEZING!
HYPNO! SLOWPOKÉ!
BOM
BOM
VOLTORB! ELECTRODE!!
VROOOOOOM
WHO IS THIS STUPID KID?!

57 Ekans the Ecstasy

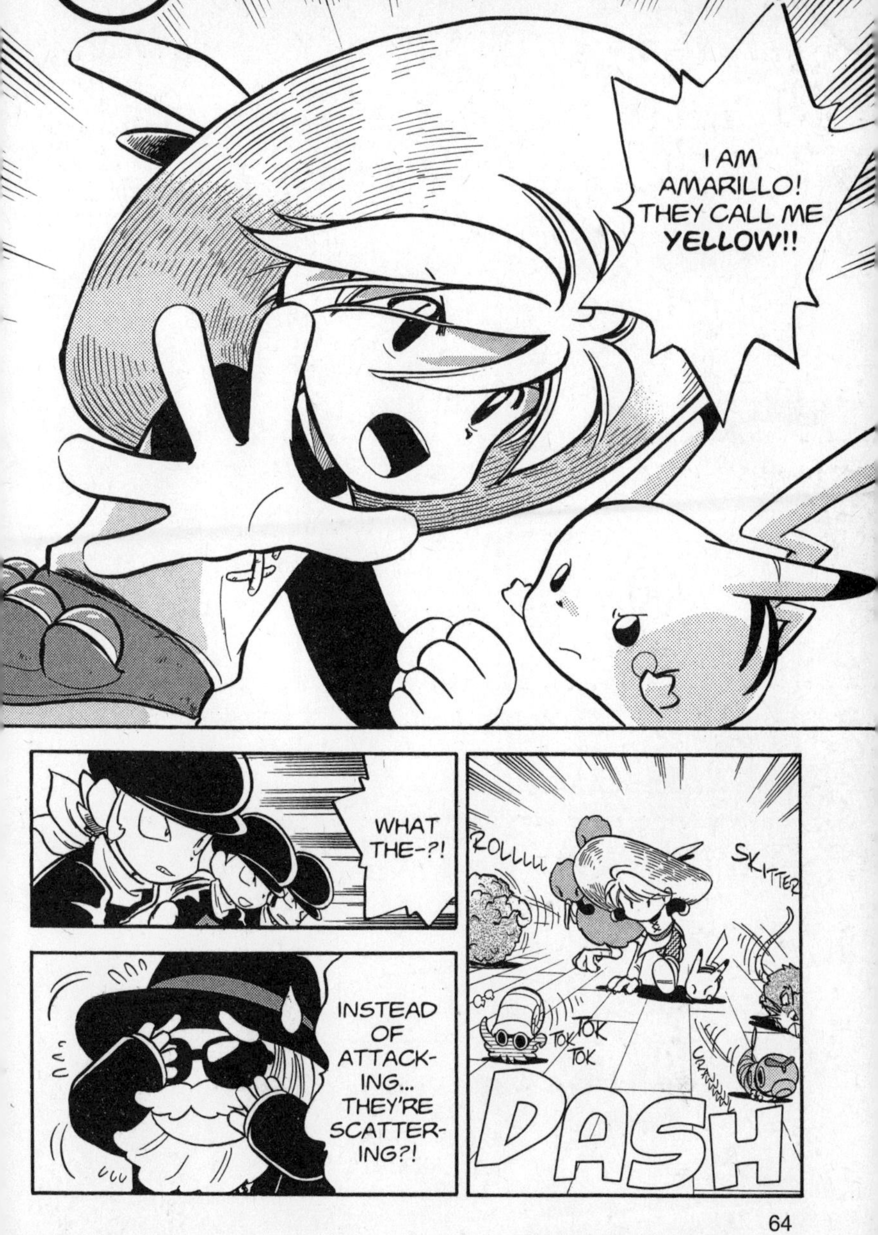
I AM AMARILLO! THEY CALL ME **YELLOW**!!
SKITTER
ROLLLLL
TOK TOK TOK
DASH
WHAT THE-?!
INSTEAD OF ATTACK-ING... THEY'RE SCATTER-ING?!

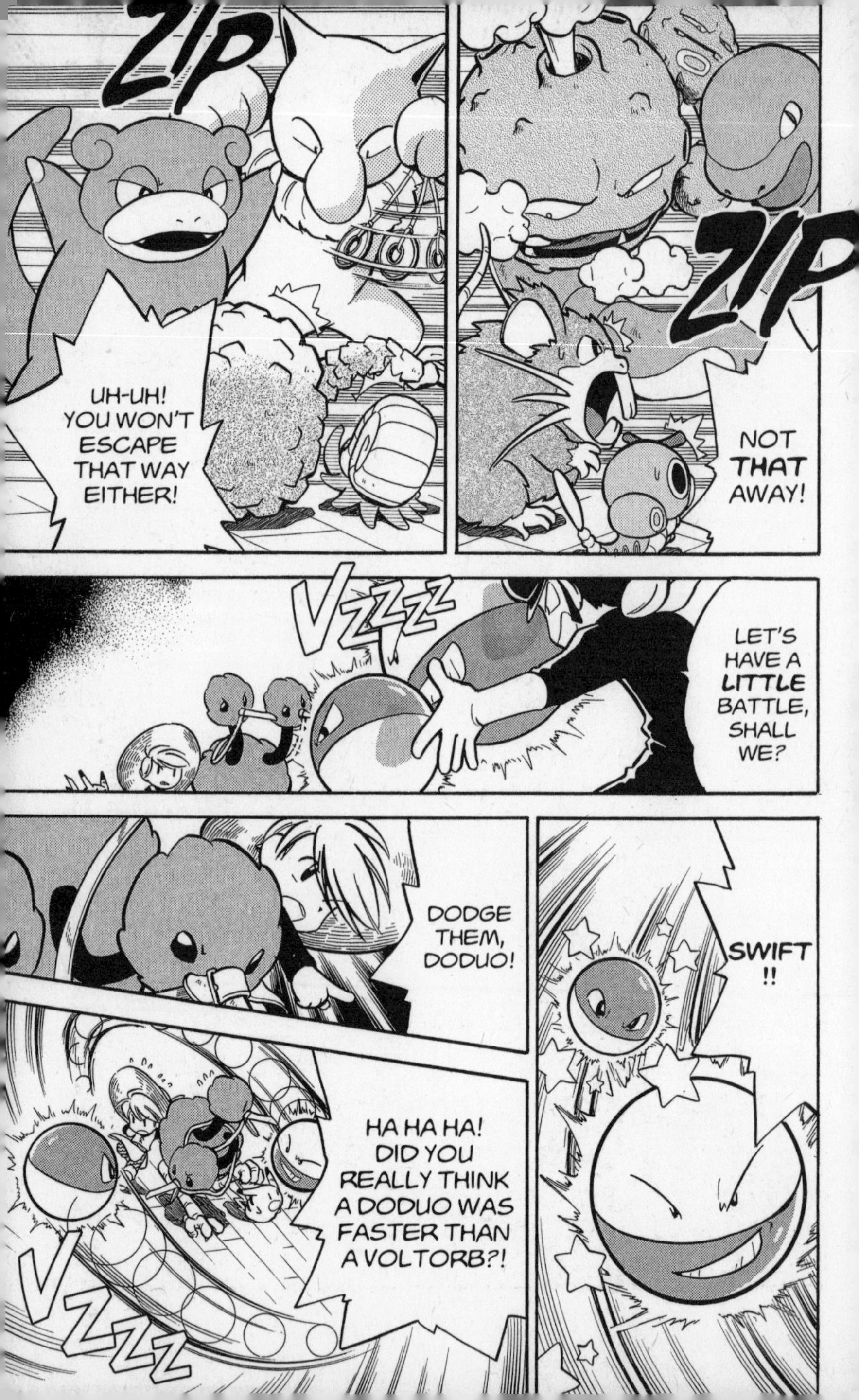
ZIP
NOT THAT AWAY!
ZIP
UH-UH! YOU WON'T ESCAPE THAT WAY EITHER!
VZZZZ
LET'S HAVE A LITTLE BATTLE, SHALL WE?
SWIFT!!
DODGE THEM, DODUO!
HA HA HA! DID YOU REALLY THINK A DODUO WAS FASTER THAN A VOLTORB?!
VZZZZ

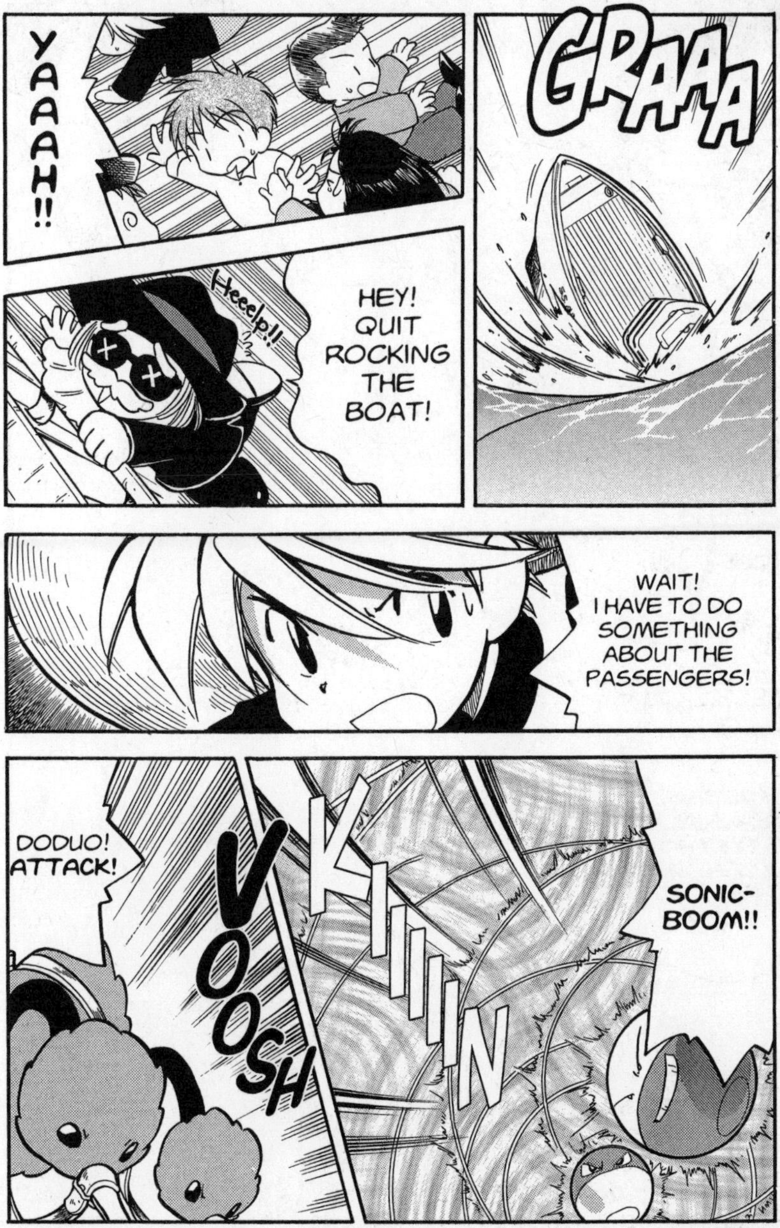
GRAAAA
YAAAAH!!
Heeelp!!
HEY! QUIT ROCKING THE BOAT!
WAIT! I HAVE TO DO SOMETHING ABOUT THE PASSENGERS!
SONIC-BOOM!!
KIIIIIN
VOOOSH
DODUO! ATTACK!

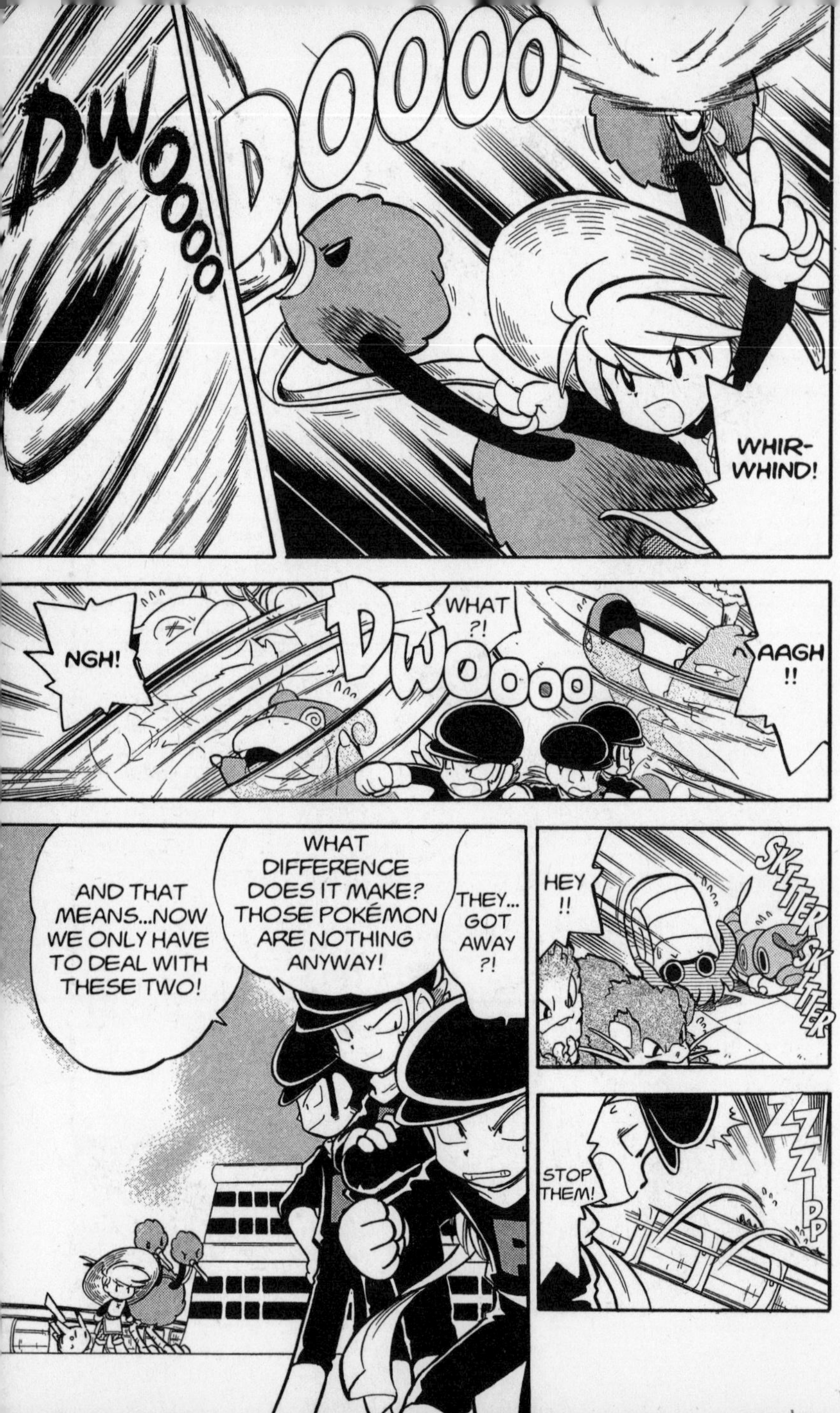

WHIR-WHIND!
DWOOOO
DOOOOO
AAGH!!
WHAT?!
DWOOOO
NGH!
SKITTER SKITTER
HEY!!
ZZZIPP
STOP THEM!
THEY... GOT AWAY?!
WHAT DIFFERENCE DOES IT MAKE? THOSE POKÉMON ARE NOTHING ANYWAY!
AND THAT MEANS...NOW WE ONLY HAVE TO DEAL WITH THESE TWO!

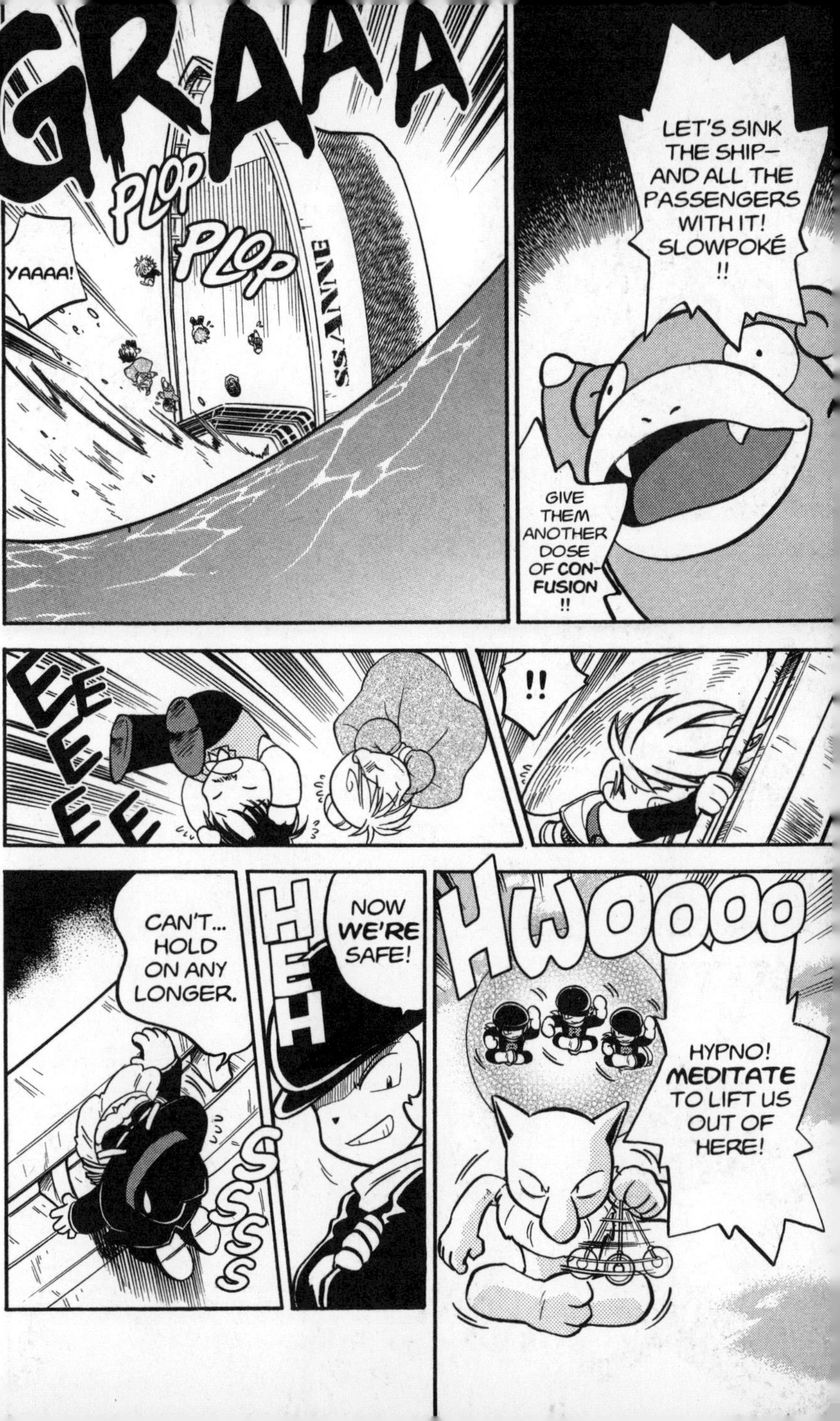
LET'S SINK THE SHIP—AND ALL THE PASSENGERS WITH IT! SLOWPOKÉ !!
GIVE THEM ANOTHER DOSE OF **CONFUSION** !!
GRAAA
PLOP
PLOP
YAAAA!
SS ANNE
!!
EEEEE
HWOOOO
HYPNO! **MEDITATE** TO LIFT US OUT OF HERE!
NOW **WE'RE** SAFE!
HEH
CAN'T... HOLD ON ANY LONGER.
SSSSS

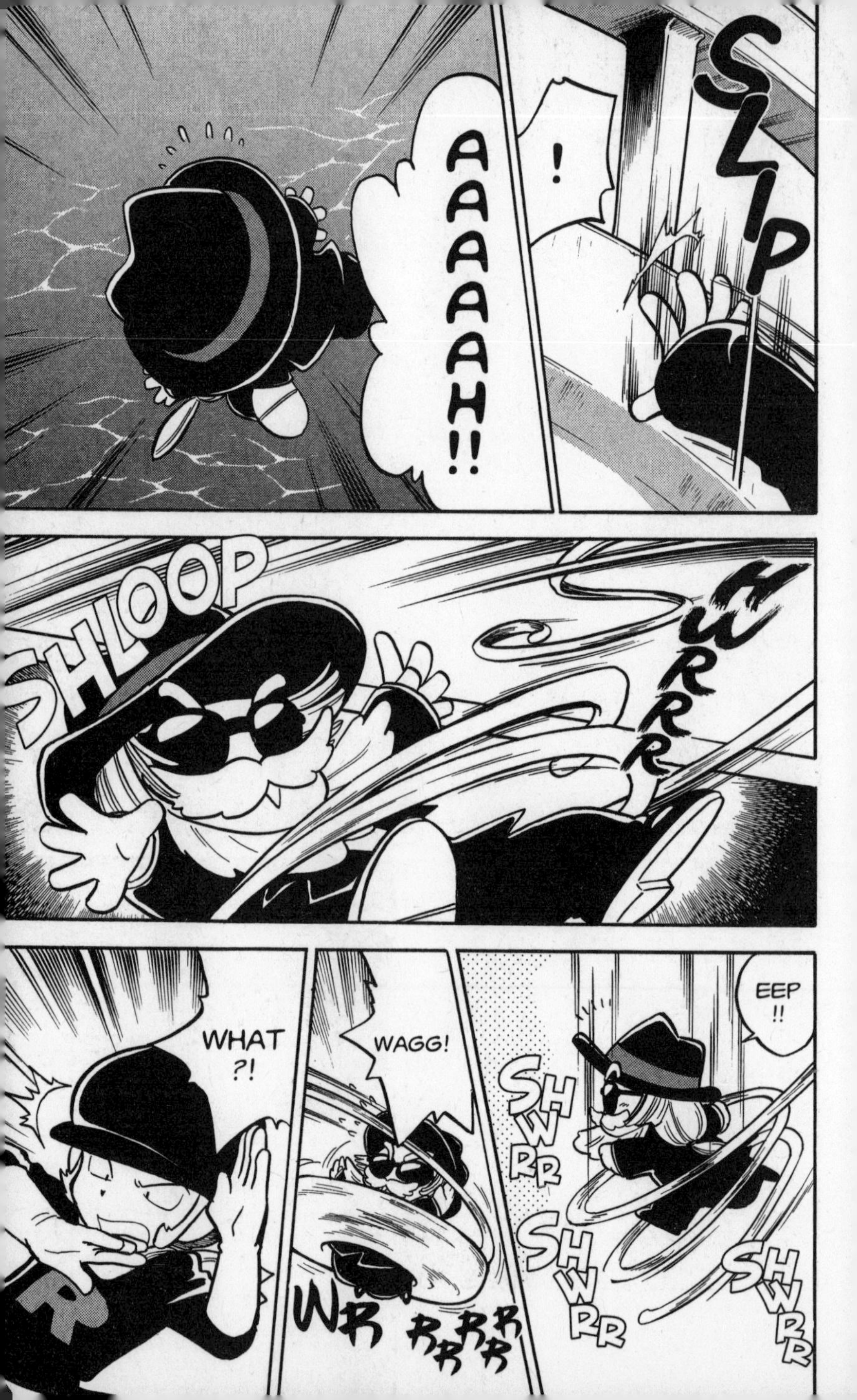
SLIP
!
AAAAAAH!!
WHURRRR
SHLOOP
EEP !!
SHWRR
SHWRR
SHWRR
WAGG!
WRRRRRR
WHAT ?!

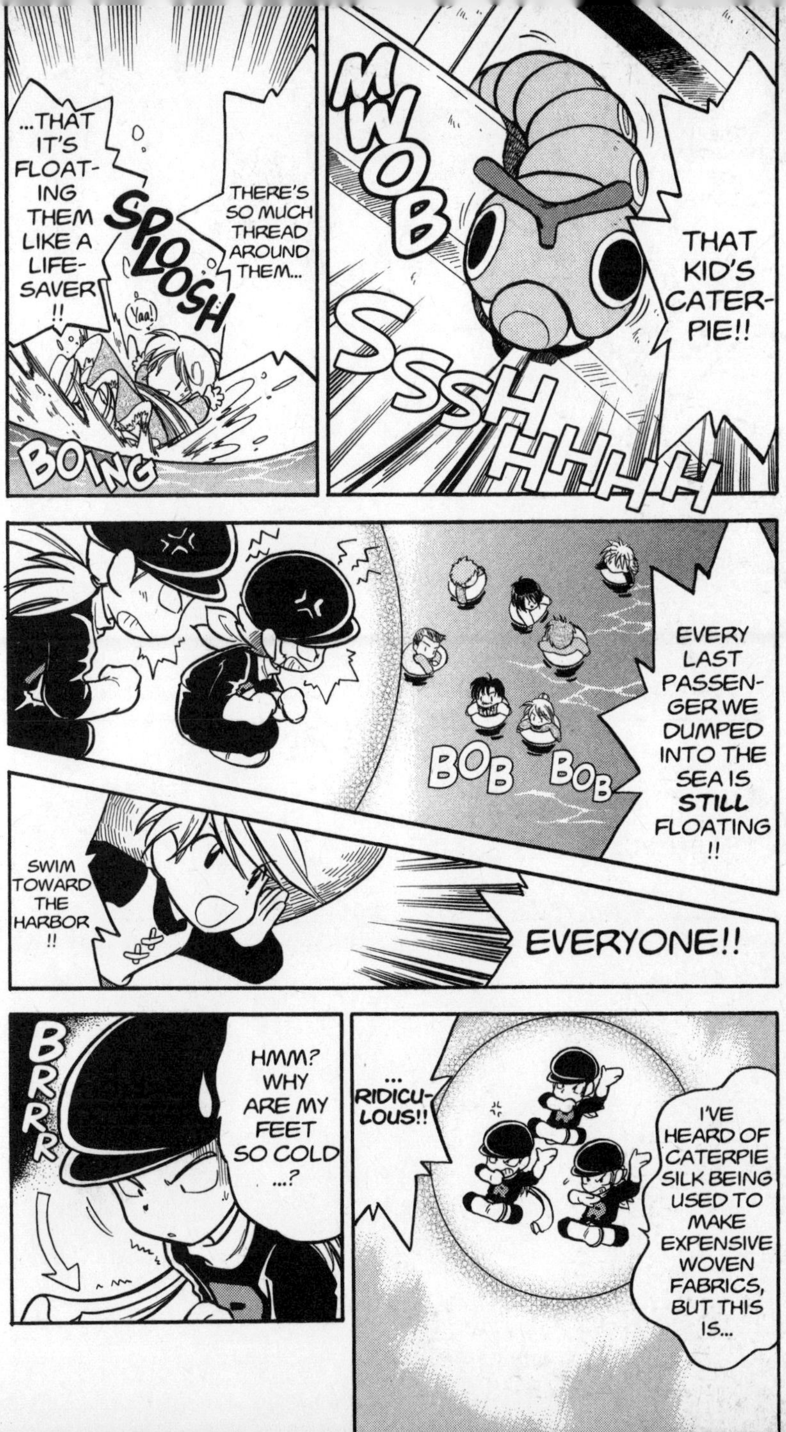
MWOB
SSSHHHHHH
THAT KID'S CATERPIE!!
THERE'S SO MUCH THREAD AROUND THEM...
...THAT IT'S FLOATING THEM LIKE A LIFE-SAVER!!
SPLOOSH
Yaa!
BOING
EVERY LAST PASSENGER WE DUMPED INTO THE SEA IS **STILL** FLOATING!!
BOB BOB
EVERYONE!!
SWIM TOWARD THE HARBOR!!
I'VE HEARD OF CATERPIE SILK BEING USED TO MAKE EXPENSIVE WOVEN FABRICS, BUT THIS IS...
...RIDICULOUS!!
HMM? WHY ARE MY FEET SO COLD...?
BRRR

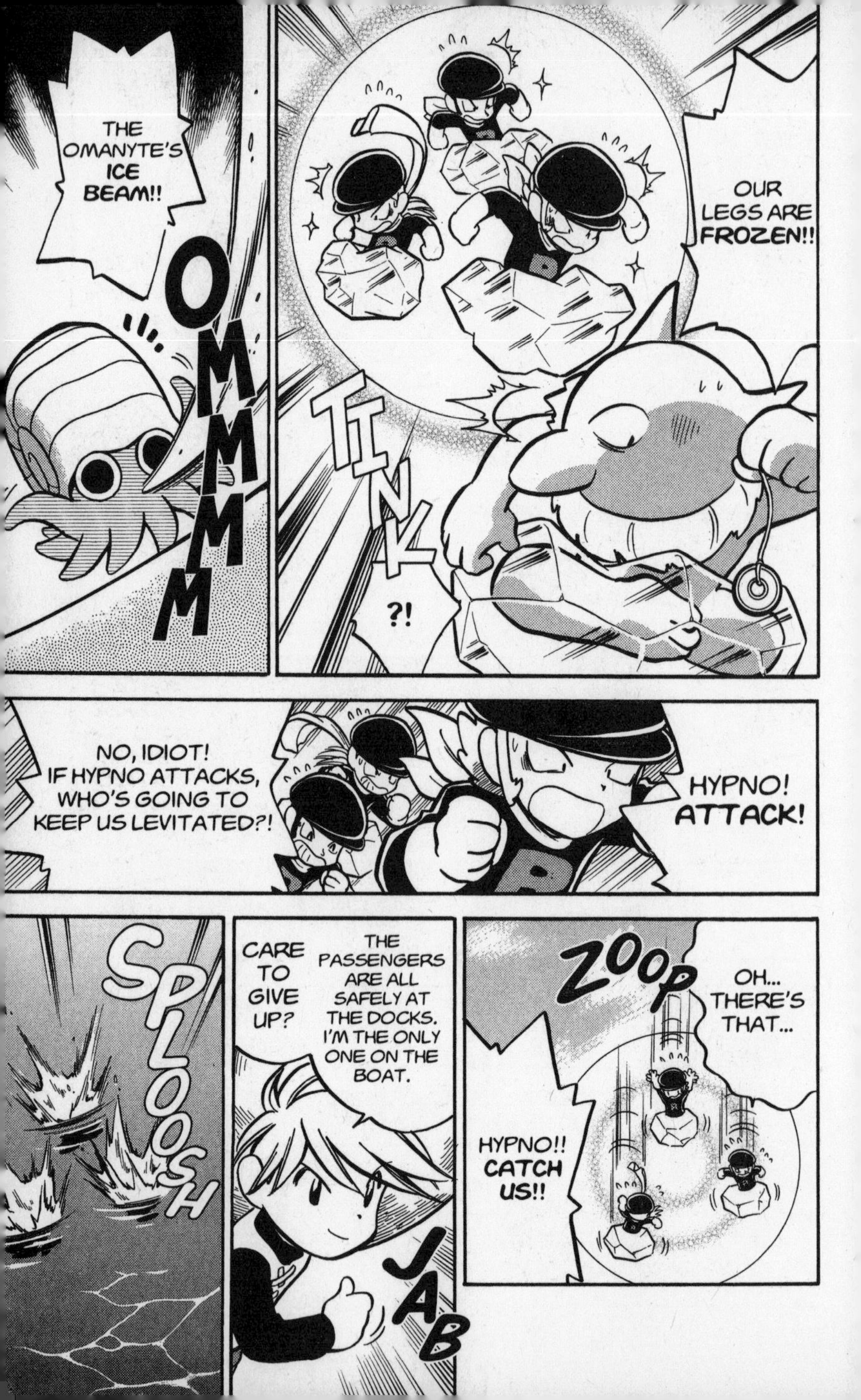
OUR LEGS ARE FROZEN!!
TINK
?!
THE OMANYTE'S ICE BEAM!!
OMMMMM
HYPNO! ATTACK!
NO, IDIOT! IF HYPNO ATTACKS, WHO'S GOING TO KEEP US LEVITATED?!
ZOOP
OH... THERE'S THAT...
HYPNO!! CATCH US!!
THE PASSENGERS ARE ALL SAFELY AT THE DOCKS. I'M THE ONLY ONE ON THE BOAT.
CARE TO GIVE UP?
JAB
SPLOOSH

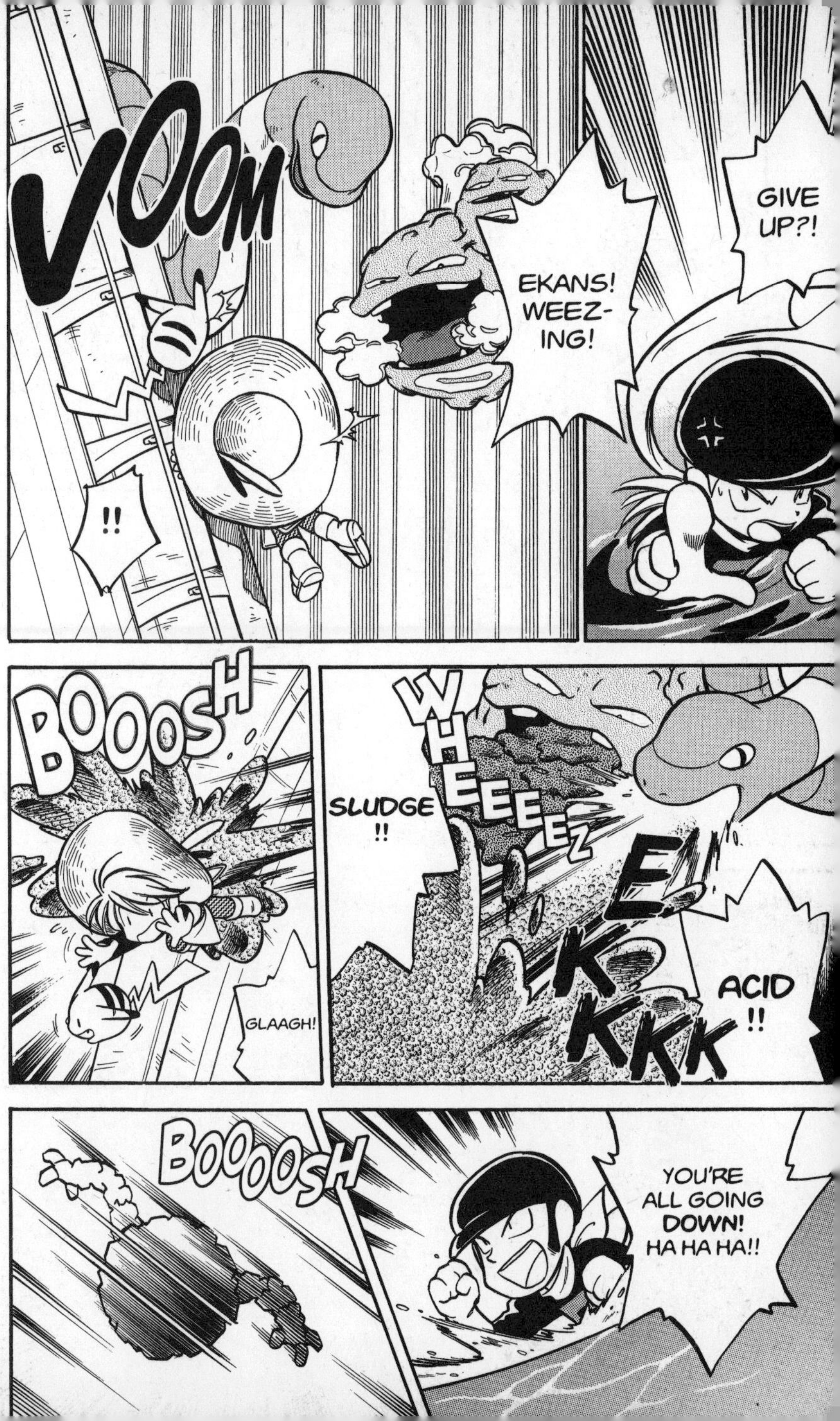
GIVE UP?!
EKANS! WEEZ-ING!
VOOM
!!
WHEEEEEZ
SLUDGE!!
EKKKKK
ACID!!
BOOOSH
GLAAGH!
YOU'RE ALL GOING DOWN! HA HA HA!!
BOOOOOSH

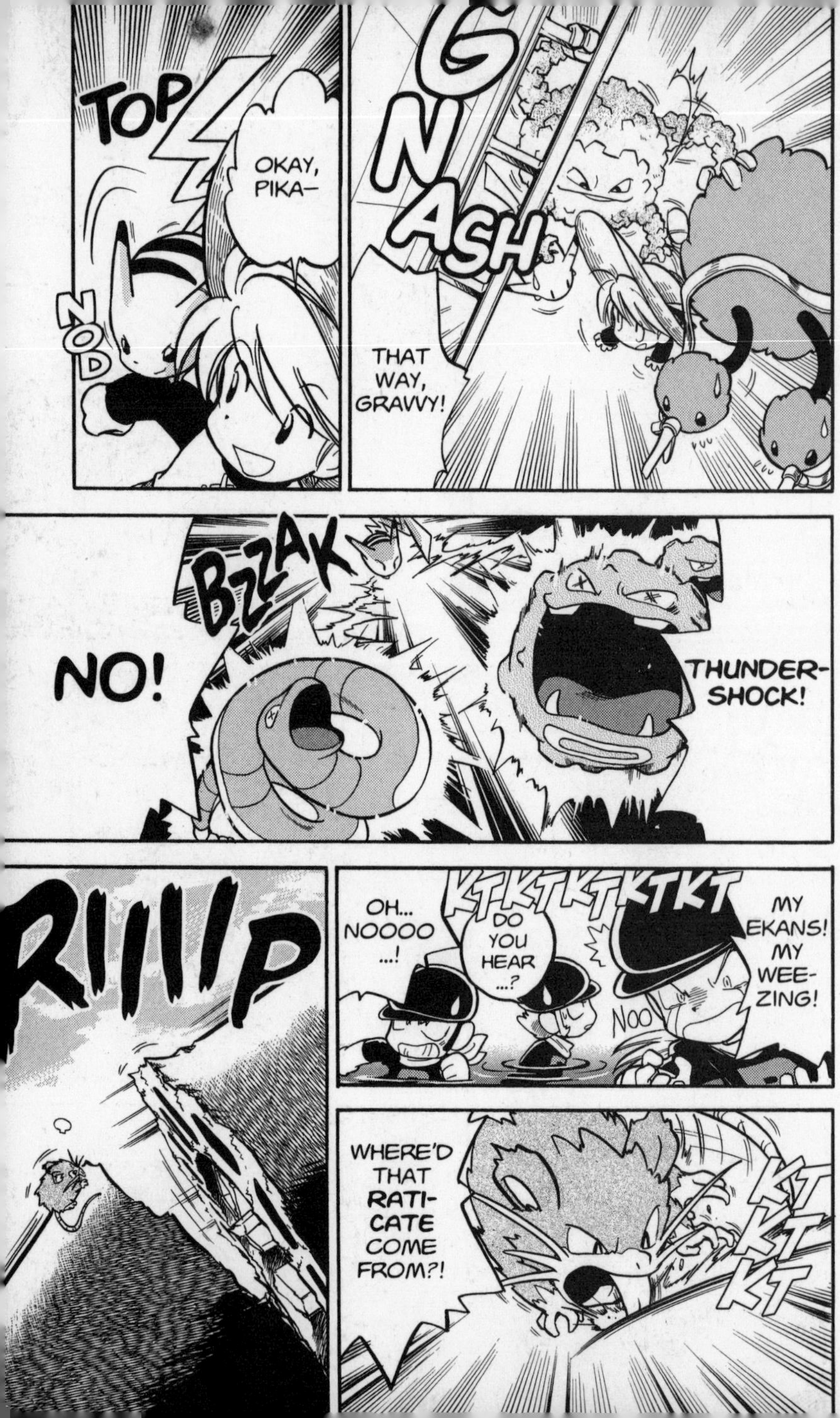
GNASH
THAT WAY, GRAVVY!
TOP
OKAY, PIKA–
NOD
THUNDER-SHOCK!
BZZAK
NO!
KTKTKTKTKT
MY EKANS! MY WEE-ZING!
DO YOU HEAR ...?
OH... NOOOO ...!
NOO
KT KT KT
WHERE'D THAT RATI-CATE COME FROM?!
RIIIP

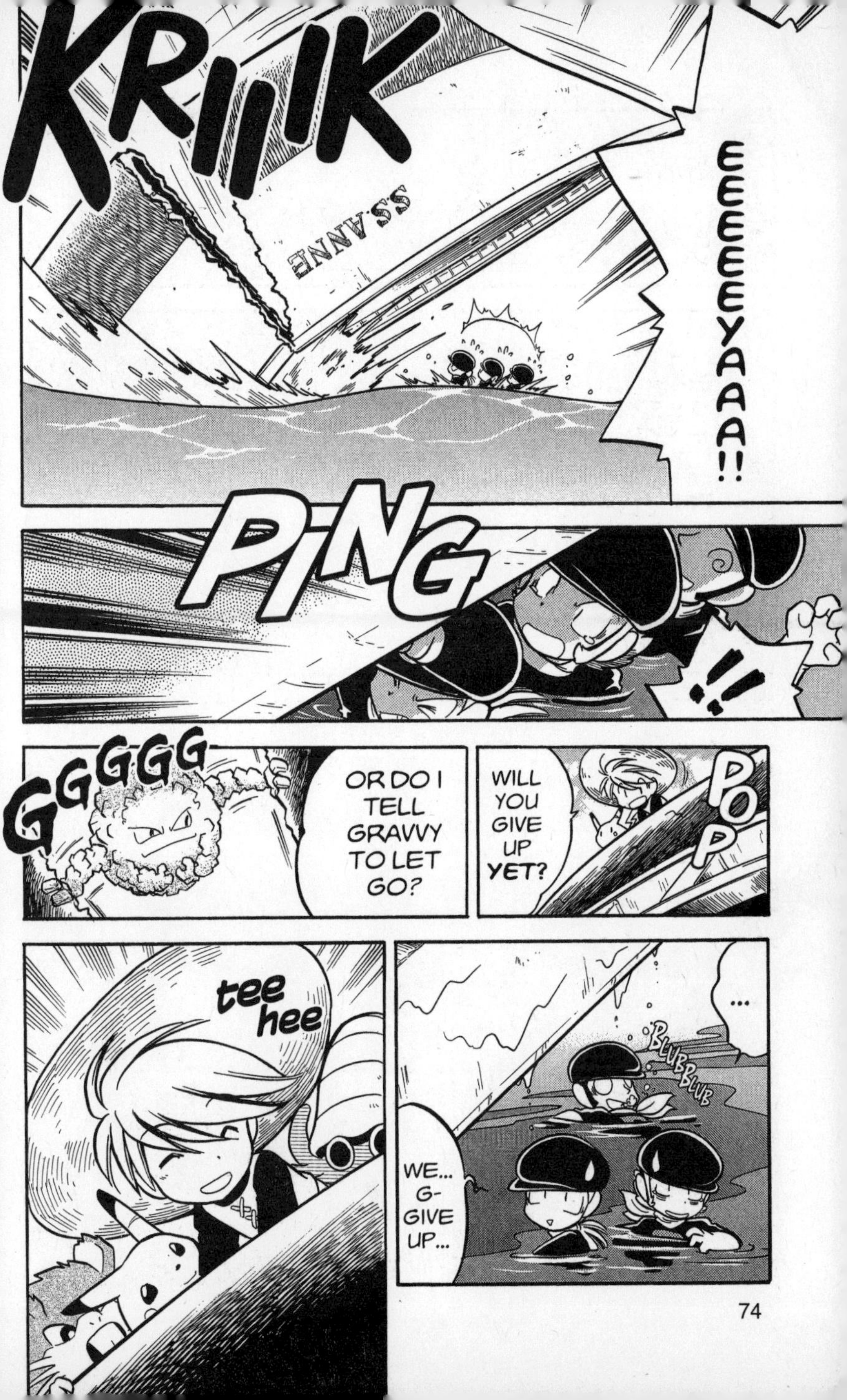
EEEEEYAAA!!
S.S. ANNE
KRIIIK
!!
PING
POP
WILL YOU GIVE UP YET?
OR DO I TELL GRAVVY TO LET GO?
GGGGG
...
BLUB BLUB
WE... G-GIVE UP...
tee hee

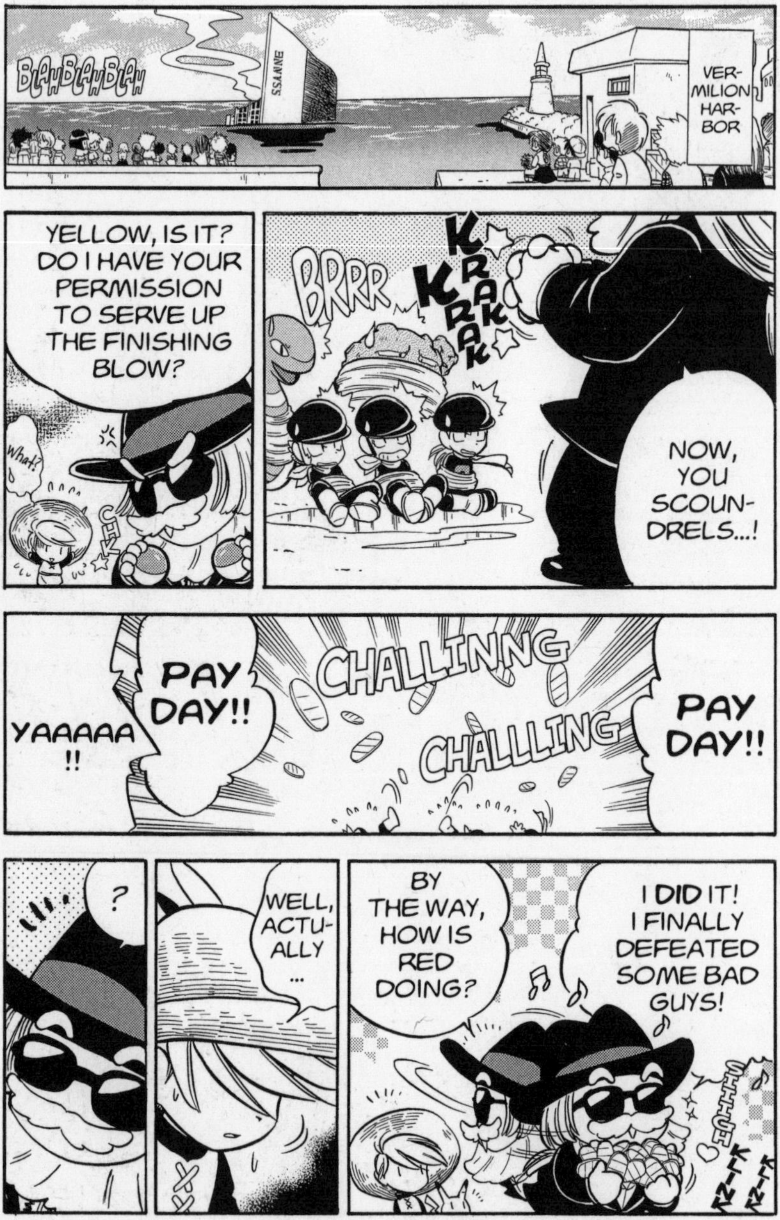
VERMILION HARBOR
S.S.ANNE
BLAHBLAHBLAH
KRAK KRAK
BRRR
NOW, YOU SCOUNDRELS...!
YELLOW, IS IT? DO I HAVE YOUR PERMISSION TO SERVE UP THE FINISHING BLOW?
What?
PAY DAY!!
CHALLLING
CHALLINNG
PAY DAY!!
YAAAAA!!
I DID IT! I FINALLY DEFEATED SOME BAD GUYS!
BY THE WAY, HOW IS RED DOING?
KLINK KLINK
WELL, ACTUALLY ...
?

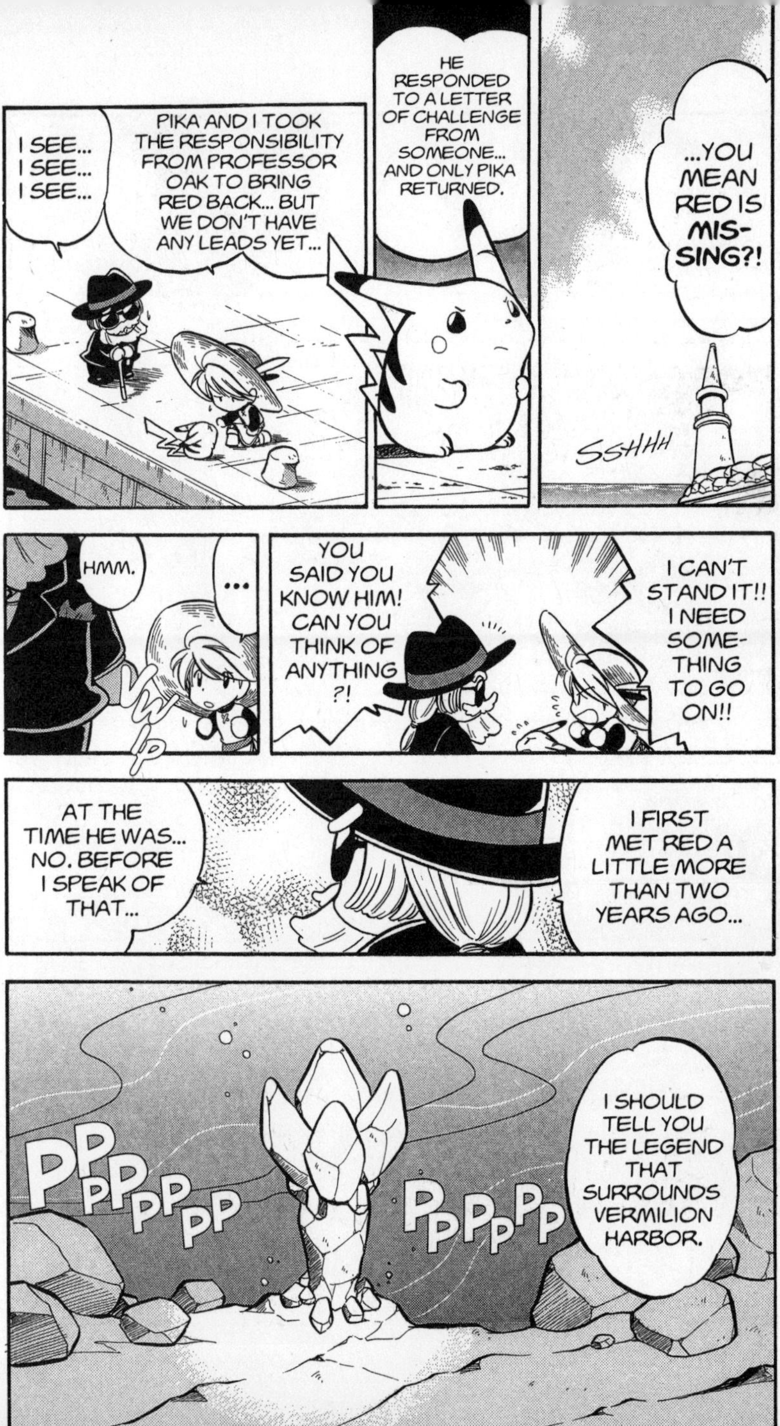
...YOU MEAN RED IS MIS-SING?!
SSHHH
HE RESPONDED TO A LETTER OF CHALLENGE FROM SOMEONE... AND ONLY PIKA RETURNED.
PIKA AND I TOOK THE RESPONSIBILITY FROM PROFESSOR OAK TO BRING RED BACK... BUT WE DON'T HAVE ANY LEADS YET...
I SEE... I SEE... I SEE...
I CAN'T STAND IT!! I NEED SOME-THING TO GO ON!!
YOU SAID YOU KNOW HIM! CAN YOU THINK OF ANYTHING ?!
...
HMM.
VWIP
I FIRST MET RED A LITTLE MORE THAN TWO YEARS AGO...
AT THE TIME HE WAS... NO. BEFORE I SPEAK OF THAT...
I SHOULD TELL YOU THE LEGEND THAT SURROUNDS VERMILION HARBOR.
PPPPPP
PPPPPPP

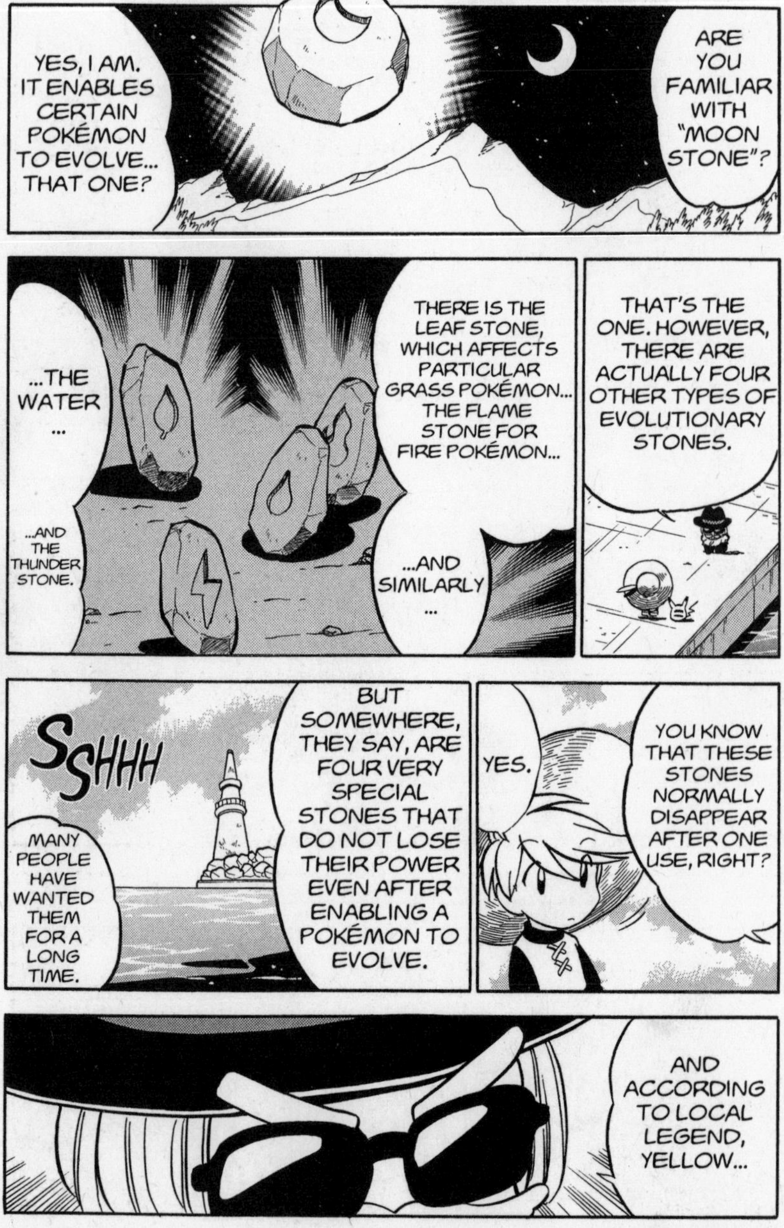
ARE YOU FAMILIAR WITH "MOON STONE"?
YES, I AM. IT ENABLES CERTAIN POKÉMON TO EVOLVE... THAT ONE?
THAT'S THE ONE. HOWEVER, THERE ARE ACTUALLY FOUR OTHER TYPES OF EVOLUTIONARY STONES.
THERE IS THE LEAF STONE, WHICH AFFECTS PARTICULAR GRASS POKÉMON... THE FLAME STONE FOR FIRE POKÉMON...
...AND SIMILARLY ...
...THE WATER ...
...AND THE THUNDER STONE.
YOU KNOW THAT THESE STONES NORMALLY DISAPPEAR AFTER ONE USE, RIGHT?
YES.
BUT SOMEWHERE, THEY SAY, ARE FOUR VERY SPECIAL STONES THAT DO NOT LOSE THEIR POWER EVEN AFTER ENABLING A POKÉMON TO EVOLVE.
SSHHH
MANY PEOPLE HAVE WANTED THEM FOR A LONG TIME.
AND ACCORDING TO LOCAL LEGEND, YELLOW...

58 The Kindest Tentacruel

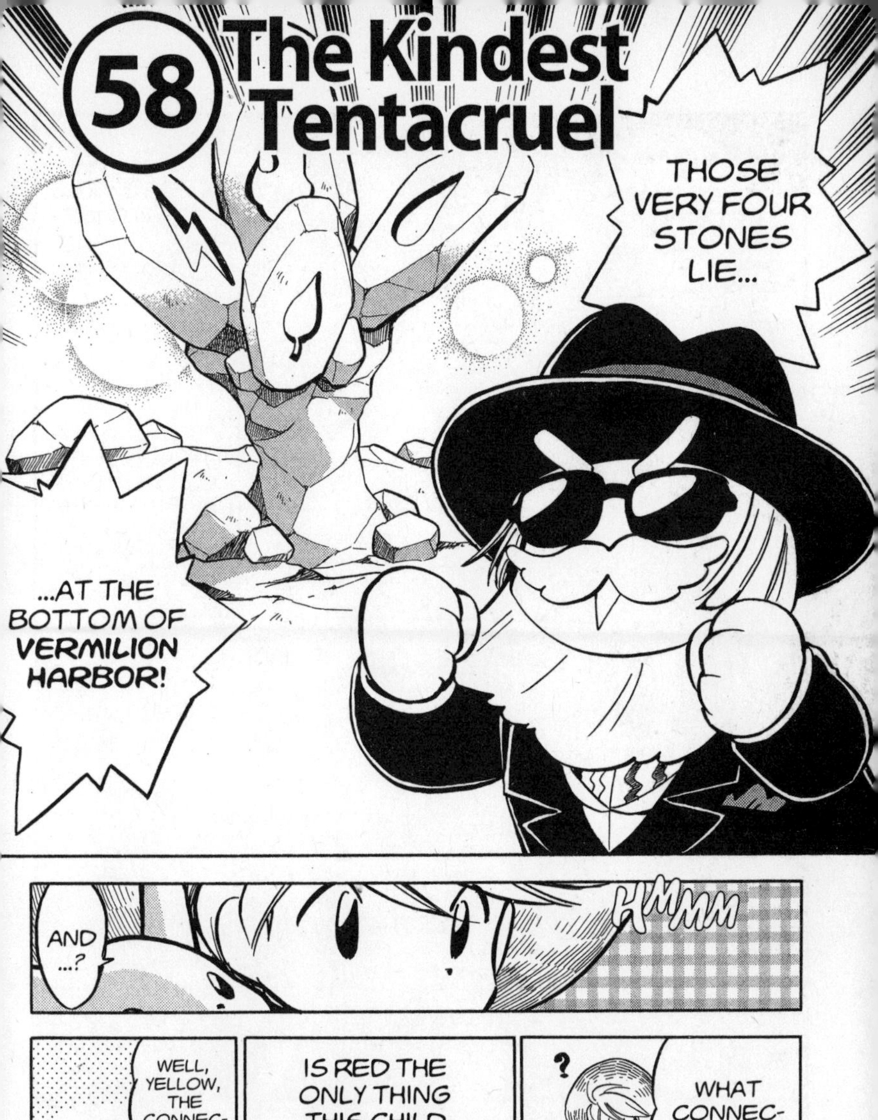
THOSE VERY FOUR STONES LIE...
...AT THE BOTTOM OF VERMILION HARBOR!
HMMM
AND ...?
WHAT CONNECTION DOES THIS HAVE WITH RED?
FUMP
IS RED THE ONLY THING THIS CHILD THINKS ABOUT?
SIGH
WELL, YELLOW, THE CONNECTION IS THIS...

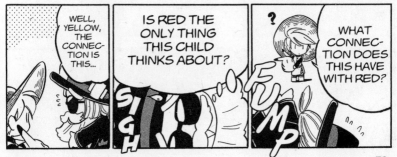

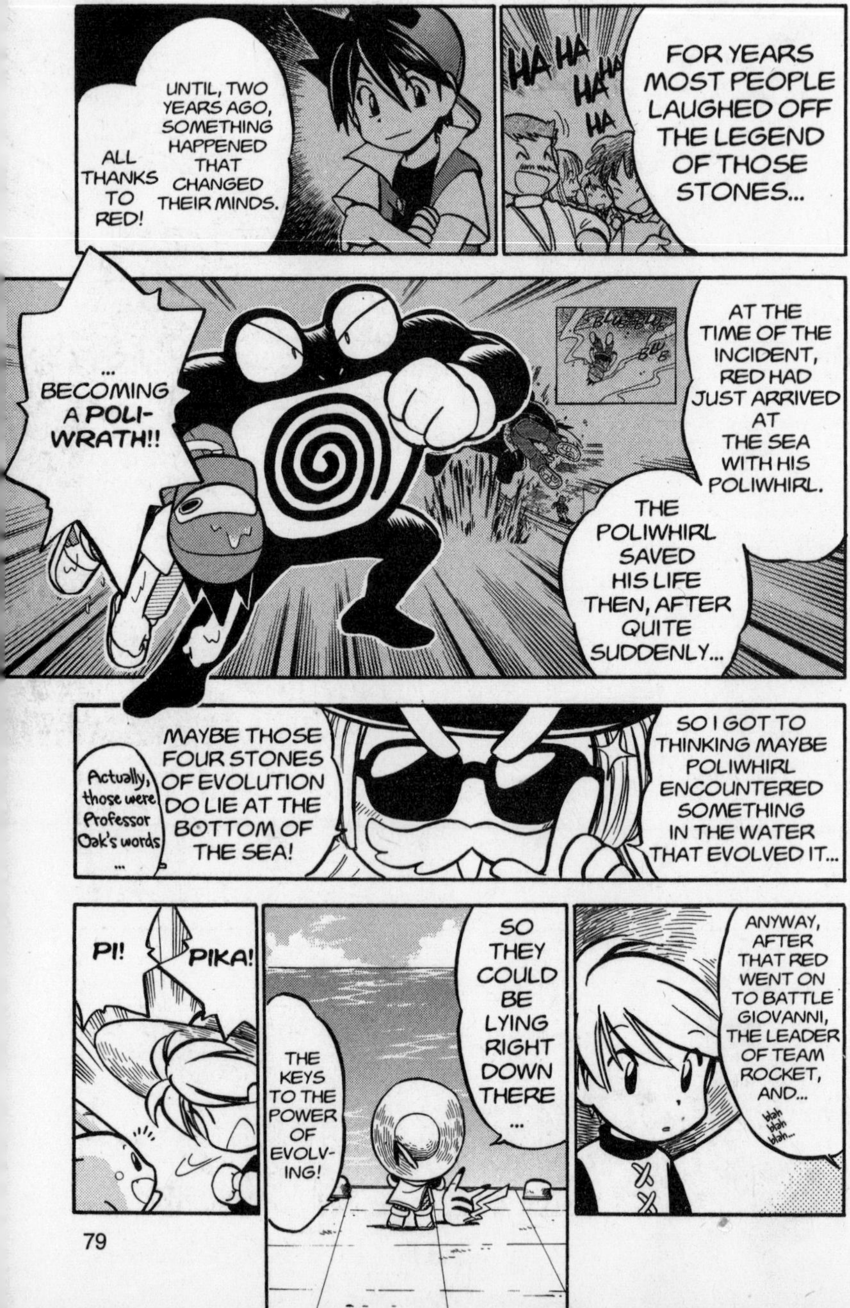
HA HA HA HA HA
FOR YEARS MOST PEOPLE LAUGHED OFF THE LEGEND OF THOSE STONES...
UNTIL, TWO YEARS AGO, SOMETHING HAPPENED THAT CHANGED THEIR MINDS.
ALL THANKS TO RED!
AT THE TIME OF THE INCIDENT, RED HAD JUST ARRIVED AT THE SEA WITH HIS POLIWHIRL.
THE POLIWHIRL SAVED HIS LIFE THEN, AFTER QUITE SUDDENLY...
... BECOMING A **POLIWRATH**!!
SO I GOT TO THINKING MAYBE POLIWHIRL ENCOUNTERED SOMETHING IN THE WATER THAT EVOLVED IT...
MAYBE THOSE FOUR STONES OF EVOLUTION DO LIE AT THE BOTTOM OF THE SEA!
Actually, those were Professor Oak's words ...
ANYWAY, AFTER THAT RED WENT ON TO BATTLE GIOVANNI, THE LEADER OF TEAM ROCKET, AND...
blah blah blah...
SO THEY COULD BE LYING RIGHT DOWN THERE ...
THE KEYS TO THE POWER OF EVOLVING!
PIKA!
PI!

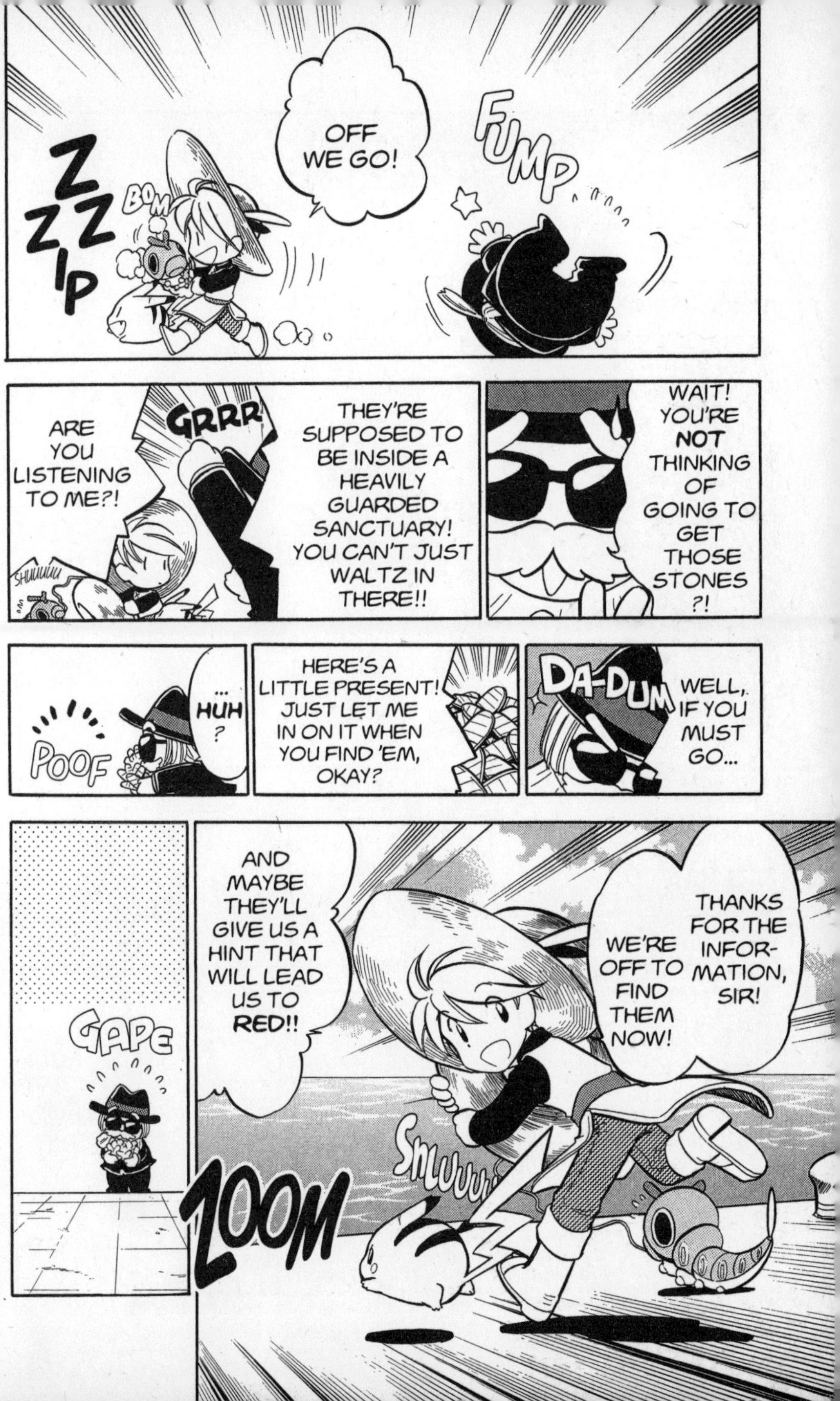
FUMP
OFF WE GO!
BOM
ZZZIP
WAIT! YOU'RE NOT THINKING OF GOING TO GET THOSE STONES?!
THEY'RE SUPPOSED TO BE INSIDE A HEAVILY GUARDED SANCTUARY! YOU CAN'T JUST WALTZ IN THERE!!
GRRR
ARE YOU LISTENING TO ME?!
SHUUUUU
WELL, IF YOU MUST GO...
DA-DUM
HERE'S A LITTLE PRESENT! JUST LET ME IN ON IT WHEN YOU FIND 'EM, OKAY?
...HUH?
POOF
THANKS FOR THE INFORMATION, SIR!
WE'RE OFF TO FIND THEM NOW!
AND MAYBE THEY'LL GIVE US A HINT THAT WILL LEAD US TO RED!!
ZOOM
GAPE

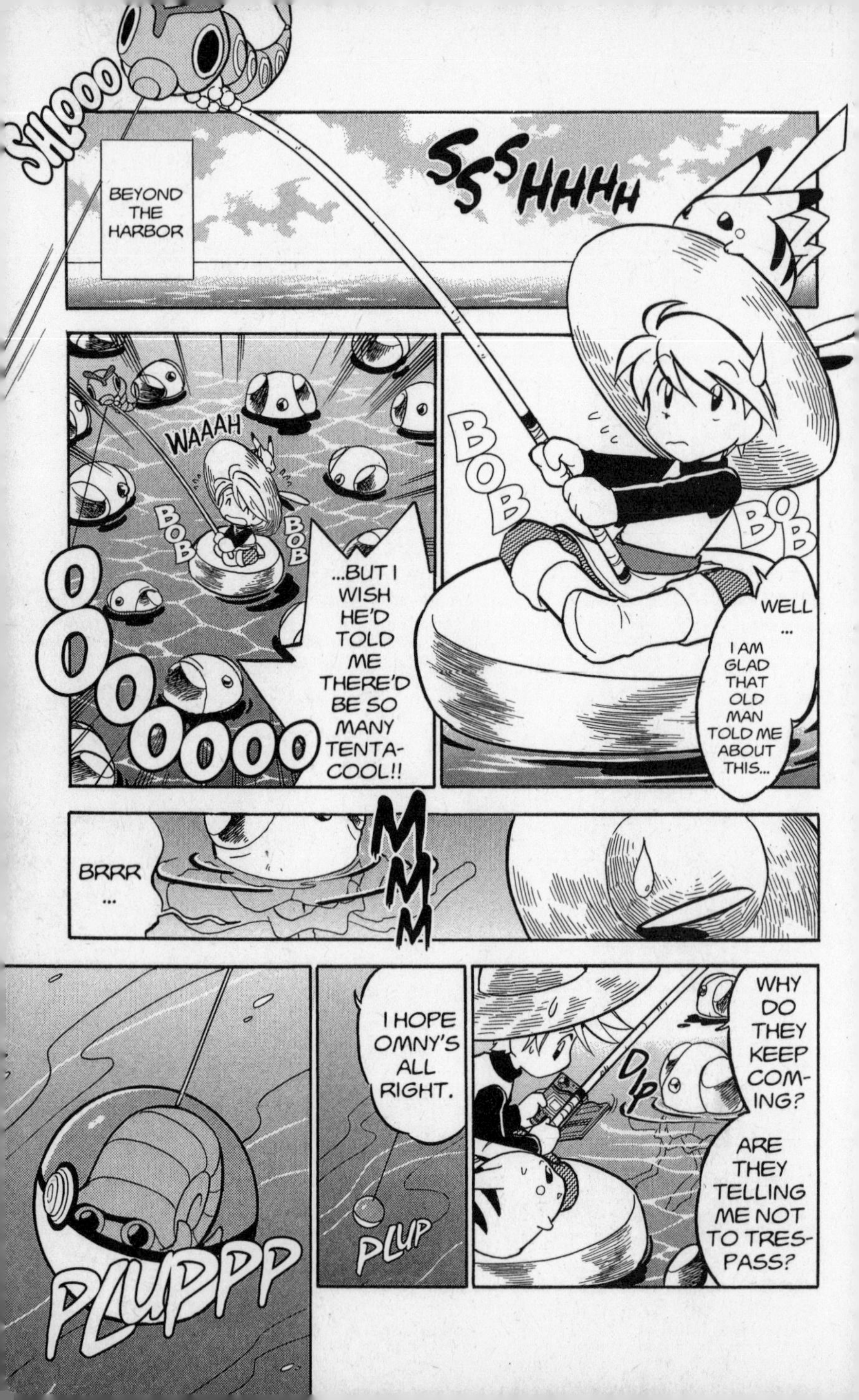
SSSHHHH
SHOOOO
BEYOND THE HARBOR
BOB
BOB
WELL ...
I AM GLAD THAT OLD MAN TOLD ME ABOUT THIS...
WAAAH
BOB
BOB
...BUT I WISH HE'D TOLD ME THERE'D BE SO MANY TENTA-COOL!!
OOOOOOOO
MMMM
BRRR ...
WHY DO THEY KEEP COM-ING?
ARE THEY TELLING ME NOT TO TRES-PASS?
DIP
I HOPE OMNY'S ALL RIGHT.
PLUP
PLUPPP

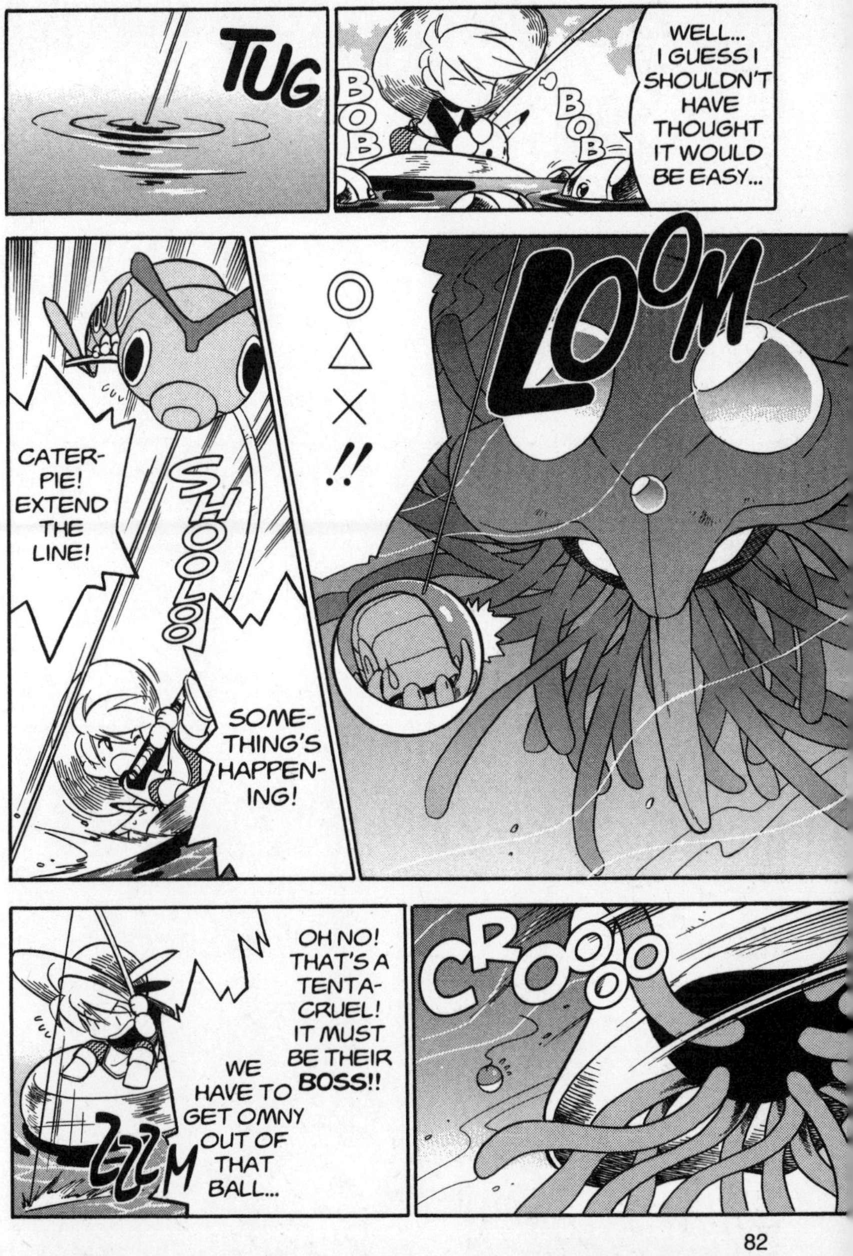

BOB
BOB
WELL... I GUESS I SHOULDN'T HAVE THOUGHT IT WOULD BE EASY...
TUG
LOOOM
○ △ × !!
SHOOLOO
CATER-PIE! EXTEND THE LINE!
SOME-THING'S HAPPEN-ING!
CROOOOO
OH NO! THAT'S A TENTA-CRUEL! IT MUST BE THEIR **BOSS**!!
WE HAVE TO GET OMNY OUT OF THAT BALL...
ZZZM

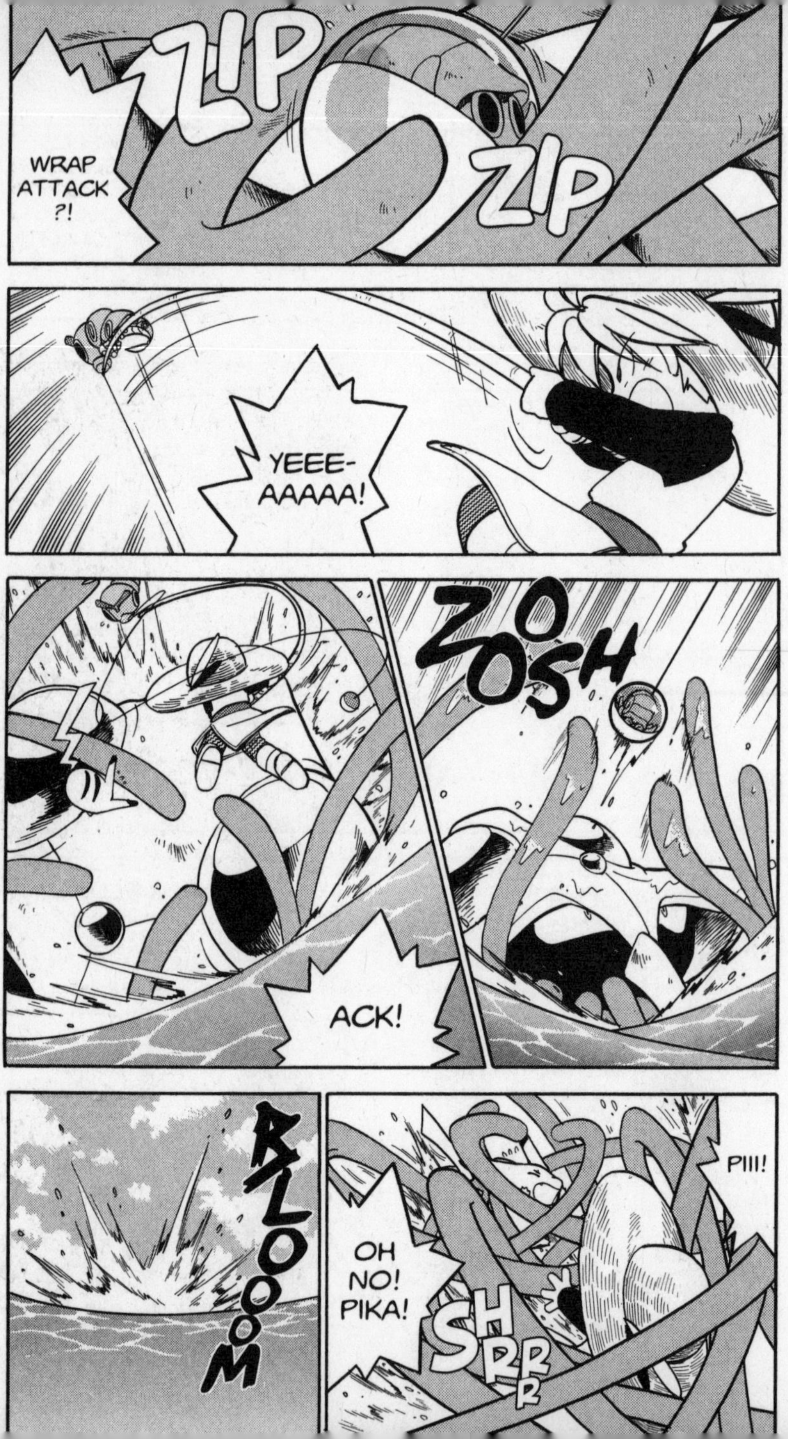
ZIP
ZIP
WRAP ATTACK ?!
YEEE-AAAAA!
ZOSH
ACK!
PIII!
OH NO! PIKA!
SHRRR
BLOOOOM

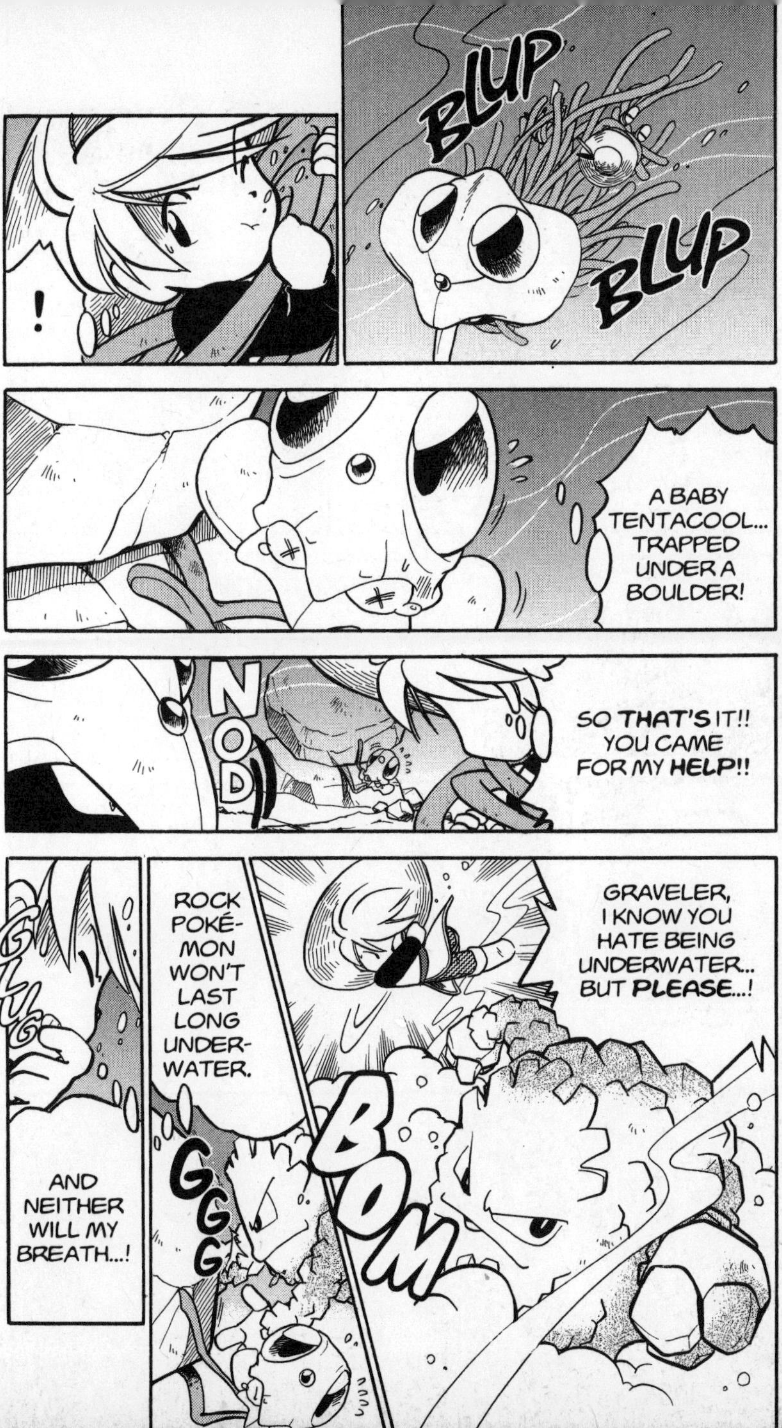
BLUP
BLUP
!
A BABY TENTACOOL... TRAPPED UNDER A BOULDER!
NOD
SO THAT'S IT!! YOU CAME FOR MY HELP!!
GRAVELER, I KNOW YOU HATE BEING UNDERWATER... BUT PLEASE...!
ROCK POKÉ-MON WON'T LAST LONG UNDER-WATER.
BOM
GGG
GLUG
AND NEITHER WILL MY BREATH...!

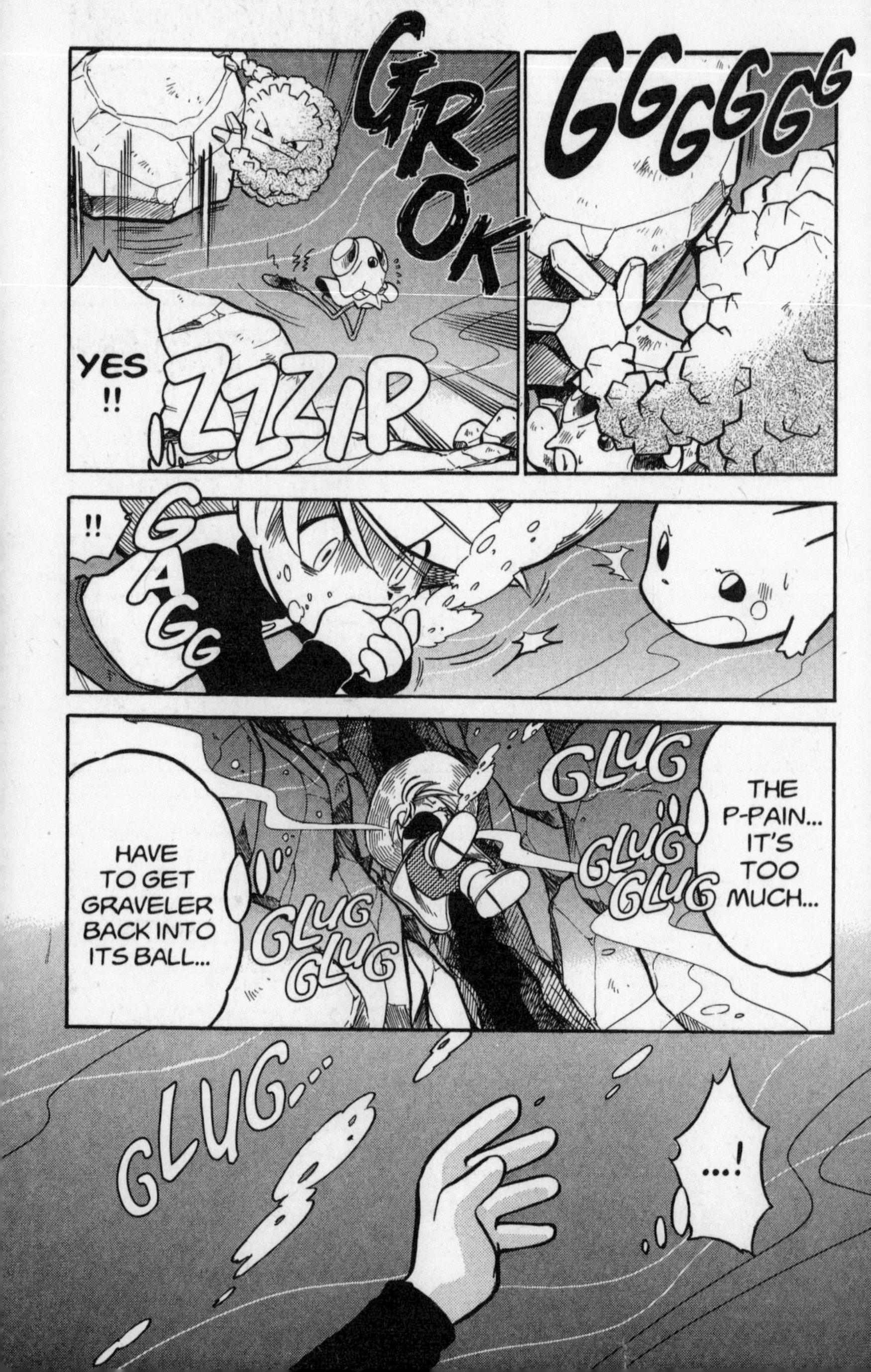
GGGGGG
GROK
YES !!
ZZZIP
!!
GAGG
THE P-PAIN... IT'S TOO MUCH...
GLUG
GLUG GLUG
HAVE TO GET GRAVELER BACK INTO ITS BALL...
GLUG GLUG
...!
GLUG...

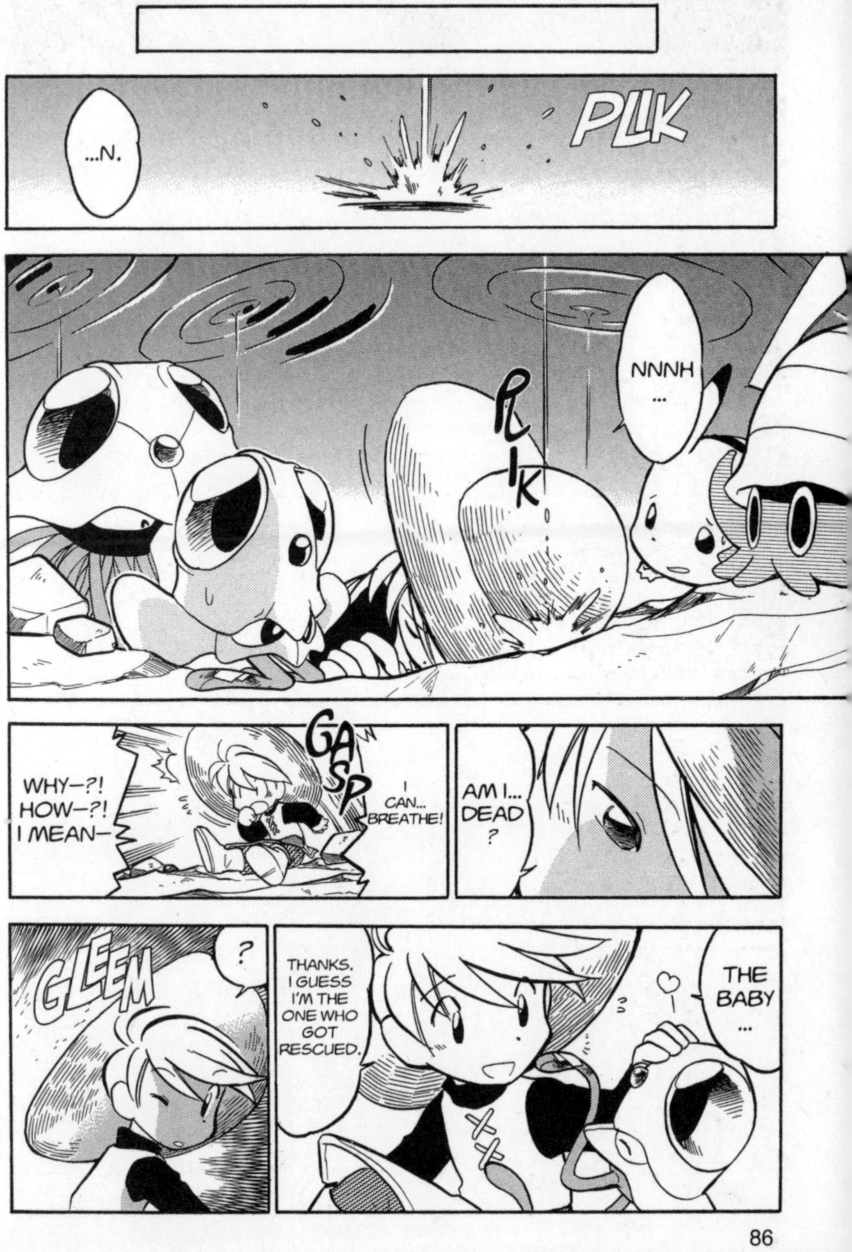
PLIK
...N.
NNNH ...
PLIK
AM I... DEAD ?
I CAN... BREATHE!
GASP
WHY–?! HOW–?! I MEAN–
THE BABY ...
THANKS. I GUESS I'M THE ONE WHO GOT RESCUED.
?
GLEEM

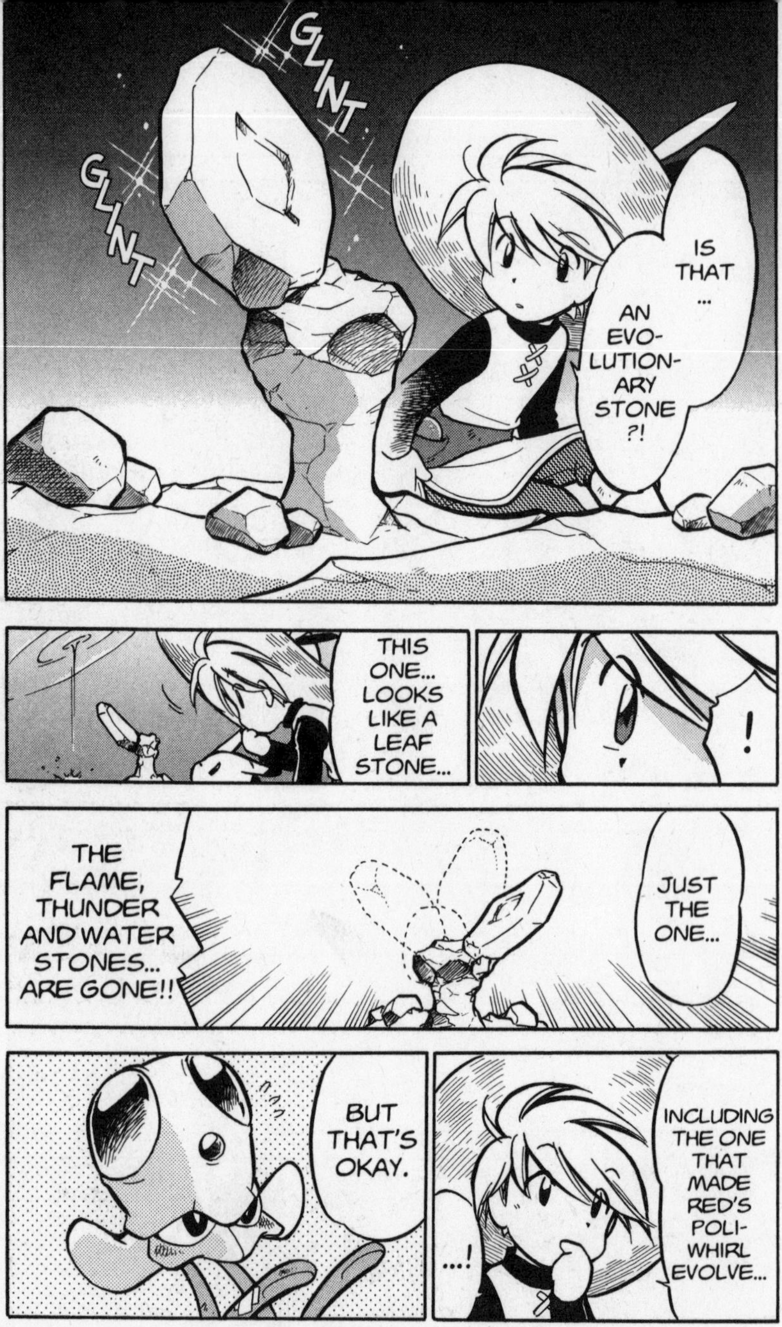
GLINT
GLINT
IS THAT ... AN EVOLUTIONARY STONE ?!
!
THIS ONE... LOOKS LIKE A LEAF STONE...
JUST THE ONE...
THE FLAME, THUNDER AND WATER STONES... ARE GONE!!
INCLUDING THE ONE THAT MADE RED'S POLIWHIRL EVOLVE...
...!
BUT THAT'S OKAY.

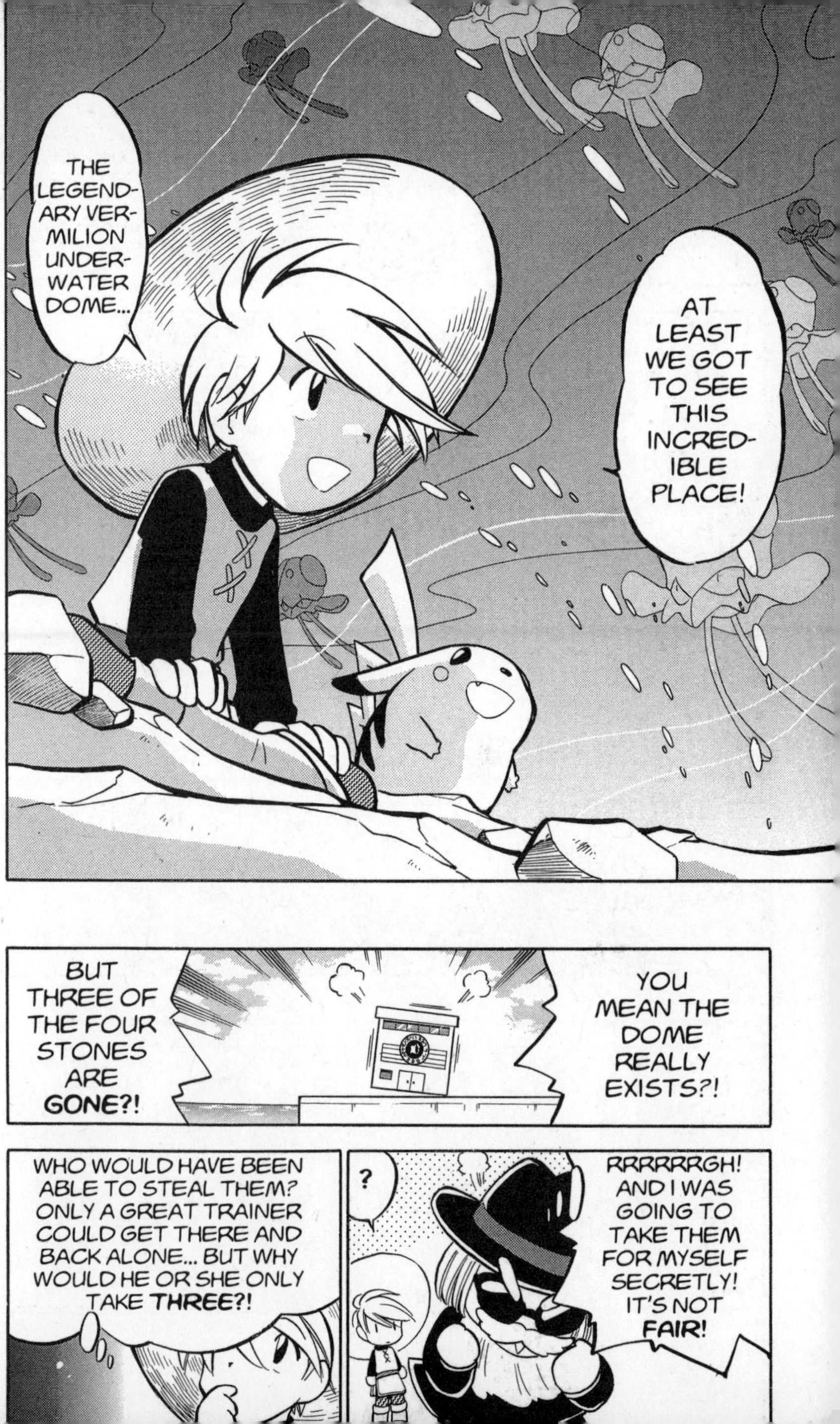
THE LEGENDARY VERMILION UNDERWATER DOME...
AT LEAST WE GOT TO SEE THIS INCREDIBLE PLACE!
YOU MEAN THE DOME REALLY EXISTS?!
BUT THREE OF THE FOUR STONES ARE GONE?!
RRRRRRGH! AND I WAS GOING TO TAKE THEM FOR MYSELF SECRETLY! IT'S NOT FAIR!
?
WHO WOULD HAVE BEEN ABLE TO STEAL THEM? ONLY A GREAT TRAINER COULD GET THERE AND BACK ALONE... BUT WHY WOULD HE OR SHE ONLY TAKE THREE?!

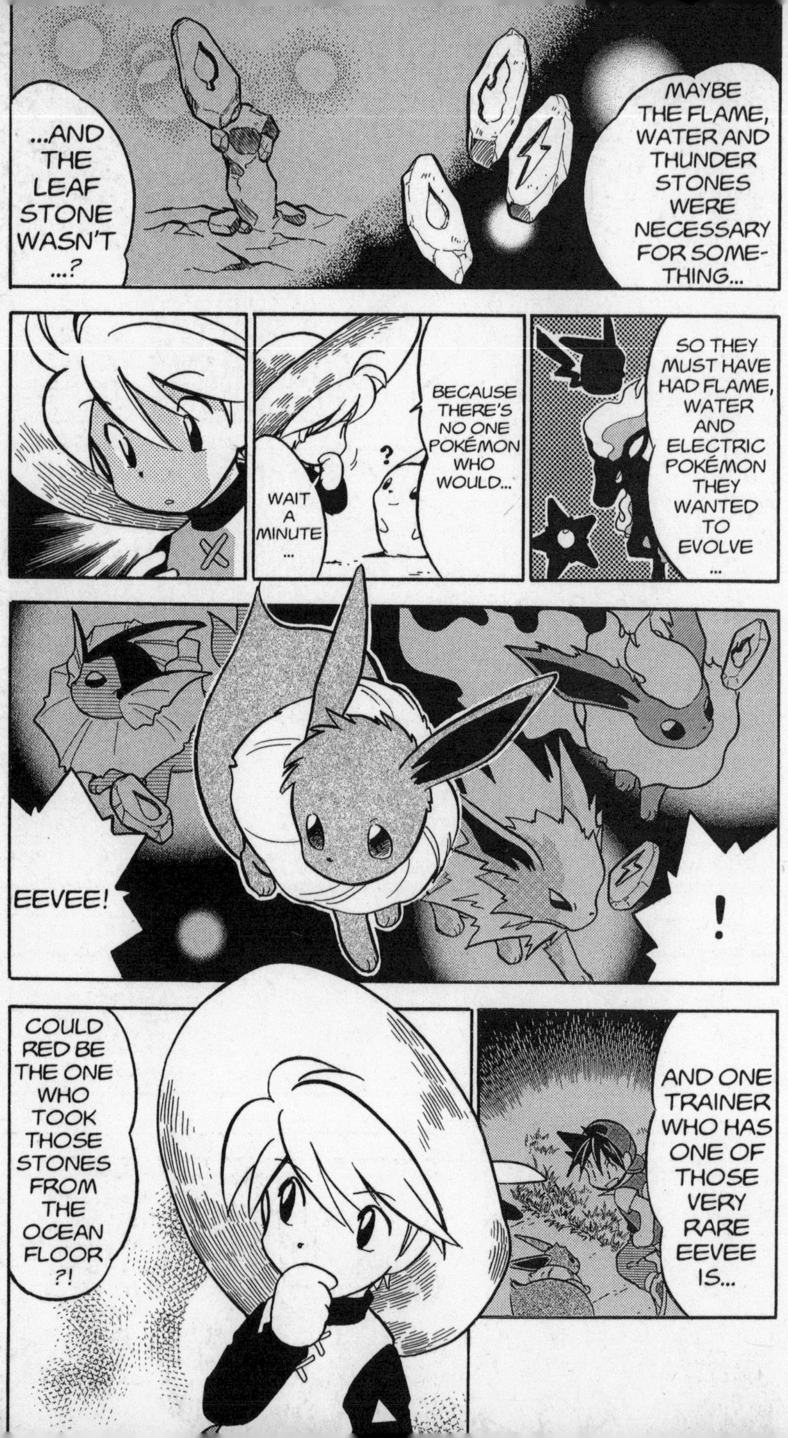
MAYBE THE FLAME, WATER AND THUNDER STONES WERE NECESSARY FOR SOME-THING...
...AND THE LEAF STONE WASN'T ...?
SO THEY MUST HAVE HAD FLAME, WATER AND ELECTRIC POKÉMON THEY WANTED TO EVOLVE ...
BECAUSE THERE'S NO ONE POKÉMON WHO WOULD...
?
WAIT A MINUTE ...
!
EEVEE!
AND ONE TRAINER WHO HAS ONE OF THOSE VERY RARE EEVEE IS...
COULD RED BE THE ONE WHO TOOK THOSE STONES FROM THE OCEAN FLOOR ?!

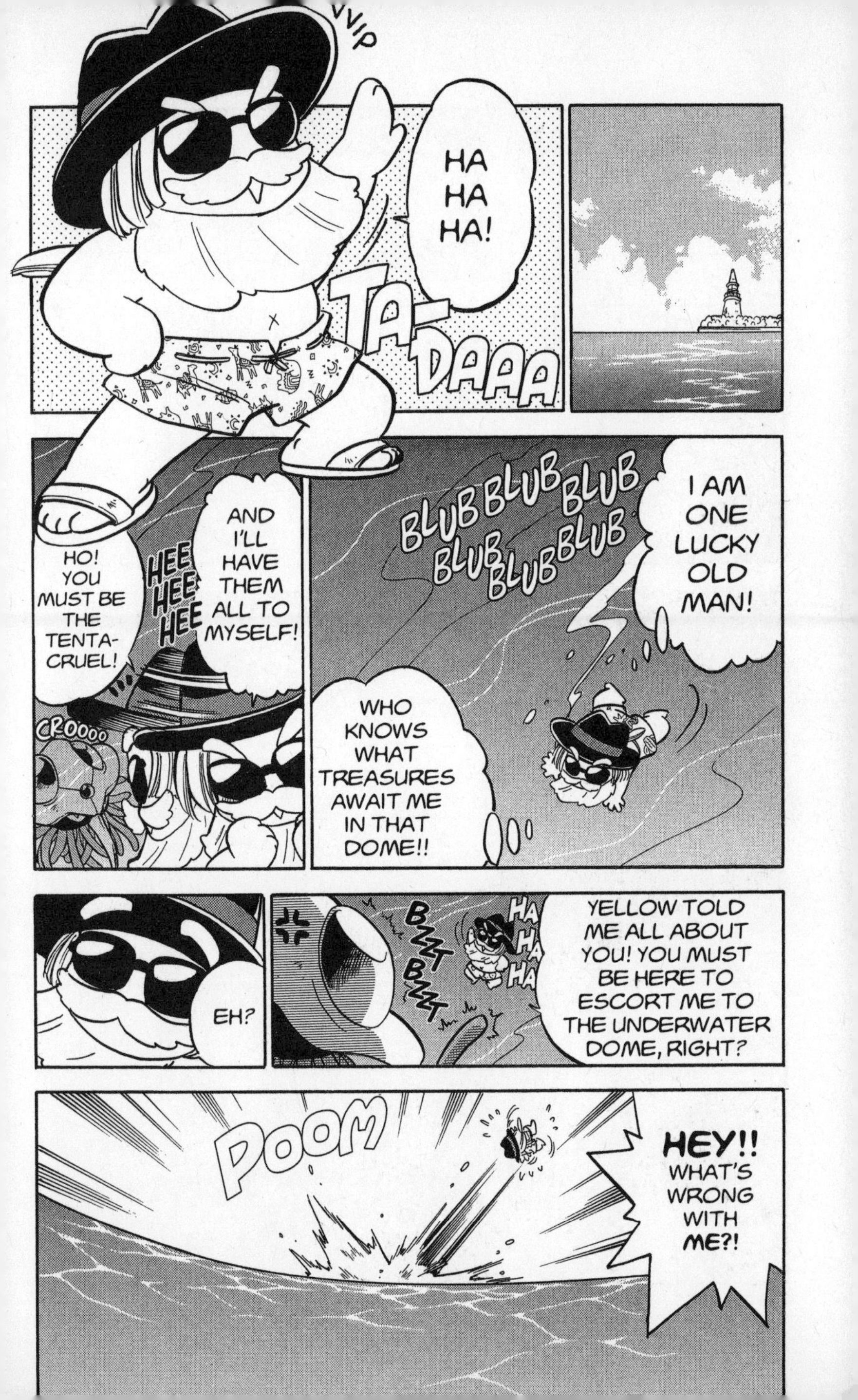
VVIP
HA HA HA!
TA-DAAAA
I AM ONE LUCKY OLD MAN!
BLUB BLUB BLUB BLUB BLUB BLUB
WHO KNOWS WHAT TREASURES AWAIT ME IN THAT DOME!!
AND I'LL HAVE THEM ALL TO MYSELF!
HEE HEE HEE
HO! YOU MUST BE THE TENTA-CRUEL!
CROOOO
YELLOW TOLD ME ALL ABOUT YOU! YOU MUST BE HERE TO ESCORT ME TO THE UNDERWATER DOME, RIGHT?
HA HA HA
BZZZT BZZZT
EH?
HEY!! WHAT'S WRONG WITH ME?!
POOM

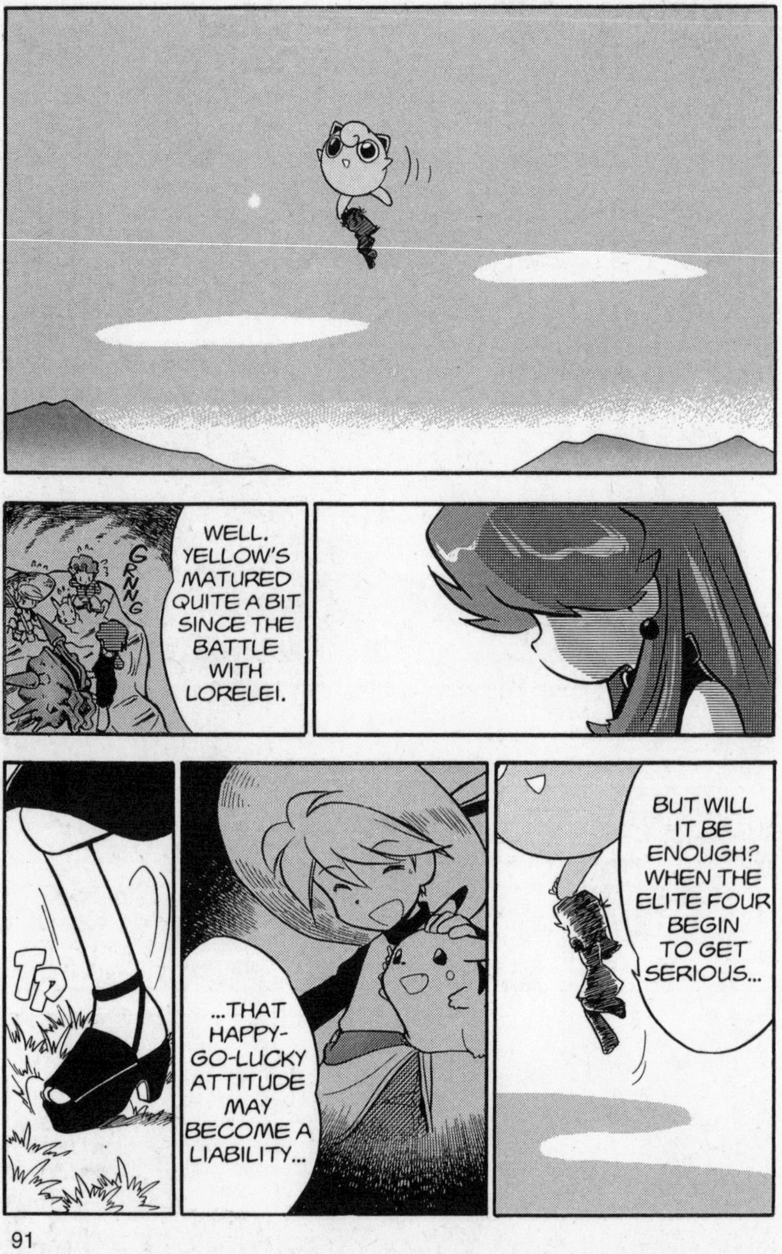
WELL. YELLOW'S MATURED QUITE A BIT SINCE THE BATTLE WITH LORELEI.
GRNNG
BUT WILL IT BE ENOUGH? WHEN THE ELITE FOUR BEGIN TO GET SERIOUS...
...THAT HAPPY-GO-LUCKY ATTITUDE MAY BECOME A LIABILITY...
TP

59 Hitmonlee, Baby! (One More Time)

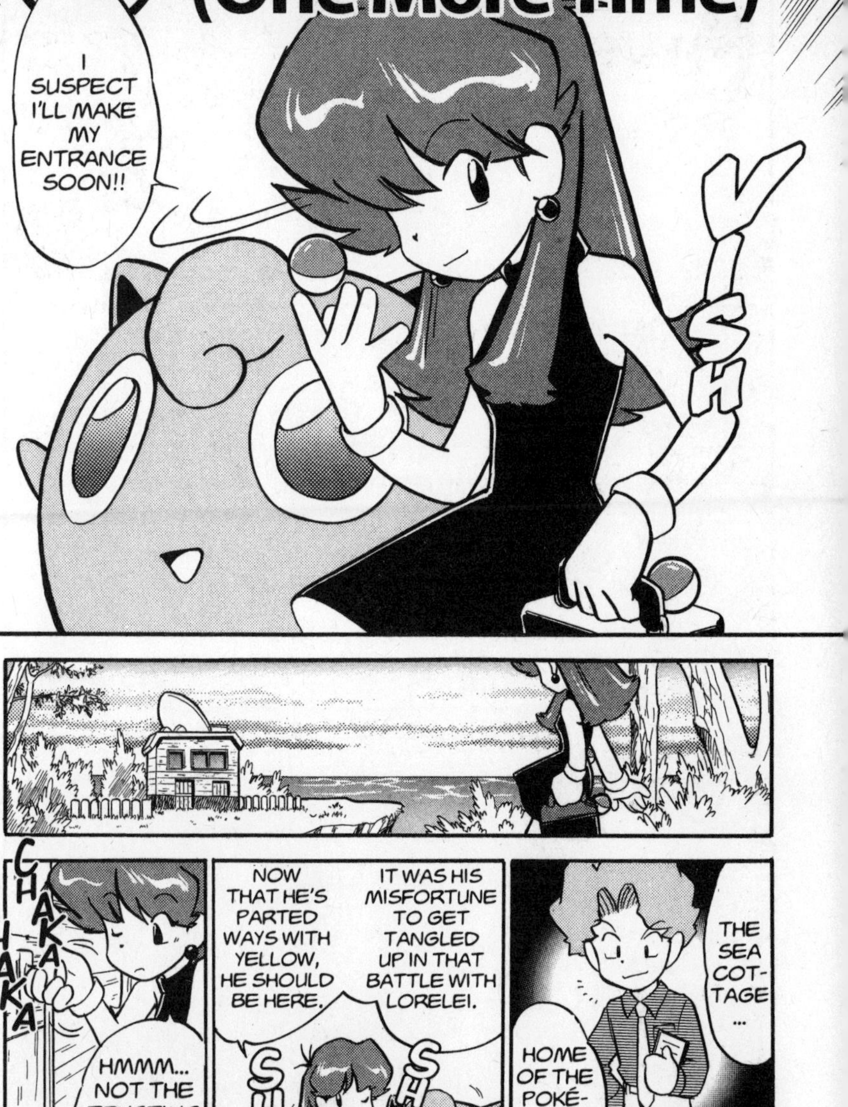

I SUSPECT I'LL MAKE MY ENTRANCE SOON!!
VISH
THE SEA COT-TAGE ...
HOME OF THE POKÉ-MON EXPERT BILL.
IT WAS HIS MISFORTUNE TO GET TANGLED UP IN THAT BATTLE WITH LORELEI.
NOW THAT HE'S PARTED WAYS WITH YELLOW, HE SHOULD BE HERE.
SHH
SHH
CHAKA
CHAKA
HMMM... NOT THE TRUSTING TYPE. NO MATTER.

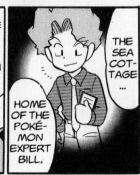

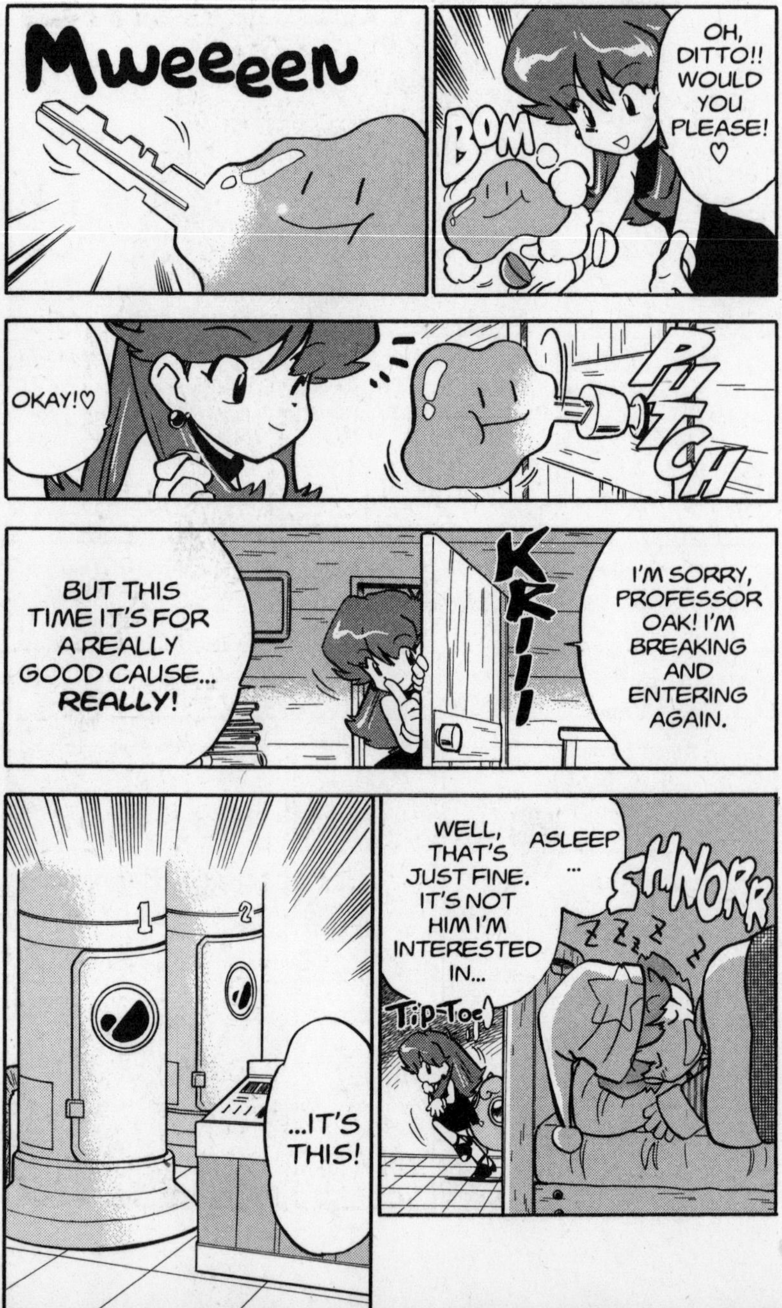

OH, DITTO!! WOULD YOU PLEASE! ♡
BOM
Mweeeen
PITCH
OKAY!♡
I'M SORRY, PROFESSOR OAK! I'M BREAKING AND ENTERING AGAIN.
KRIII
BUT THIS TIME IT'S FOR A REALLY GOOD CAUSE... **REALLY**!
SHNORR
ZZZZZ
ASLEEP...
WELL, THAT'S JUST FINE. IT'S NOT HIM I'M INTERESTED IN...
Tip-Toe
...IT'S THIS!

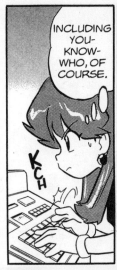

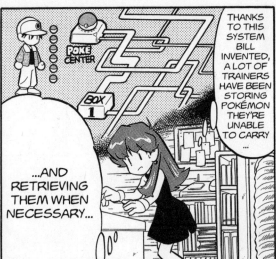

THANKS TO THIS SYSTEM BILL INVENTED, A LOT OF TRAINERS HAVE BEEN STORING POKéMON THEY'RE UNABLE TO CARRY ...
POKE CENTER
BOX 1
...AND RETRIEVING THEM WHEN NECESSARY...
INCLUDING YOU-KNOW-WHO, OF COURSE.
KCH
IF I TAP THE RECORDS... ANYONE ASSOCIATED WITH A POKéMON TRANSACTION...
KCHKCH
... SHOULD COME UP!!
NN... NNN ...?
WH...? WHAT THE-?!
IT'S A BURGLAR !!
OKAY, THEN !!
KCH
KCH

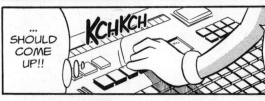

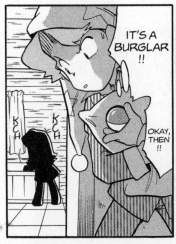

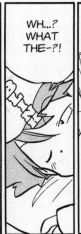

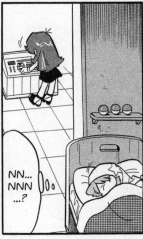

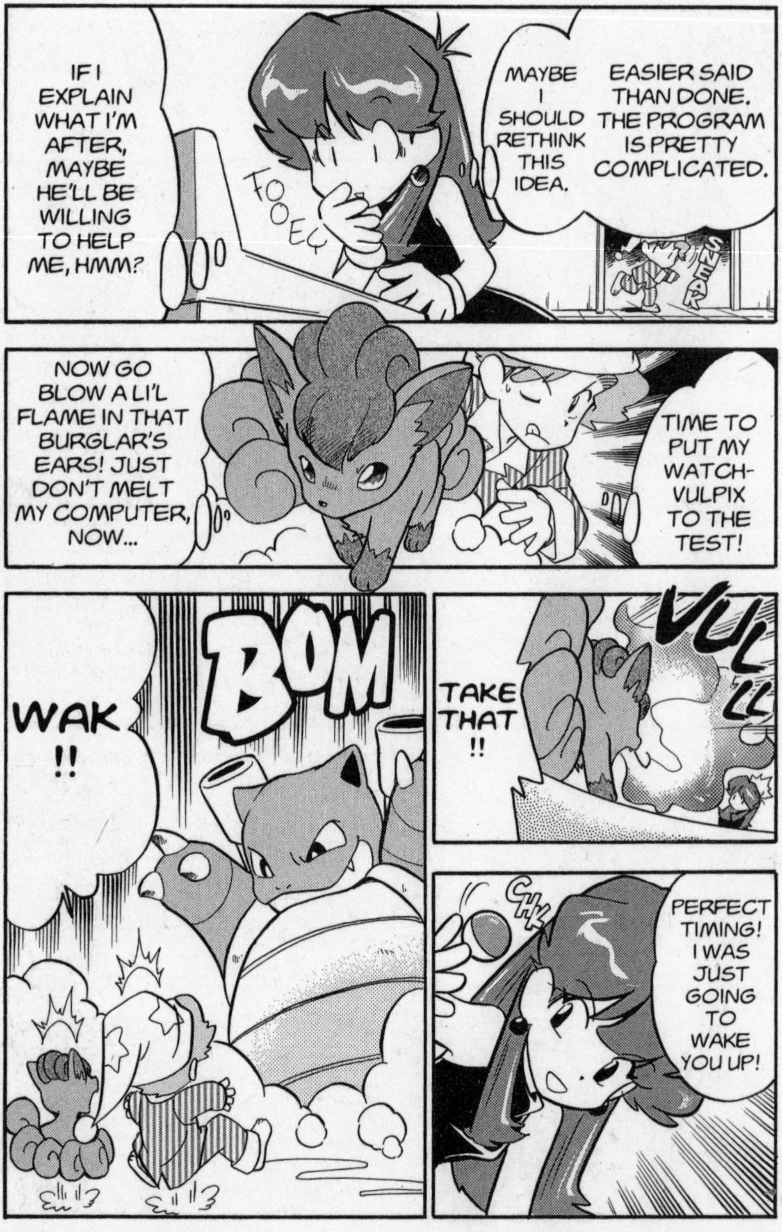
EASIER SAID THAN DONE. THE PROGRAM IS PRETTY COMPLICATED.
MAYBE I SHOULD RETHINK THIS IDEA.
SNEAK
FOOEY
IF I EXPLAIN WHAT I'M AFTER, MAYBE HE'LL BE WILLING TO HELP ME, HMM?
TIME TO PUT MY WATCH-VULPIX TO THE TEST!
NOW GO BLOW A LI'L FLAME IN THAT BURGLAR'S EARS! JUST DON'T MELT MY COMPUTER, NOW...
VULLL
TAKE THAT !!
CHK
PERFECT TIMING! I WAS JUST GOING TO WAKE YOU UP!
BOM
WAK !!

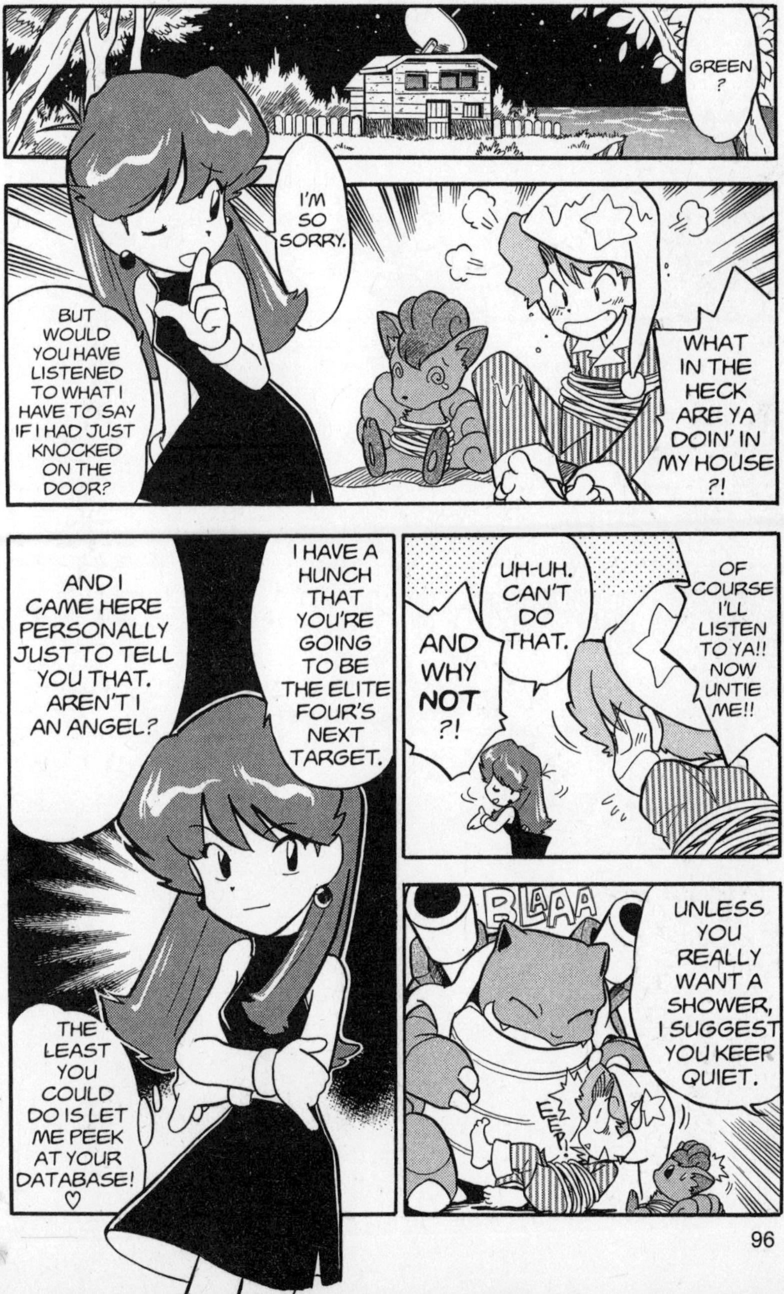
GREEN?
WHAT IN THE HECK ARE YA DOIN' IN MY HOUSE?!
I'M SO SORRY.
BUT WOULD YOU HAVE LISTENED TO WHAT I HAVE TO SAY IF I HAD JUST KNOCKED ON THE DOOR?
OF COURSE I'LL LISTEN TO YA!! NOW UNTIE ME!!
UH-UH. CAN'T DO THAT.
AND WHY **NOT**?!
BLAAA
UNLESS YOU REALLY WANT A SHOWER, I SUGGEST YOU KEEP QUIET.
EEEP!
I HAVE A HUNCH THAT YOU'RE GOING TO BE THE ELITE FOUR'S NEXT TARGET.
AND I CAME HERE PERSONALLY JUST TO TELL YOU THAT. AREN'T I AN ANGEL?
THE LEAST YOU COULD DO IS LET ME PEEK AT YOUR DATABASE! ♡

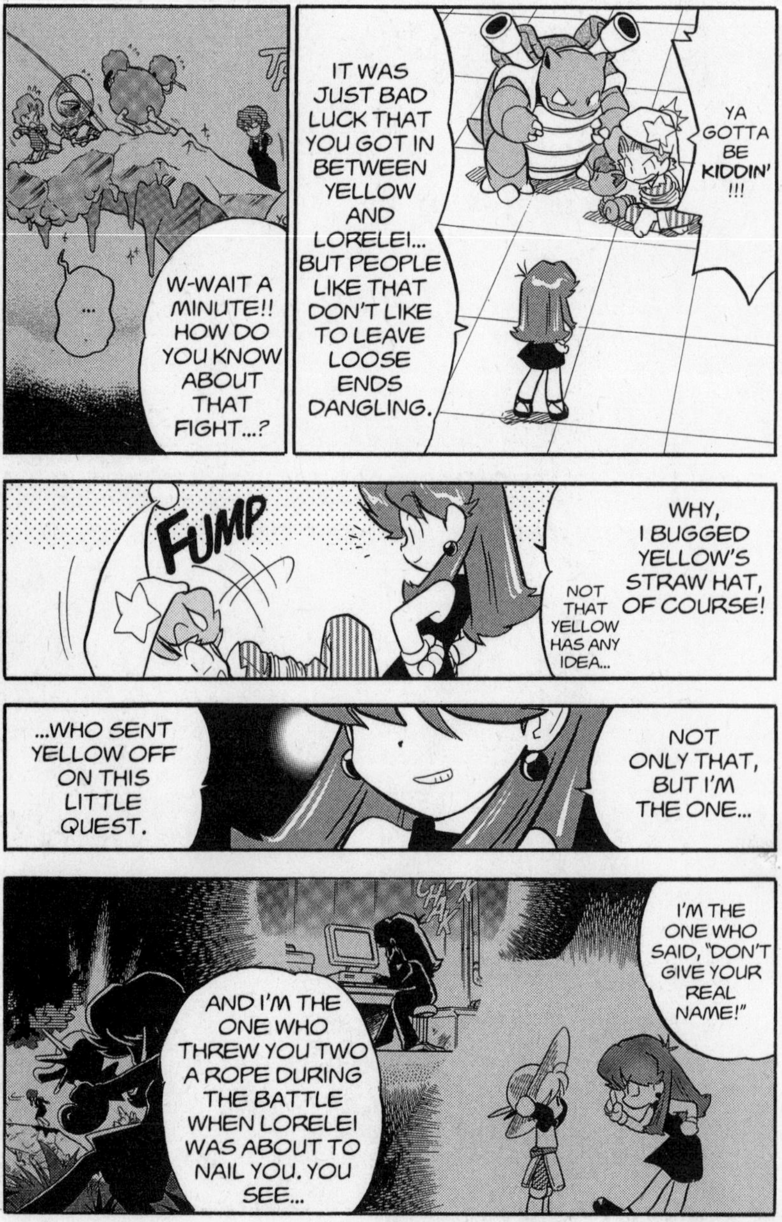
IT WAS JUST BAD LUCK THAT YOU GOT IN BETWEEN YELLOW AND LORELEI... BUT PEOPLE LIKE THAT DON'T LIKE TO LEAVE LOOSE ENDS DANGLING.
YA GOTTA BE KIDDIN' !!!
W-WAIT A MINUTE!! HOW DO YOU KNOW ABOUT THAT FIGHT...?
...
WHY, I BUGGED YELLOW'S STRAW HAT, OF COURSE!
NOT THAT YELLOW HAS ANY IDEA...
FUMP
NOT ONLY THAT, BUT I'M THE ONE...
...WHO SENT YELLOW OFF ON THIS LITTLE QUEST.
I'M THE ONE WHO SAID, "DON'T GIVE YOUR REAL NAME!"
CHAK CHAK
AND I'M THE ONE WHO THREW YOU TWO A ROPE DURING THE BATTLE WHEN LORELEI WAS ABOUT TO NAIL YOU. YOU SEE...

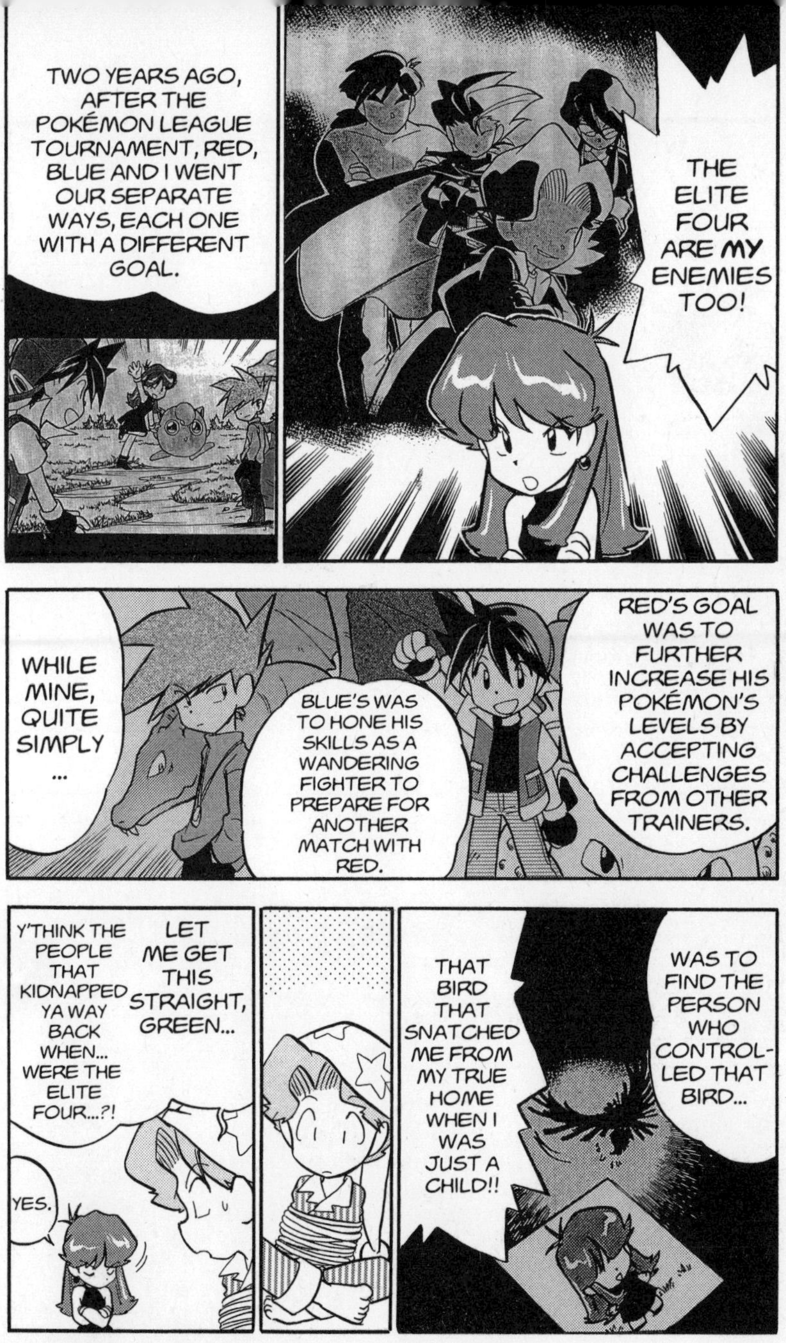
THE ELITE FOUR ARE MY ENEMIES TOO!
TWO YEARS AGO, AFTER THE POKÉMON LEAGUE TOURNAMENT, RED, BLUE AND I WENT OUR SEPARATE WAYS, EACH ONE WITH A DIFFERENT GOAL.
RED'S GOAL WAS TO FURTHER INCREASE HIS POKÉMON'S LEVELS BY ACCEPTING CHALLENGES FROM OTHER TRAINERS.
BLUE'S WAS TO HONE HIS SKILLS AS A WANDERING FIGHTER TO PREPARE FOR ANOTHER MATCH WITH RED.
WHILE MINE, QUITE SIMPLY ...
WAS TO FIND THE PERSON WHO CONTROL-LED THAT BIRD...
THAT BIRD THAT SNATCHED ME FROM MY TRUE HOME WHEN I WAS JUST A CHILD!!
LET ME GET THIS STRAIGHT, GREEN...
Y'THINK THE PEOPLE THAT KIDNAPPED YA WAY BACK WHEN... WERE THE ELITE FOUR...?!
YES.

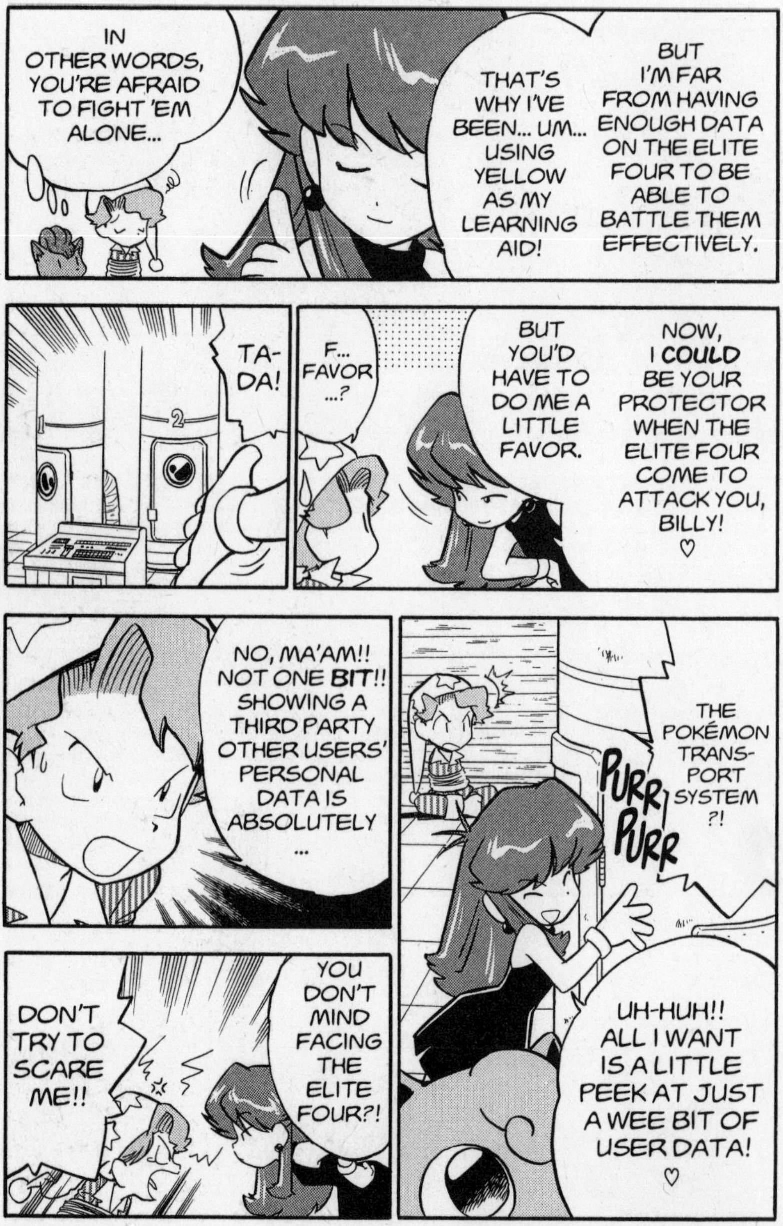
BUT I'M FAR FROM HAVING ENOUGH DATA ON THE ELITE FOUR TO BE ABLE TO BATTLE THEM EFFECTIVELY.
THAT'S WHY I'VE BEEN... UM... USING YELLOW AS MY LEARNING AID!
IN OTHER WORDS, YOU'RE AFRAID TO FIGHT 'EM ALONE...
NOW, I **COULD** BE YOUR PROTECTOR WHEN THE ELITE FOUR COME TO ATTACK YOU, BILLY! ♡
BUT YOU'D HAVE TO DO ME A LITTLE FAVOR.
F... FAVOR ...?
TA-DA!
THE POKéMON TRANS-PORT SYSTEM ?!
PURR PURR
UH-HUH!! ALL I WANT IS A LITTLE PEEK AT JUST A WEE BIT OF USER DATA! ♡
NO, MA'AM!! NOT ONE **BIT**!! SHOWING A THIRD PARTY OTHER USERS' PERSONAL DATA IS ABSOLUTELY ...
YOU DON'T MIND FACING THE ELITE FOUR?!
DON'T TRY TO SCARE ME!!

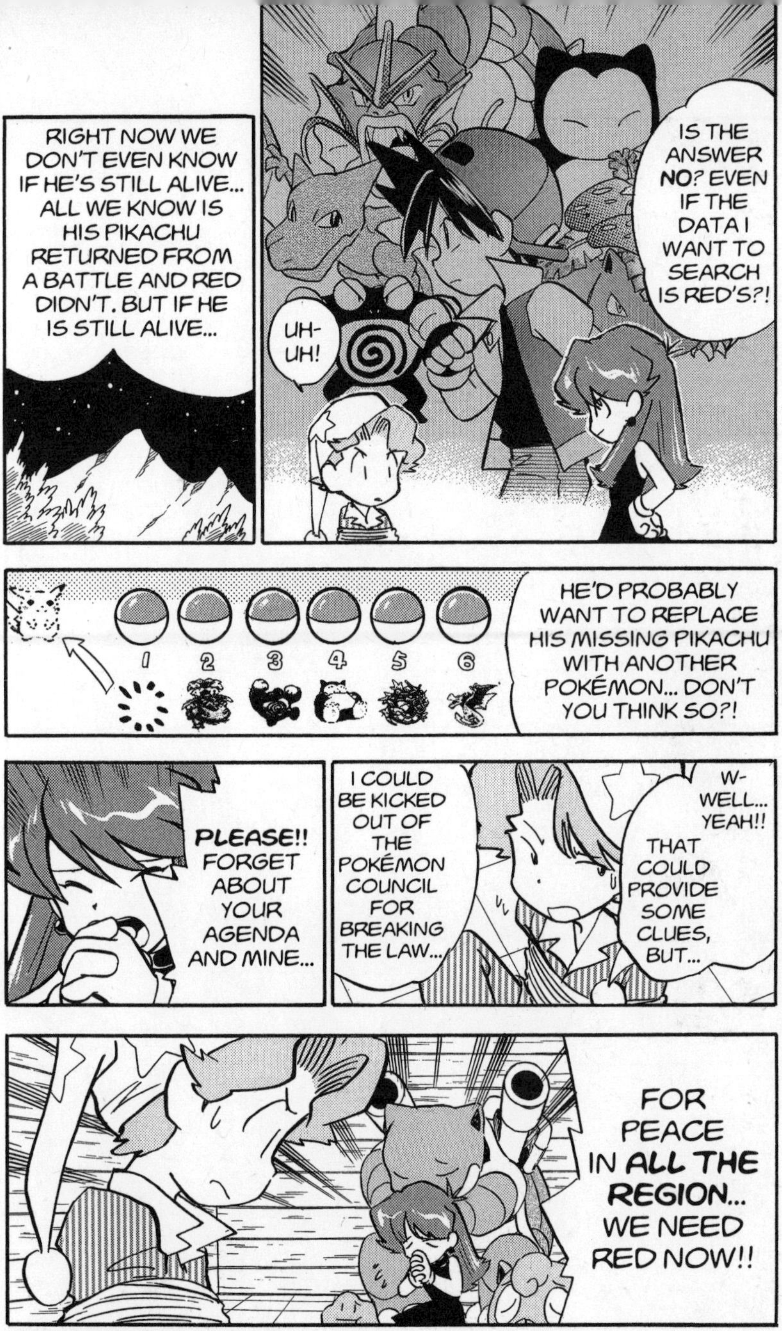
IS THE ANSWER NO? EVEN IF THE DATA I WANT TO SEARCH IS RED'S?!
UH-UH!
RIGHT NOW WE DON'T EVEN KNOW IF HE'S STILL ALIVE... ALL WE KNOW IS HIS PIKACHU RETURNED FROM A BATTLE AND RED DIDN'T. BUT IF HE IS STILL ALIVE...
1
2
3
4
5
6
HE'D PROBABLY WANT TO REPLACE HIS MISSING PIKACHU WITH ANOTHER POKÉMON... DON'T YOU THINK SO?!
W-WELL... YEAH!!
THAT COULD PROVIDE SOME CLUES, BUT...
I COULD BE KICKED OUT OF THE POKÉMON COUNCIL FOR BREAKING THE LAW...
PLEASE!! FORGET ABOUT YOUR AGENDA AND MINE...
FOR PEACE IN ALL THE REGION... WE NEED RED NOW!!

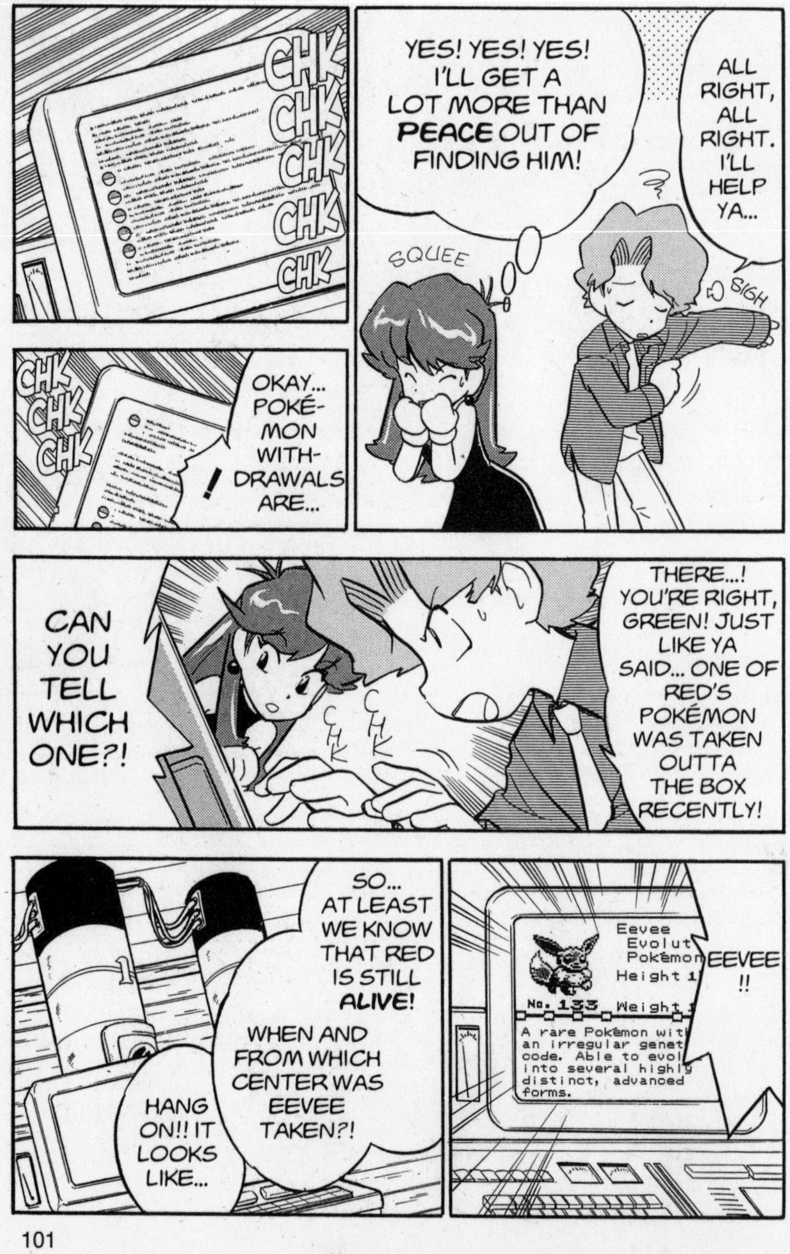

ALL RIGHT, ALL RIGHT. I'LL HELP YA...
YES! YES! YES! I'LL GET A LOT MORE THAN **PEACE** OUT OF FINDING HIM!
SIGH
SQUEE
CHK CHK CHK CHK CHK
OKAY... POKÉ-MON WITH-DRAWALS ARE...
!
CHK CHK CHK
THERE...! YOU'RE RIGHT, GREEN! JUST LIKE YA SAID... ONE OF RED'S POKÉMON WAS TAKEN OUTTA THE BOX RECENTLY!
CHK CHK
CAN YOU TELL WHICH ONE?!
EEVEE!!
Eevee
Evolut
Pokémon
Height 1
No. 133
Weight 1
A rare Pokémon wit an irregular genet code. Able to evol into several highly distinct, advanced forms.
SO... AT LEAST WE KNOW THAT RED IS STILL **ALIVE**!
WHEN AND FROM WHICH CENTER WAS EEVEE TAKEN?!
HANG ON!! IT LOOKS LIKE...

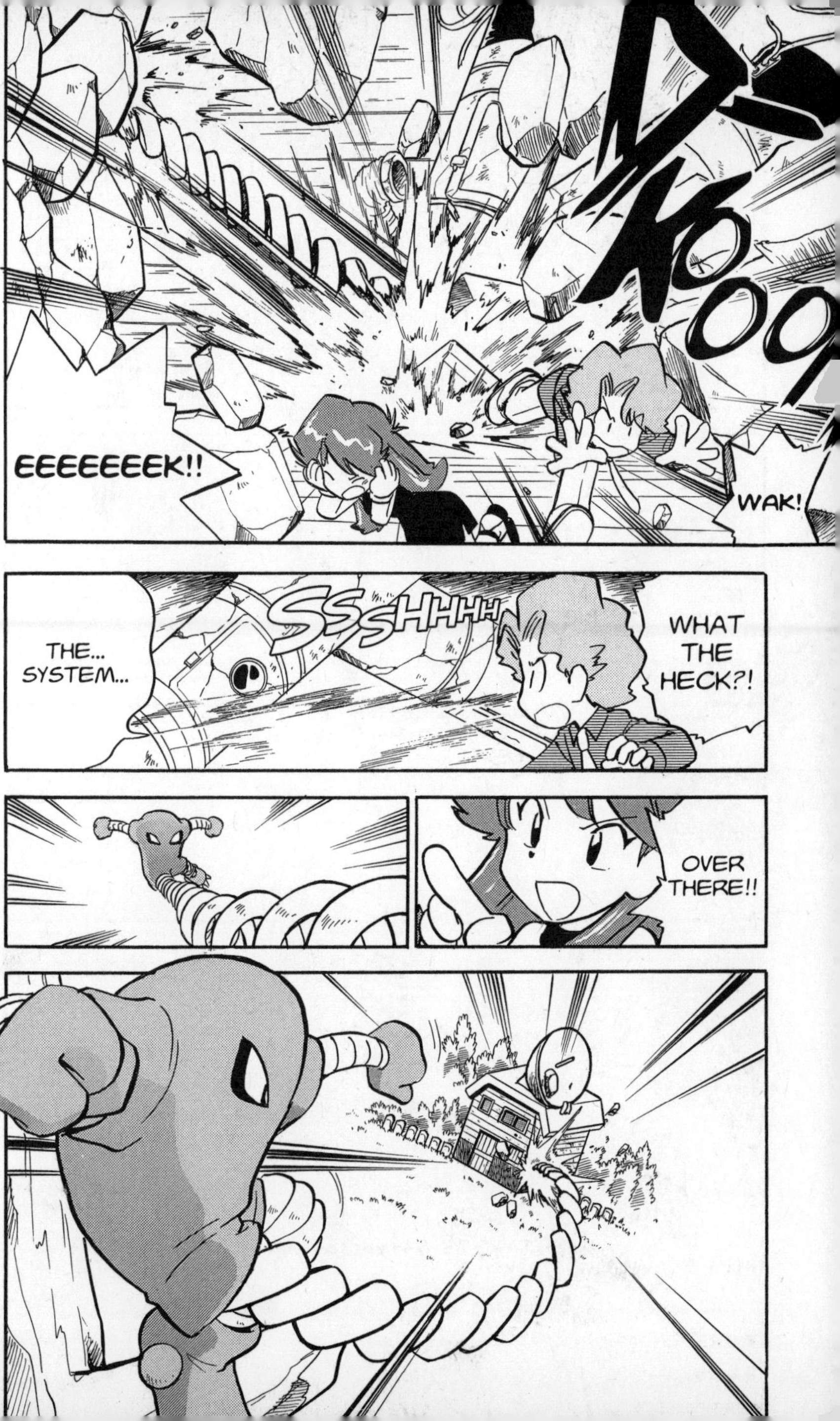
WAK!
EEEEEEEK!!
WHAT THE HECK?!
SSSHHHH
THE... SYSTEM...
OVER THERE!!

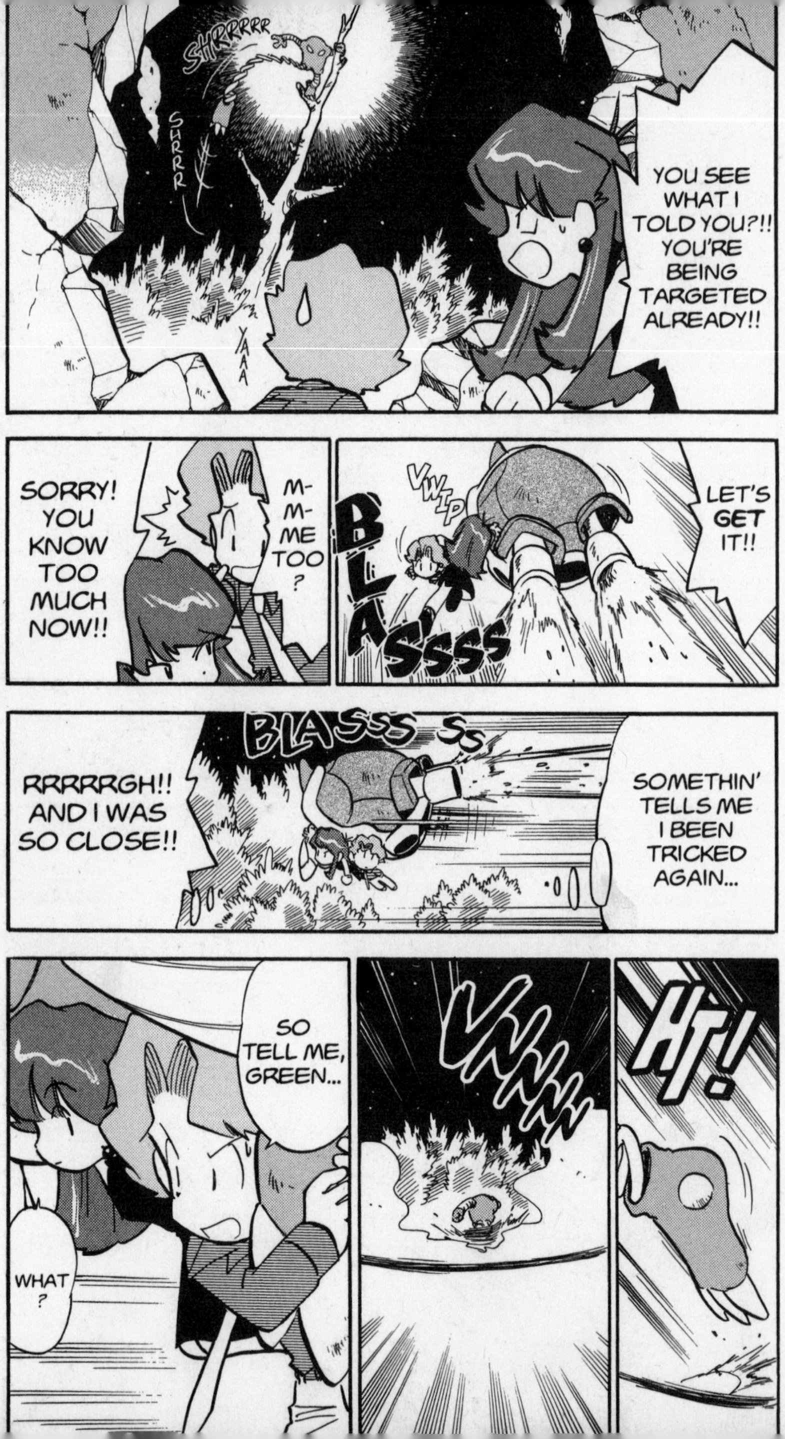
YOU SEE WHAT I TOLD YOU?!! YOU'RE BEING TARGETED ALREADY!!
SHRRRRR
SHRRR
YAAA
LET'S GET IT!!
VWIP
BLASSSSS
M-M-ME TOO?
SORRY! YOU KNOW TOO MUCH NOW!!
SOMETHIN' TELLS ME I BEEN TRICKED AGAIN...
BLASSS SS
RRRRRGH!! AND I WAS SO CLOSE!!
HT!
VNNNN
SO TELL ME, GREEN...
WHAT?

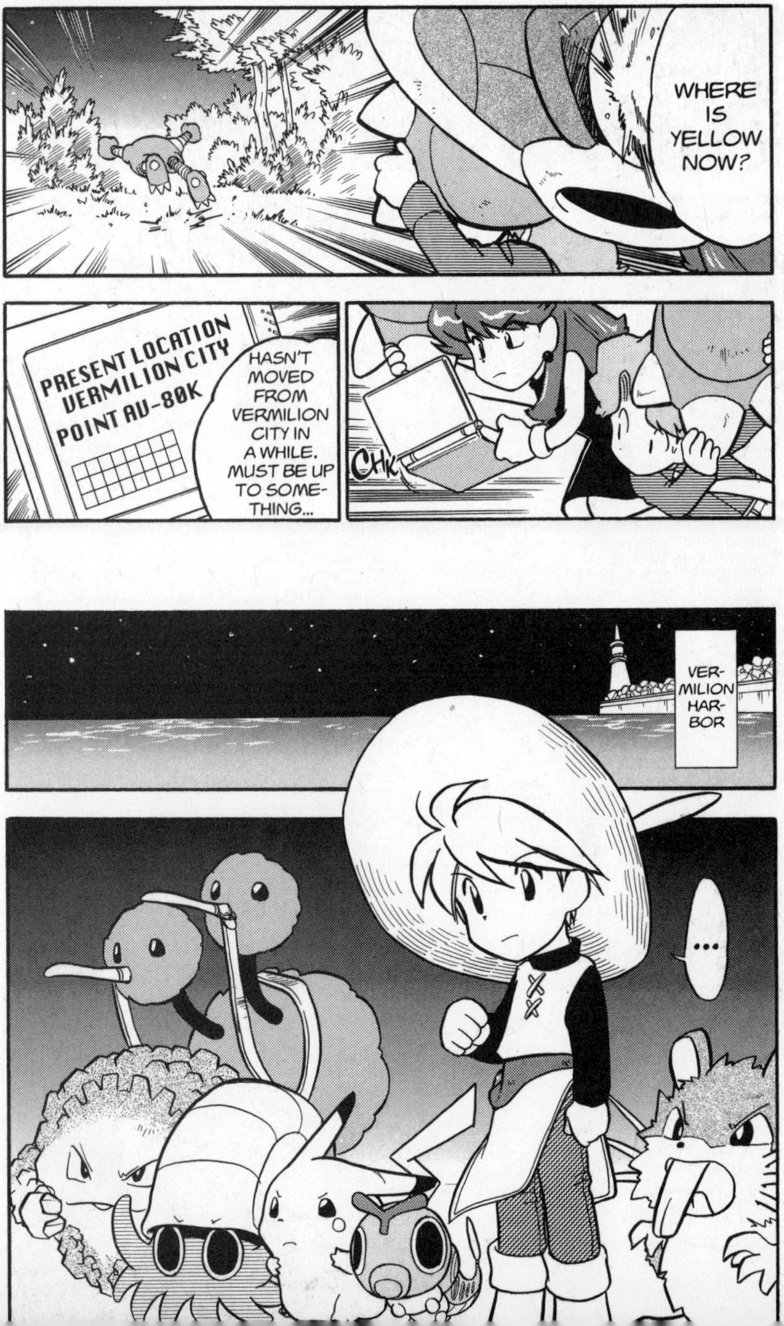
WHERE IS YELLOW NOW?
CHK
PRESENT LOCATION
VERMILION CITY
POINT AV-80K
HASN'T MOVED FROM VERMILION CITY IN A WHILE. MUST BE UP TO SOME-THING...
VER-MILION HAR-BOR
...

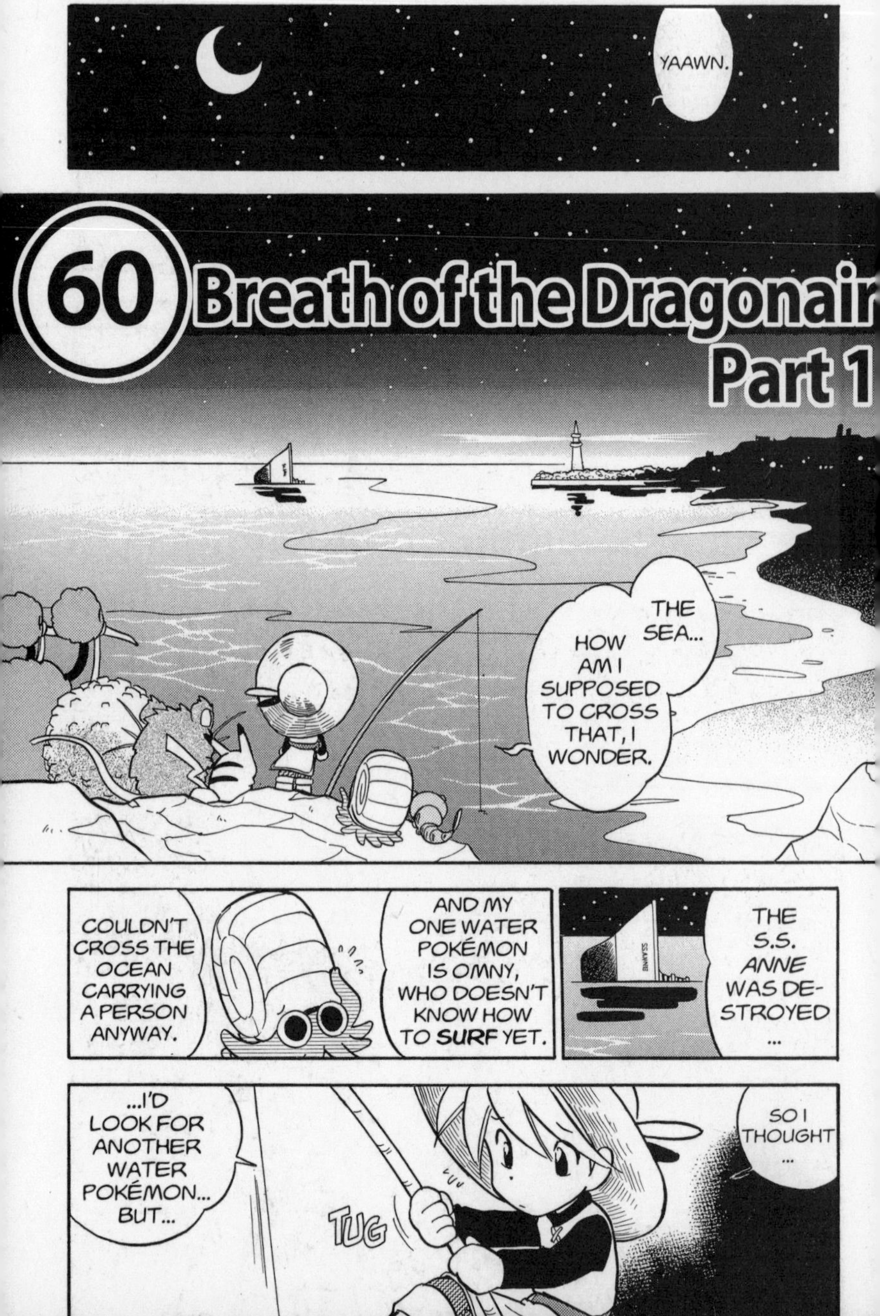
YAAWN.
60 Breath of the Dragonair Part 1
THE SEA... HOW AM I SUPPOSED TO CROSS THAT, I WONDER.
THE S.S. ANNE WAS DE-STROYED...
AND MY ONE WATER POKÉMON IS OMNY, WHO DOESN'T KNOW HOW TO **SURF** YET.
COULDN'T CROSS THE OCEAN CARRYING A PERSON ANYWAY.
SO I THOUGHT...
...I'D LOOK FOR ANOTHER WATER POKÉMON... BUT...
TUG

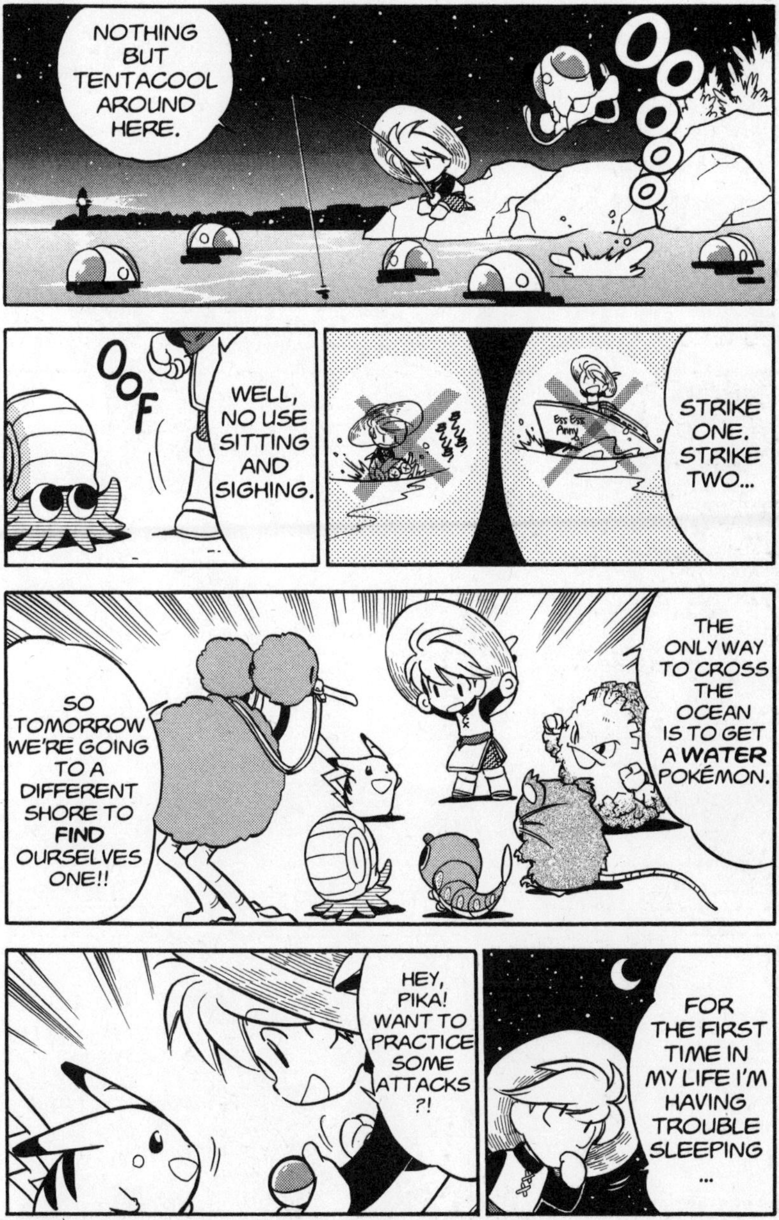
NOTHING BUT TENTACOOL AROUND HERE.
STRIKE ONE. STRIKE TWO...
WELL, NO USE SITTING AND SIGHING.
OOF
THE ONLY WAY TO CROSS THE OCEAN IS TO GET A **WATER** POKÉMON.
SO TOMORROW WE'RE GOING TO A DIFFERENT SHORE TO **FIND** OURSELVES ONE!!
FOR THE FIRST TIME IN MY LIFE I'M HAVING TROUBLE SLEEPING ...
HEY, PIKA! WANT TO PRACTICE SOME ATTACKS ?!

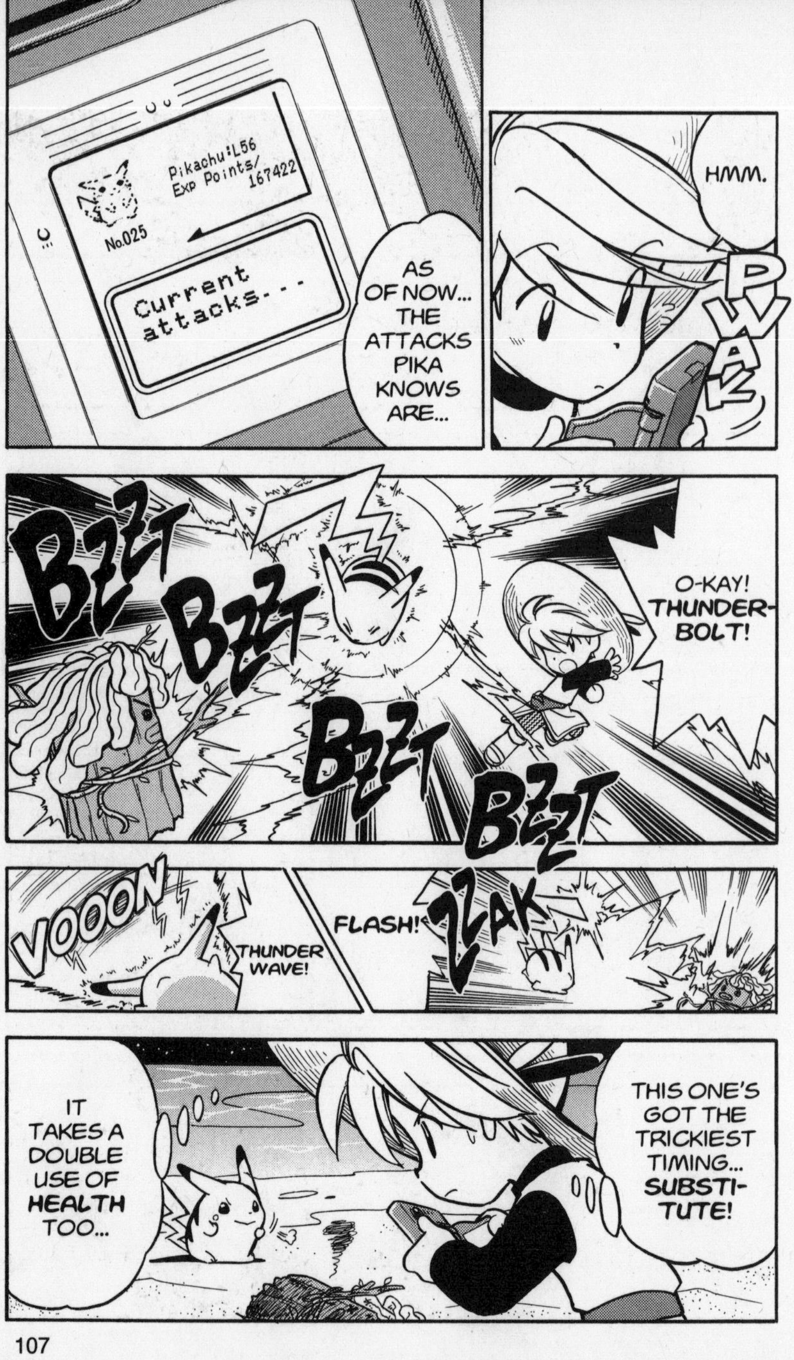
HMM.
PWAK
Pikachu:L56
Exp Points/
167422
No.025
Current attacks...
AS OF NOW... THE ATTACKS PIKA KNOWS ARE...
O-KAY! THUNDER-BOLT!
BZZT
BZZT
BZZT
BZZT
FLASH!
ZZAK
VOOON
THUNDER WAVE!
THIS ONE'S GOT THE TRICKIEST TIMING... SUBSTI-TUTE!
IT TAKES A DOUBLE USE OF HEALTH TOO...

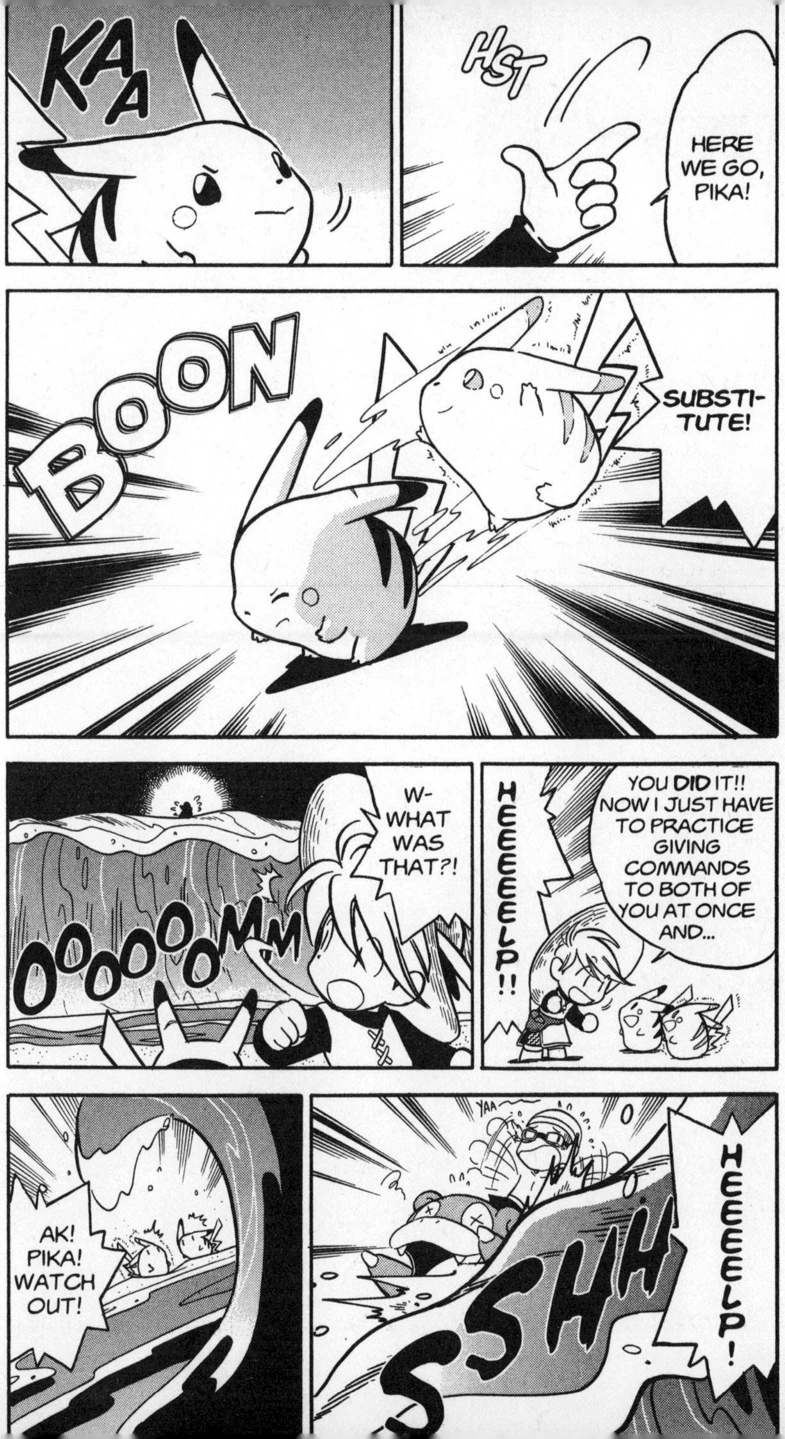

HERE WE GO, PIKA!
HST
KAA
SUBSTI-TUTE!
BOON
YOU DID IT!! NOW I JUST HAVE TO PRACTICE GIVING COMMANDS TO BOTH OF YOU AT ONCE AND...
HEEEEELP!!
W-WHAT WAS THAT?!
OOOOOOMM
HEEEELP!
YAA
SSHH
AK! PIKA! WATCH OUT!

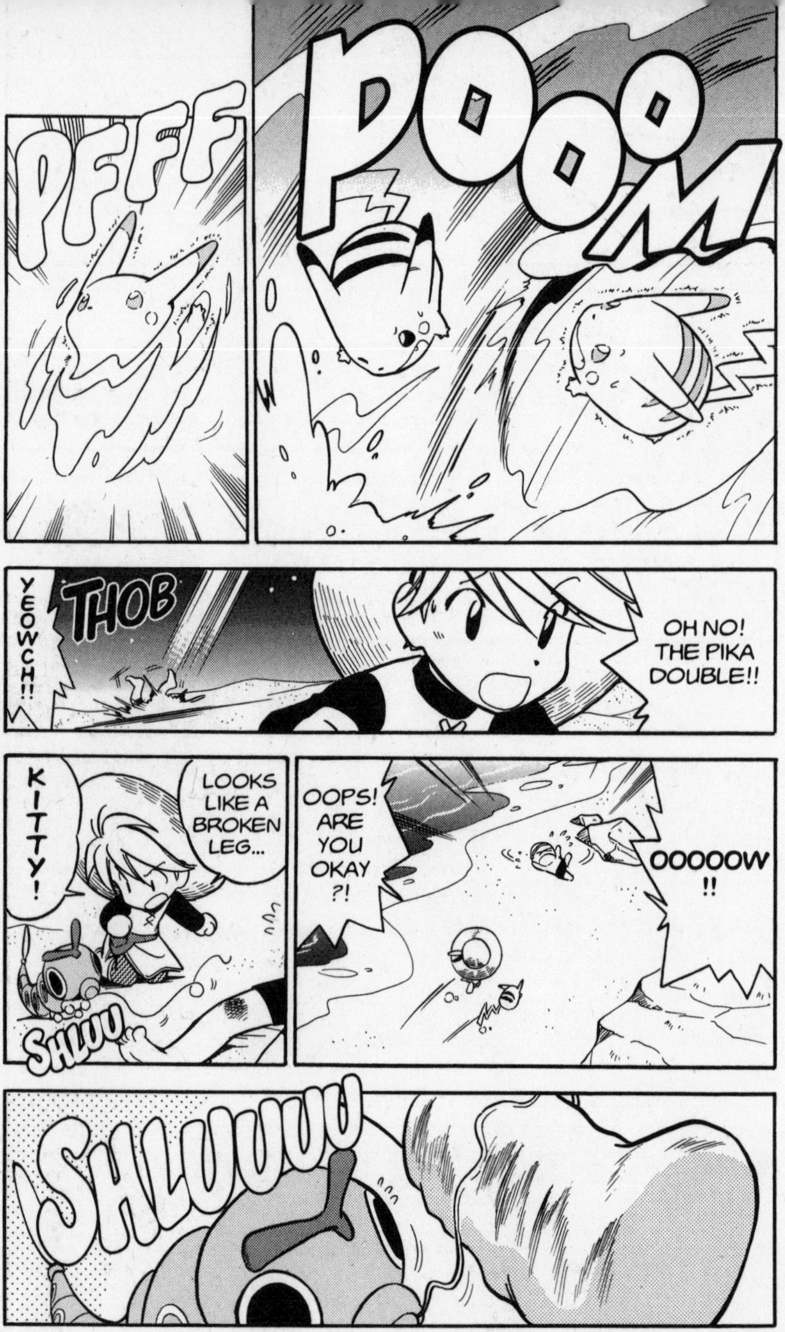
POOOM
PFFF
OH NO! THE PIKA DOUBLE!!
THOB
YEOWCH!!
OOOOOW!!
OOPS! ARE YOU OKAY?!
LOOKS LIKE A BROKEN LEG...
KITTY!
SHLUU
SHLUUUUU

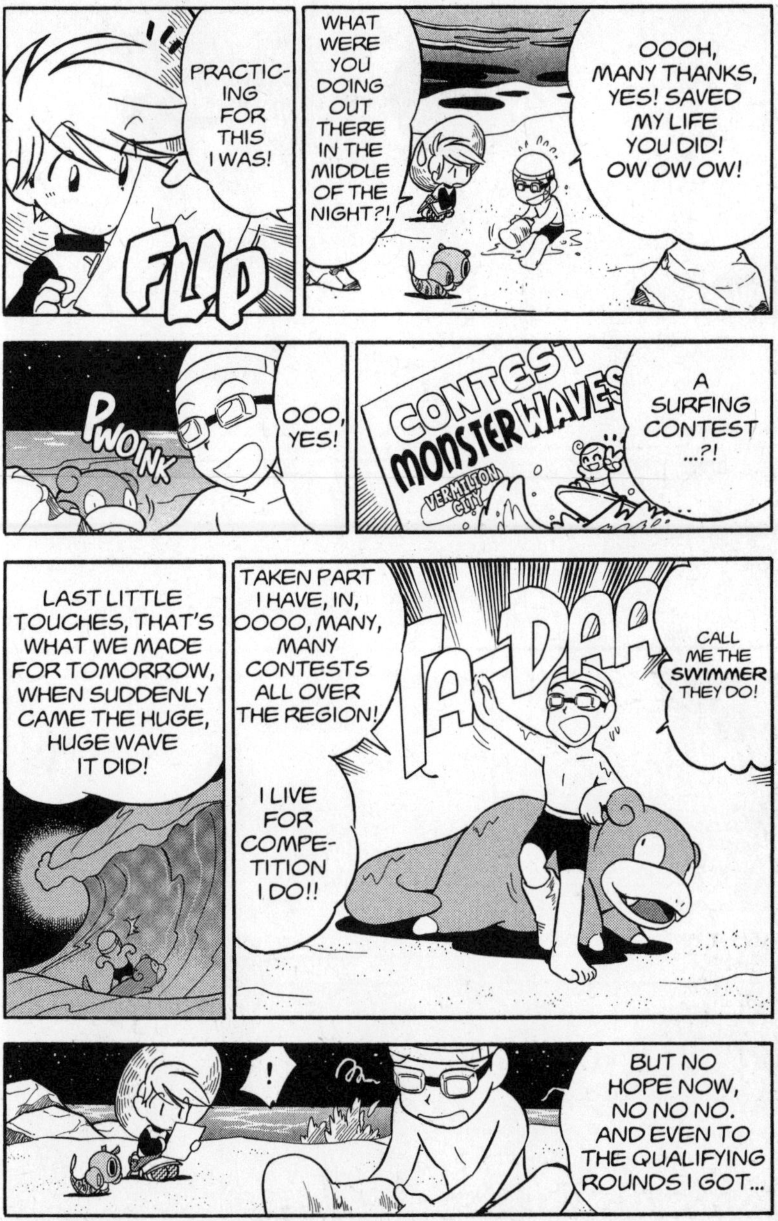
OOOH, MANY THANKS, YES! SAVED MY LIFE YOU DID! OW OW OW!
WHAT WERE YOU DOING OUT THERE IN THE MIDDLE OF THE NIGHT?!
PRACTIC-ING FOR THIS I WAS!
FLIP
CONTEST
MONSTER WAVES
VERMILION CITY
A SURFING CONTEST ...?!
OOO, YES!
PWOINK
CALL ME THE SWIMMER THEY DO!
TA-DAA
TAKEN PART I HAVE, IN, OOOO, MANY, MANY CONTESTS ALL OVER THE REGION!
I LIVE FOR COMPE-TITION I DO!!
LAST LITTLE TOUCHES, THAT'S WHAT WE MADE FOR TOMORROW, WHEN SUDDENLY CAME THE HUGE, HUGE WAVE IT DID!
BUT NO HOPE NOW, NO NO NO. AND EVEN TO THE QUALIFYING ROUNDS I GOT...
!

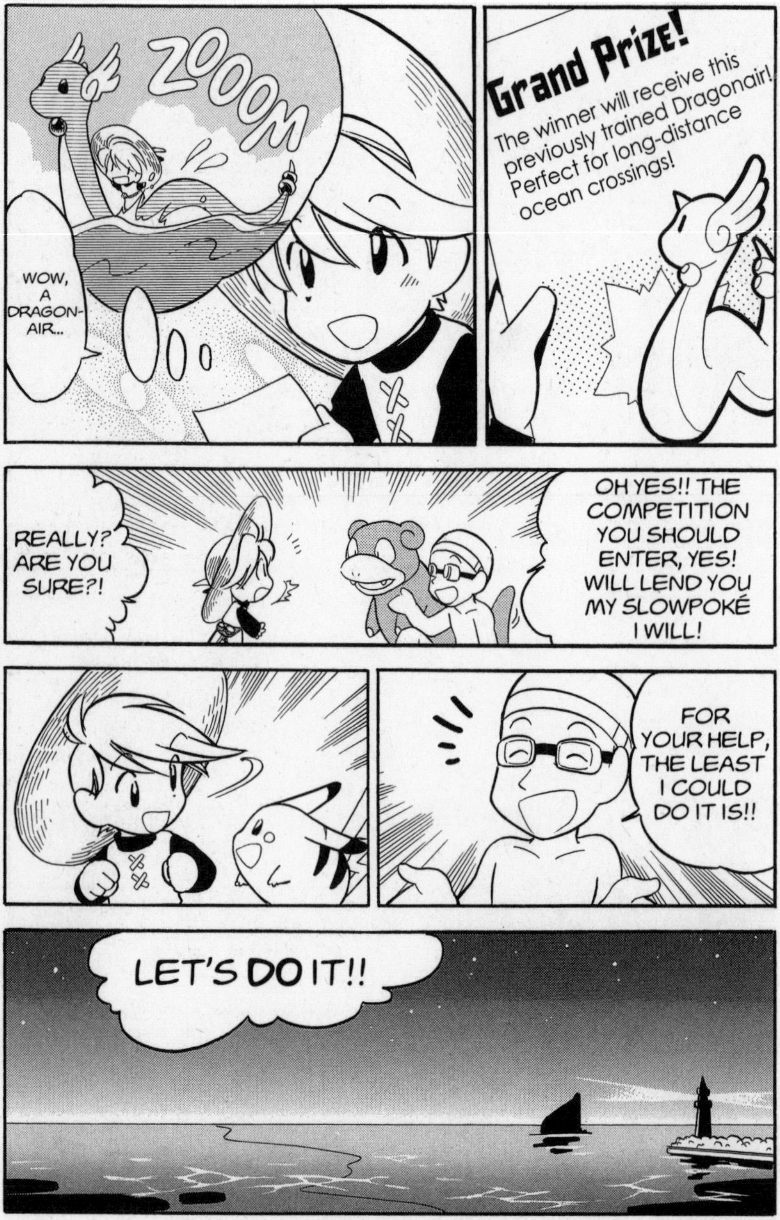
Grand Prize!
The winner will receive this previously trained Dragonair! Perfect for long-distance ocean crossings!
ZOOOM
WOW, A DRAGON-AIR...
OH YES!! THE COMPETITION YOU SHOULD ENTER, YES! WILL LEND YOU MY SLOWPOKÉ I WILL!
REALLY? ARE YOU SURE?!
FOR YOUR HELP, THE LEAST I COULD DO IT IS!!
LET'S DO IT!!

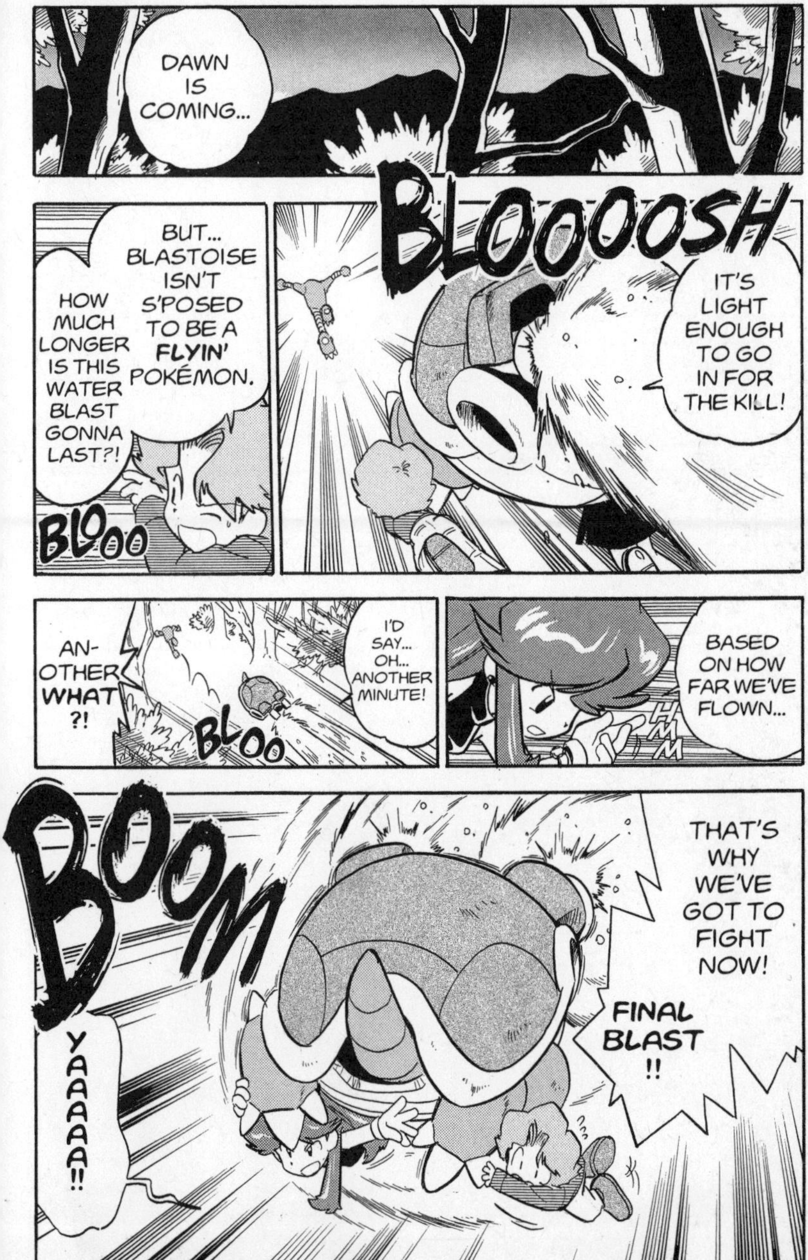
DAWN IS COMING...
BLOOOOSH
IT'S LIGHT ENOUGH TO GO IN FOR THE KILL!
BUT... BLASTOISE ISN'T S'POSED TO BE A **FLYIN'** POKÉMON.
HOW MUCH LONGER IS THIS WATER BLAST GONNA LAST?!
BLOOO
BASED ON HOW FAR WE'VE FLOWN...
HMM
I'D SAY... OH... ANOTHER MINUTE!
AN-OTHER **WHAT** ?!
BLOO
THAT'S WHY WE'VE GOT TO FIGHT NOW!
FINAL BLAST !!
BOOM
YAAAAAA!!

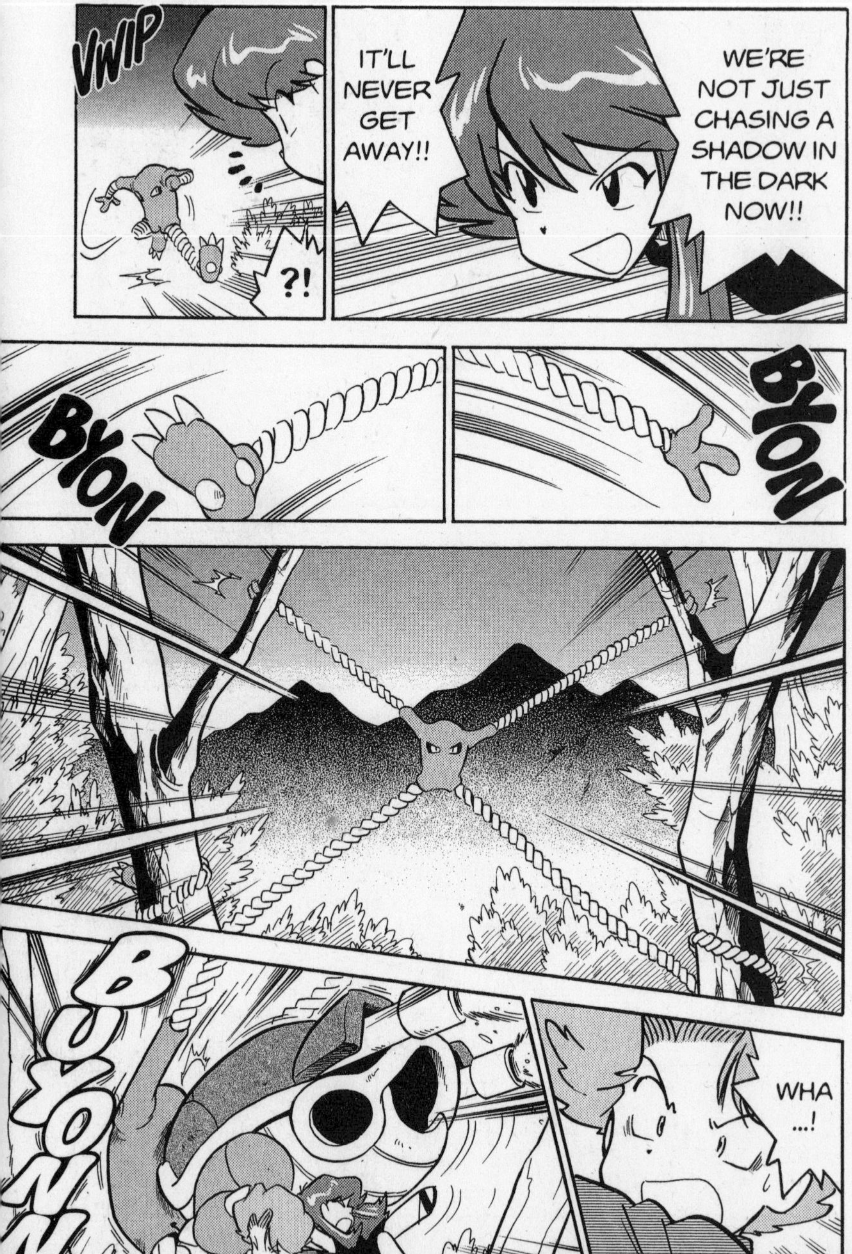
WE'RE NOT JUST CHASING A SHADOW IN THE DARK NOW!!
IT'LL NEVER GET AWAY!!
VWIP
...
?!
BYON
BYON
WHA ...!
BUYONN

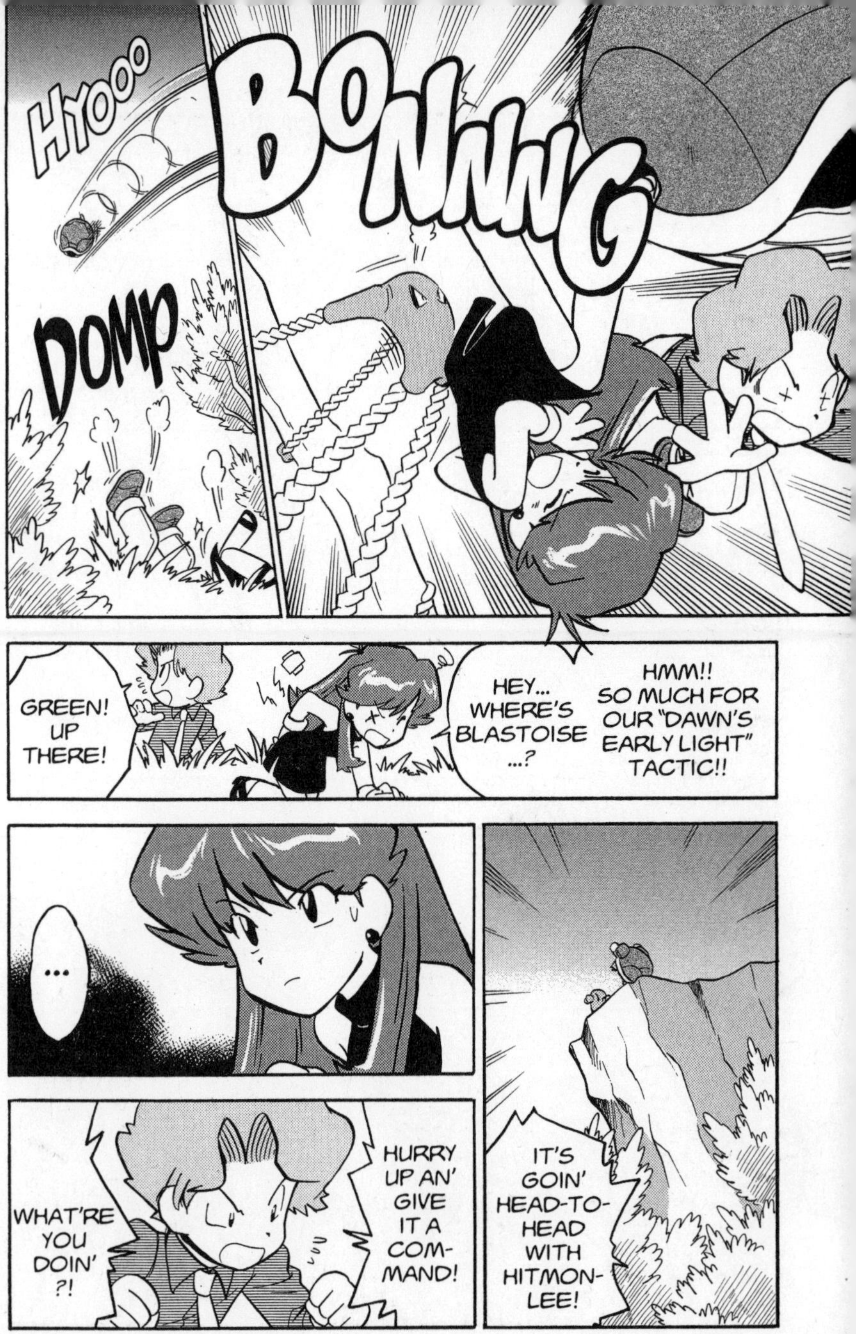
BONNNG
HYOOO
DOMP
HMM!! SO MUCH FOR OUR "DAWN'S EARLY LIGHT" TACTIC!!
HEY... WHERE'S BLASTOISE ...?
GREEN! UP THERE!
IT'S GOIN' HEAD-TO-HEAD WITH HITMON-LEE!
...
HURRY UP AN' GIVE IT A COM-MAND!
WHAT'RE YOU DOIN' ?!

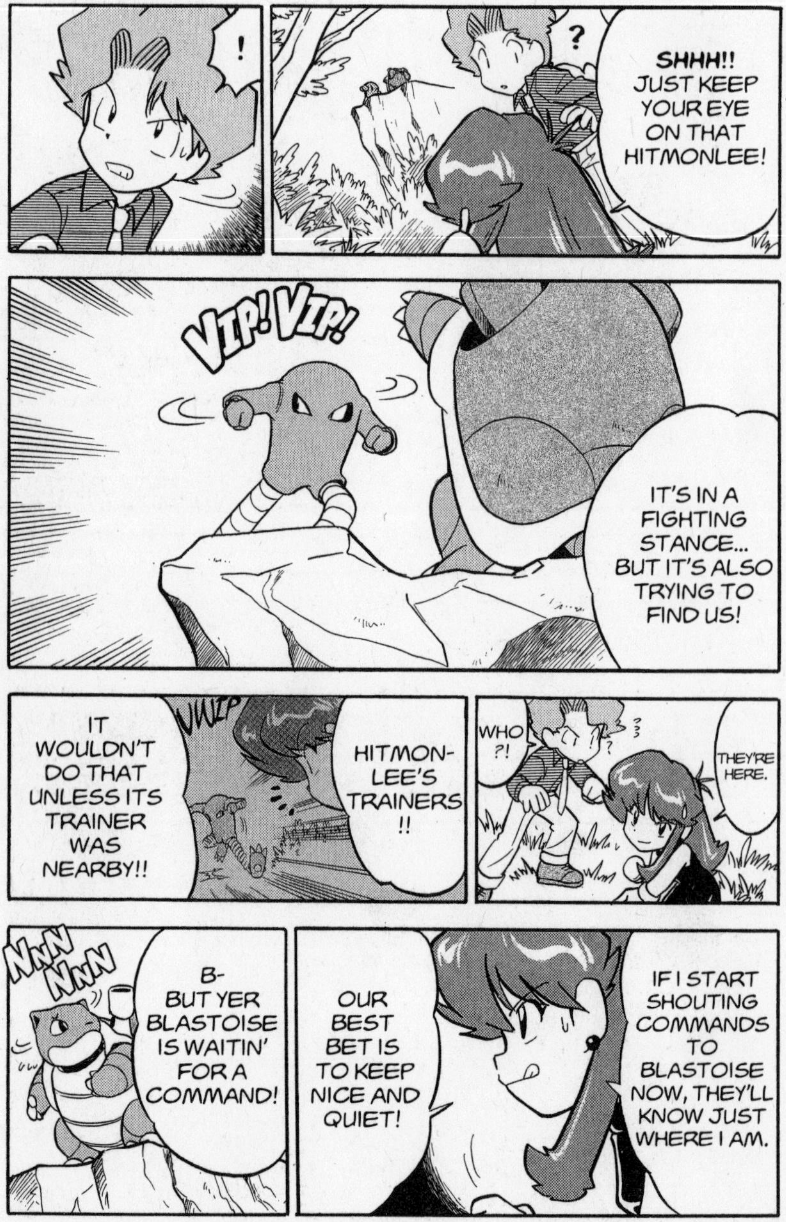
SHHH!! JUST KEEP YOUR EYE ON THAT HITMONLEE!
?
!
VIP! VIP!
IT'S IN A FIGHTING STANCE... BUT IT'S ALSO TRYING TO FIND US!
THEY'RE HERE.
WHO ?!
HITMON-LEE'S TRAINERS !!
VWIP
IT WOULDN'T DO THAT UNLESS ITS TRAINER WAS NEARBY!!
IF I START SHOUTING COMMANDS TO BLASTOISE NOW, THEY'LL KNOW JUST WHERE I AM.
OUR BEST BET IS TO KEEP NICE AND QUIET!
B- BUT YER BLASTOISE IS WAITIN' FOR A COMMAND!
NNN NNN

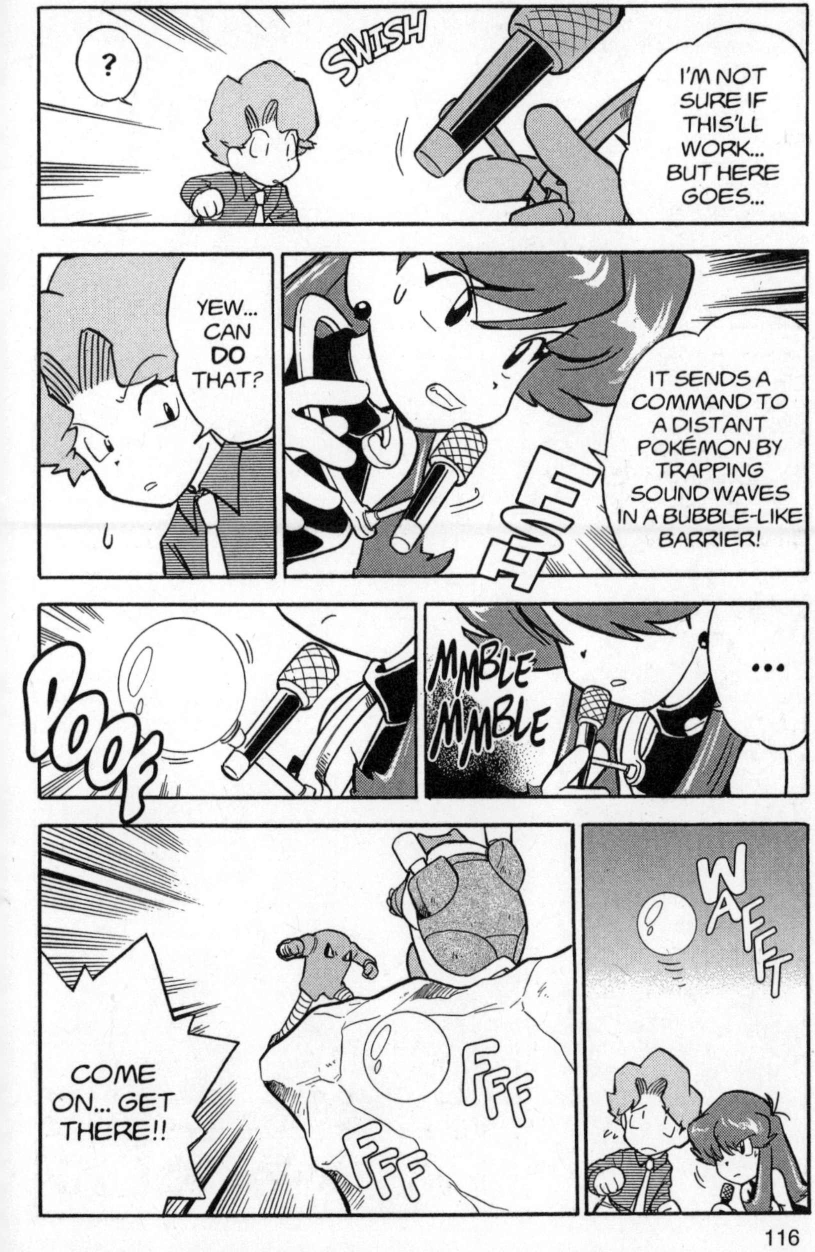
I'M NOT SURE IF THIS'LL WORK... BUT HERE GOES...
SWISH
?
IT SENDS A COMMAND TO A DISTANT POKÉMON BY TRAPPING SOUND WAVES IN A BUBBLE-LIKE BARRIER!
FSH
YEW... CAN DO THAT?
...
MMBLE MMBLE
POOF
WAFFT
FFF
FFF
COME ON... GET THERE!!

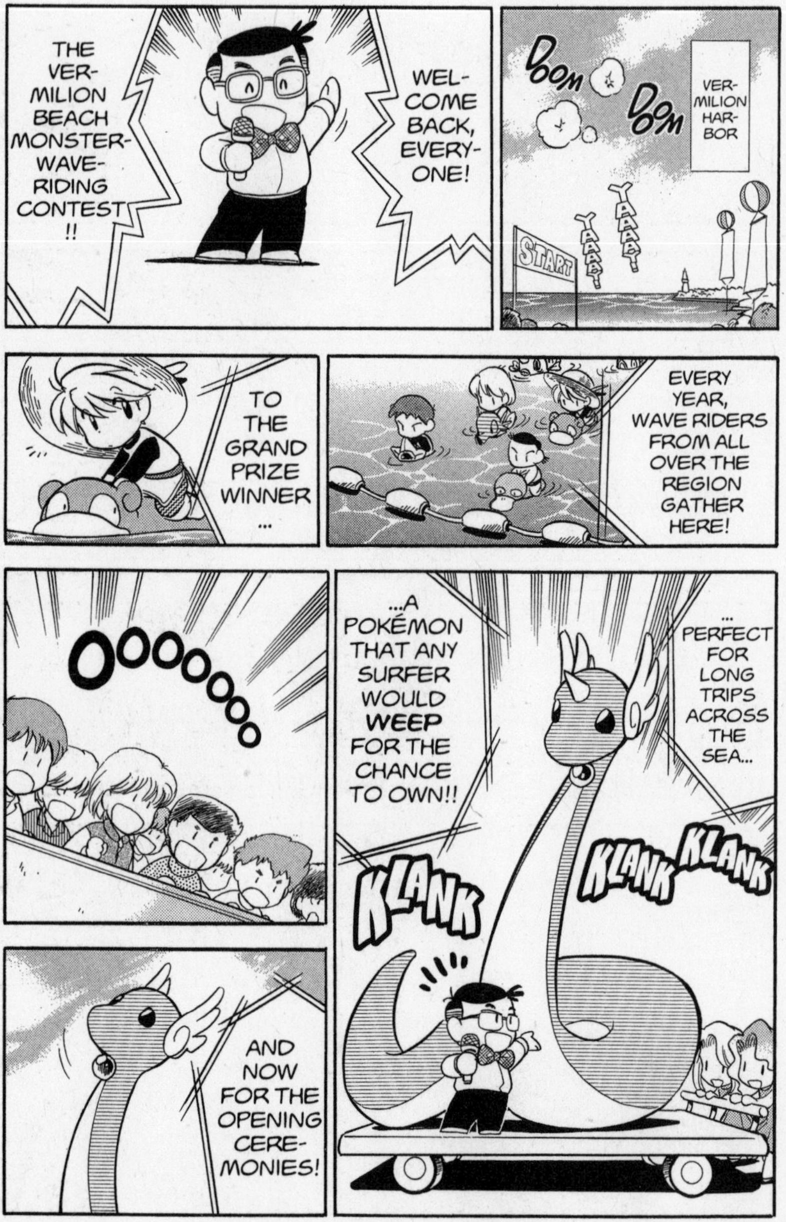
VERMILION HARBOR
DOOM
DOOM
YAAAA!
YAAAA!
START
WELCOME BACK, EVERYONE!
THE VERMILION BEACH MONSTER-WAVE-RIDING CONTEST!!
EVERY YEAR, WAVE RIDERS FROM ALL OVER THE REGION GATHER HERE!
TO THE GRAND PRIZE WINNER...
...A POKÉMON THAT ANY SURFER WOULD **WEEP** FOR THE CHANCE TO OWN!!
...PERFECT FOR LONG TRIPS ACROSS THE SEA...
KLANK KLANK
KLANK
OOOOOOO
AND NOW FOR THE OPENING CEREMONIES!

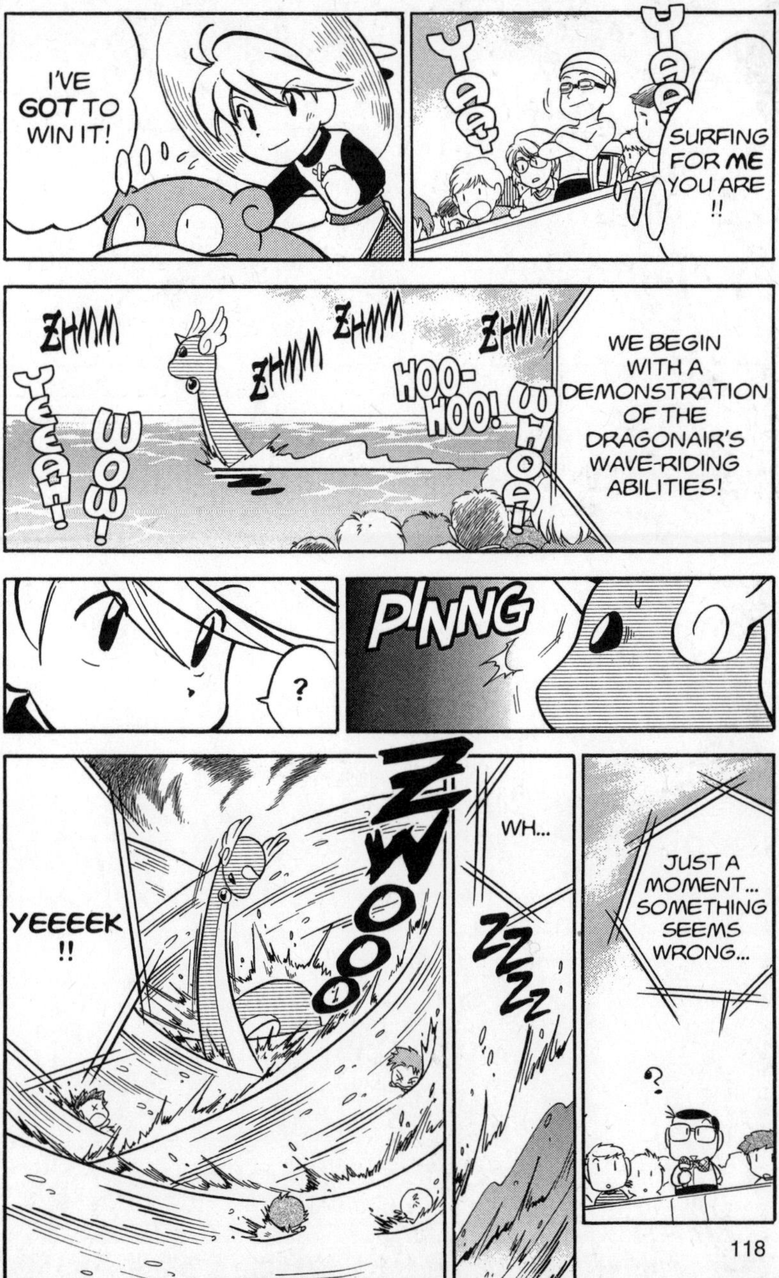

SURFING FOR ME YOU ARE !!
I'VE GOT TO WIN IT!
WE BEGIN WITH A DEMONSTRATION OF THE DRAGONAIR'S WAVE-RIDING ABILITIES!
ZHMM
HOO-HOO!
WHOA!
ZHMM
ZHMM
ZHMM
WOW!
PINNG
?
JUST A MOMENT... SOMETHING SEEMS WRONG...
WH...
ZZZZ
ZWOOOO
YEEEEK !!

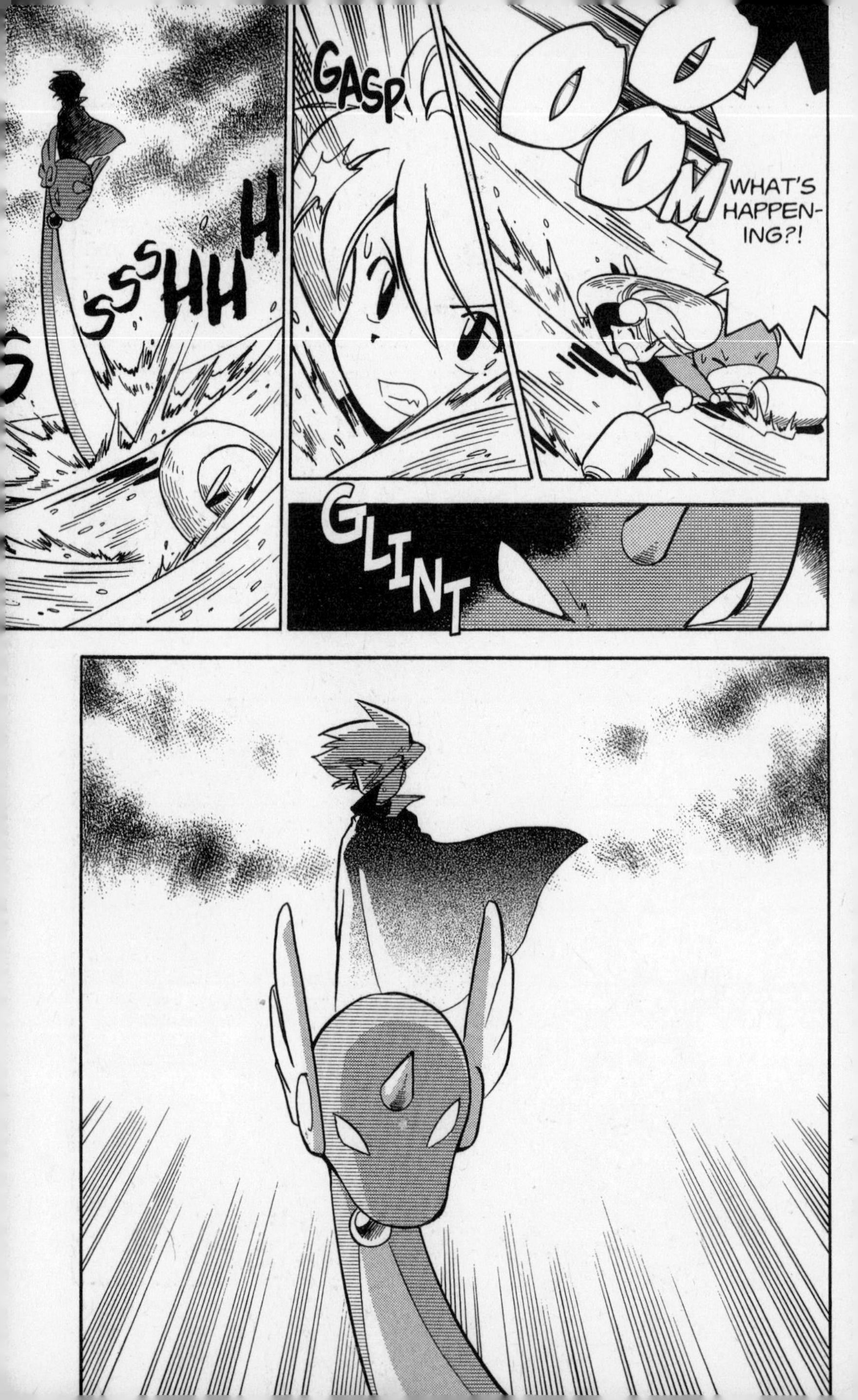
OOOM
WHAT'S HAPPEN-ING?!
GASP
SSSHHHH
GLINT

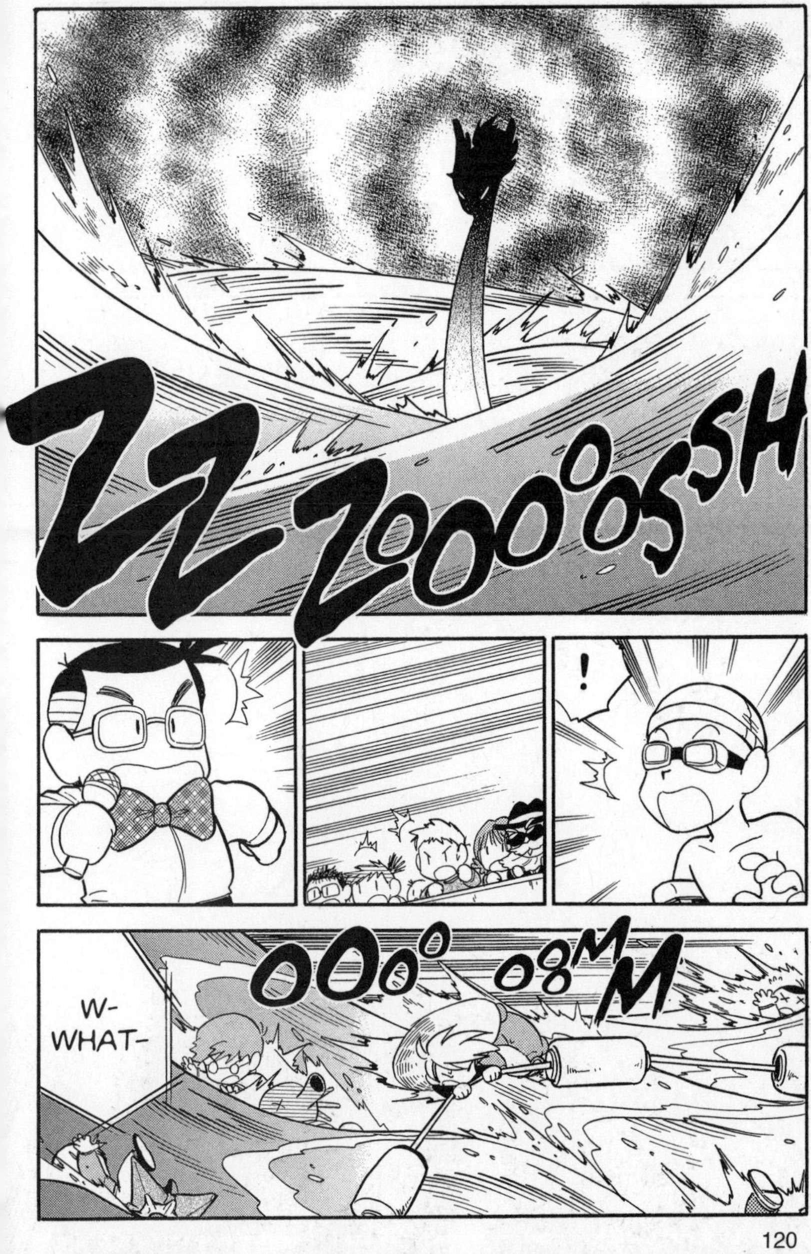
ZZZOOOOOSSH
!
W-
WHAT-

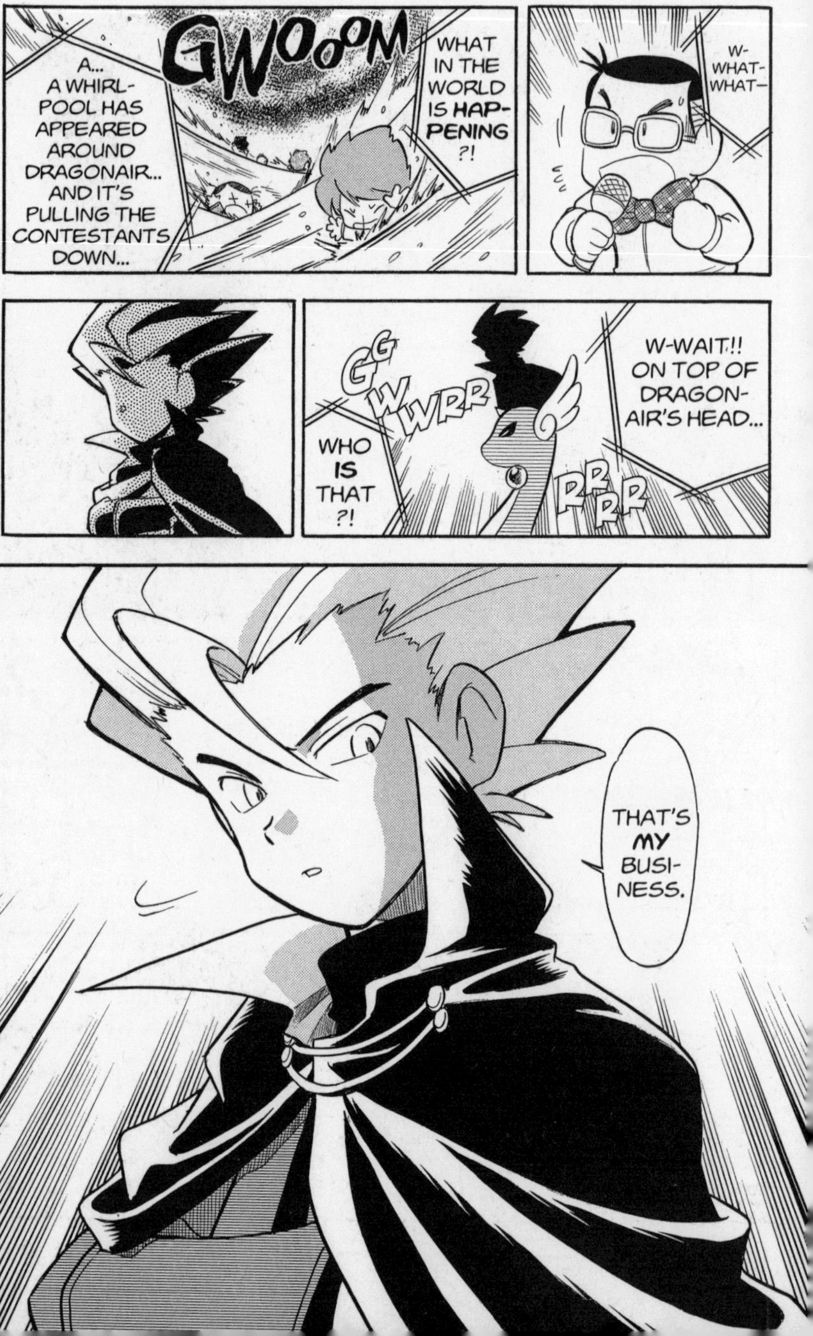
W-WHAT-WHAT—
WHAT IN THE WORLD IS HAPPENING?!
GWOOOM
A... A WHIRLPOOL HAS APPEARED AROUND DRAGONAIR... AND IT'S PULLING THE CONTESTANTS DOWN...
W-WAIT!! ON TOP OF DRAGONAIR'S HEAD...
RRRR
GGWWWRR
WHO IS THAT?!
THAT'S MY BUSINESS.

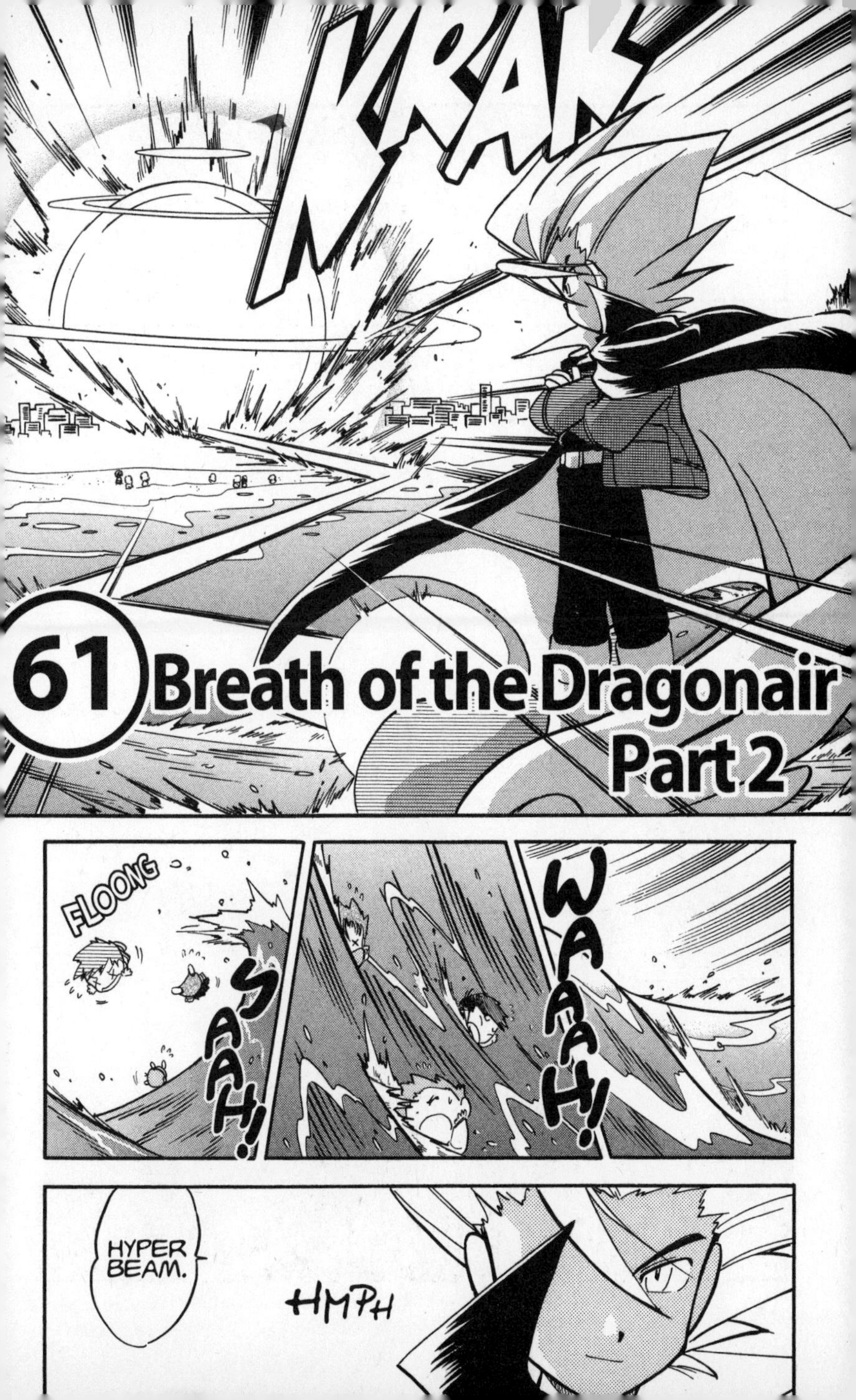
61
Breath of the Dragonair Part 2
WAAAAH!
SAAH!
FLOONG
HYPER BEAM.
HMPH

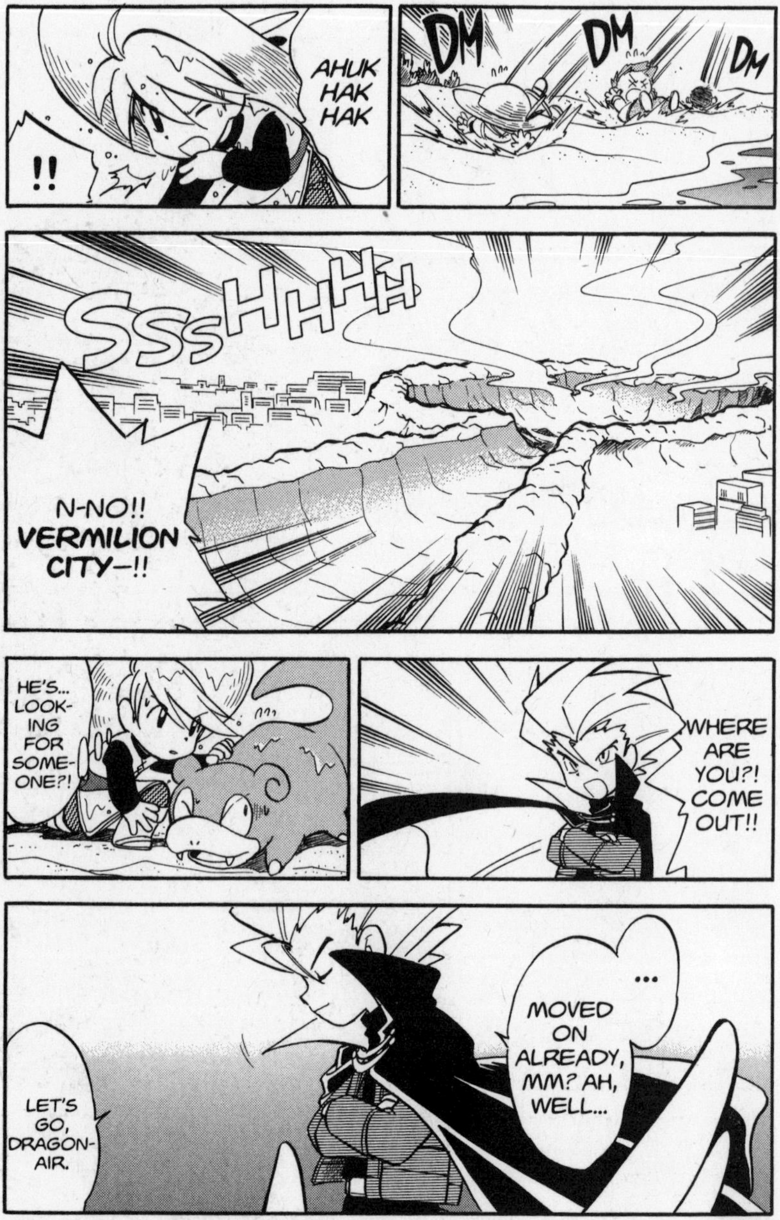
DM DM DM
AHUK HAK HAK
!!
SSSHHHHH
N-NO!! VERMILION CITY—!!
WHERE ARE YOU?! COME OUT!!
HE'S... LOOKING FOR SOMEONE?!
... MOVED ON ALREADY, MM? AH, WELL...
LET'S GO, DRAGONAIR.

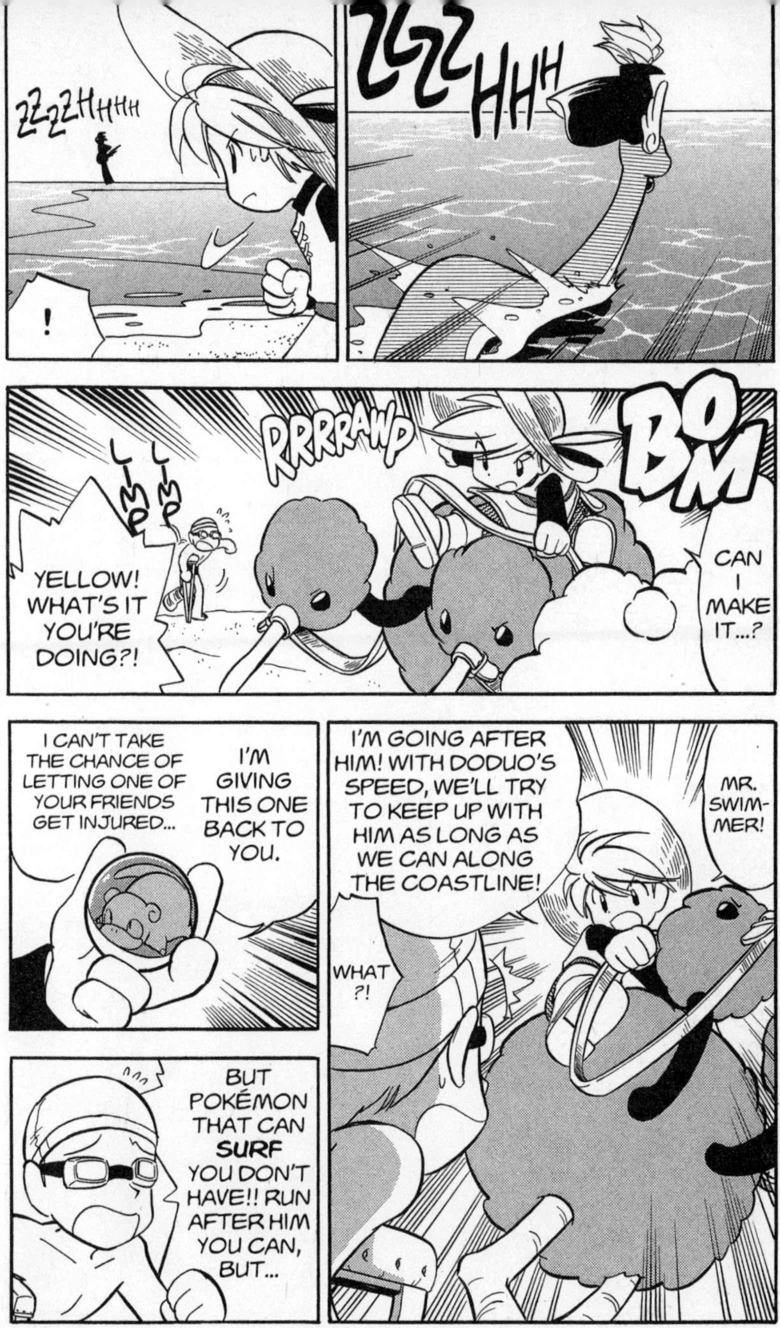
ZZZZHHH
ZZZZHHHH
!
BOM
CAN I MAKE IT...?
RRRRAWP
LIMP LIMP
YELLOW! WHAT'S IT YOU'RE DOING?!
MR. SWIM-MER!
I'M GOING AFTER HIM! WITH DODUO'S SPEED, WE'LL TRY TO KEEP UP WITH HIM AS LONG AS WE CAN ALONG THE COASTLINE!
WHAT?!
I'M GIVING THIS ONE BACK TO YOU.
I CAN'T TAKE THE CHANCE OF LETTING ONE OF YOUR FRIENDS GET INJURED...
BUT POKÉMON THAT CAN **SURF** YOU DON'T HAVE!! RUN AFTER HIM YOU CAN, BUT...

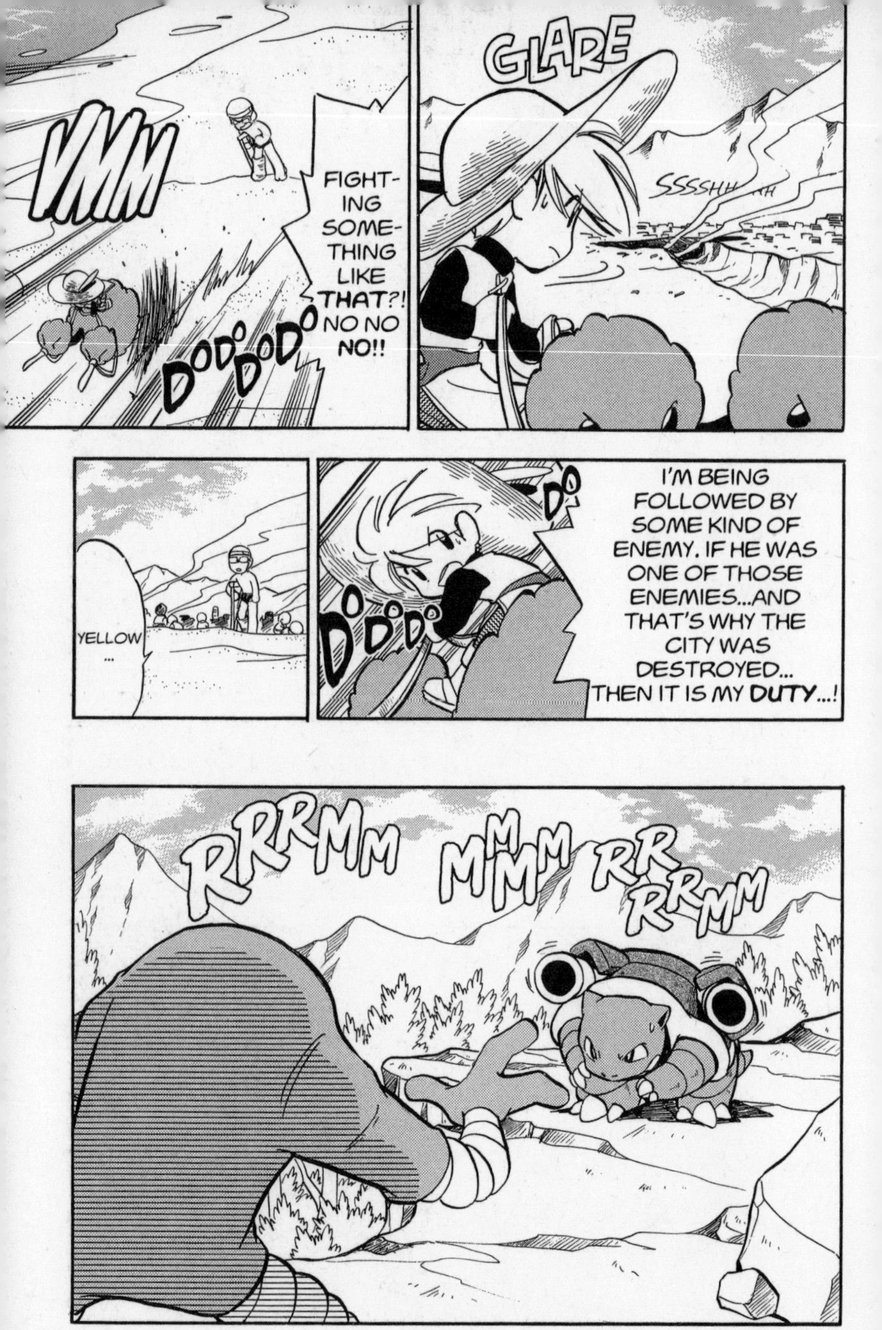
GLARE
VMM
DODODODO
FIGHTING-ING SOMETHING LIKE THAT?! NO NO NO!!
DO
I'M BEING FOLLOWED BY SOME KIND OF ENEMY. IF HE WAS ONE OF THOSE ENEMIES...AND THAT'S WHY THE CITY WAS DESTROYED... THEN IT IS MY **DUTY**...!
DODODO
YELLOW ...
RRRMM MMMM RRRRMM

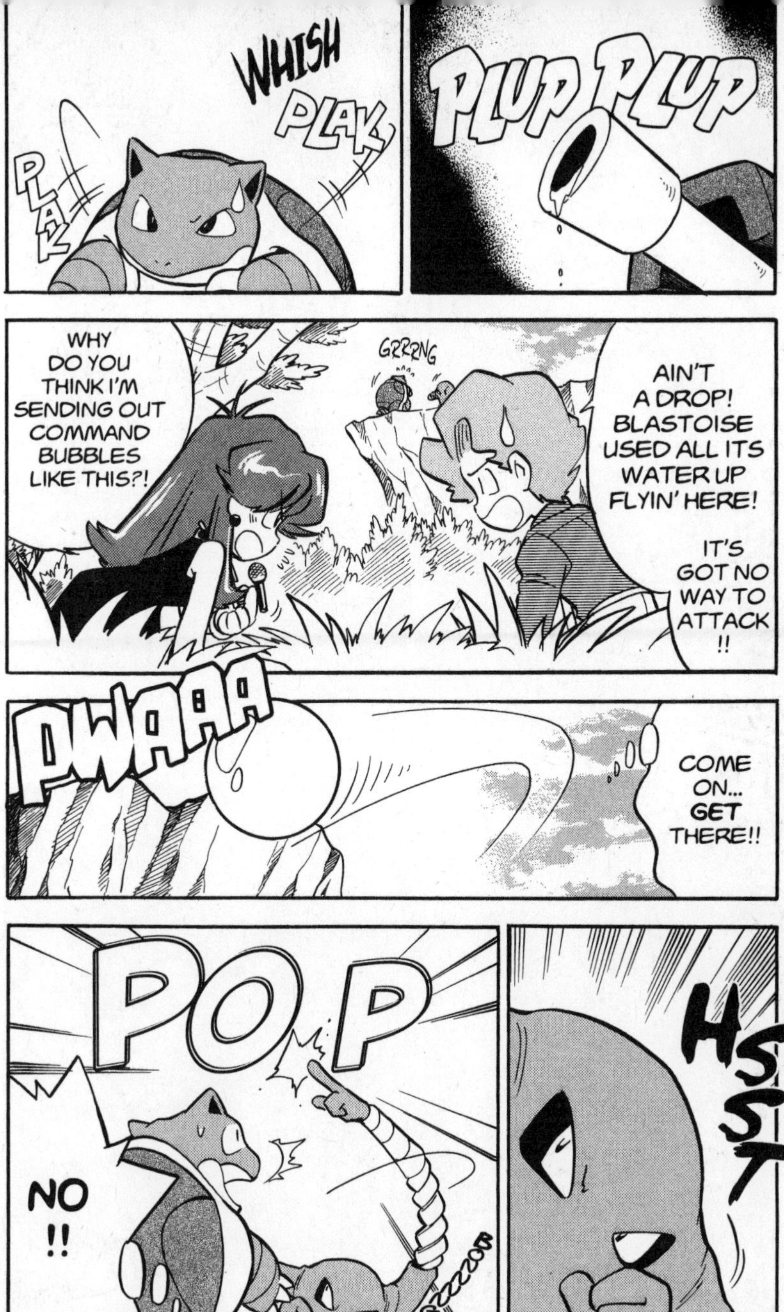
PLUP PLUP
WHISH
PLAK
PLAK
AIN'T A DROP! BLASTOISE USED ALL ITS WATER UP FLYIN' HERE!
IT'S GOT NO WAY TO ATTACK!!
GRRRNG
WHY DO YOU THINK I'M SENDING OUT COMMAND BUBBLES LIKE THIS?!
COME ON... GET THERE!!
PWAAA
HSSST
POP
NO!!
GZZZZOB

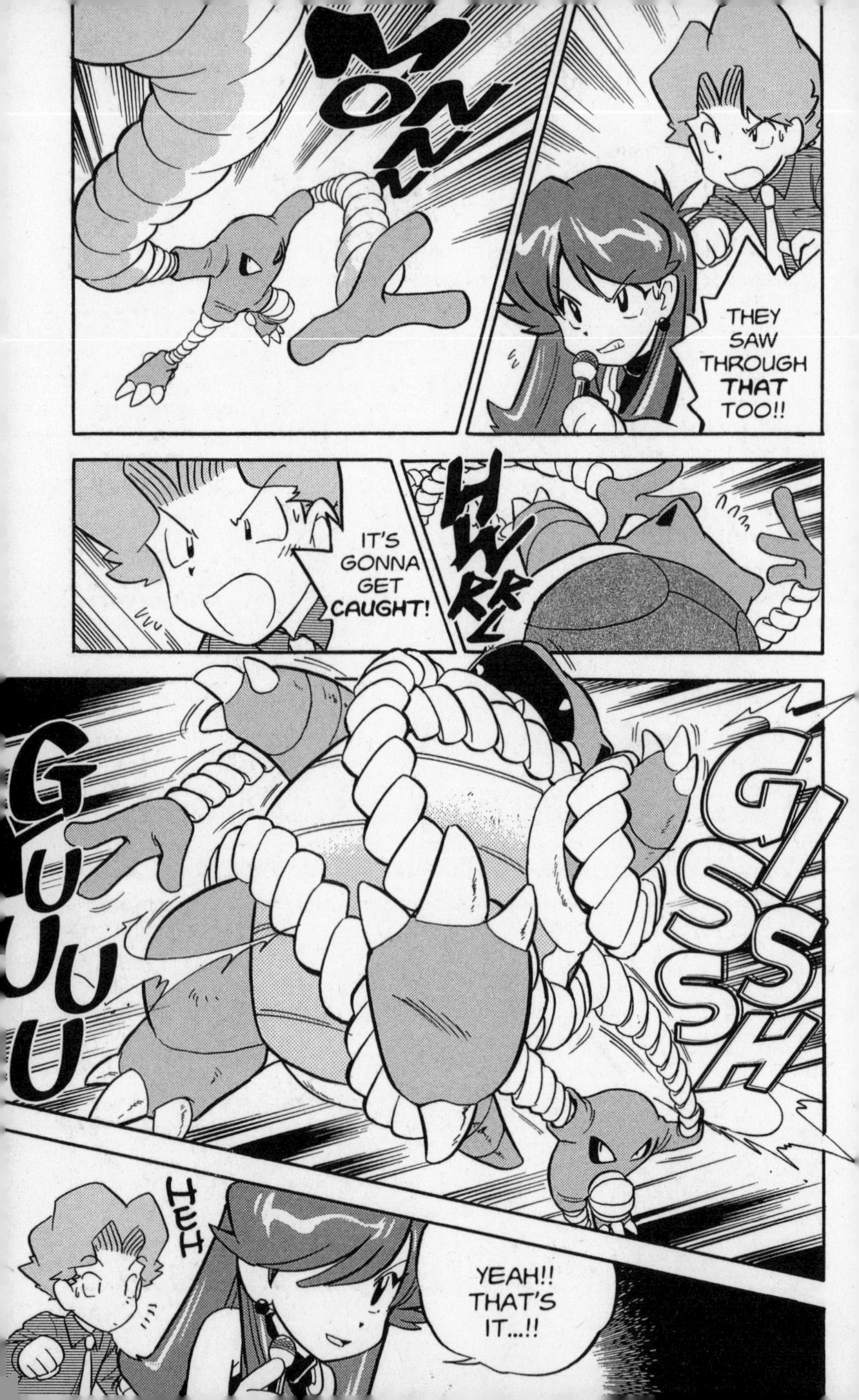
MONNN
THEY SAW THROUGH THAT TOO!!
HWRRL
IT'S GONNA GET CAUGHT!
GISSSH
GUUUU
YEAH!! THAT'S IT...!!
HEH

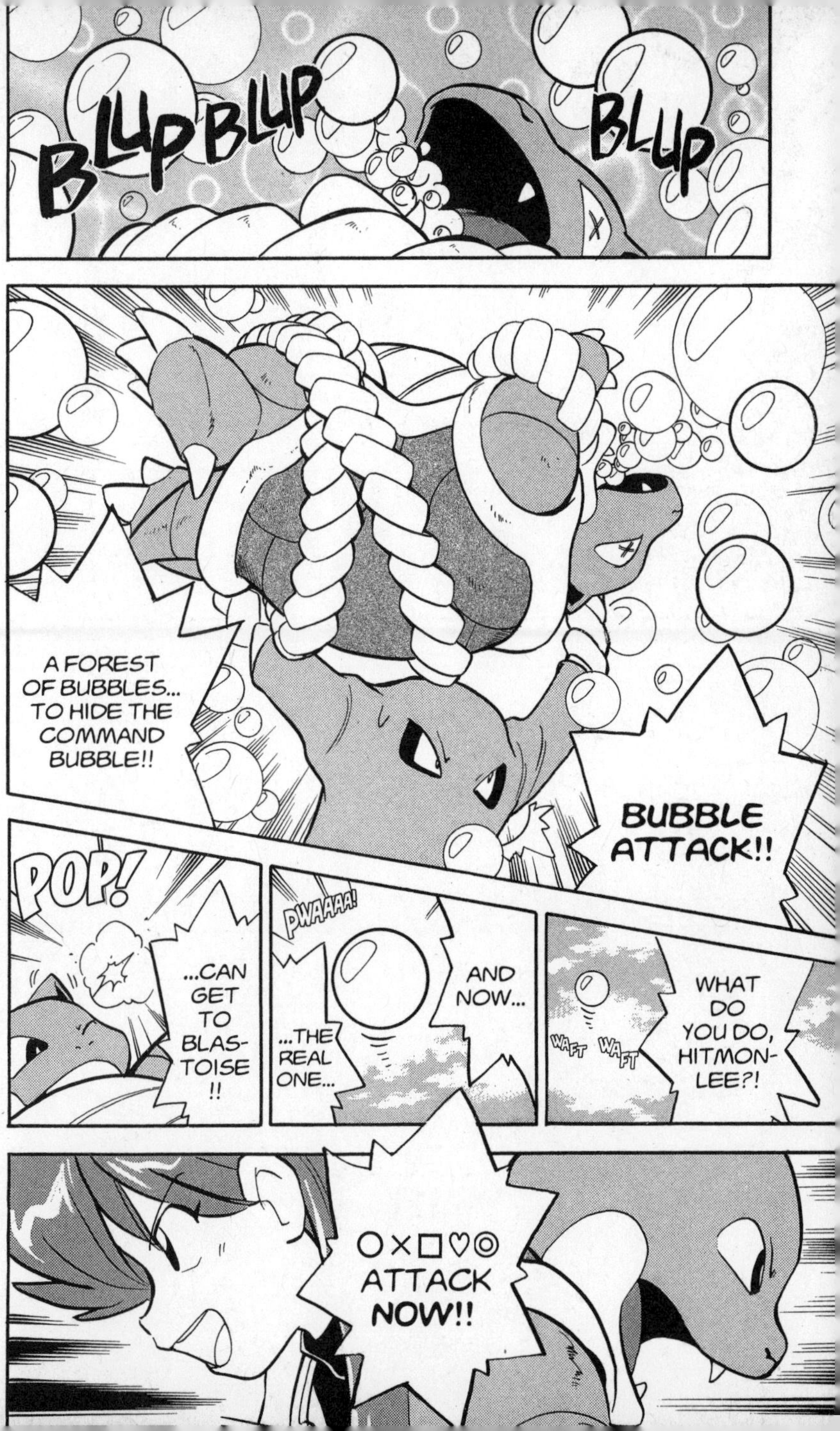
BLUP
BLUP BLUP
BUBBLE ATTACK!!
A FOREST OF BUBBLES... TO HIDE THE COMMAND BUBBLE!!
WAFT WAFT
WHAT DO YOU DO, HITMON-LEE?!
PWAAAAA!
AND NOW...
...THE REAL ONE...
POP!
...CAN GET TO BLAS-TOISE!!
○×□♡◎ ATTACK NOW!!

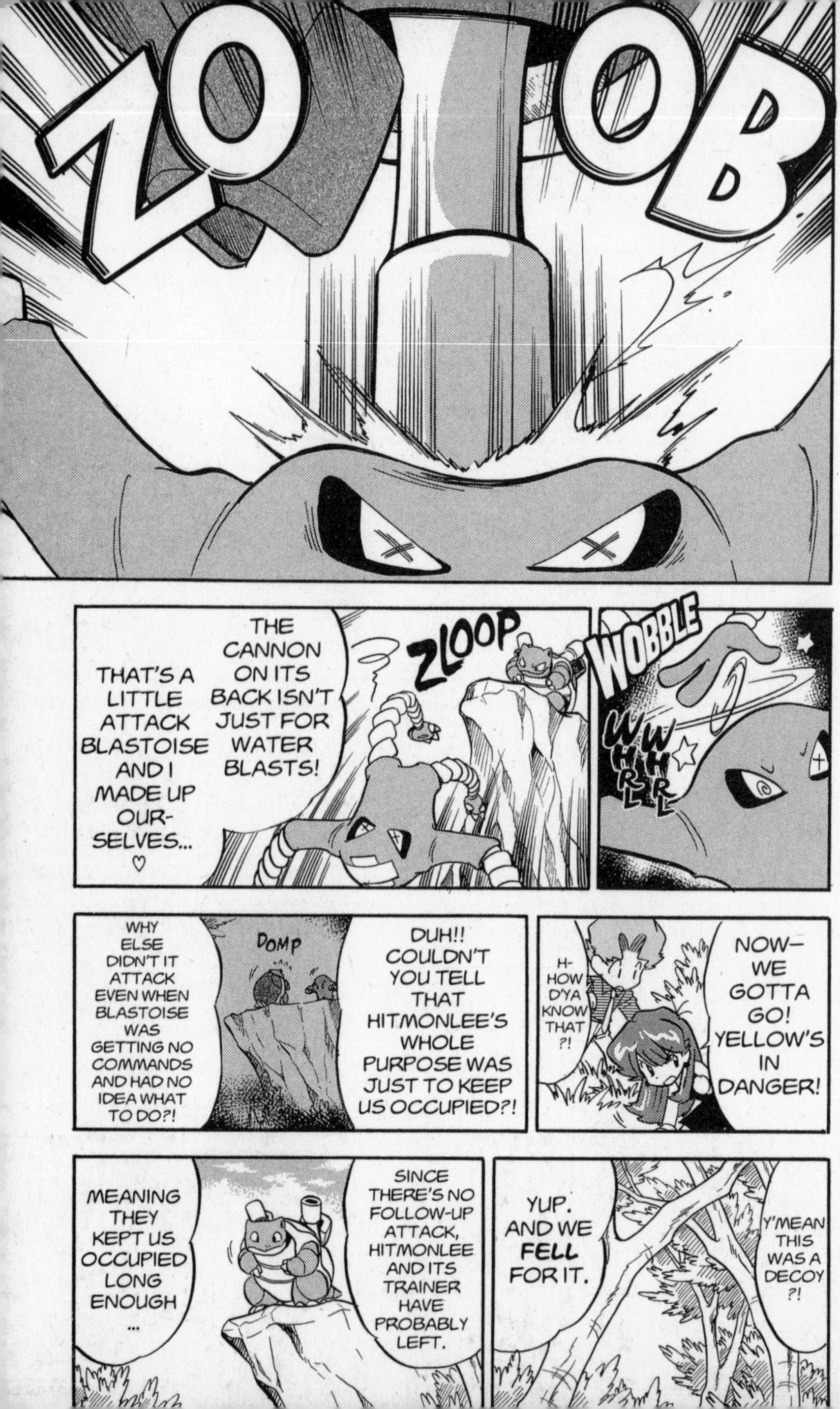
ZOOB
WOBBLE
WHRL WHRL
ZLOOP
THE CANNON ON ITS BACK ISN'T JUST FOR WATER BLASTS!
THAT'S A LITTLE ATTACK BLASTOISE AND I MADE UP OURSELVES... ♡
NOW— WE GOTTA GO! YELLOW'S IN DANGER!
H-HOW D'YA KNOW THAT?!
DUH!! COULDN'T YOU TELL THAT HITMONLEE'S WHOLE PURPOSE WAS JUST TO KEEP US OCCUPIED?!
DOMP
WHY ELSE DIDN'T IT ATTACK EVEN WHEN BLASTOISE WAS GETTING NO COMMANDS AND HAD NO IDEA WHAT TO DO?!
Y'MEAN THIS WAS A DECOY?!
YUP. AND WE **FELL** FOR IT.
SINCE THERE'S NO FOLLOW-UP ATTACK, HITMONLEE AND ITS TRAINER HAVE PROBABLY LEFT.
MEANING THEY KEPT US OCCUPIED LONG ENOUGH ...

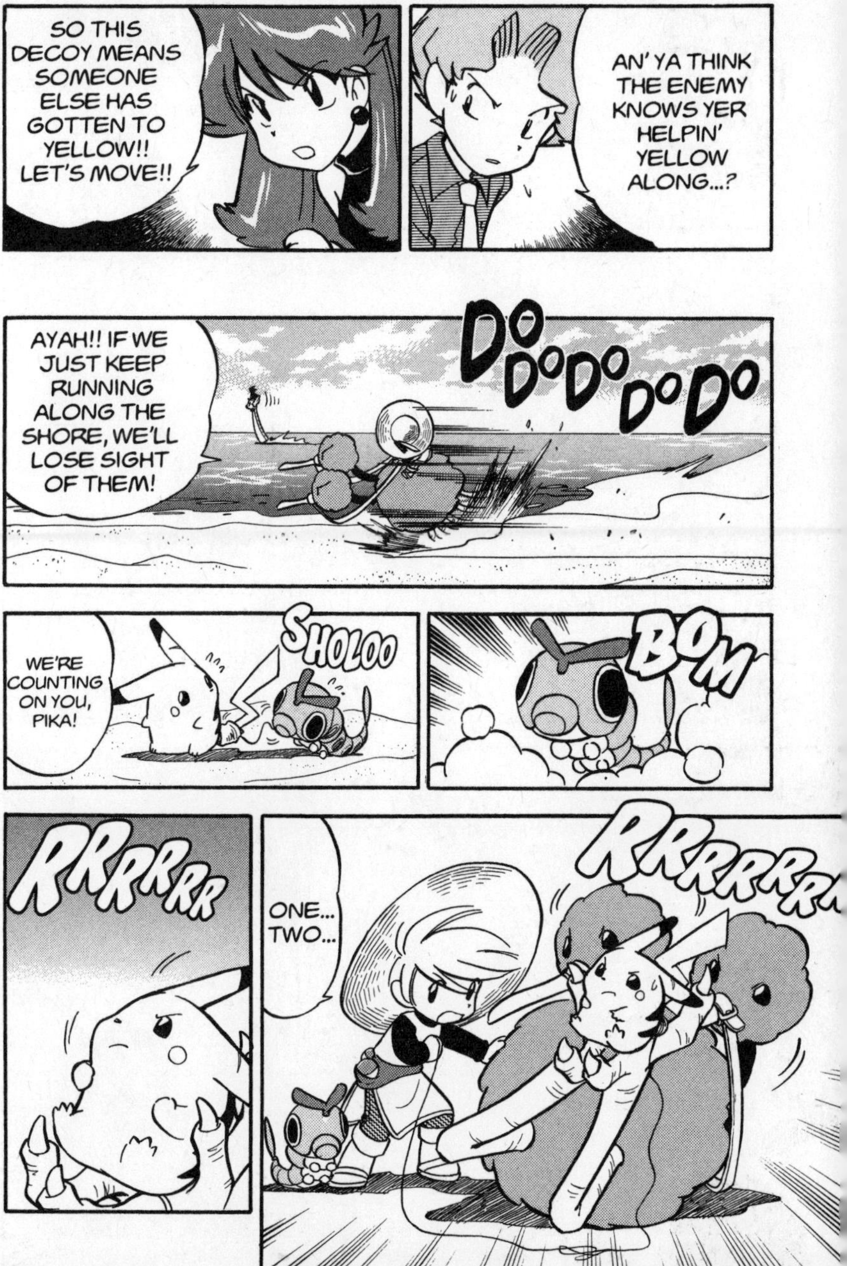
SO THIS DECOY MEANS SOMEONE ELSE HAS GOTTEN TO YELLOW!! LET'S MOVE!!
AN' YA THINK THE ENEMY KNOWS YER HELPIN' YELLOW ALONG...?
AYAH!! IF WE JUST KEEP RUNNING ALONG THE SHORE, WE'LL LOSE SIGHT OF THEM!
DODODODODO
WE'RE COUNTING ON YOU, PIKA!
SHOLOO
BOM
RRRRRR
ONE... TWO...
RRRRRRR

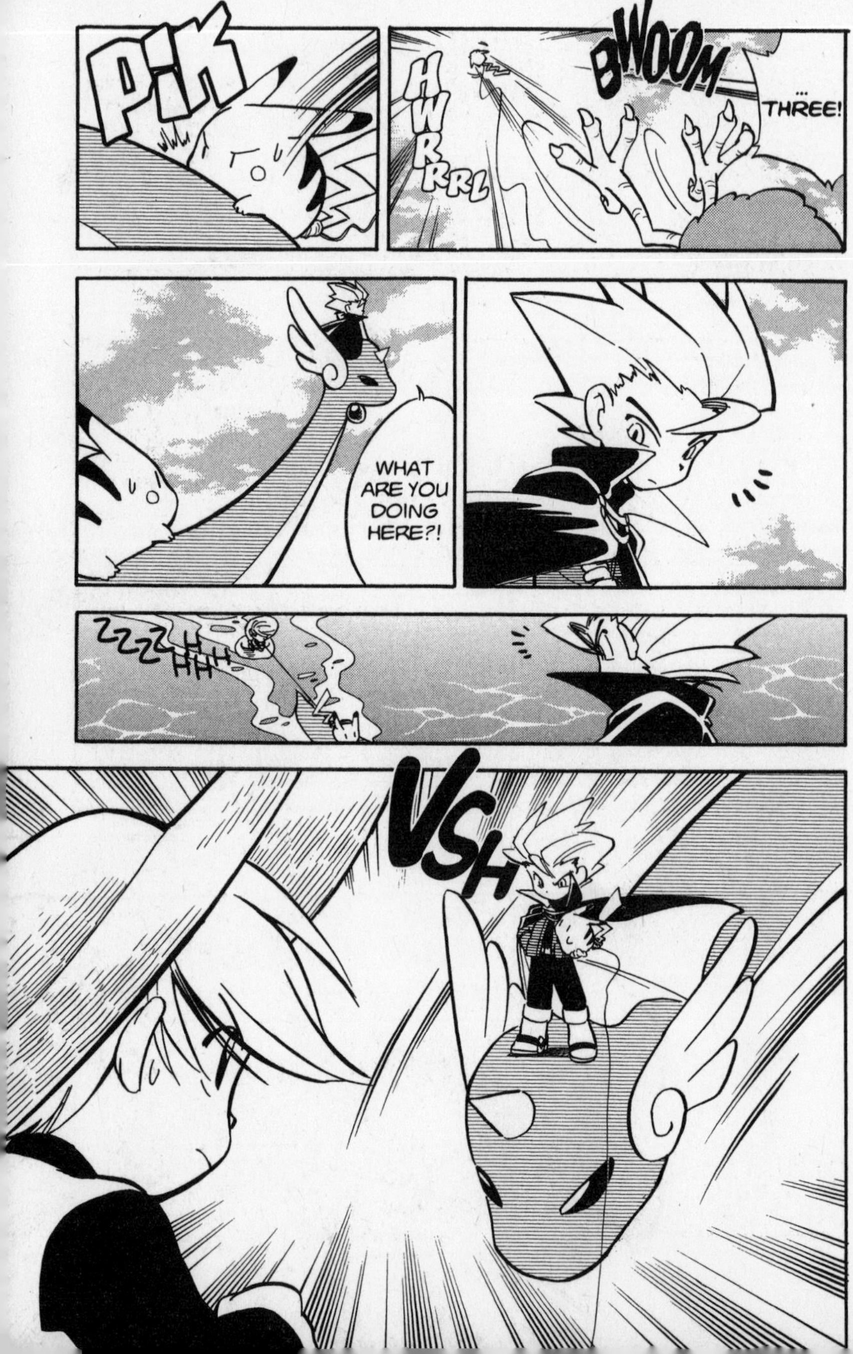
BWOOM
...THREE!
HWRRRL
PIK
WHAT ARE YOU DOING HERE?!
ZZZZ HHHH
VSH

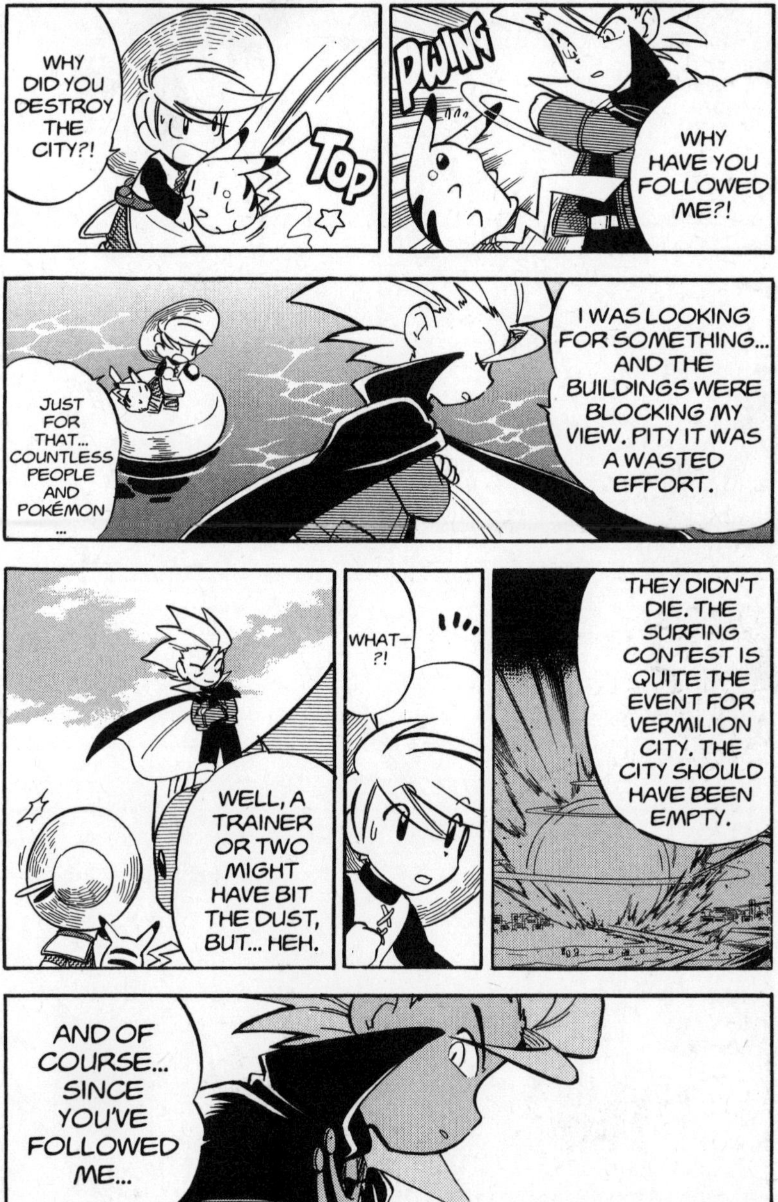
PWING
WHY HAVE YOU FOLLOWED ME?!
WHY DID YOU DESTROY THE CITY?!
TOP
I WAS LOOKING FOR SOMETHING... AND THE BUILDINGS WERE BLOCKING MY VIEW. PITY IT WAS A WASTED EFFORT.
JUST FOR THAT... COUNTLESS PEOPLE AND POKÉMON ...
THEY DIDN'T DIE. THE SURFING CONTEST IS QUITE THE EVENT FOR VERMILION CITY. THE CITY SHOULD HAVE BEEN EMPTY.
WHAT—?!
WELL, A TRAINER OR TWO MIGHT HAVE BIT THE DUST, BUT... HEH.
AND OF COURSE... SINCE YOU'VE FOLLOWED ME...

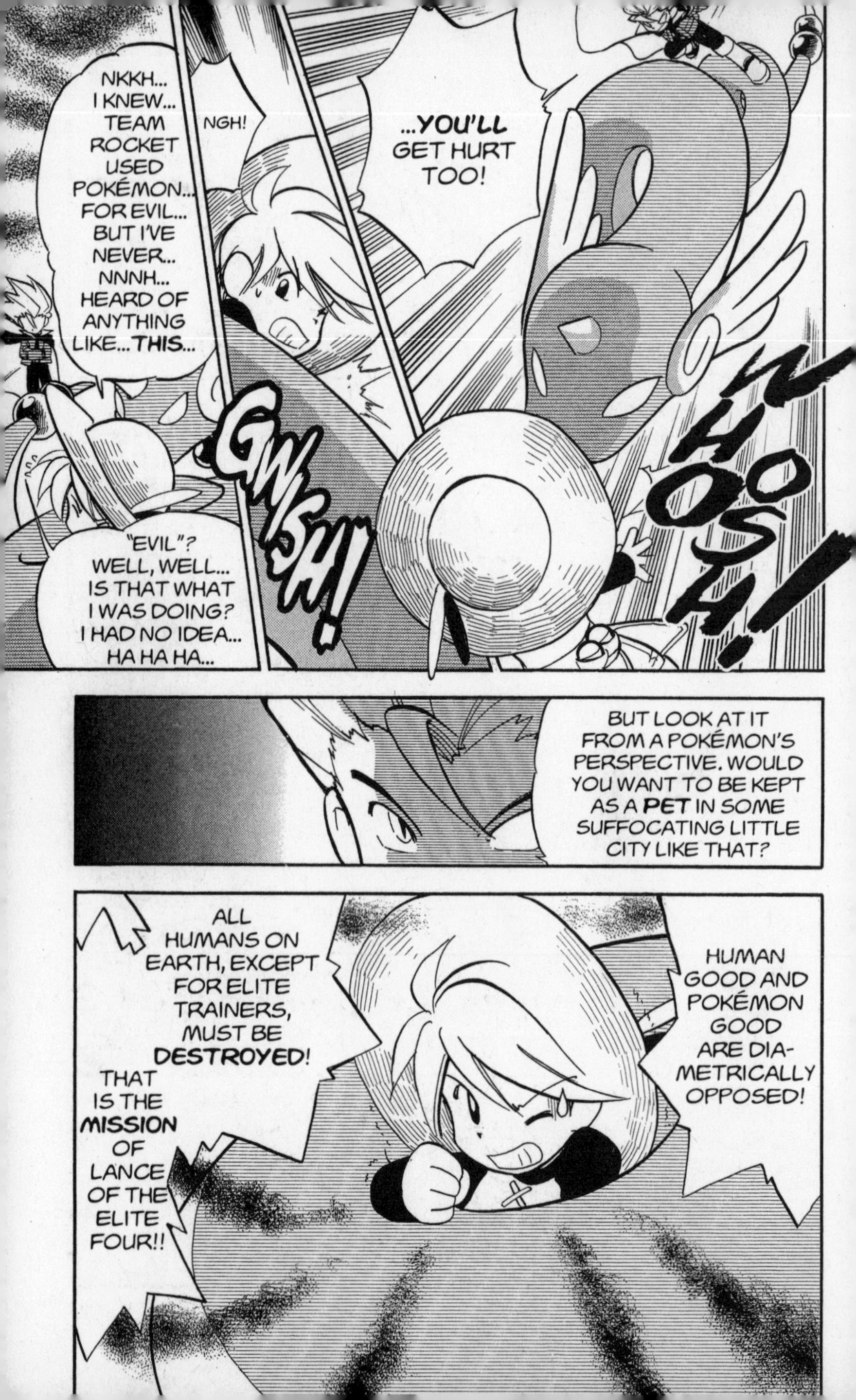
...YOU'LL GET HURT TOO!
WHOOSH!
GWISH!
NGH!
NKKH... I KNEW... TEAM ROCKET USED POKÉMON... FOR EVIL... BUT I'VE NEVER... NNNH... HEARD OF ANYTHING LIKE... THIS...
"EVIL"? WELL, WELL... IS THAT WHAT I WAS DOING? I HAD NO IDEA... HA HA HA...
BUT LOOK AT IT FROM A POKÉMON'S PERSPECTIVE. WOULD YOU WANT TO BE KEPT AS A PET IN SOME SUFFOCATING LITTLE CITY LIKE THAT?
HUMAN GOOD AND POKÉMON GOOD ARE DIAMETRICALLY OPPOSED!
ALL HUMANS ON EARTH, EXCEPT FOR ELITE TRAINERS, MUST BE DESTROYED!
THAT IS THE MISSION OF LANCE OF THE ELITE FOUR!!

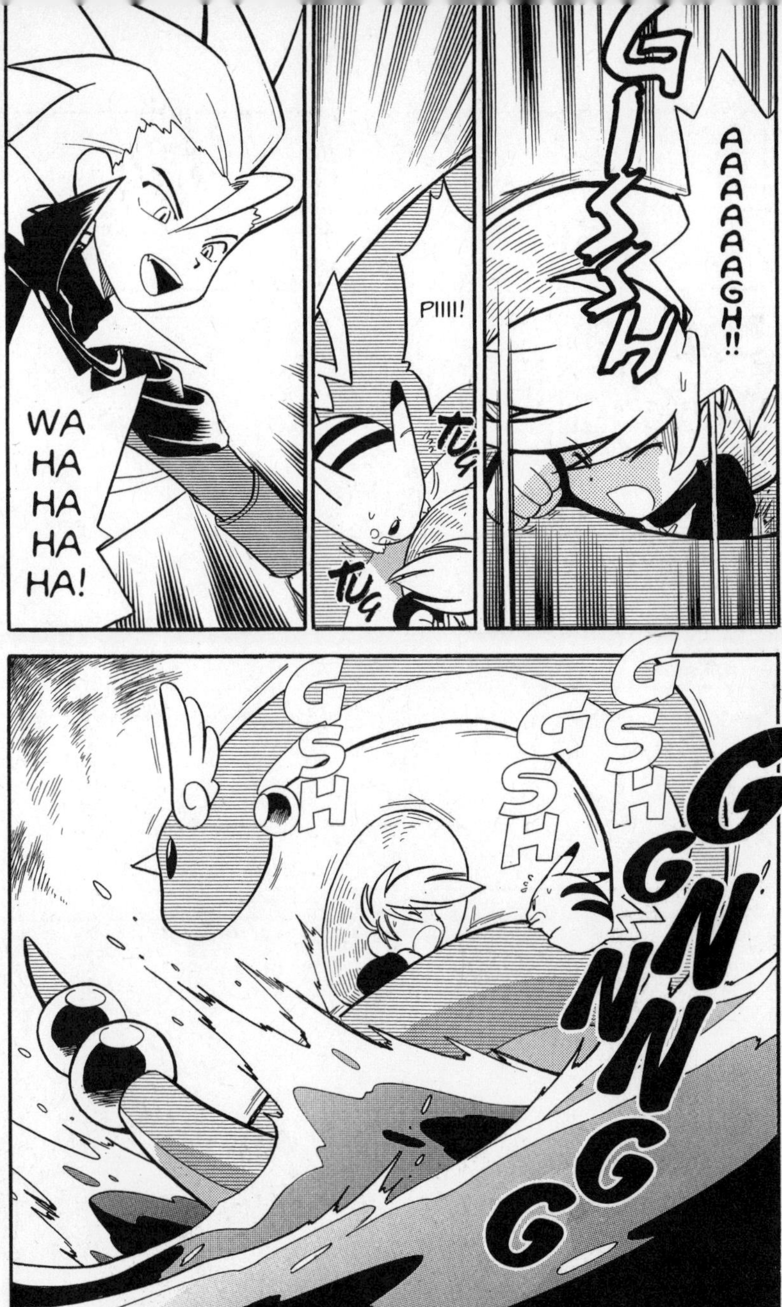
AAAAAAAGH!!
PIIII!
TUG
TUG
WA HA HA HA HA!
GSH
GSH
GSH

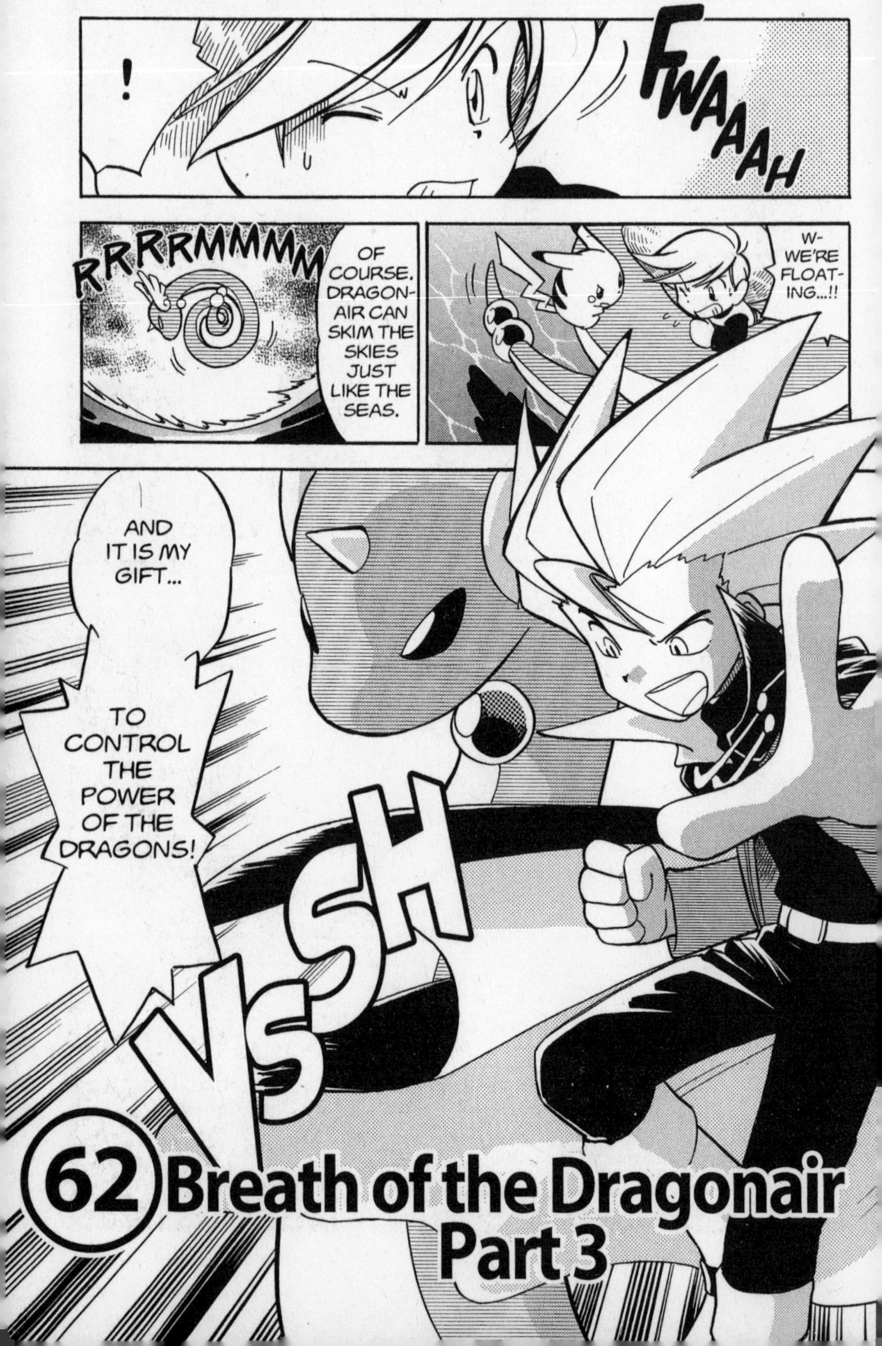
FWAAAAH
!
W-WE'RE FLOATING...!!
OF COURSE. DRAGONAIR CAN SKIM THE SKIES JUST LIKE THE SEAS.
RRRRMMMMM
AND IT IS MY GIFT...
TO CONTROL THE POWER OF THE DRAGONS!
VSSH

62 Breath of the Dragonair Part 3

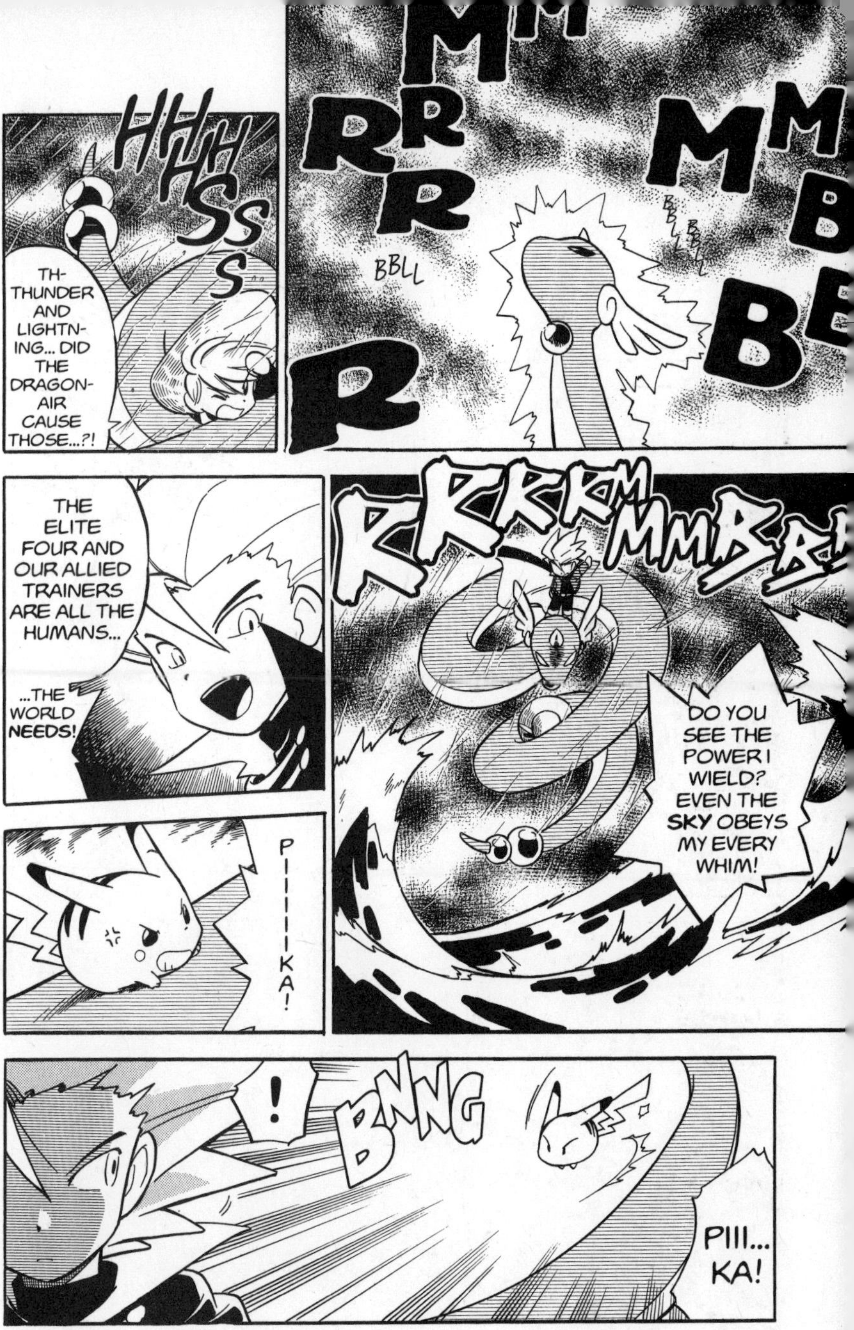
MMRRRR
MMMBB
BBLL
BBLL
BBLL
HHHHSSS
TH-THUNDER AND LIGHTNING... DID THE DRAGONAIR CAUSE THOSE...?!
RRRRMMMBB
DO YOU SEE THE POWER I WIELD? EVEN THE **SKY** OBEYS MY EVERY WHIM!
THE ELITE FOUR AND OUR ALLIED TRAINERS ARE ALL THE HUMANS...
...THE WORLD **NEEDS**!
PIIIKA!
BNNG
!
PIII... KA!

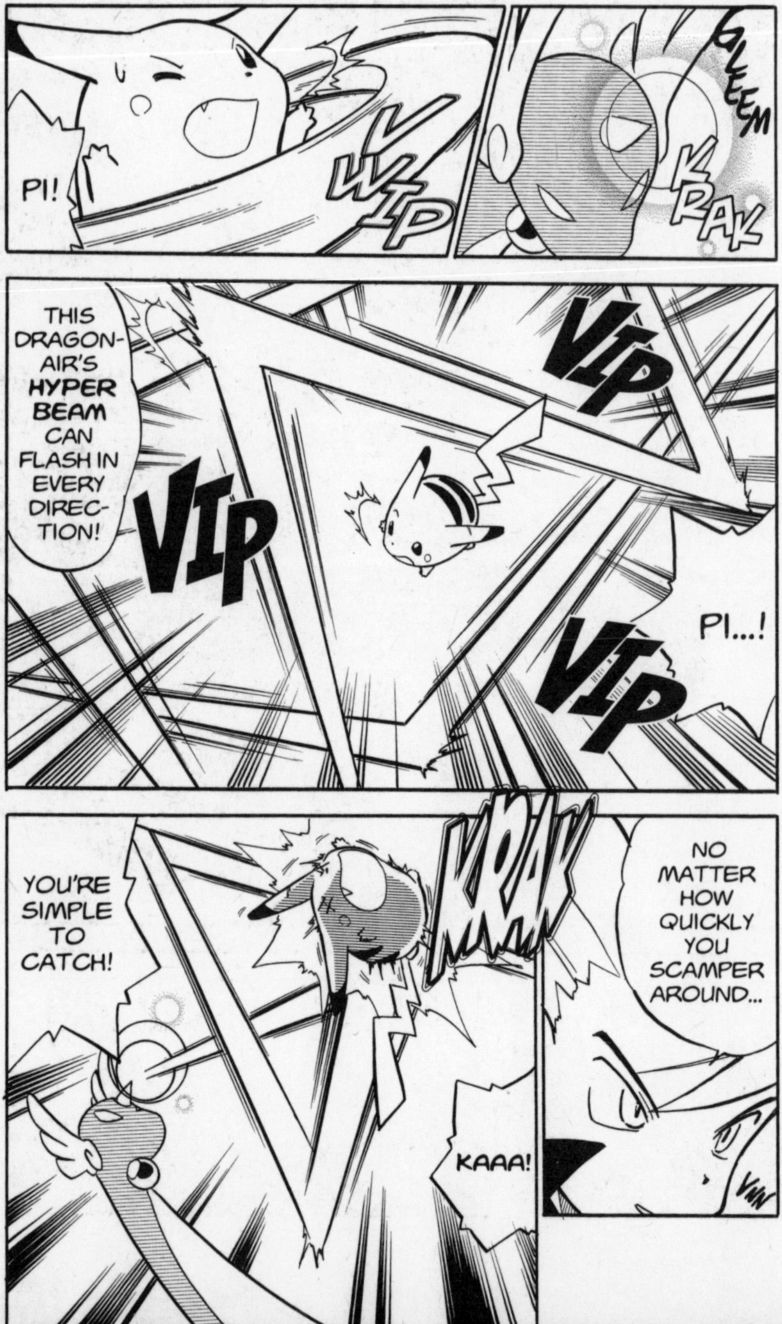
GLEEM
KRAK
VWIP
PI!
VIP
THIS DRAGON-AIR'S **HYPER BEAM** CAN FLASH IN EVERY DIREC-TION!
PI...!
VIP
VIP
NO MATTER HOW QUICKLY YOU SCAMPER AROUND...
VNN
YOU'RE SIMPLE TO CATCH!
KAAA!

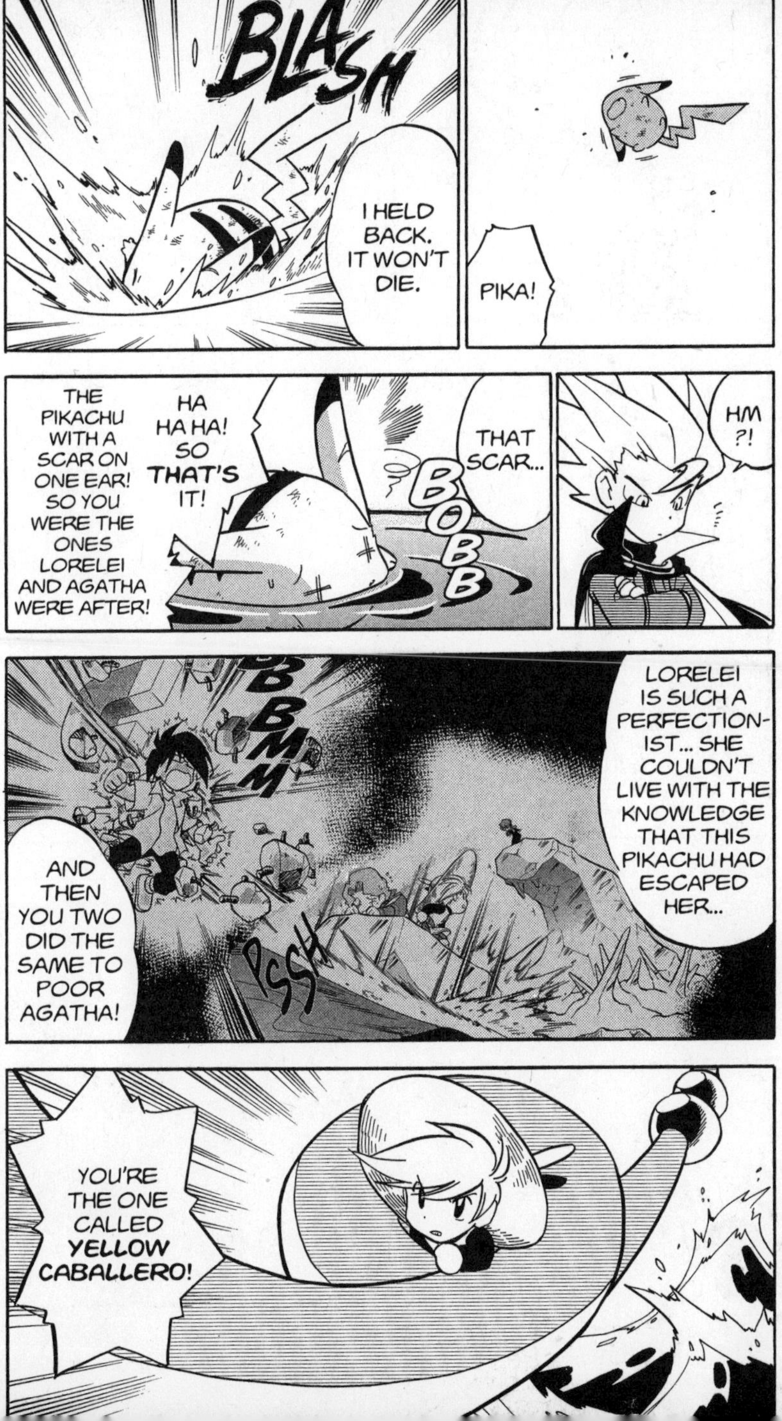
PIKA!
BLASH
I HELD BACK. IT WON'T DIE.
HM ?!
THAT SCAR...
BOBB
HA HA HA! SO THAT'S IT!
THE PIKACHU WITH A SCAR ON ONE EAR! SO YOU WERE THE ONES LORELEI AND AGATHA WERE AFTER!
LORELEI IS SUCH A PERFECTION-IST... SHE COULDN'T LIVE WITH THE KNOWLEDGE THAT THIS PIKACHU HAD ESCAPED HER...
BBMM
PSSH
AND THEN YOU TWO DID THE SAME TO POOR AGATHA!
YOU'RE THE ONE CALLED YELLOW CABALLERO!

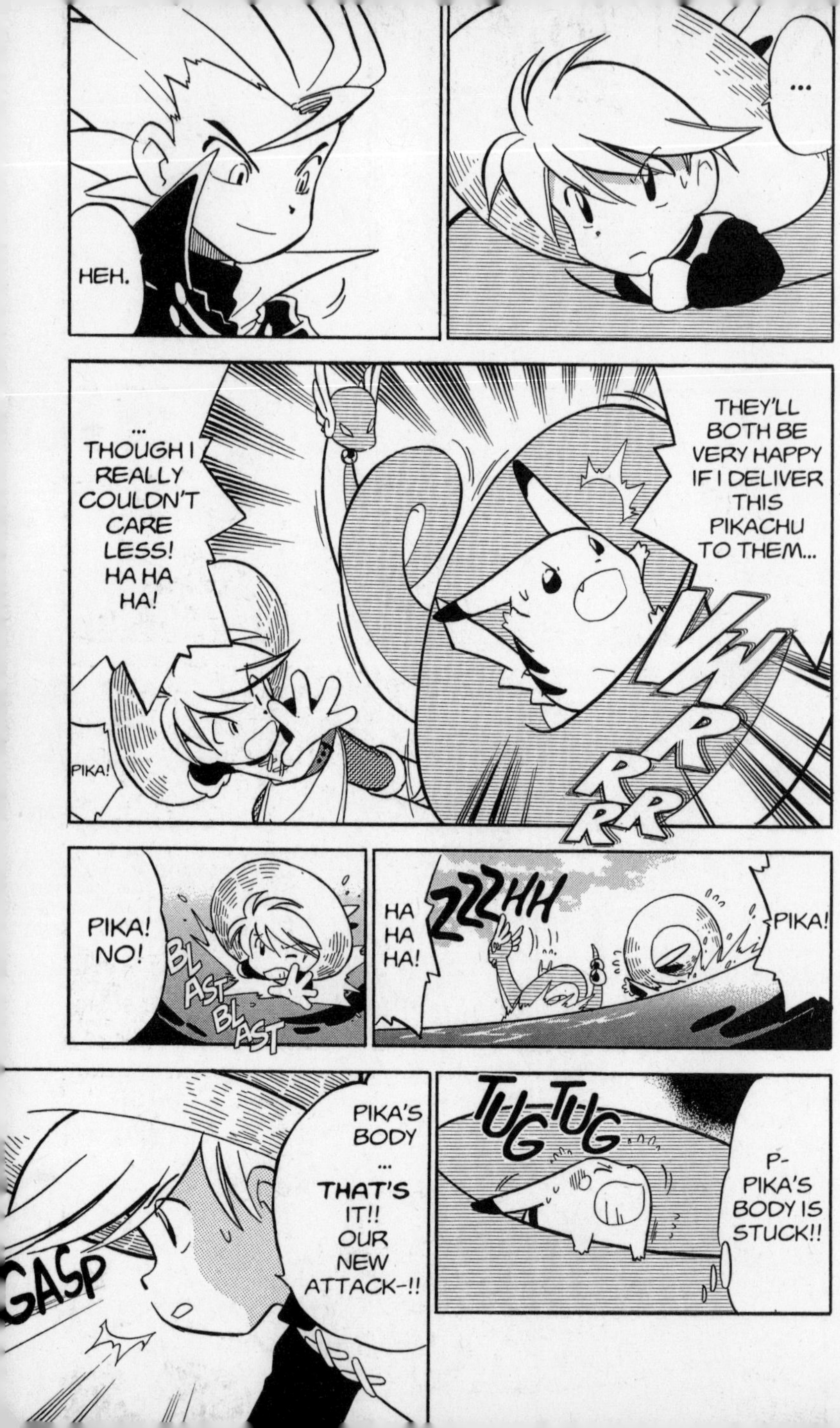
...
HEH.
THEY'LL BOTH BE VERY HAPPY IF I DELIVER THIS PIKACHU TO THEM...
... THOUGH I REALLY COULDN'T CARE LESS! HA HA HA!
VWRRRR
PIKA!
PIKA!
ZZZHH
HA HA HA!
PIKA! NO!
BLAST BLAST
TUG TUG
P- PIKA'S BODY IS STUCK!!
PIKA'S BODY ... THAT'S IT!! OUR NEW ATTACK-!!
GASP

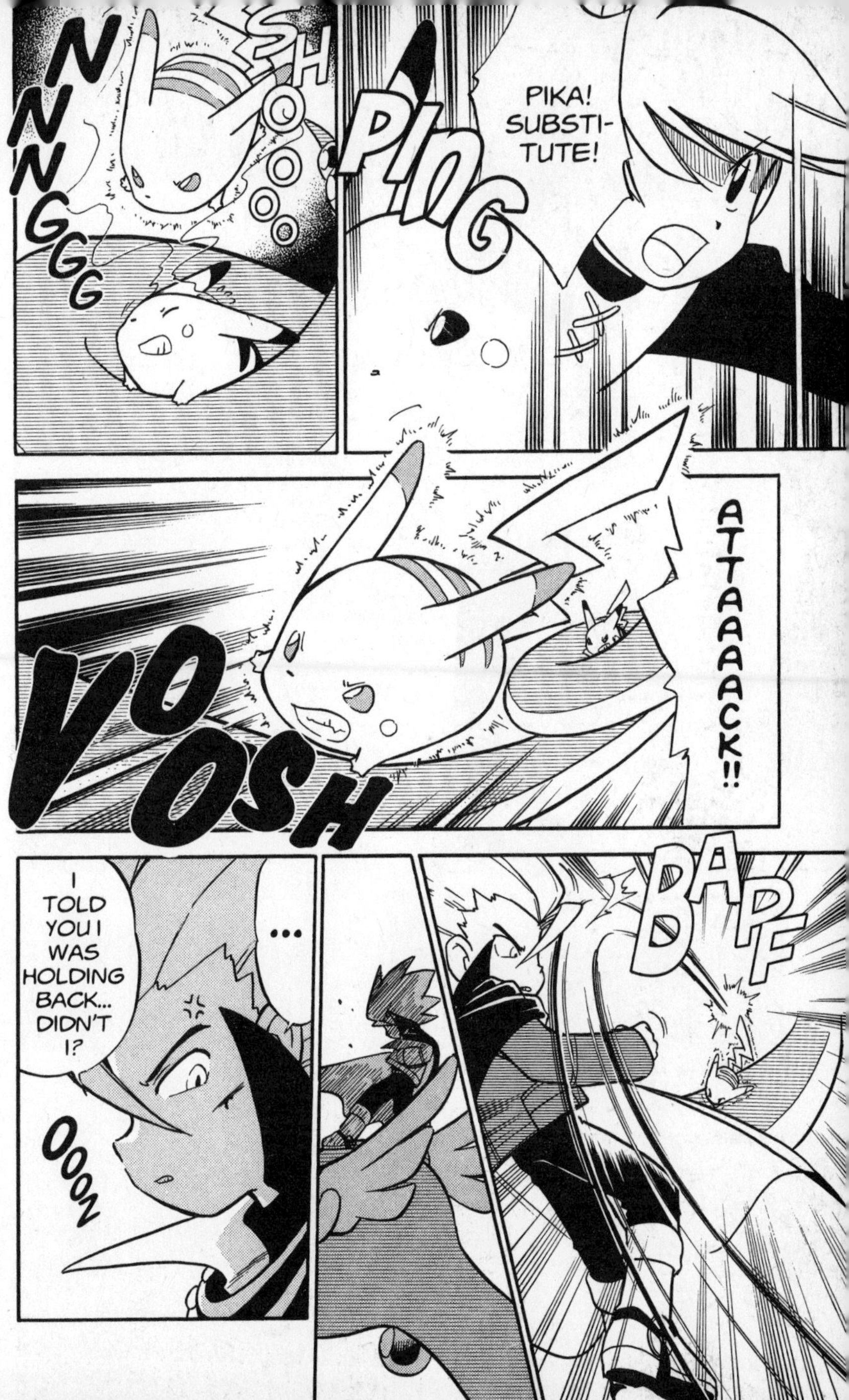
PIKA! SUBSTITUTE!
PING
SHOOOOO
NNNNGGG
ATTAAAACK!!
VOOSH
BAPF
...
I TOLD YOU I WAS HOLDING BACK... DIDN'T I?
OOOON

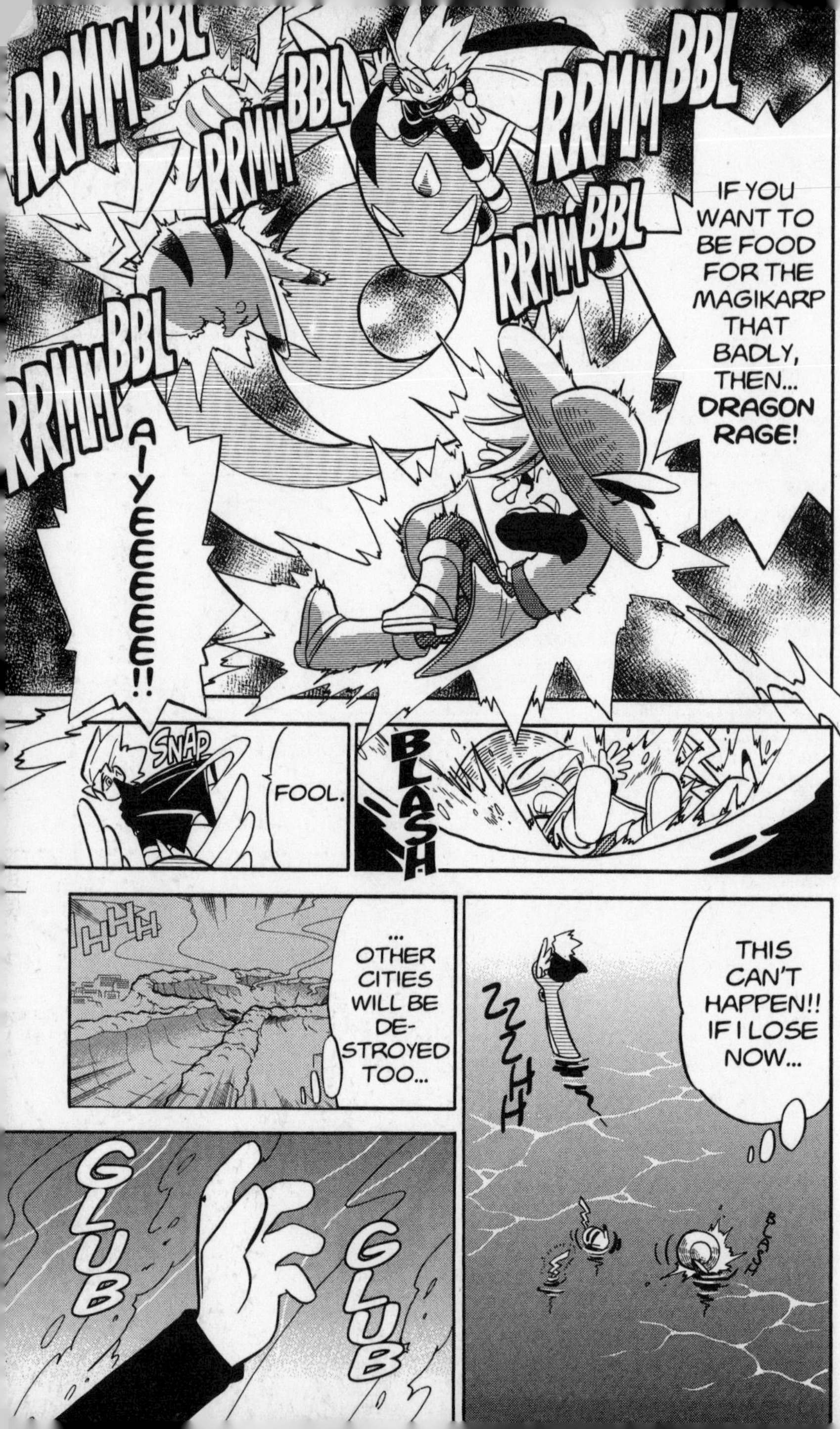

RRMM BBL
IF YOU WANT TO BE FOOD FOR THE MAGIKARP THAT BADLY, THEN... DRAGON RAGE!
RRMM BBL
RRMM BBL
RRMM BBL
RRMM BBL
AIYEEEEEE!!
BLASH
FOOL.
SNAP
THIS CAN'T HAPPEN!! IF I LOSE NOW...
ZZZHH
... OTHER CITIES WILL BE DE-STROYED TOO...
HHHH
GLUB
GLUB

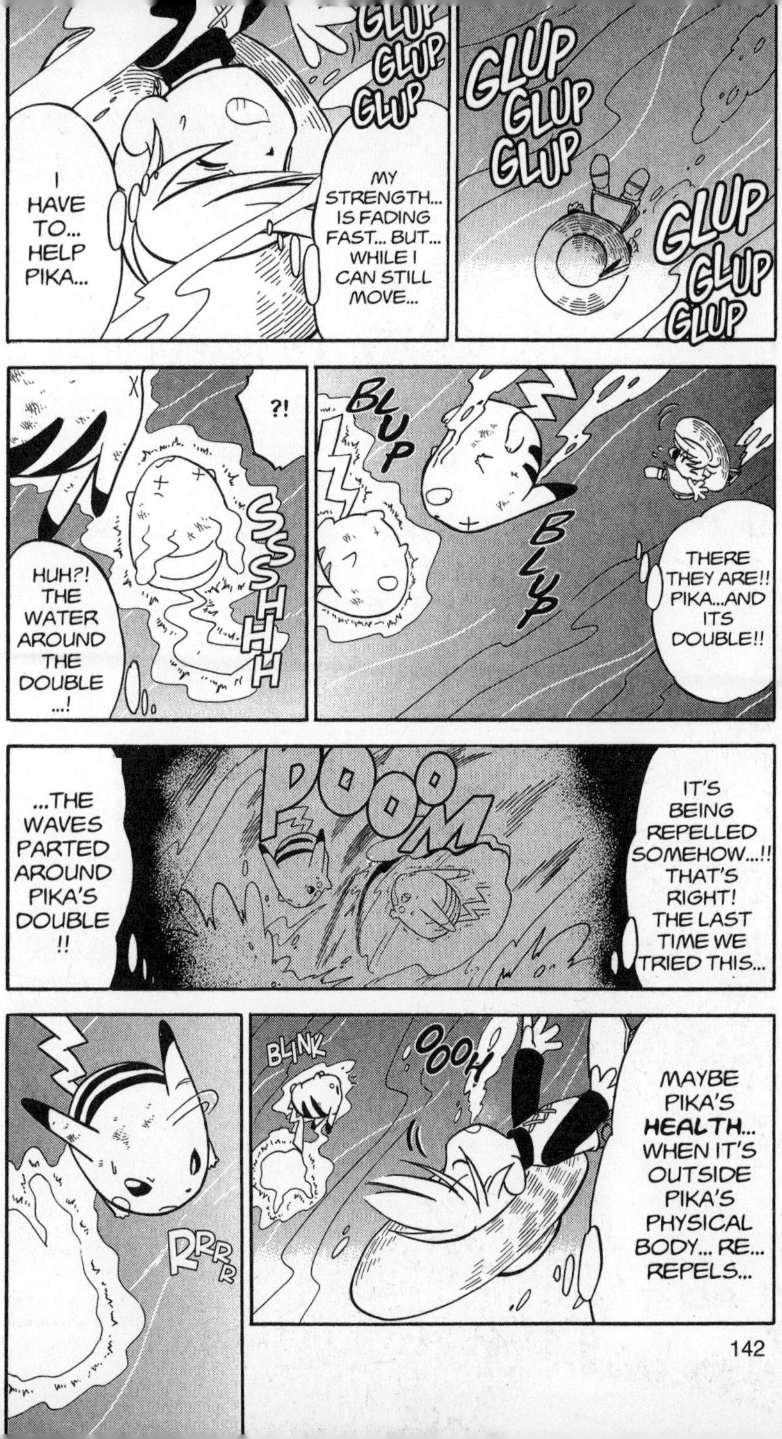
GLUP GLUP GLUP
GLUP GLUP GLUP
GLUP GLUP GLUP
MY STRENGTH... IS FADING FAST... BUT... WHILE I CAN STILL MOVE...
I HAVE TO... HELP PIKA...
THERE THEY ARE!! PIKA...AND ITS DOUBLE!!
BLUP
BLUP
?!
SSSHHHH
HUH?! THE WATER AROUND THE DOUBLE ...!
IT'S BEING REPELLED SOMEHOW...!! THAT'S RIGHT! THE LAST TIME WE TRIED THIS...
DOOOM
...THE WAVES PARTED AROUND PIKA'S DOUBLE !!
MAYBE PIKA'S **HEALTH**... WHEN IT'S OUTSIDE PIKA'S PHYSICAL BODY... RE... REPELS...
OOOH
BLINK
RRRR

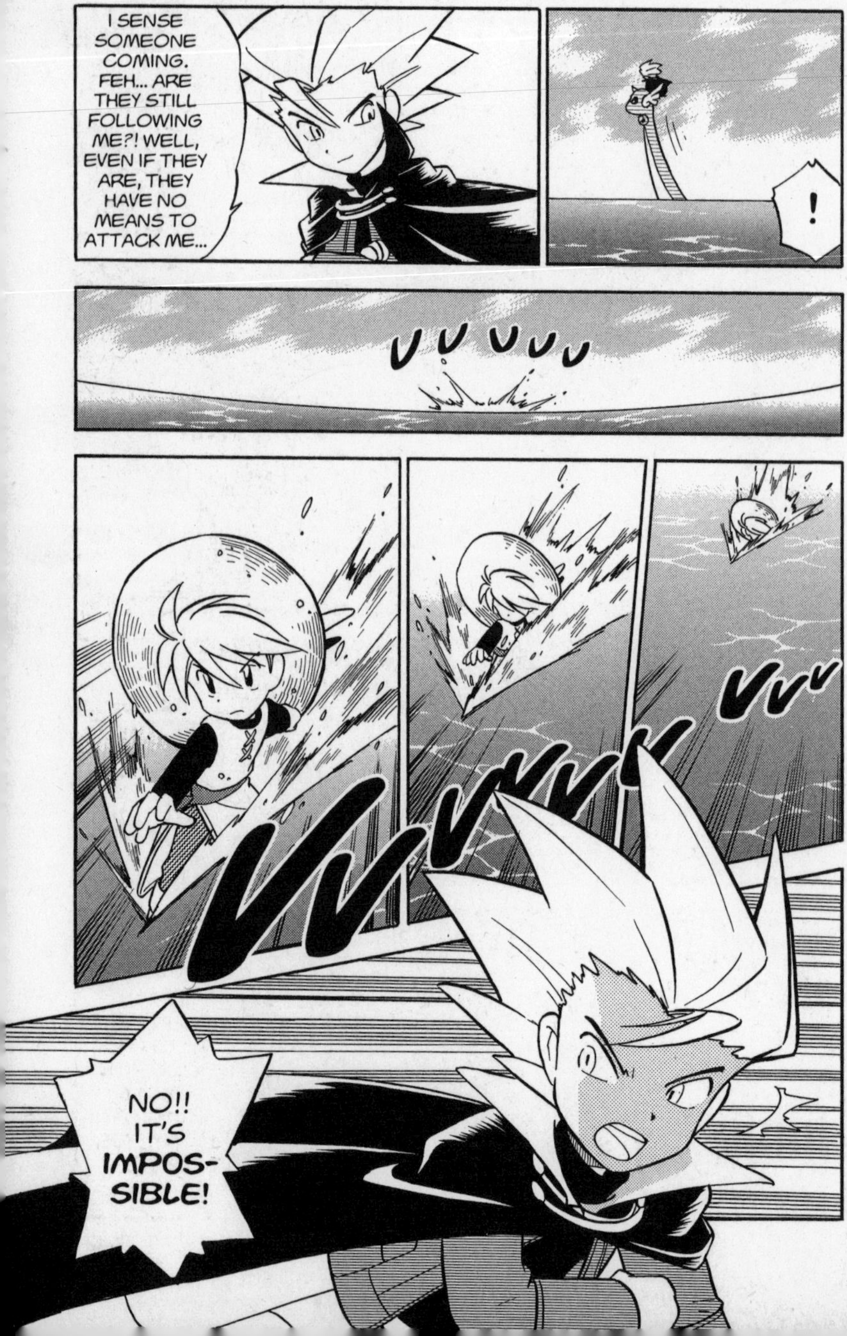
!
I SENSE SOMEONE COMING. FEH... ARE THEY STILL FOLLOWING ME?! WELL, EVEN IF THEY ARE, THEY HAVE NO MEANS TO ATTACK ME...
VVVVV
VVV
VVVVVV
NO!! IT'S IMPOS-SIBLE!

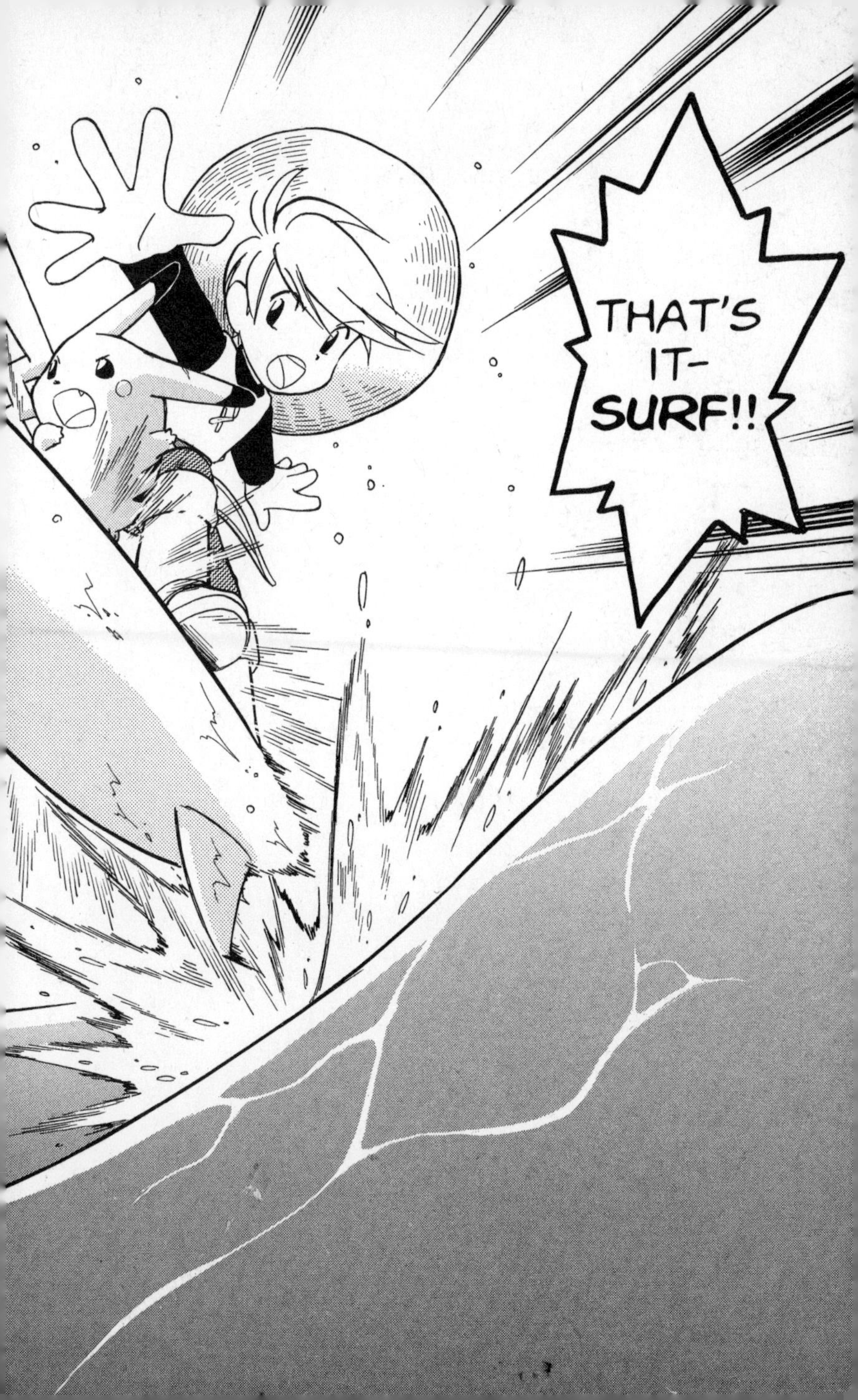
THAT'S IT- SURF!!

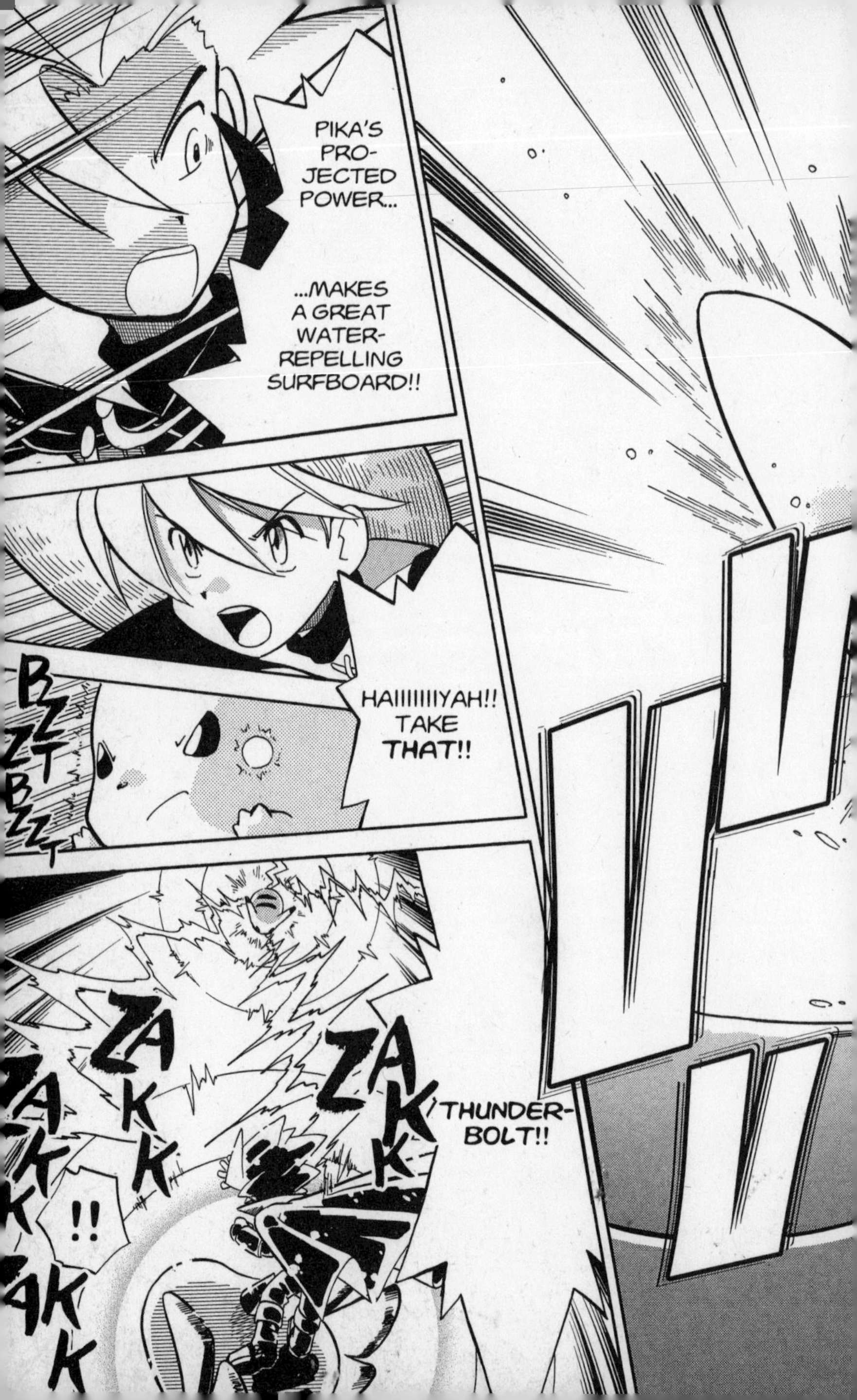
PIKA'S PROJECTED POWER...
...MAKES A GREAT WATER-REPELLING SURFBOARD!!
HAIIIIIIIYAH!! TAKE THAT!!
BZZT BZZZT
THUNDER-BOLT!!
ZAKK
ZAKK
!!

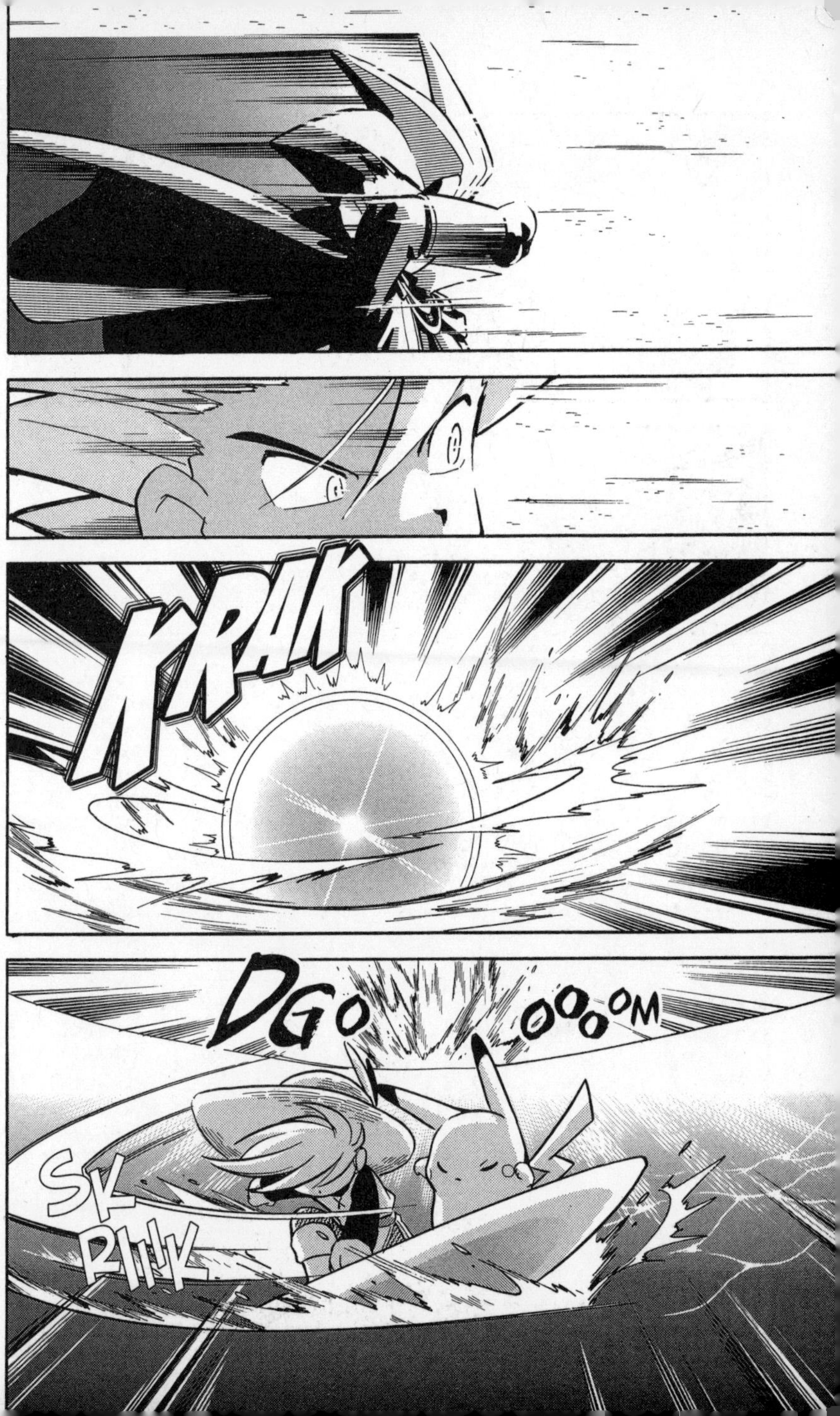

KRAK
DGO OOOOM
SK RIIIK

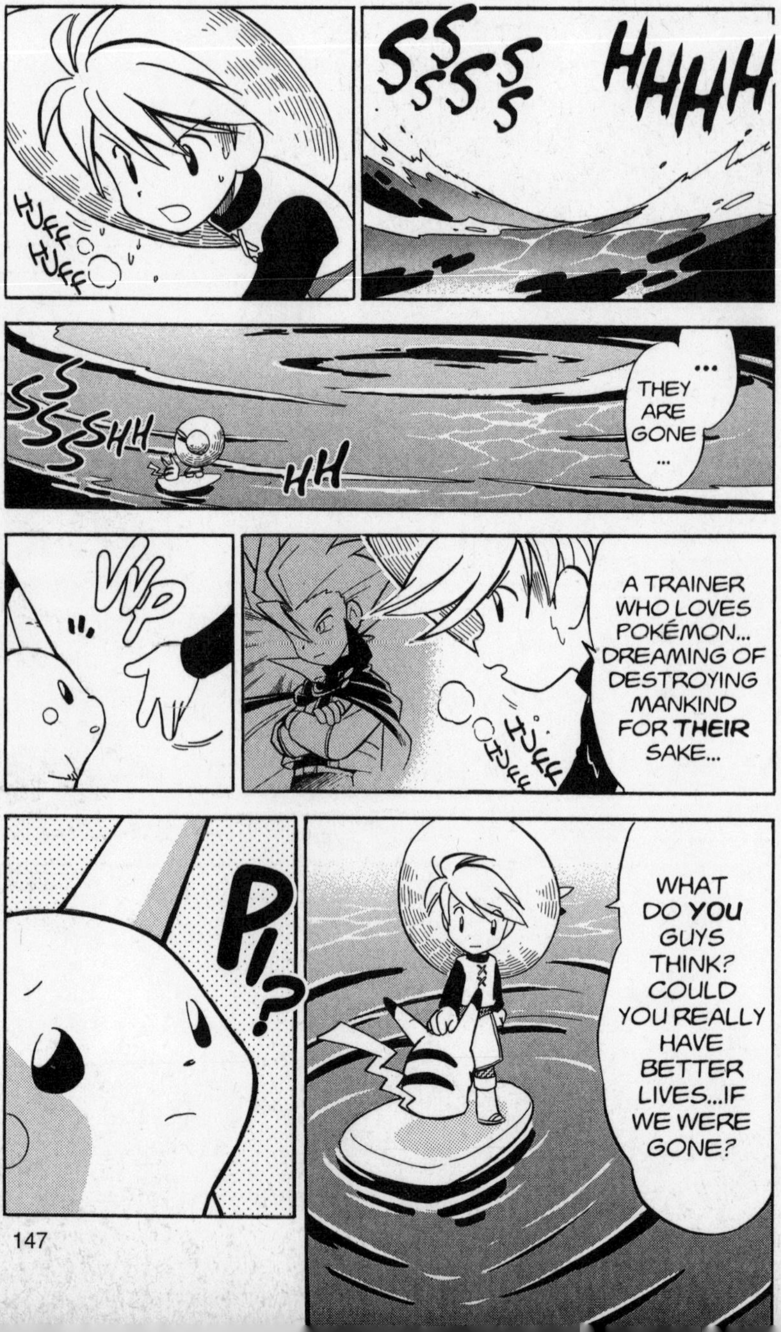
SSSSSSS HHHH
HUFF HUFF
SSSSSSHH HH
... THEY ARE GONE ...
A TRAINER WHO LOVES POKÉMON... DREAMING OF DESTROYING MANKIND FOR THEIR SAKE...
HUFF HUFF
VWP
WHAT DO YOU GUYS THINK? COULD YOU REALLY HAVE BETTER LIVES...IF WE WERE GONE?
PI?

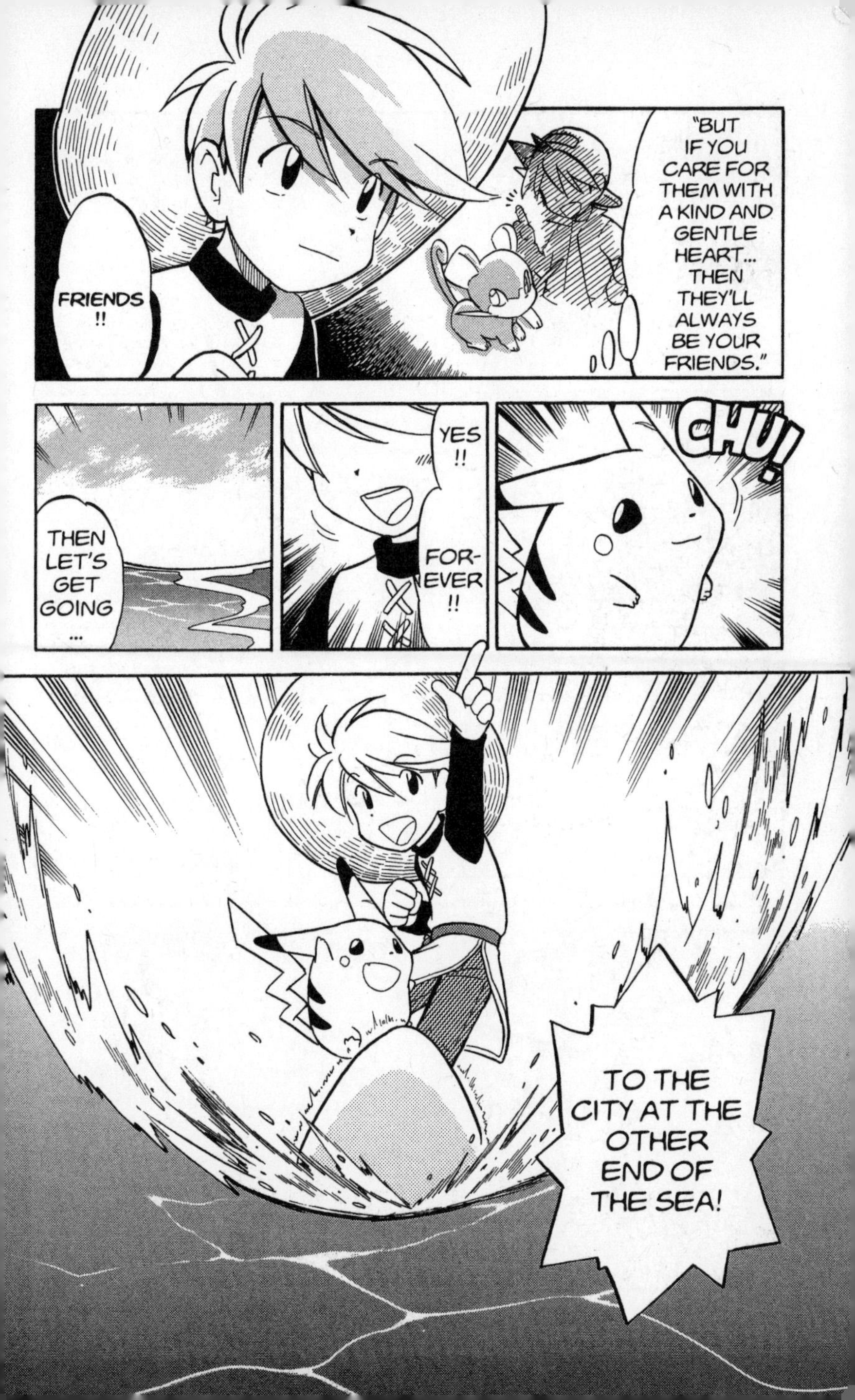
"BUT IF YOU CARE FOR THEM WITH A KIND AND GENTLE HEART... THEN THEY'LL ALWAYS BE YOUR FRIENDS."
FRIENDS !!
CHU!
YES !!
FOR-EVER !!
THEN LET'S GET GOING ...
TO THE CITY AT THE OTHER END OF THE SEA!

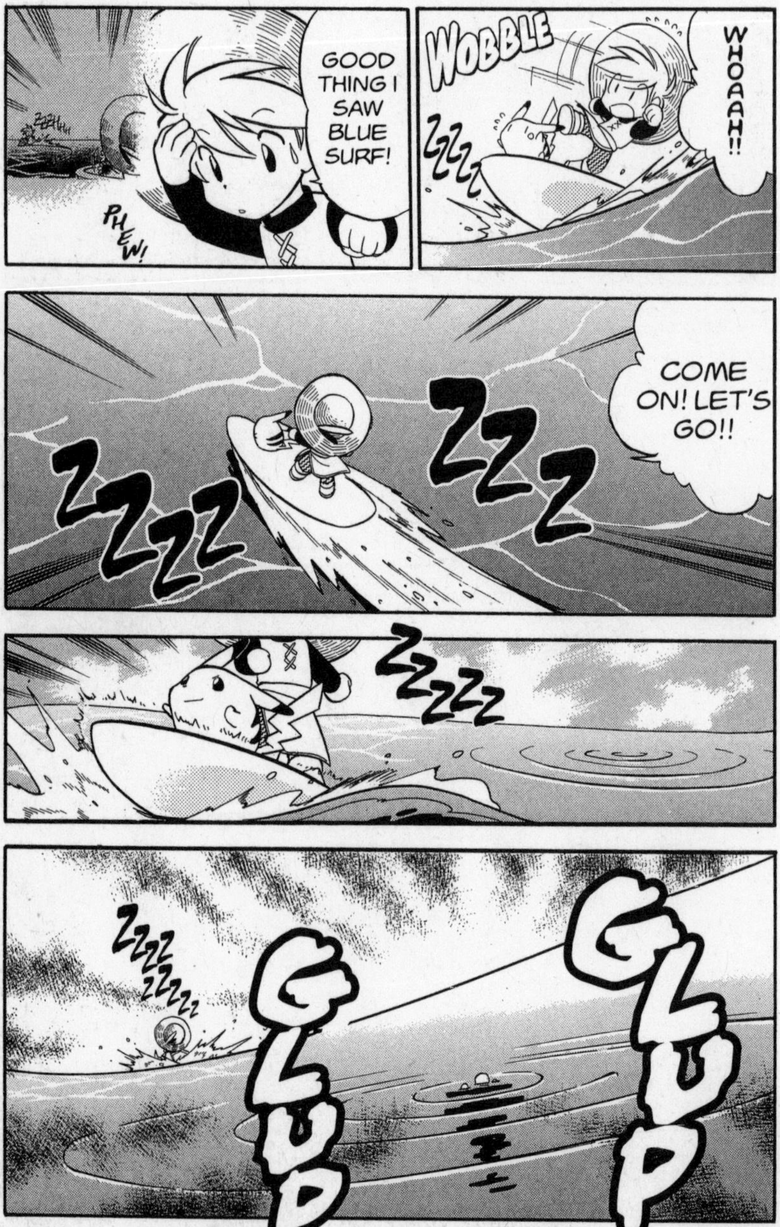
WOBBLE
WHOAAAH!!
ZZZZ
GOOD THING I SAW BLUE SURF!
PHEW!
COME ON! LET'S GO!!
ZZZ
ZZZZ
ZZZZZZ
GLUP
GLUP
ZZZZ
ZZZZZ

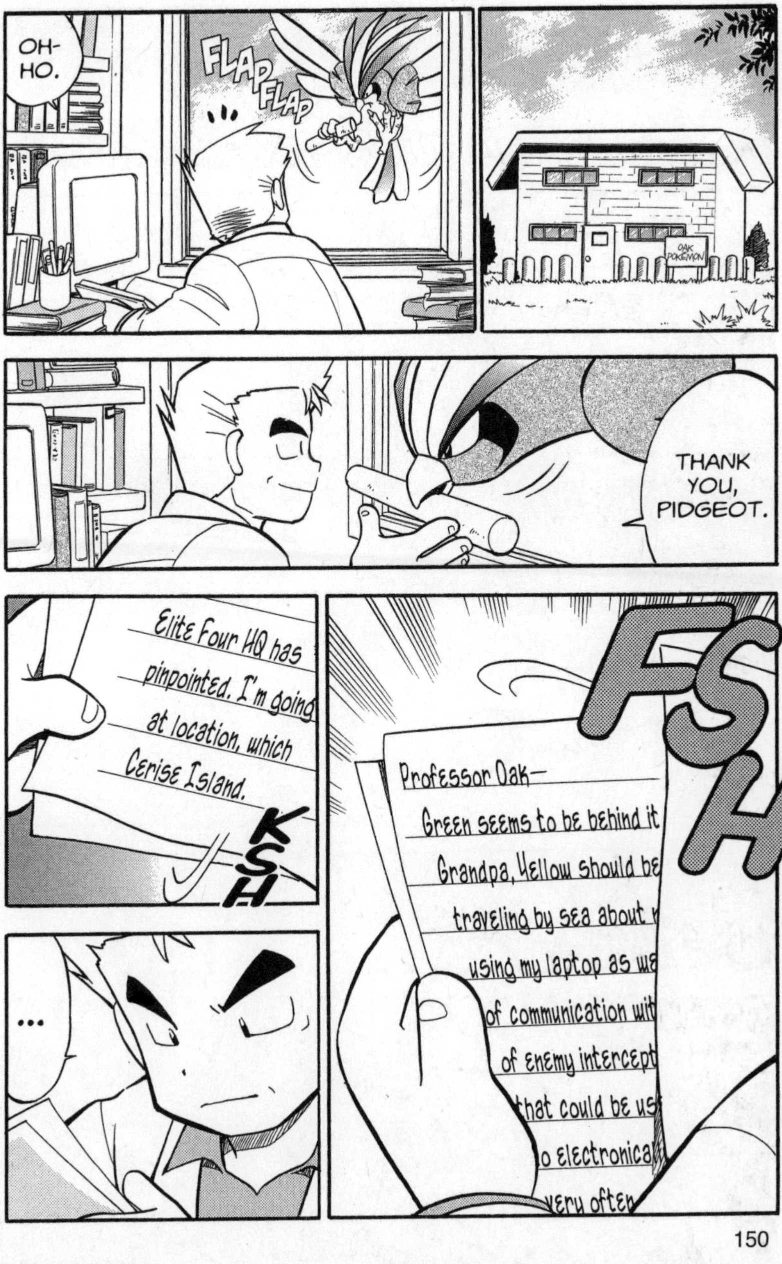
OAK POKéMON
OH-HO.
FLAP FLAP
...
THANK YOU, PIDGEOT.
FSH
Professor Oak—
Green seems to be behind it
Grandpa, Yellow should be
traveling by sea about
using my laptop as we
of communication wit
of enemy intercept
that could be us
o electronica
very often
Elite Four HQ has
pinpointed. I'm going
at location, which
Cerise Island.
KSH
...

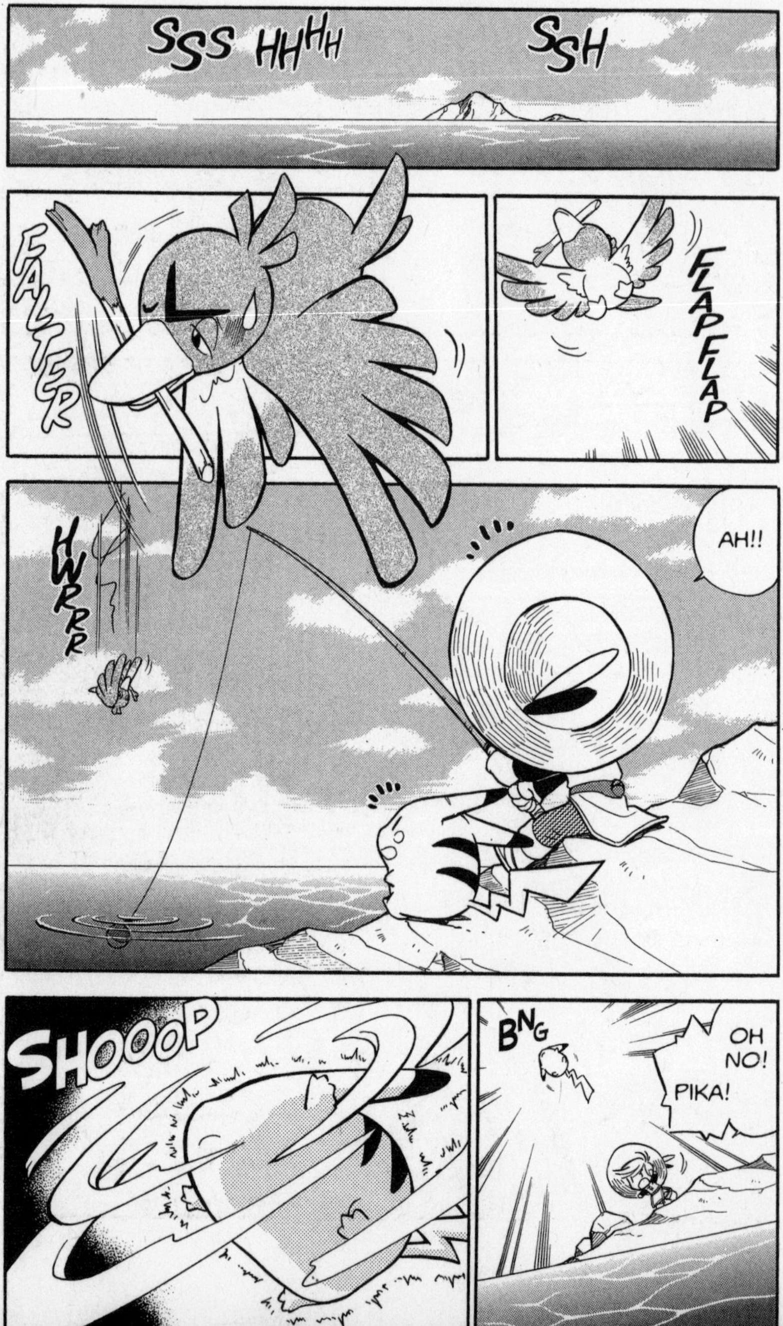
SSH
SSS HHHH
FLAPFLAP
FALTER
AH!!
HWRRR
OH NO!
BNG
PIKA!
SHOOOP

63 Extricated from Exeggutor

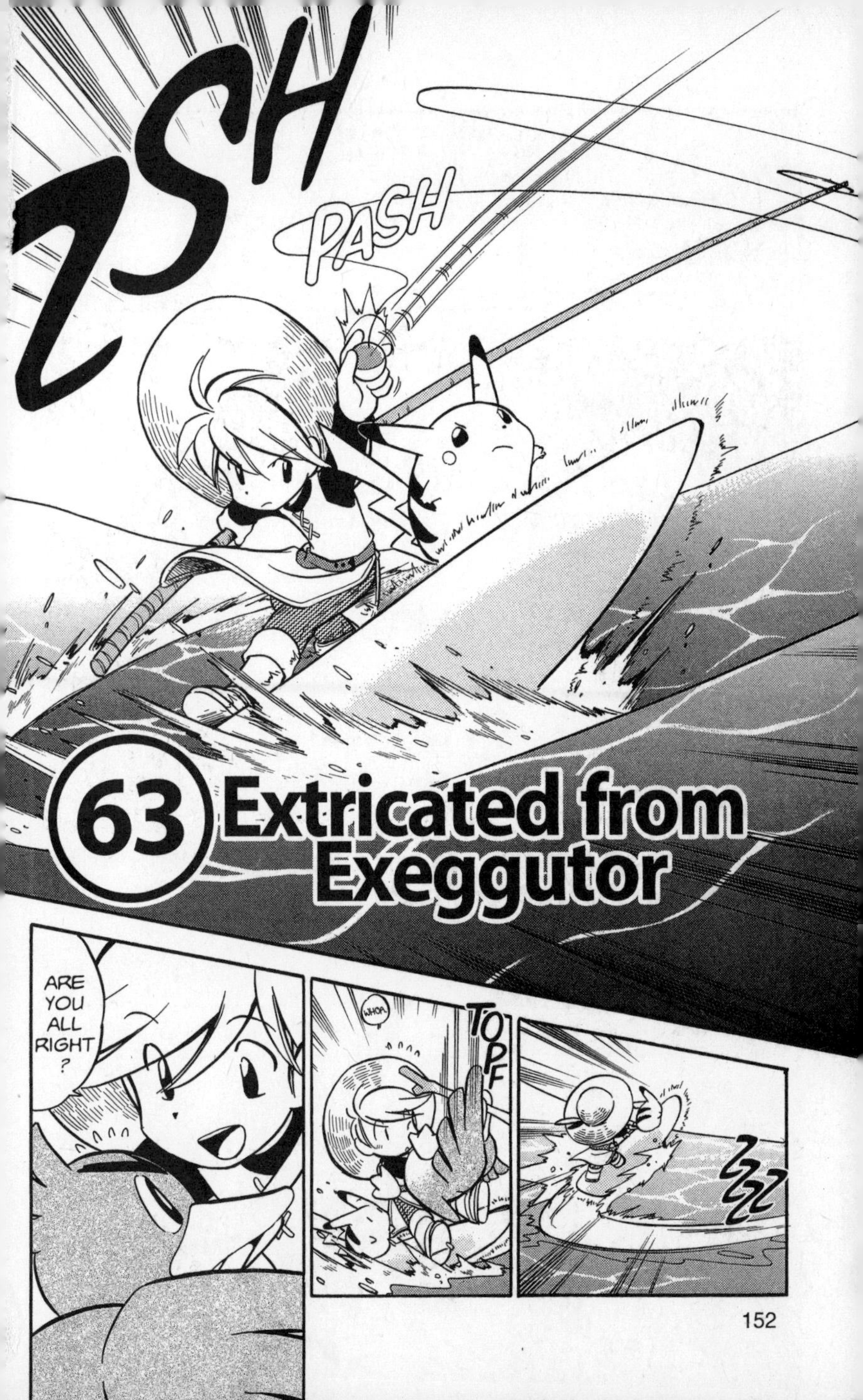
ZSH
PASH
ZZZ
WHOA
TOPF
ARE YOU ALL RIGHT?

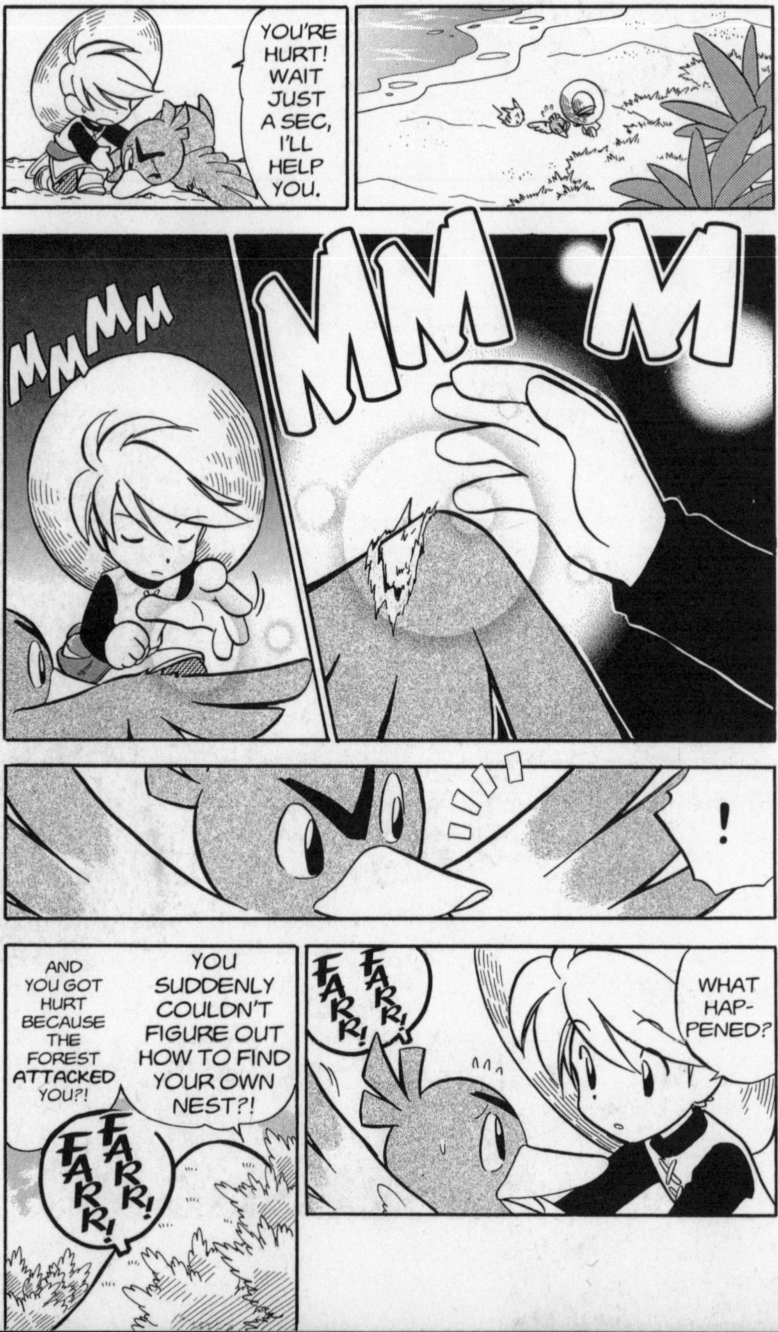
YOU'RE HURT! WAIT JUST A SEC, I'LL HELP YOU.
MM M
MMMM
!
WHAT HAP-PENED?
FARR! FARR!
YOU SUDDENLY COULDN'T FIGURE OUT HOW TO FIND YOUR OWN NEST?!
AND YOU GOT HURT BECAUSE THE FOREST ATTACKED YOU?!
FARR! FARR!

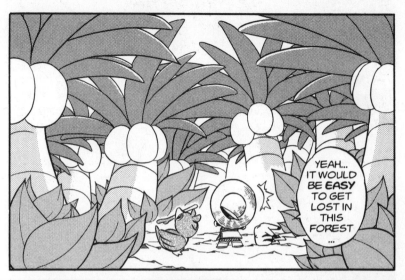

YEAH... IT WOULD BE EASY TO GET LOST IN THIS FOREST ...
PIKA... THIS FARFETCH'D SAYS THAT THE FOREST CHANGES EVERY TIME IT COMES THROUGH!
SO HOW DO WE NOT GET LOST TOO WHILE WE'RE LOOKING FOR ITS NEST...
BOM
GOT IT! CATER-PIE!
TNNG
WE'LL JUST DO THIS ...
SHOOLOLOLOO
FIRST, LET'S TRAVEL STRAIGHT FROM HERE!

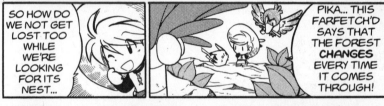

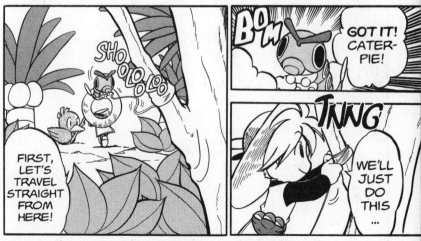

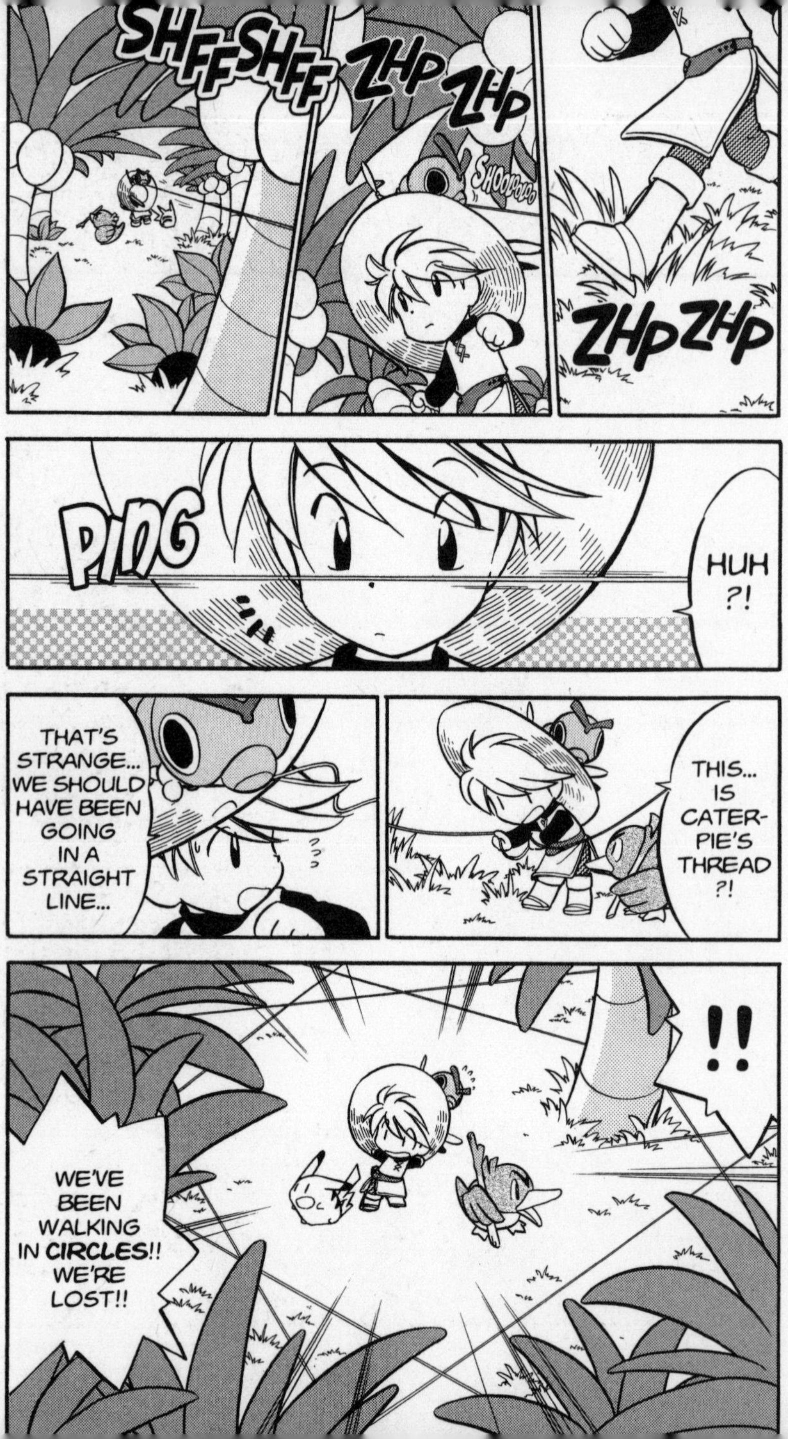
ZHP ZHP
SHOOPOOO
ZHP ZHP
SHFF SHFF
PING
HUH?!
THIS... IS CATERPIE'S THREAD?!
THAT'S STRANGE... WE SHOULD HAVE BEEN GOING IN A STRAIGHT LINE...
!!
WE'VE BEEN WALKING IN **CIRCLES**!! WE'RE LOST!!

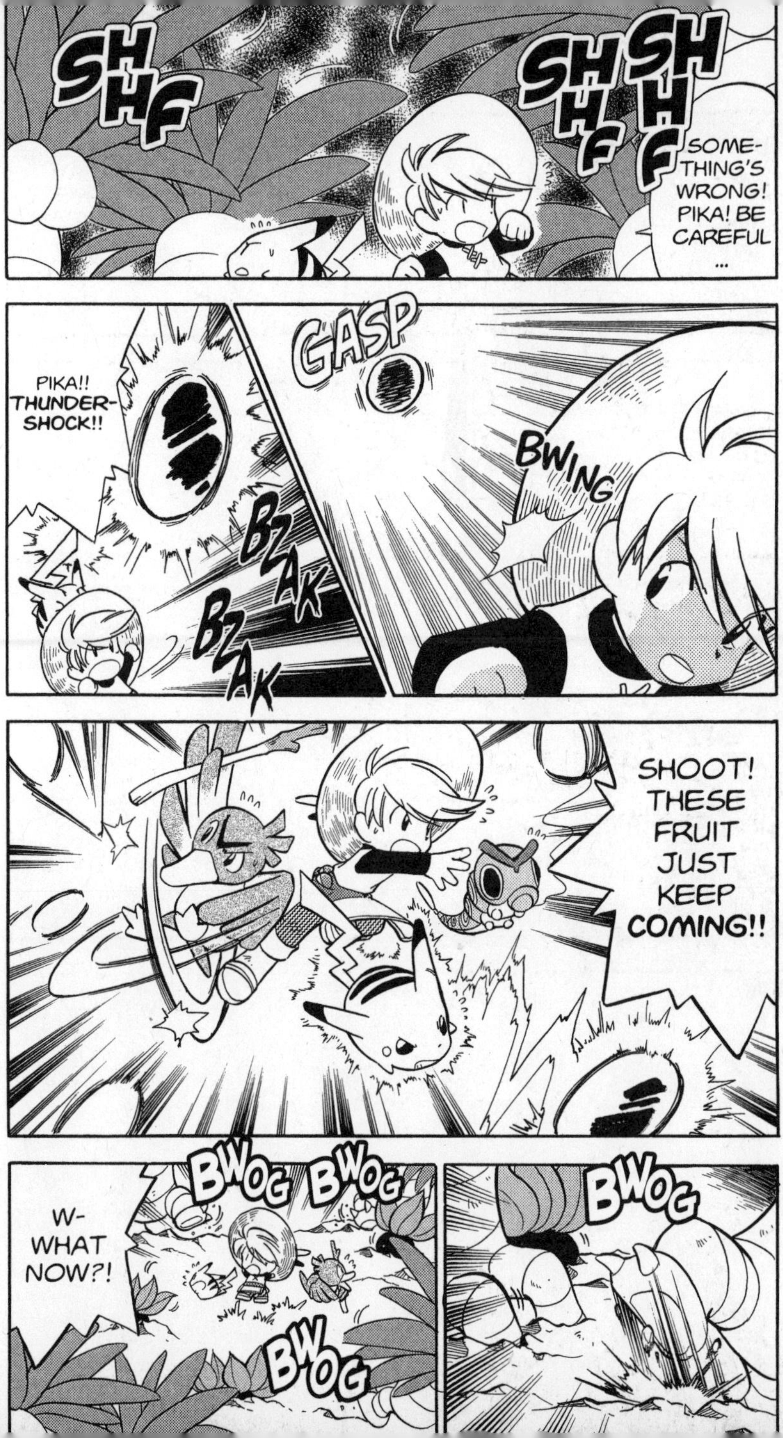
SHHF SHHF
SOME-THING'S WRONG! PIKA! BE CAREFUL ...
SHHF
GASP
BWING
PIKA!! THUNDER-SHOCK!!
BZAK BZAK
SHOOT! THESE FRUIT JUST KEEP COMING!!
BWOG
BWOG BWOG
W- WHAT NOW?!
BWOG

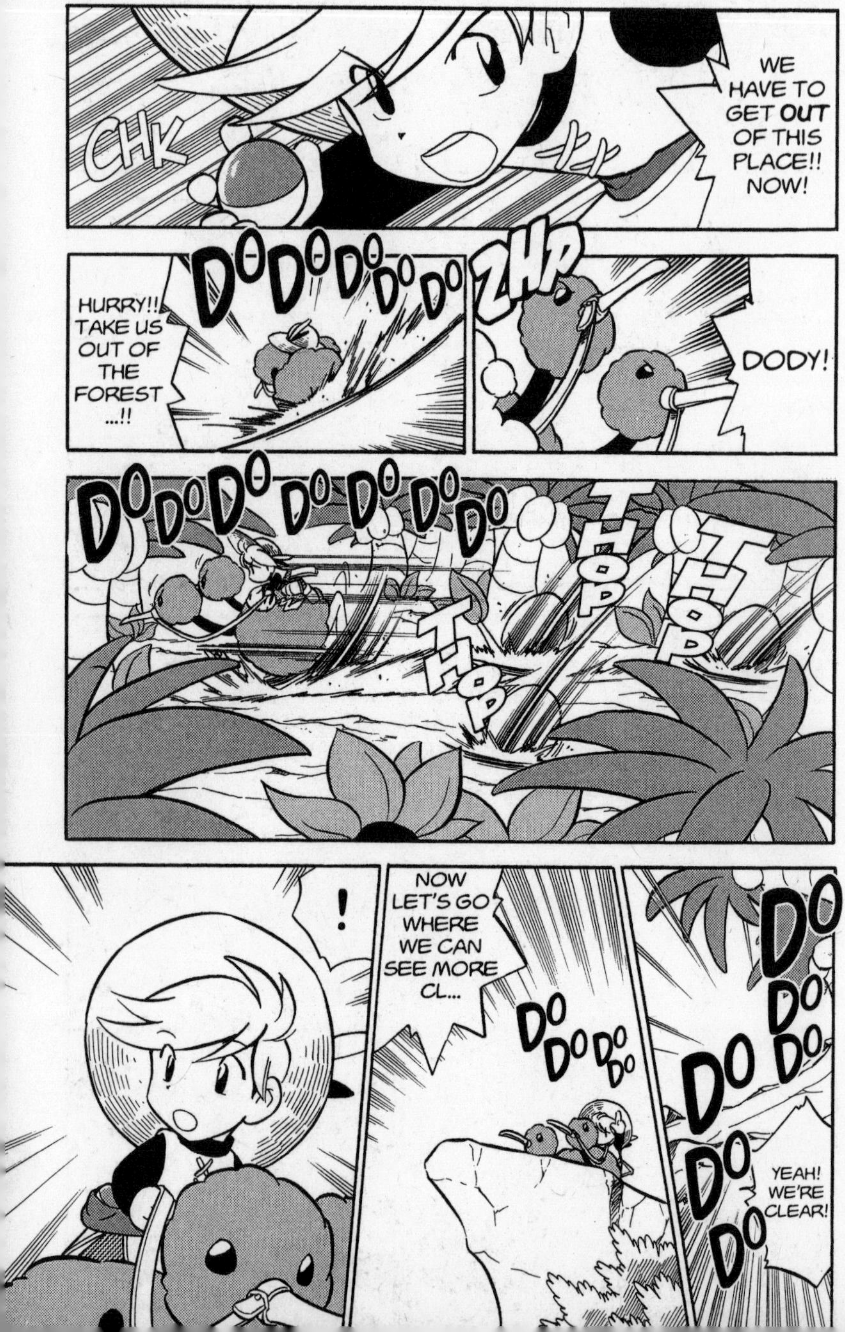
WE HAVE TO GET **OUT** OF THIS PLACE!! NOW!
CHK
ZHP
DODY!
DODODODODODO
HURRY!! TAKE US OUT OF THE FOREST ...!!
THOP
THOP
THOP
DODODODODODODODO
DO DO DO DO DO DO DO DO DO
YEAH! WE'RE CLEAR!
NOW LET'S GO WHERE WE CAN SEE MORE CL...
DO DO DO DO DO
!

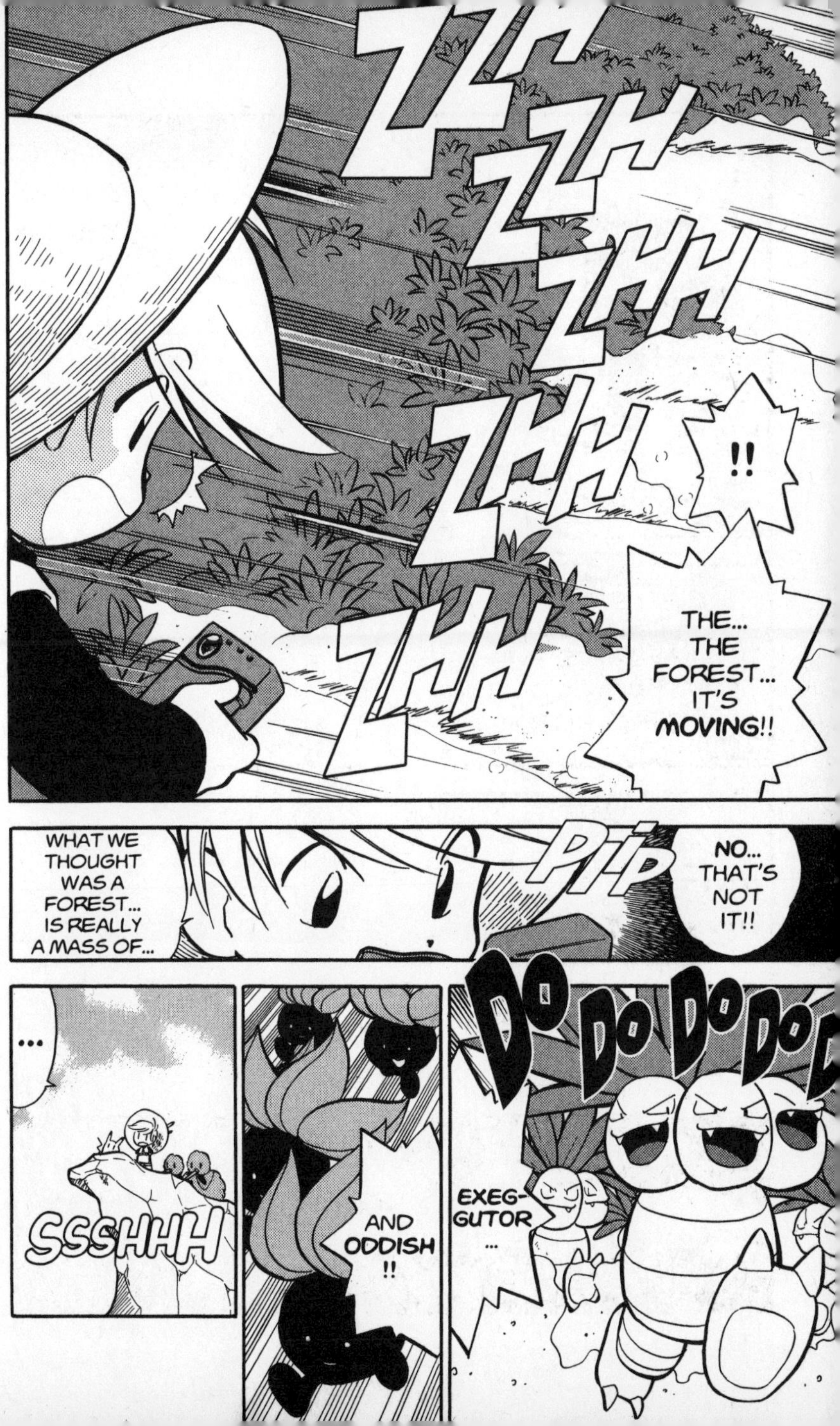
ZZH ZZH ZHH ZHH ZHH
!!
THE... THE FOREST... IT'S MOVING!!
NO... THAT'S NOT IT!!
PI-P
WHAT WE THOUGHT WAS A FOREST... IS REALLY A MASS OF...
DO DO DO DO DO
EXEG-GUTOR ...
AND ODDISH !!
...
SSSHHH

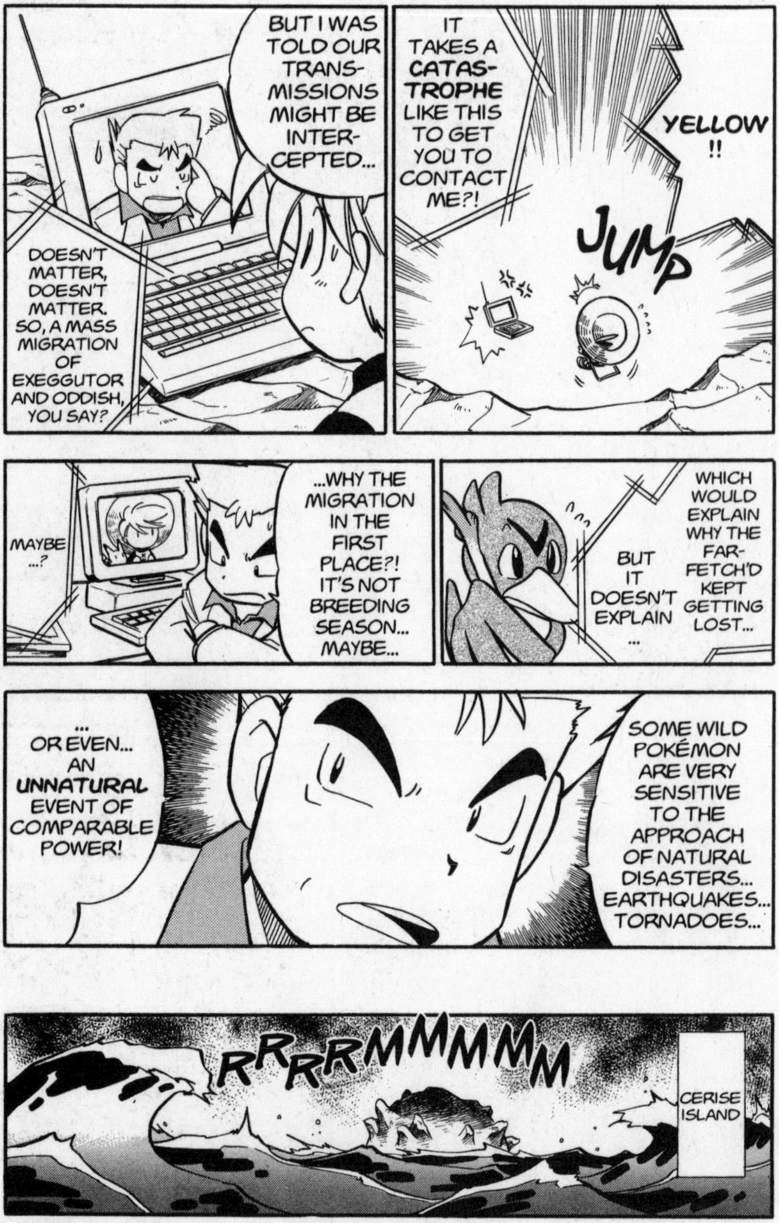
YELLOW !!
IT TAKES A CATASTROPHE LIKE THIS TO GET YOU TO CONTACT ME?!
JUMP
BUT I WAS TOLD OUR TRANSMISSIONS MIGHT BE INTERCEPTED...
DOESN'T MATTER, DOESN'T MATTER. SO, A MASS MIGRATION OF EXEGGUTOR AND ODDISH, YOU SAY?
WHICH WOULD EXPLAIN WHY THE FARFETCH'D KEPT GETTING LOST...
BUT IT DOESN'T EXPLAIN...
...WHY THE MIGRATION IN THE FIRST PLACE?! IT'S NOT BREEDING SEASON... MAYBE...
MAYBE ...?
SOME WILD POKÉMON ARE VERY SENSITIVE TO THE APPROACH OF NATURAL DISASTERS... EARTHQUAKES... TORNADOES...
... OR EVEN... AN UNNATURAL EVENT OF COMPARABLE POWER!
CERISE ISLAND
RRRRMMMMMM

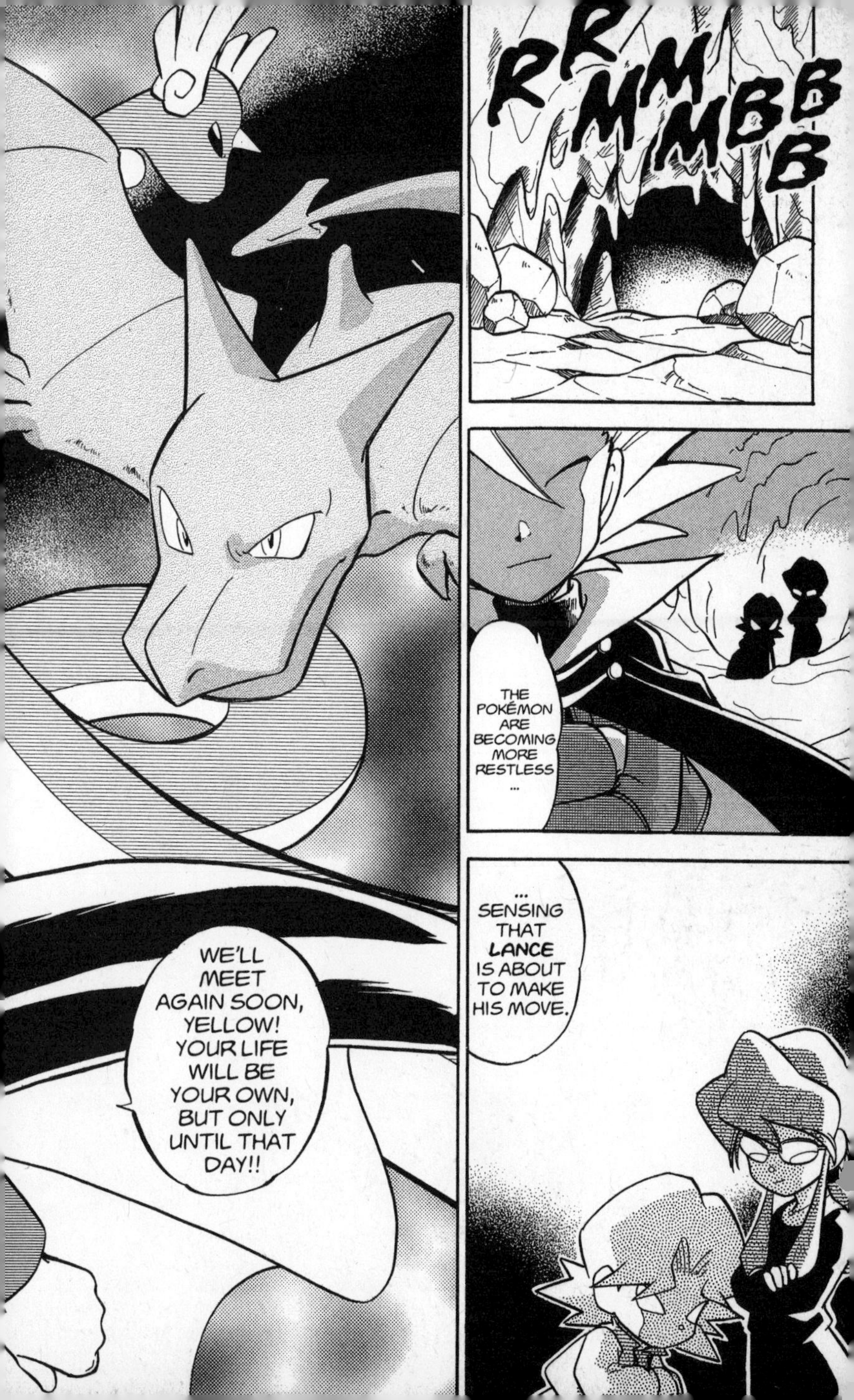
RRMMMBBB
THE POKÉMON ARE BECOMING MORE RESTLESS ...
... SENSING THAT **LANCE** IS ABOUT TO MAKE HIS MOVE.
WE'LL MEET AGAIN SOON, YELLOW! YOUR LIFE WILL BE YOUR OWN, BUT ONLY UNTIL THAT DAY!!

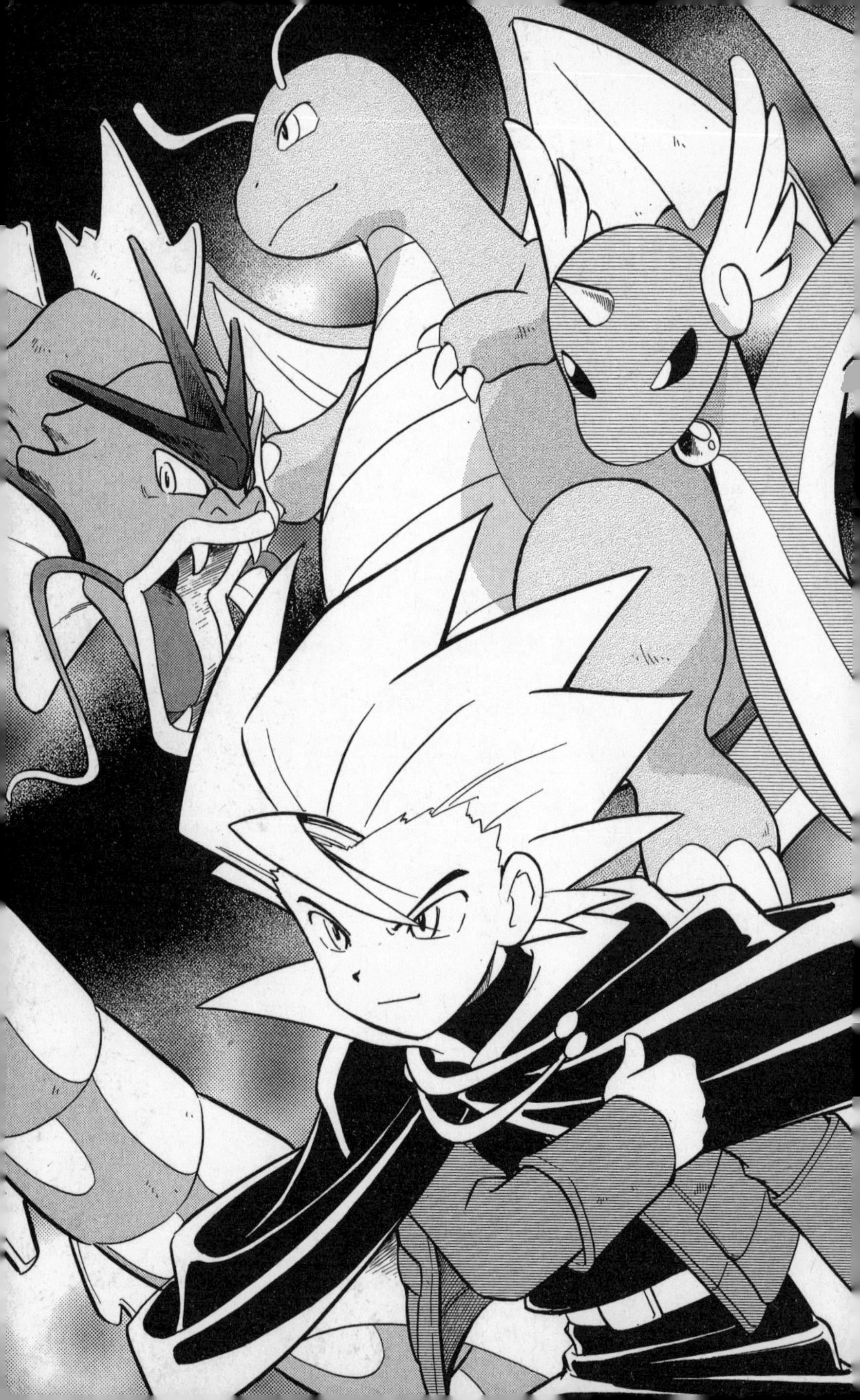

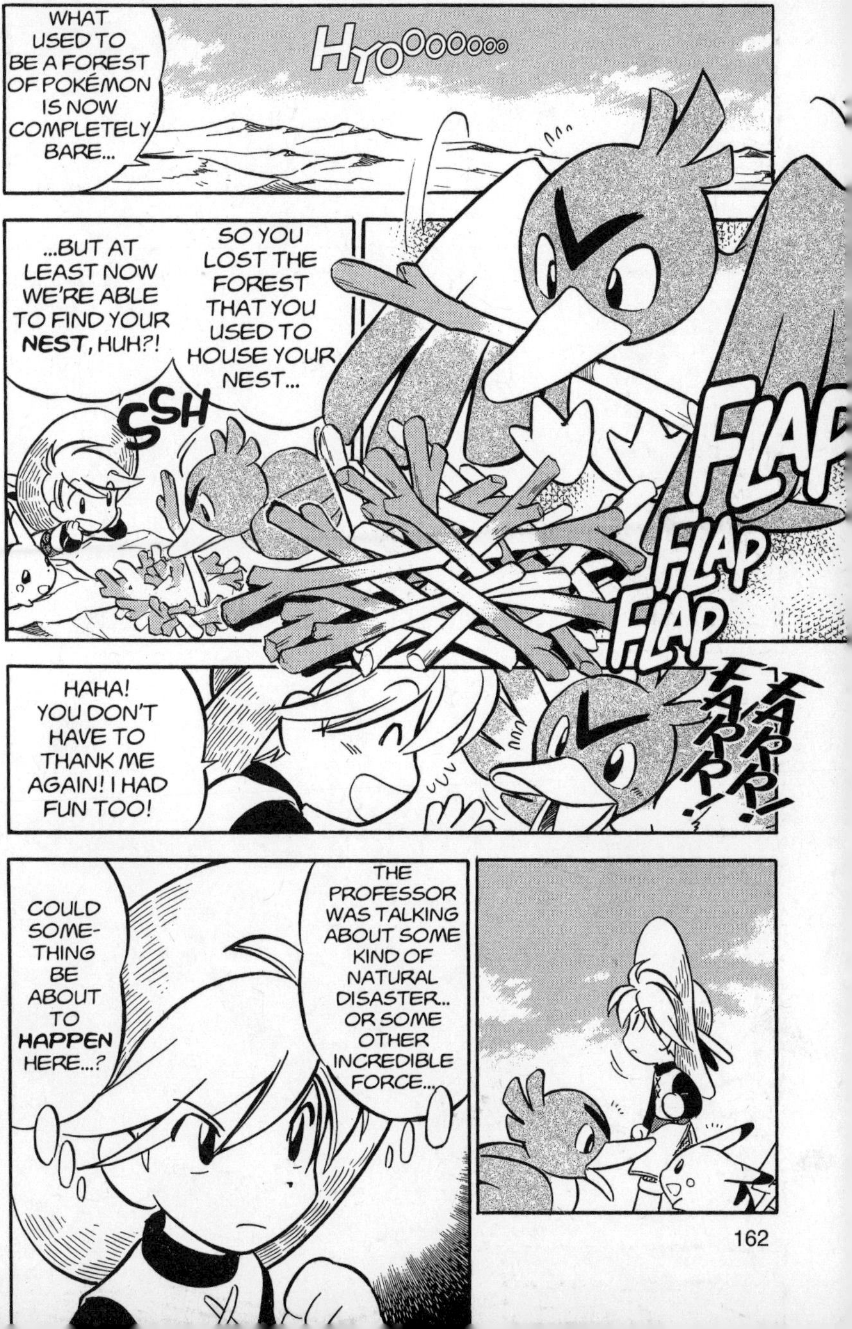
WHAT USED TO BE A FOREST OF POKÉMON IS NOW COMPLETELY BARE...
HYOOOOOOO
FLAP FLAP FLAP
SO YOU LOST THE FOREST THAT YOU USED TO HOUSE YOUR NEST...
...BUT AT LEAST NOW WE'RE ABLE TO FIND YOUR **NEST**, HUH?!
SSH
FARRR! FARRR!
HAHA! YOU DON'T HAVE TO THANK ME AGAIN! I HAD FUN TOO!
THE PROFESSOR WAS TALKING ABOUT SOME KIND OF NATURAL DISASTER... OR SOME OTHER INCREDIBLE FORCE...
COULD SOME-THING BE ABOUT TO **HAPPEN** HERE...?

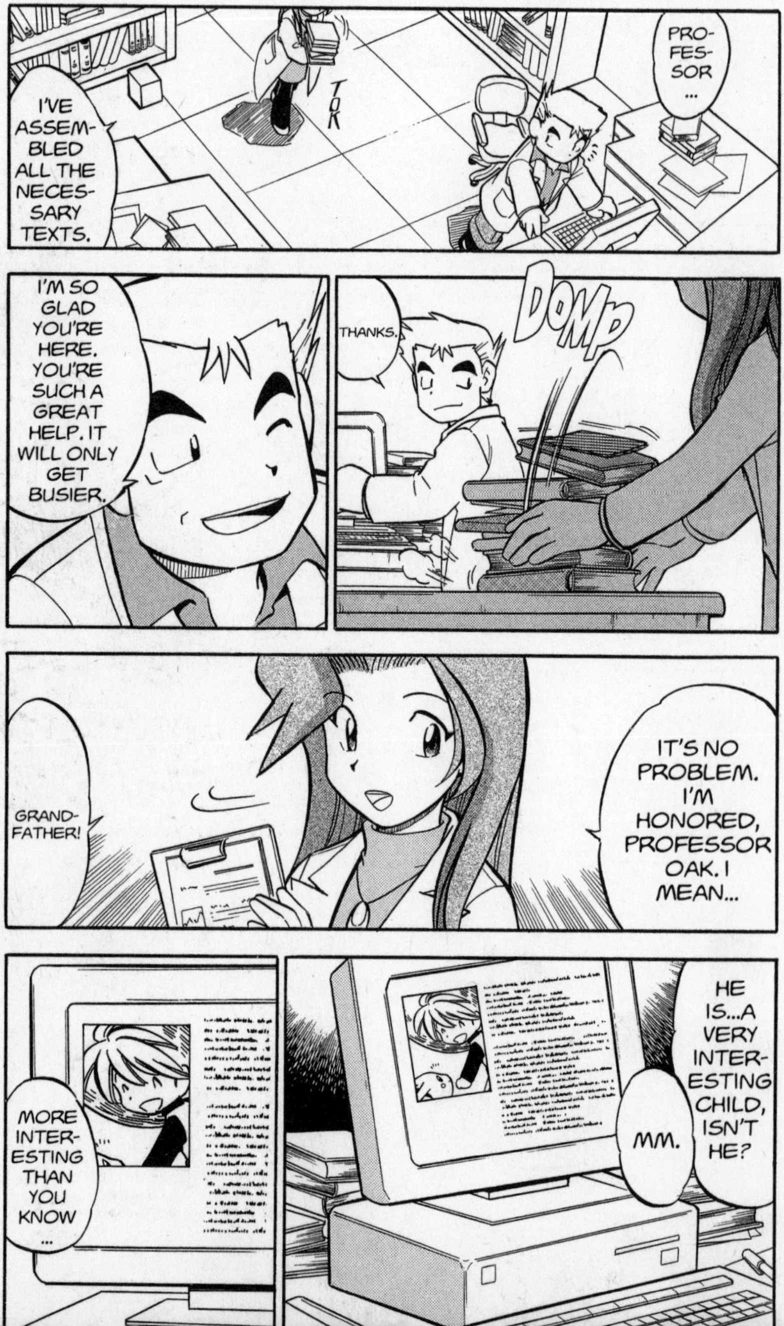
PROFESSOR...
TOK
I'VE ASSEMBLED ALL THE NECESSARY TEXTS.
DOMP
THANKS.
I'M SO GLAD YOU'RE HERE. YOU'RE SUCH A GREAT HELP. IT WILL ONLY GET BUSIER.
IT'S NO PROBLEM. I'M HONORED, PROFESSOR OAK. I MEAN...
GRANDFATHER!
HE IS...A VERY INTERESTING CHILD, ISN'T HE?
MM.
MORE INTERESTING THAN YOU KNOW...

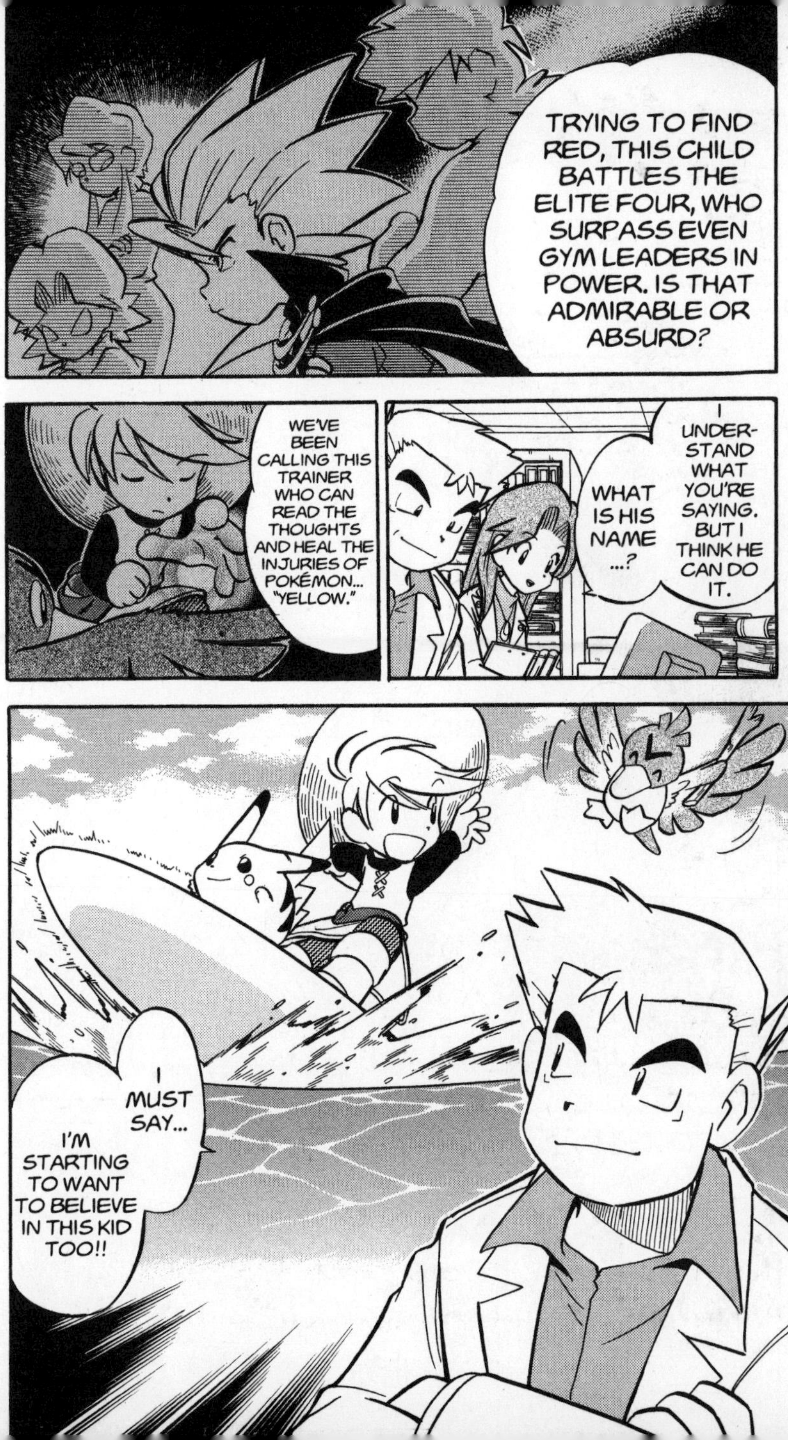
TRYING TO FIND RED, THIS CHILD BATTLES THE ELITE FOUR, WHO SURPASS EVEN GYM LEADERS IN POWER. IS THAT ADMIRABLE OR ABSURD?
I UNDERSTAND WHAT YOU'RE SAYING. BUT I THINK HE CAN DO IT.
WHAT IS HIS NAME ...?
WE'VE BEEN CALLING THIS TRAINER WHO CAN READ THE THOUGHTS AND HEAL THE INJURIES OF POKÉMON... "YELLOW."
I MUST SAY...
I'M STARTING TO WANT TO BELIEVE IN THIS KID TOO!!

64 Putting It on the Line... Against Arcanine

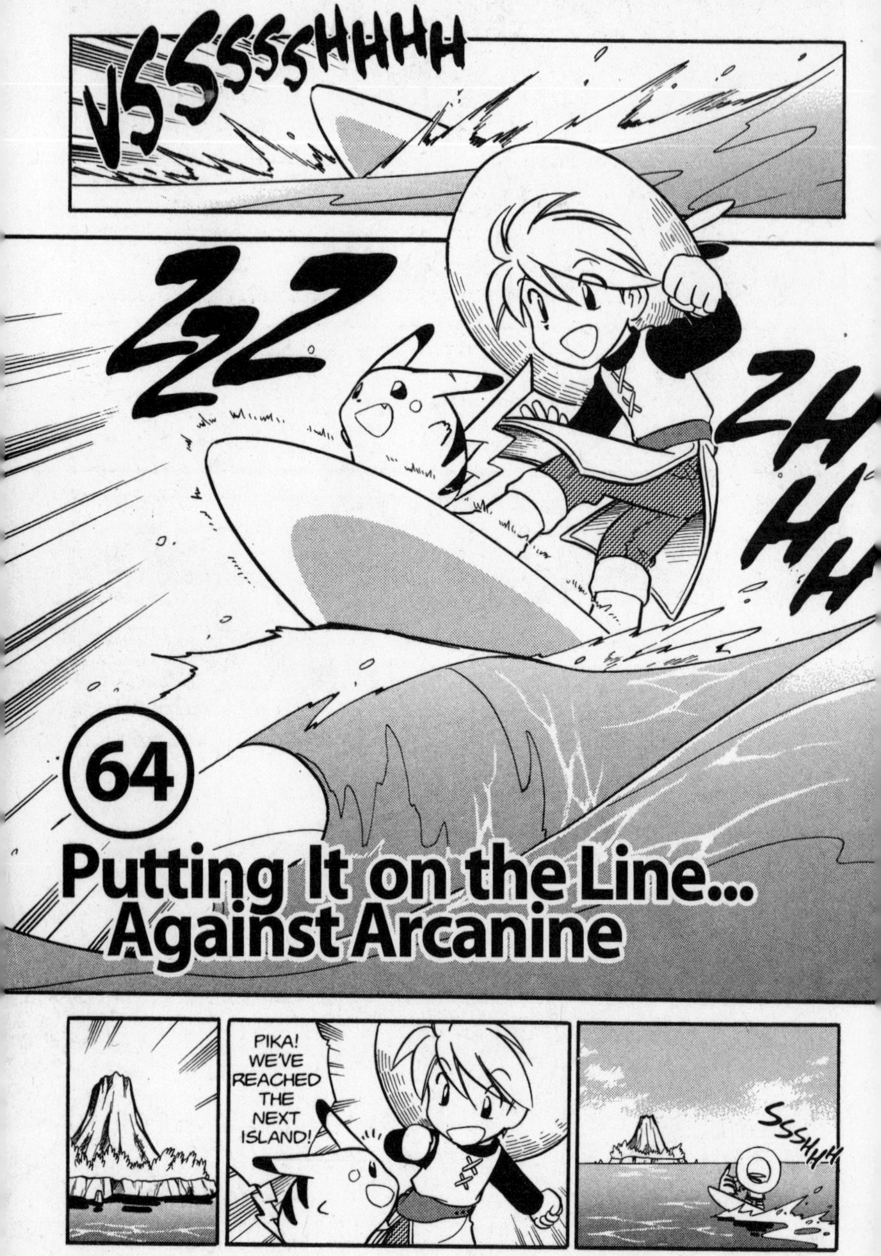
VSSSSSSHHHH
ZZZ
ZHHH
SSSHHH
PIKA! WE'VE REACHED THE NEXT ISLAND!

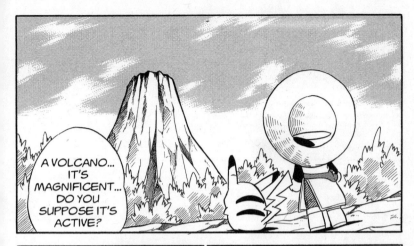

A VOLCANO... IT'S MAGNIFICENT... DO YOU SUPPOSE IT'S ACTIVE?
NOPE. THAT VOLCANO HAS BEEN DORMANT FOR DECADES.
!
WELCOME TO CINNABAR ISLAND. I'M WHAT YOU CALL A JUNIOR TRAINER.
CINNABAR ISLAND! THAT IS WHERE **BLAINE** HAS HIS GYM AND RESEARCH LAB!
WHICH MEANS, I THINK, THAT WE WON'T FIND ANY CLUES TO FINDING RED... BLAINE **MUST** HAVE SEARCHED HIS OWN ISLAND THOROUGHLY.
WHAT SHOULD WE DO, PIKA?
GLANCE GLANCE

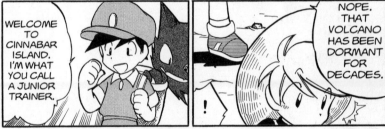

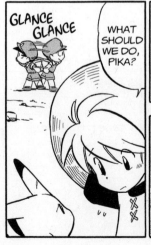

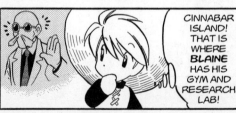

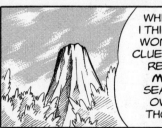

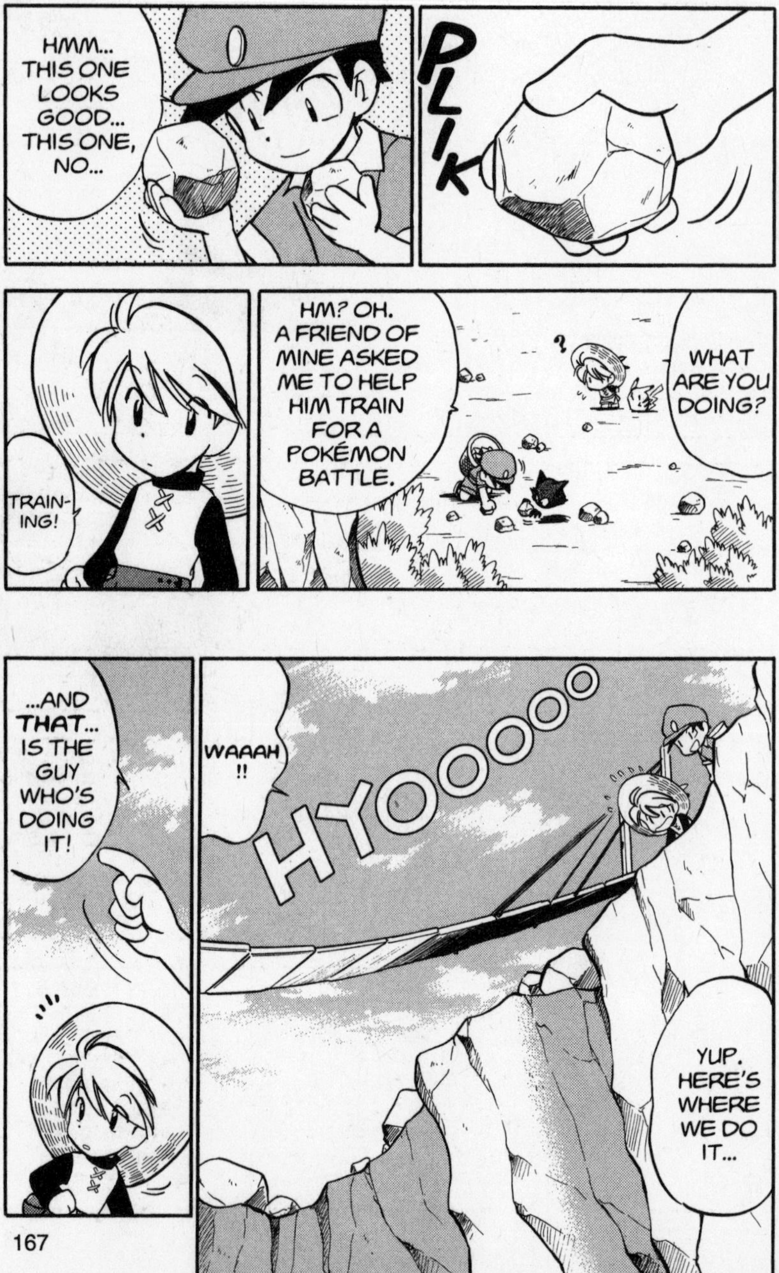
PLIK
HMM... THIS ONE LOOKS GOOD... THIS ONE, NO...
WHAT ARE YOU DOING?
HM? OH. A FRIEND OF MINE ASKED ME TO HELP HIM TRAIN FOR A POKÉMON BATTLE.
TRAIN-ING!
HYOOOOOO
WAAAH !!
YUP. HERE'S WHERE WE DO IT...
...AND THAT... IS THE GUY WHO'S DOING IT!

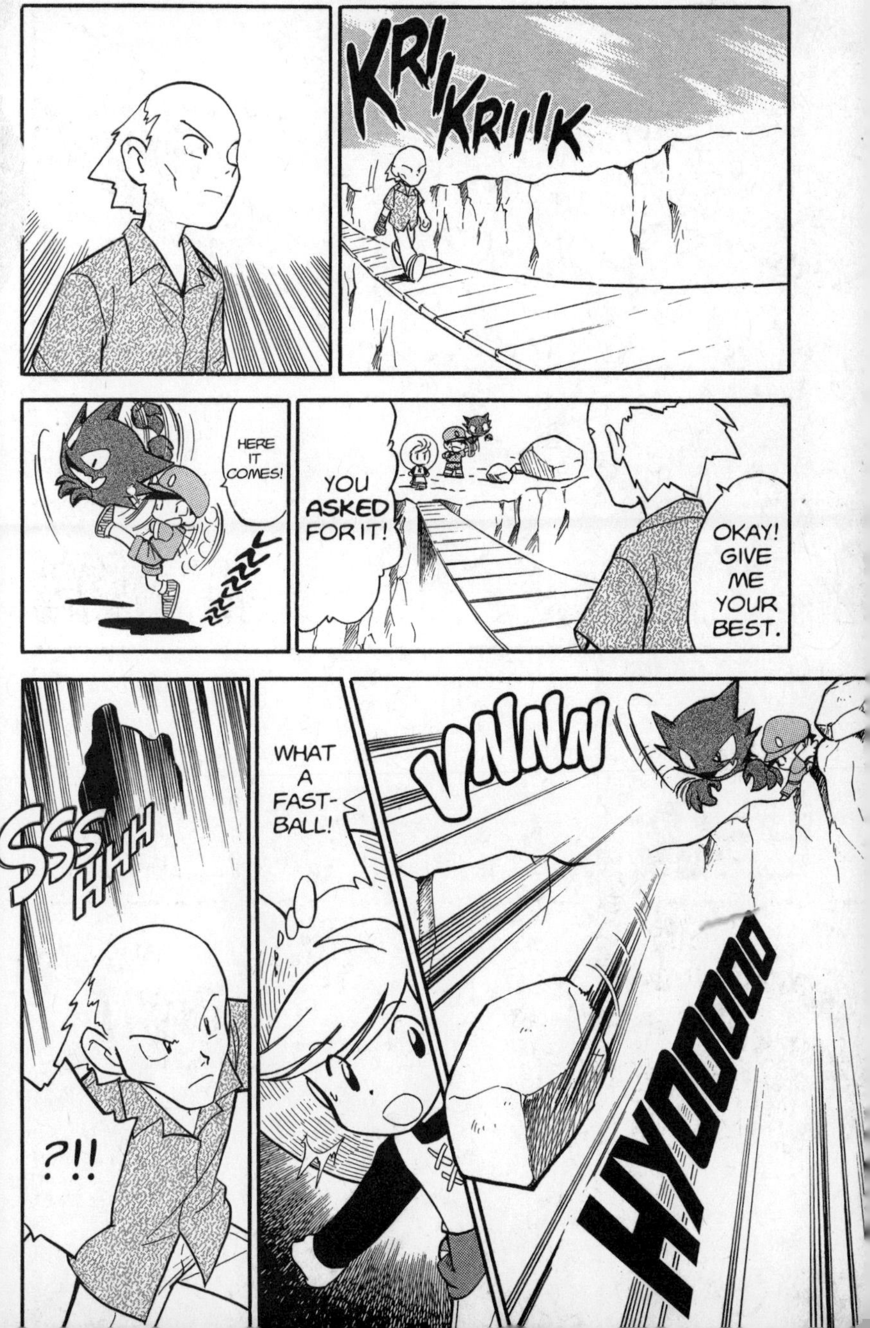
KRI KRIIIK
OKAY! GIVE ME YOUR BEST.
YOU ASKED FOR IT!
HERE IT COMES!
VNNN
WHAT A FAST-BALL!
HYOOOOO
SSSHHH
?!!

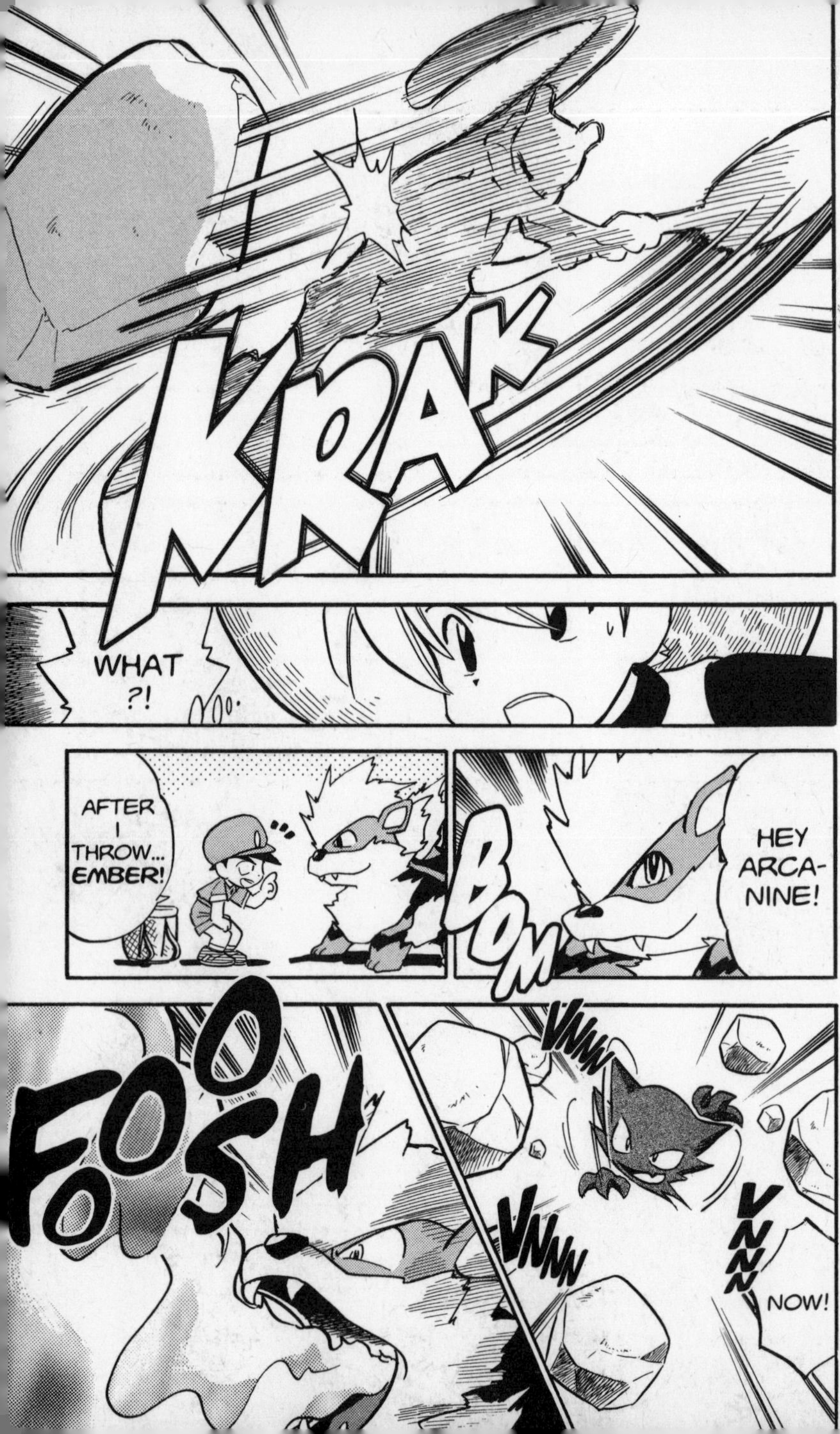
KRAK
WHAT ?!
HEY ARCA-
NINE!
BOM
AFTER I THROW... EMBER!
VNNN
VNNN
NOW!
VNNN
FOOOOSH

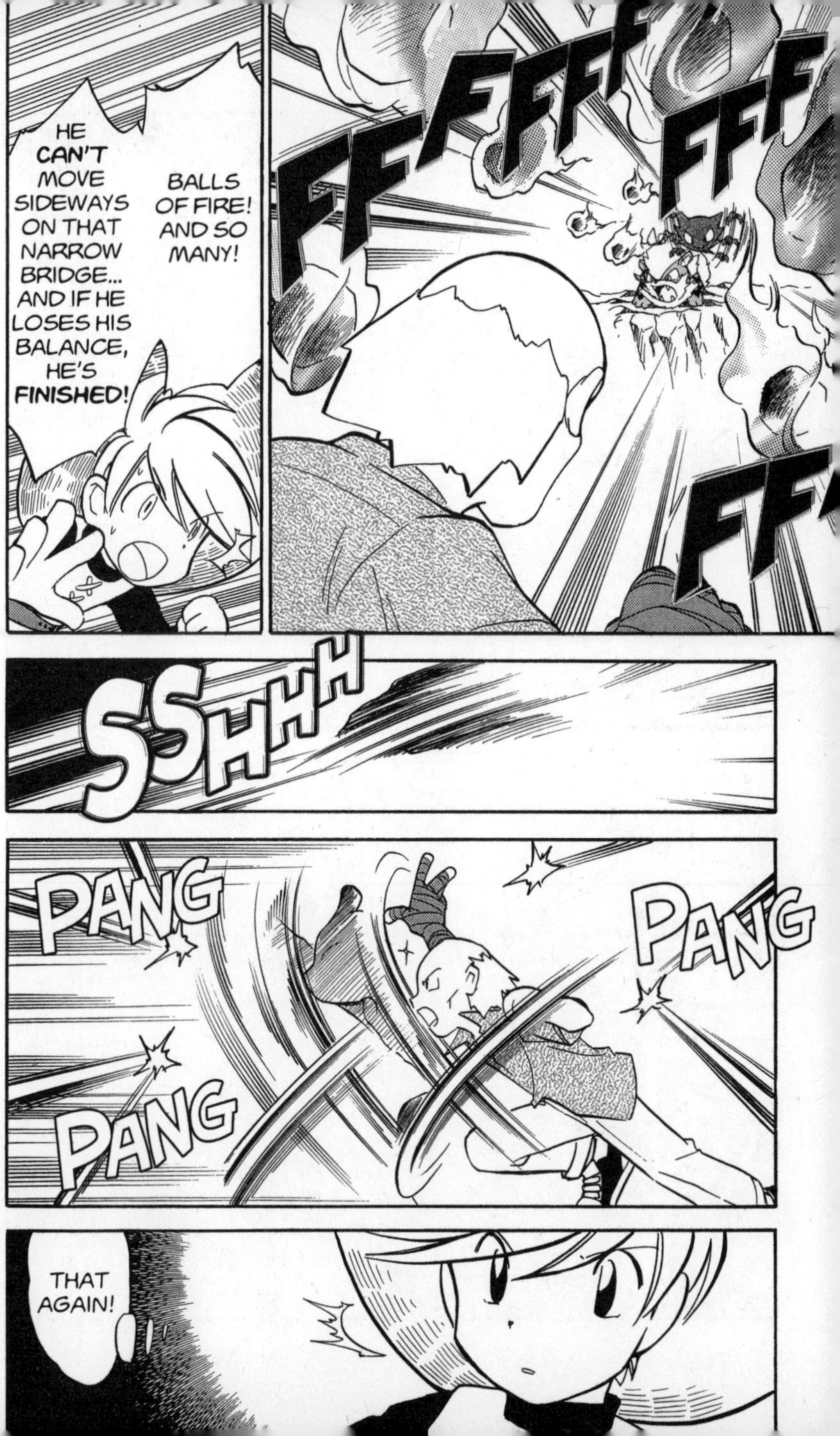
FFFFF
FFF
FF
BALLS OF FIRE! AND SO MANY!
HE CAN'T MOVE SIDEWAYS ON THAT NARROW BRIDGE... AND IF HE LOSES HIS BALANCE, HE'S FINISHED!
SSHHH
PANG
PANG
PANG
THAT AGAIN!

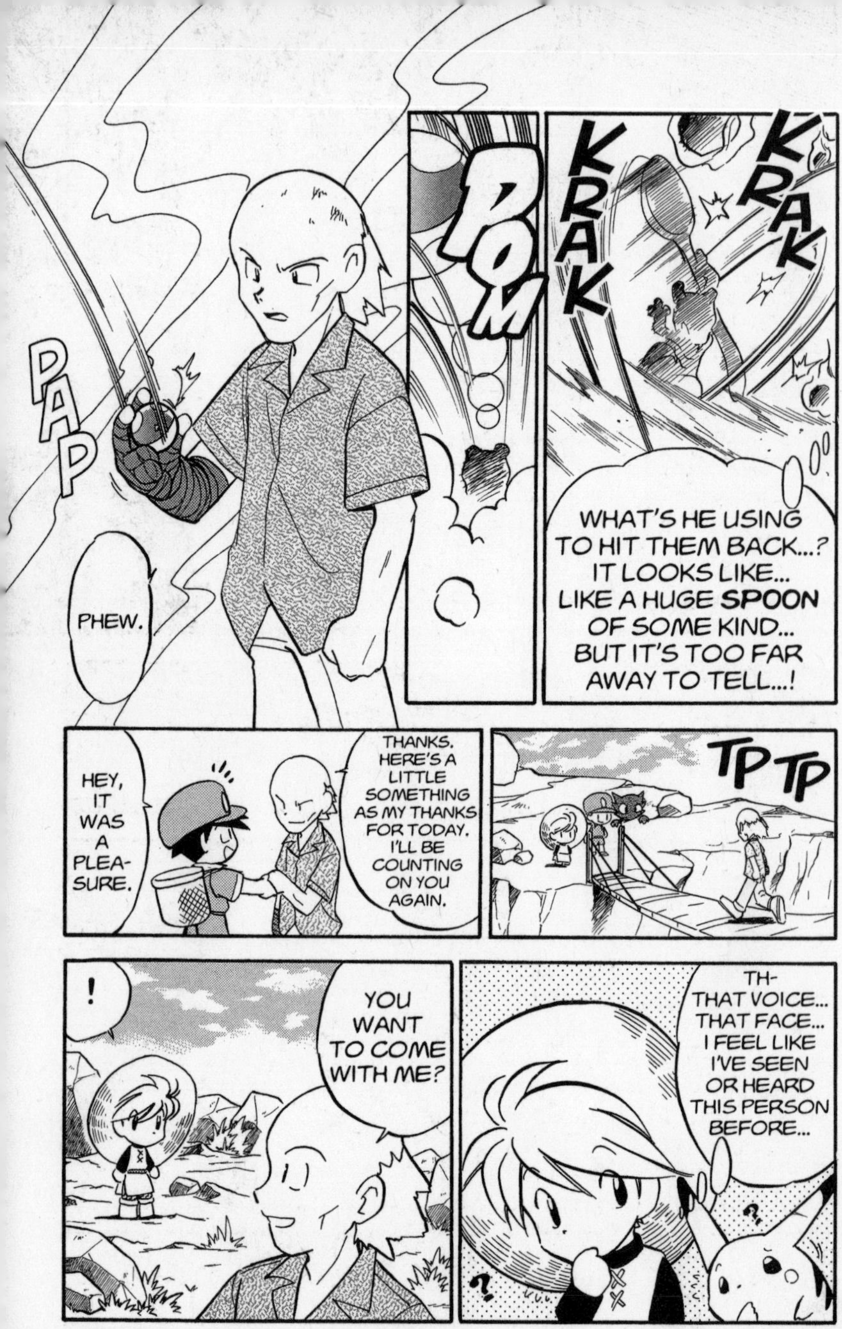
KRAK
KRAK
WHAT'S HE USING TO HIT THEM BACK...? IT LOOKS LIKE... LIKE A HUGE **SPOON** OF SOME KIND... BUT IT'S TOO FAR AWAY TO TELL...!
POM
PAP
PHEW.
TP TP
THANKS. HERE'S A LITTLE SOMETHING AS MY THANKS FOR TODAY. I'LL BE COUNTING ON YOU AGAIN.
HEY, IT WAS A PLEASURE.
TH- THAT VOICE... THAT FACE... I FEEL LIKE I'VE SEEN OR HEARD THIS PERSON BEFORE...
YOU WANT TO COME WITH ME?
!

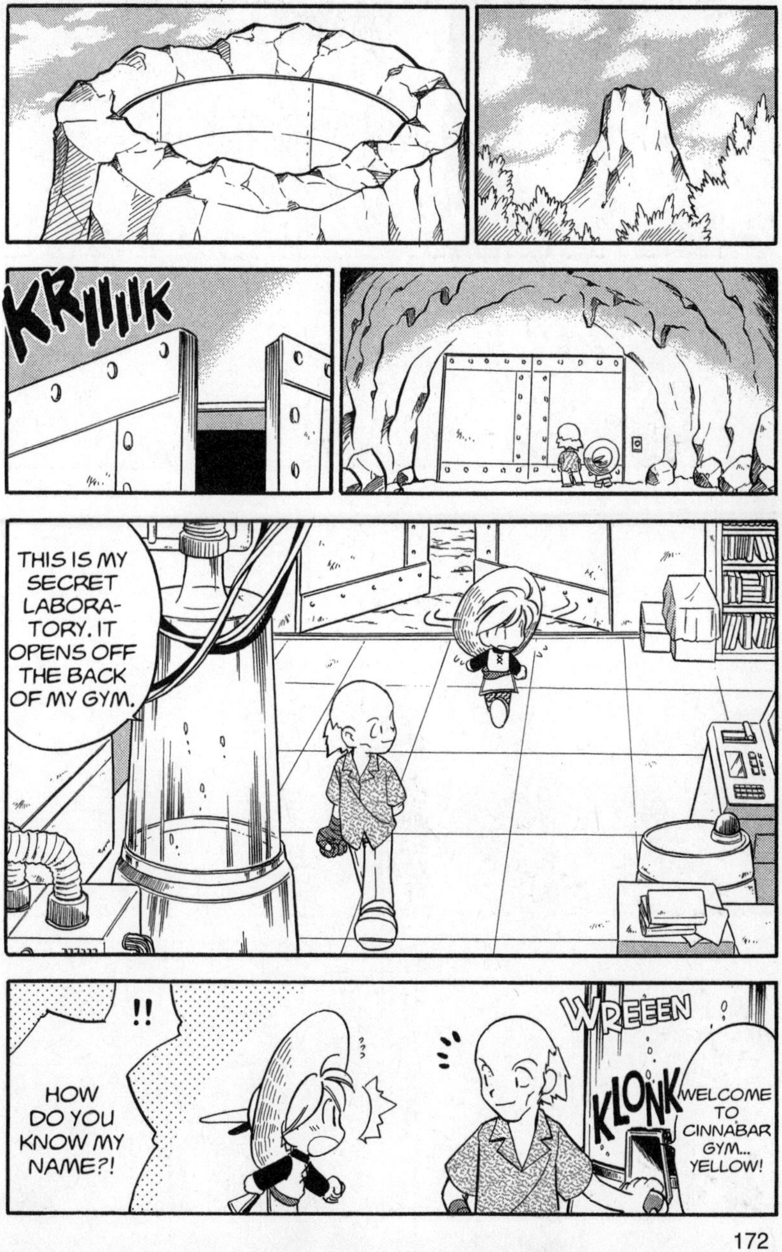
KRIIIIK
THIS IS MY SECRET LABORATORY. IT OPENS OFF THE BACK OF MY GYM.
WREEEN
KLONK
WELCOME TO CINNABAR GYM... YELLOW!
!!
HOW DO YOU KNOW MY NAME?!

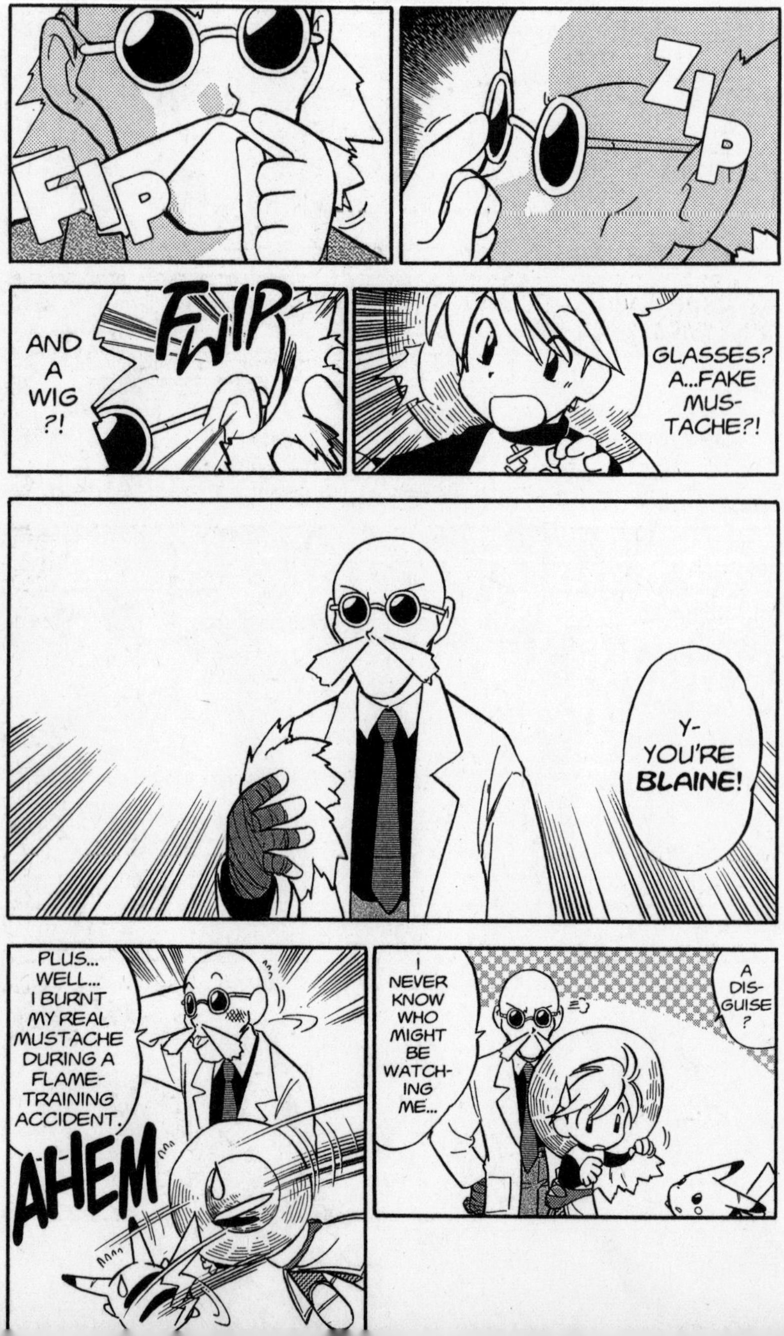
ZIP
FLIP
GLASSES? A...FAKE MUS-TACHE?!
FWIP
AND A WIG ?!
Y- YOU'RE BLAINE!
A DIS-GUISE ?
I NEVER KNOW WHO MIGHT BE WATCHING ME...
PLUS... WELL... I BURNT MY REAL MUSTACHE DURING A FLAME-TRAINING ACCIDENT.
AHEM

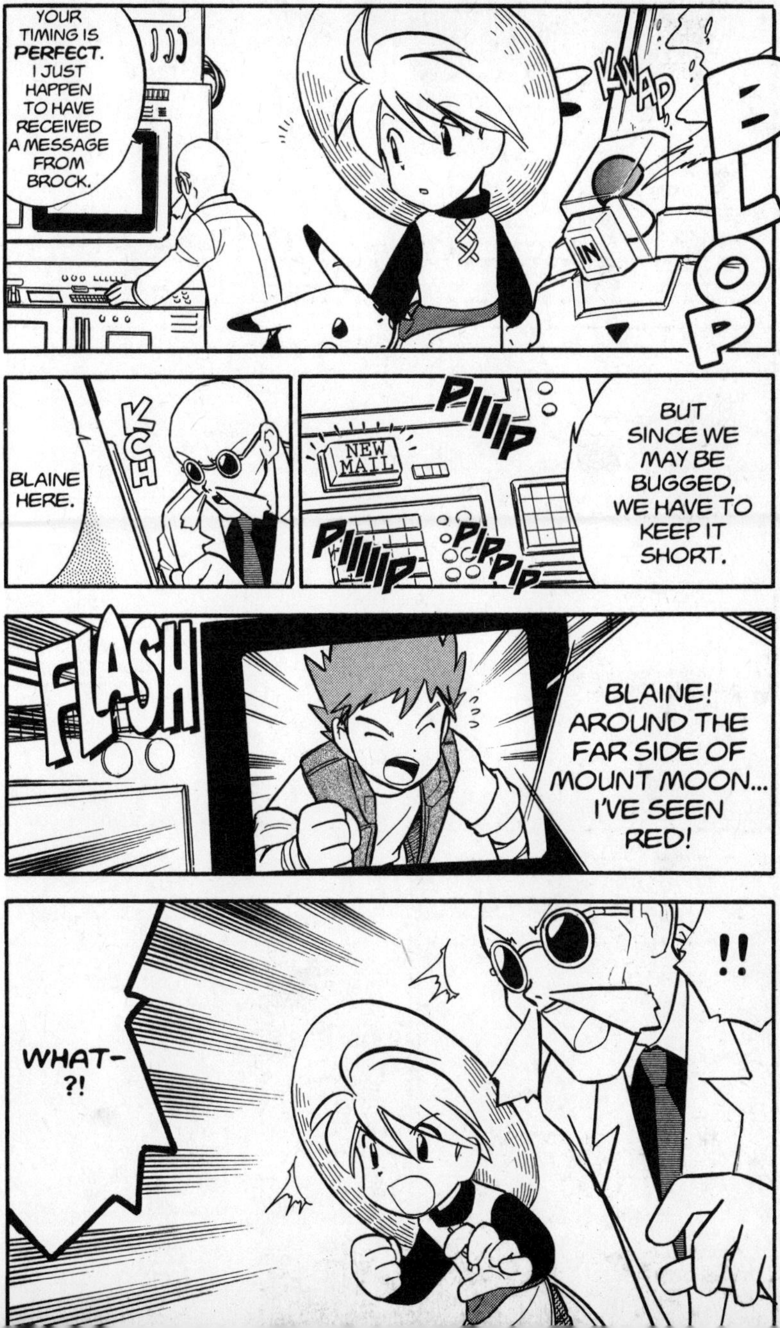
BLOOP
KWAP
IN
YOUR TIMING IS PERFECT. I JUST HAPPEN TO HAVE RECEIVED A MESSAGE FROM BROCK.
PIIIIP
BUT SINCE WE MAY BE BUGGED, WE HAVE TO KEEP IT SHORT.
NEW MAIL
PIIIIIP
PIP PIP
KCH
BLAINE HERE.
BLAINE! AROUND THE FAR SIDE OF MOUNT MOON... I'VE SEEN RED!
FLASH
!!
WHAT-?!

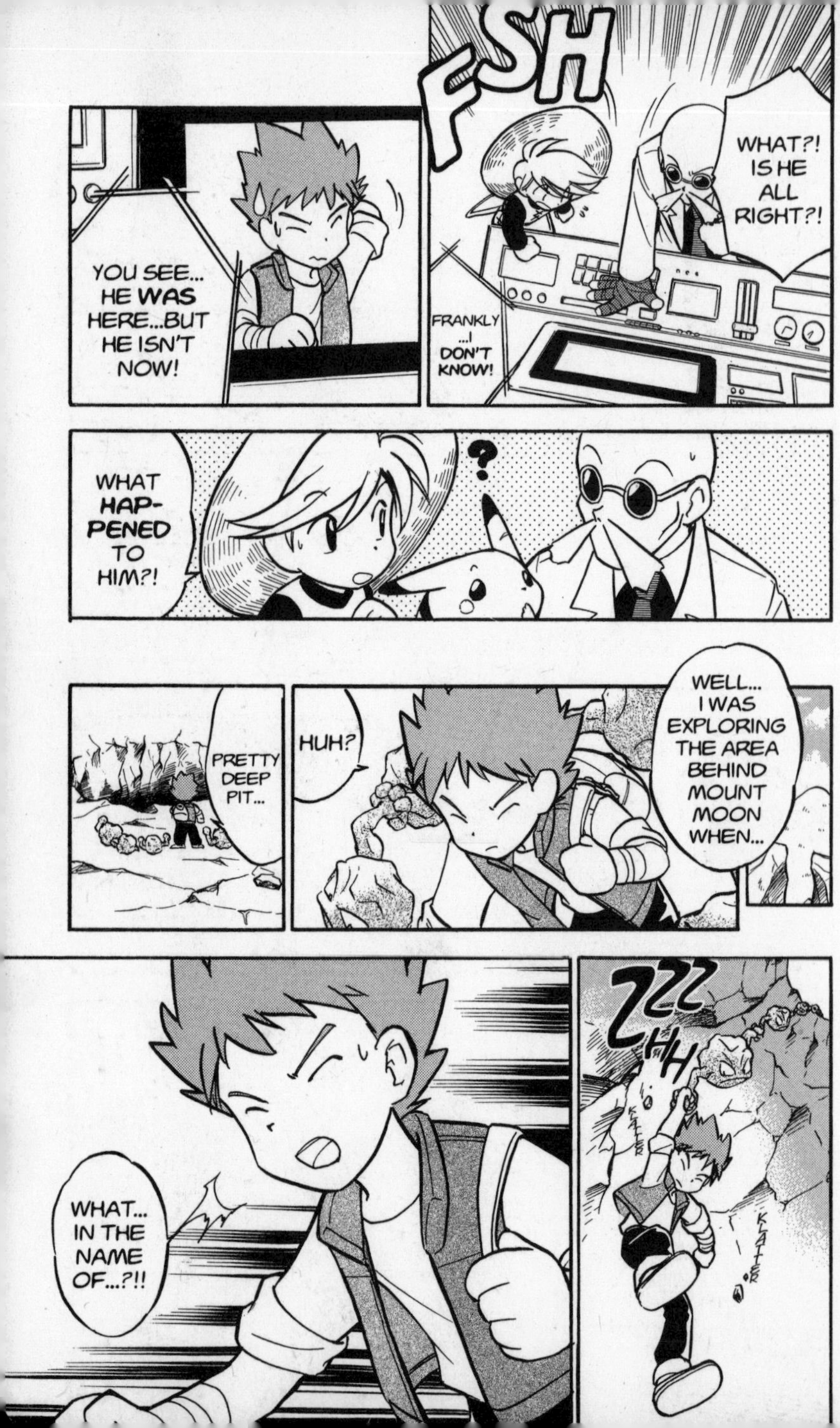
FSH
WHAT?! IS HE ALL RIGHT?!
FRANKLY ...I DON'T KNOW!
YOU SEE... HE WAS HERE...BUT HE ISN'T NOW!
WHAT HAPPENED TO HIM?!
WELL... I WAS EXPLORING THE AREA BEHIND MOUNT MOON WHEN...
HUH?
PRETTY DEEP PIT...
ZZZHH
KLATTER
KLATTER
WHAT... IN THE NAME OF...?!!

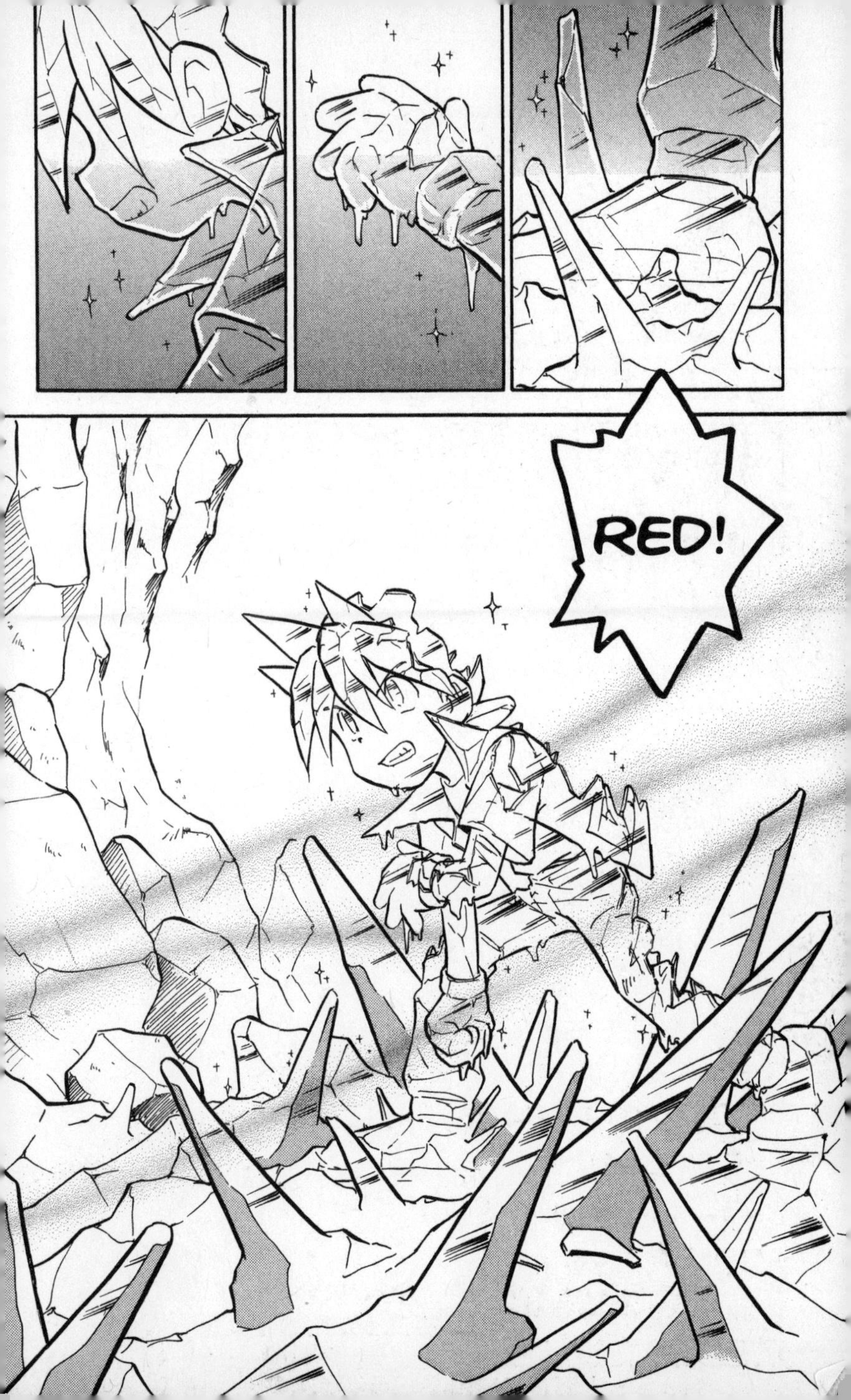
RED!

65 Karate Machop!

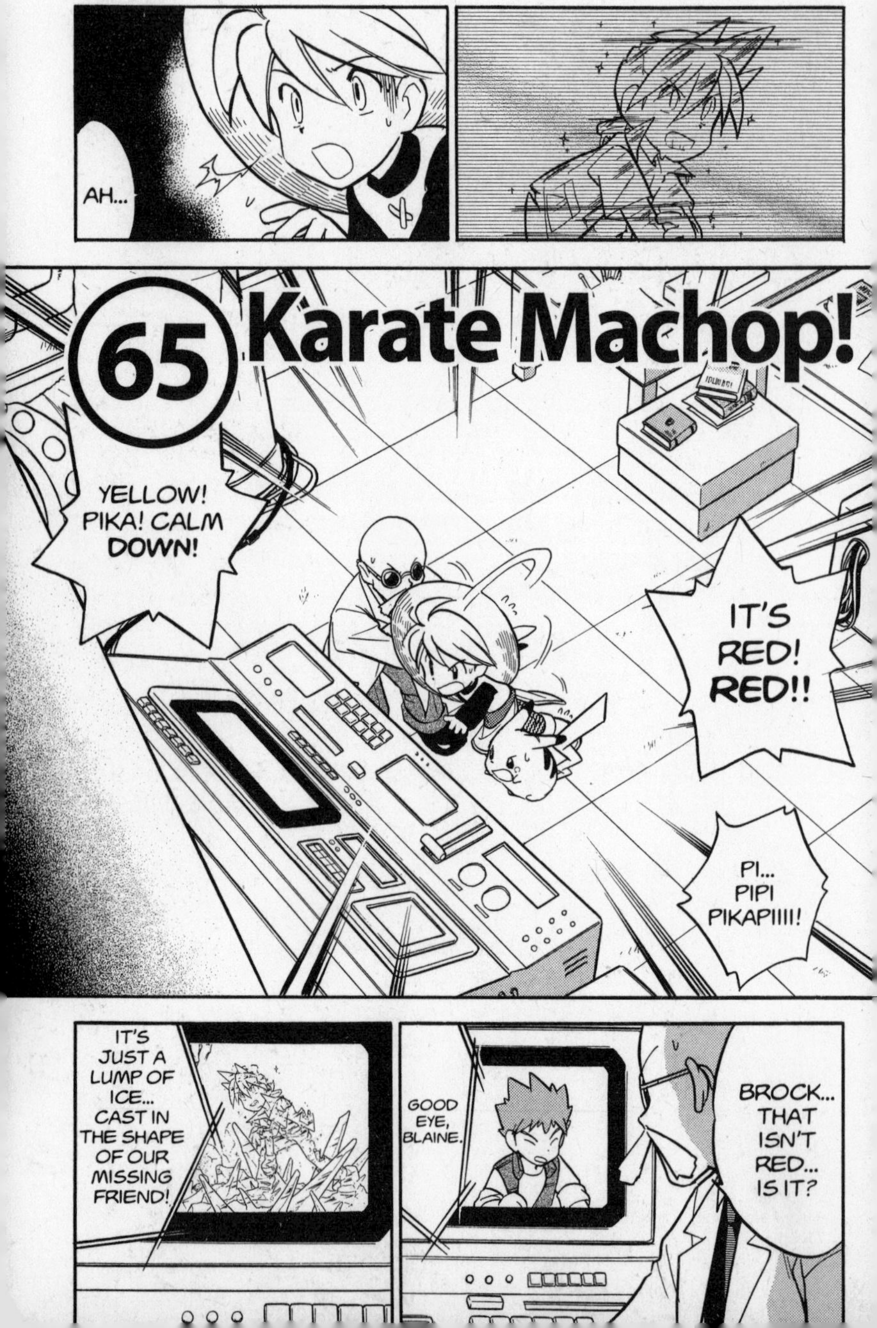
AH...
IT'S RED! RED!!
YELLOW! PIKA! CALM DOWN!
PI... PIPI PIKAPIIII!
BROCK... THAT ISN'T RED... IS IT?
GOOD EYE, BLAINE.
IT'S JUST A LUMP OF ICE... CAST IN THE SHAPE OF OUR MISSING FRIEND!

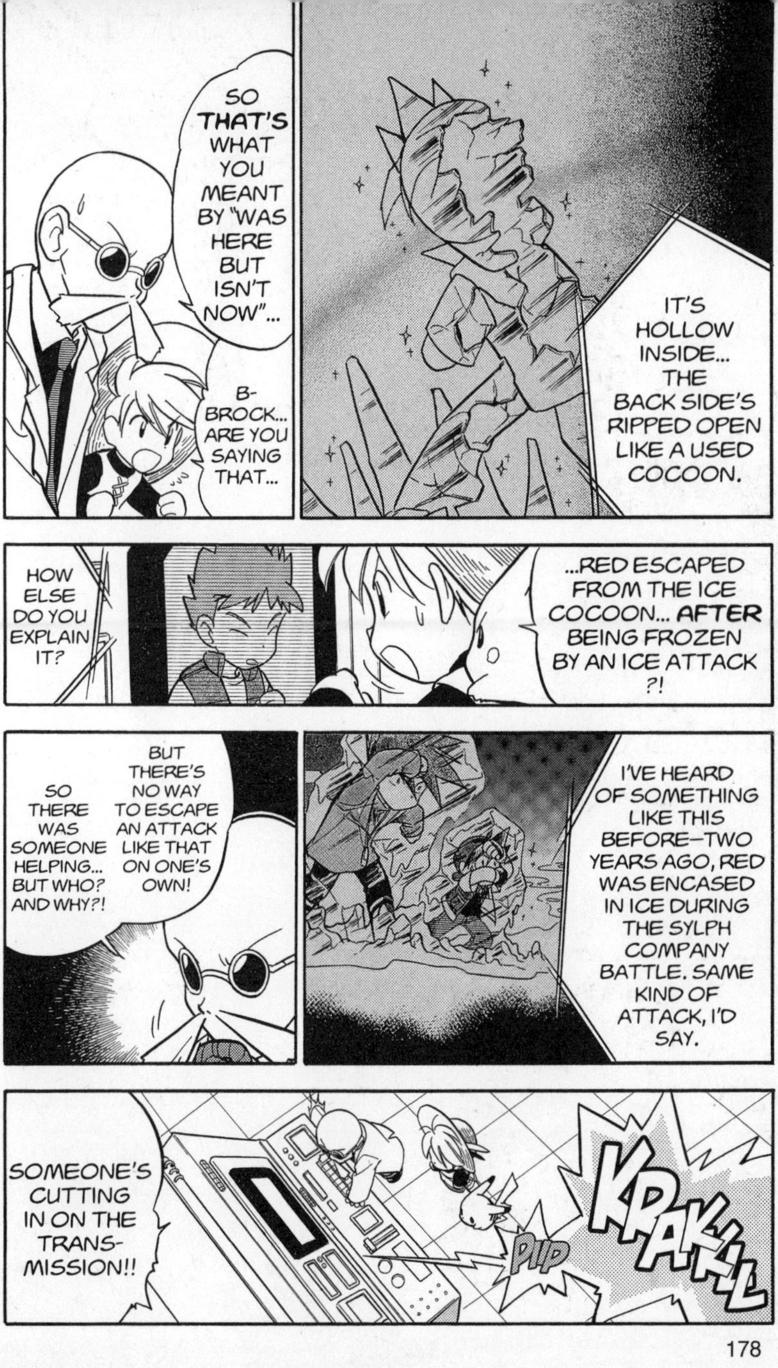
IT'S HOLLOW INSIDE... THE BACK SIDE'S RIPPED OPEN LIKE A USED COCOON.
SO **THAT'S** WHAT YOU MEANT BY "WAS HERE BUT ISN'T NOW"...
B-BROCK... ARE YOU SAYING THAT...
...RED ESCAPED FROM THE ICE COCOON... **AFTER** BEING FROZEN BY AN ICE ATTACK ?!
HOW ELSE DO YOU EXPLAIN IT?
I'VE HEARD OF SOMETHING LIKE THIS BEFORE—TWO YEARS AGO, RED WAS ENCASED IN ICE DURING THE SYLPH COMPANY BATTLE. SAME KIND OF ATTACK, I'D SAY.
BUT THERE'S NO WAY TO ESCAPE AN ATTACK LIKE THAT ON ONE'S OWN!
SO THERE WAS SOMEONE HELPING... BUT WHO? AND WHY?!
PIP
SOMEONE'S CUTTING IN ON THE TRANS-MISSION!!

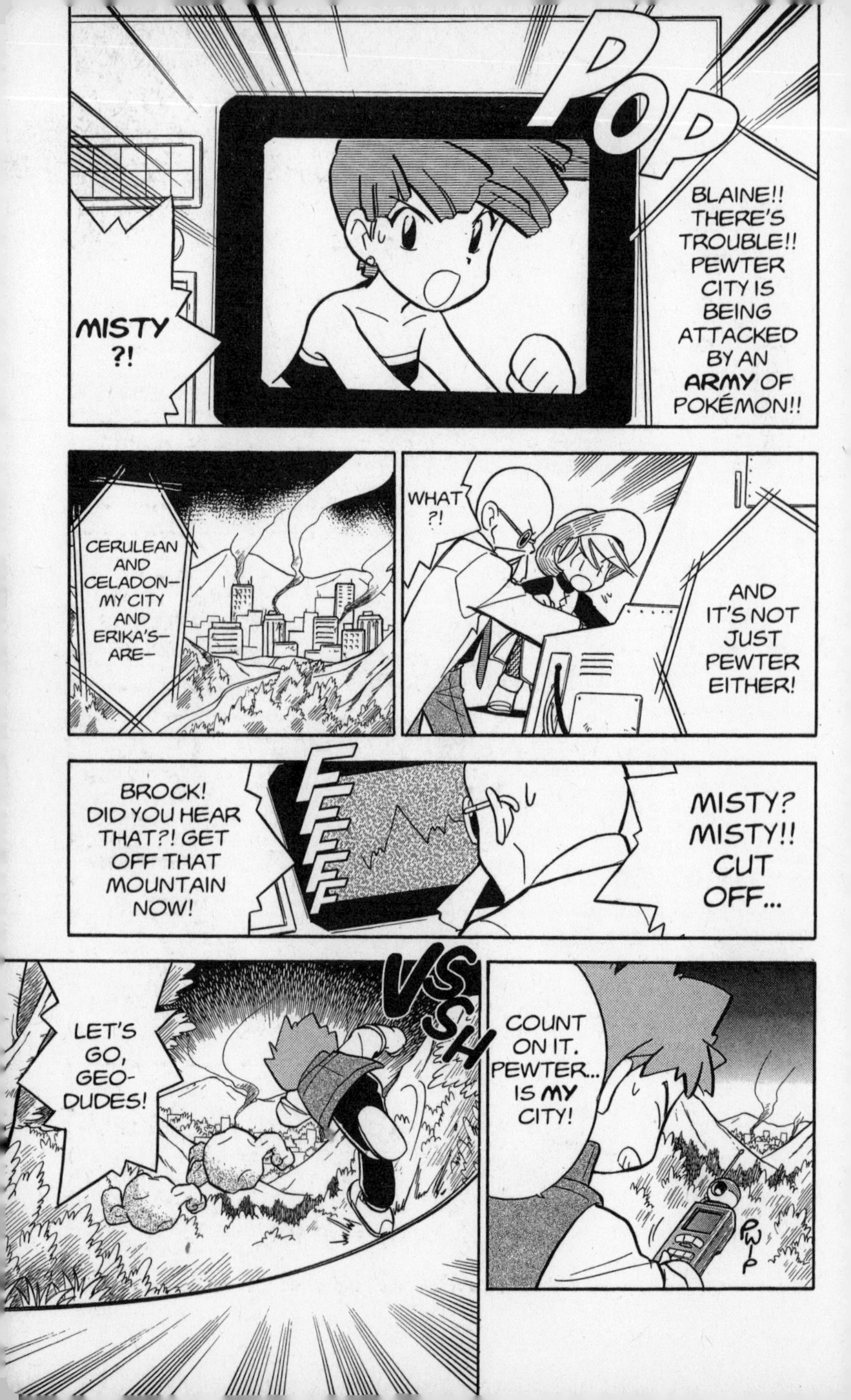
POP
BLAINE!! THERE'S TROUBLE!! PEWTER CITY IS BEING ATTACKED BY AN **ARMY** OF POKÉMON!!
MISTY ?!
WHAT ?!
AND IT'S NOT JUST PEWTER EITHER!
CERULEAN AND CELADON— MY CITY AND ERIKA'S— ARE—
MISTY? MISTY!! CUT OFF...
FFFFF
BROCK! DID YOU HEAR THAT?! GET OFF THAT MOUNTAIN NOW!
COUNT ON IT. PEWTER... IS **MY** CITY!
PWIP
VSSH
LET'S GO, GEO-DUDES!

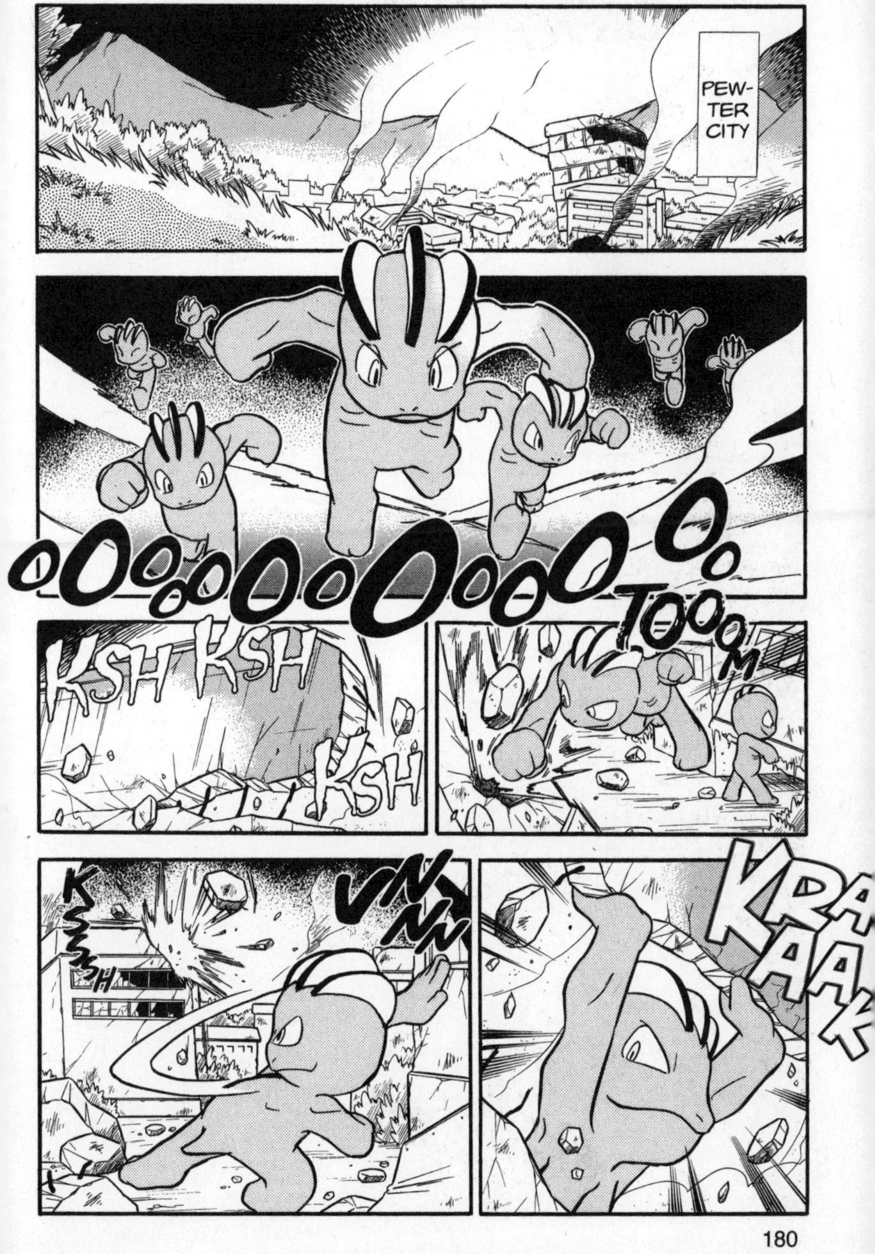
PEW-
TER
CITY
OOOOOOOOOOOOOOO
TOOOM
KSH KSH
KSH
KRAAAK
VNNN
KSSSSH

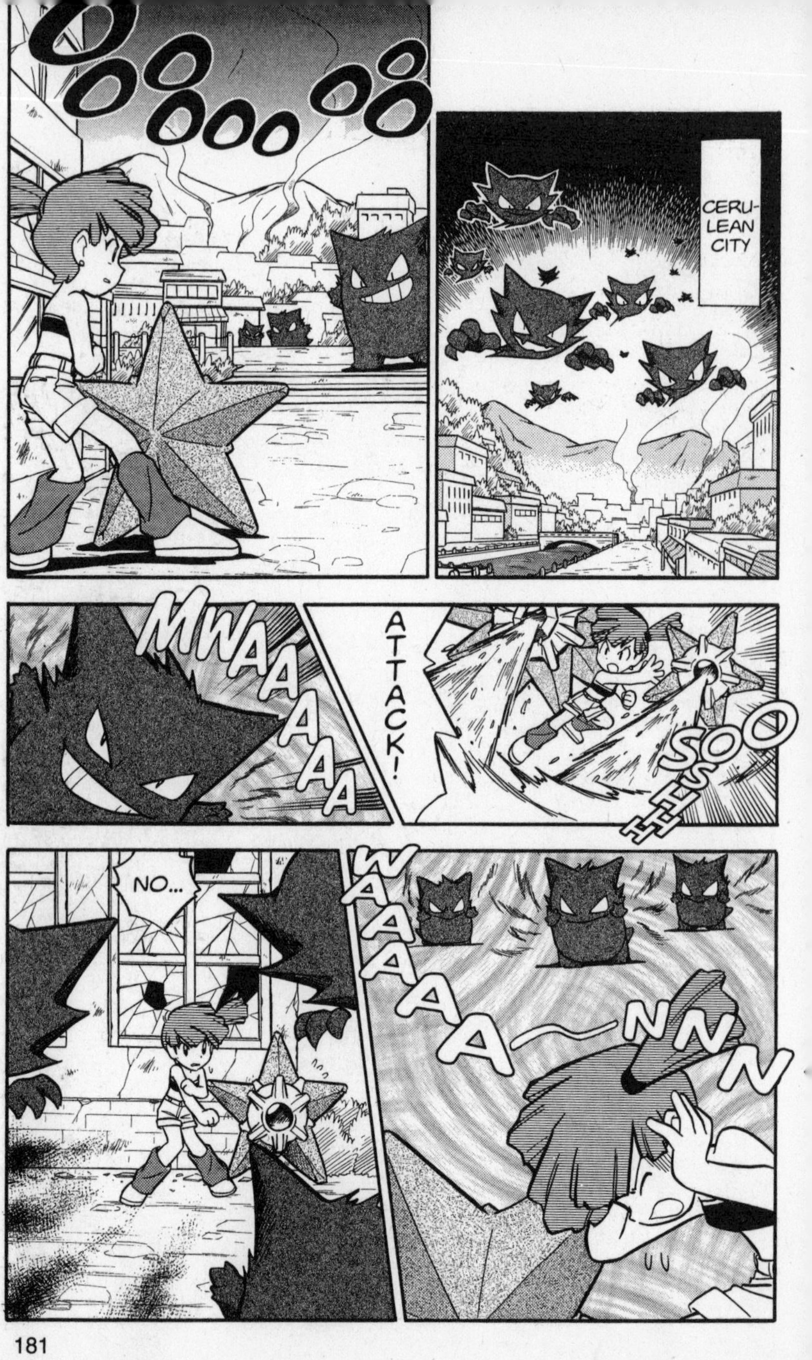
CERU-
LEAN
CITY
OOOOOOOOO
ATTACK!
SOOSHHH
MWAAAAAA
WAAAAAA—NNNN
NO...

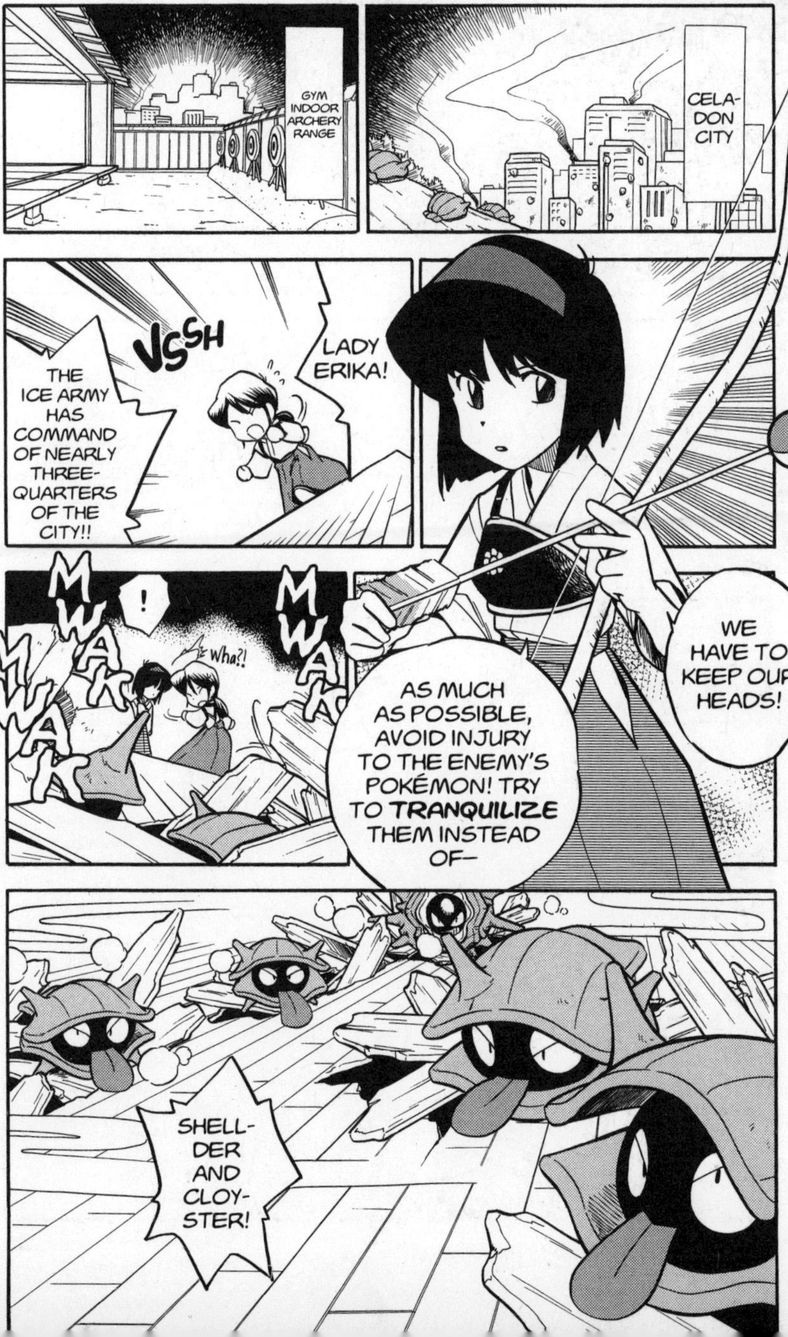
CELADON CITY
GYM INDOOR ARCHERY RANGE
LADY ERIKA!
VSSH
THE ICE ARMY HAS COMMAND OF NEARLY THREE-QUARTERS OF THE CITY!!
WE HAVE TO KEEP OUR HEADS!
AS MUCH AS POSSIBLE, AVOID INJURY TO THE ENEMY'S POKÉMON! TRY TO **TRANQUILIZE** THEM INSTEAD OF—
MWAK
!
Wha?!
MWAK
MWAK
SHELLDER AND CLOYSTER!

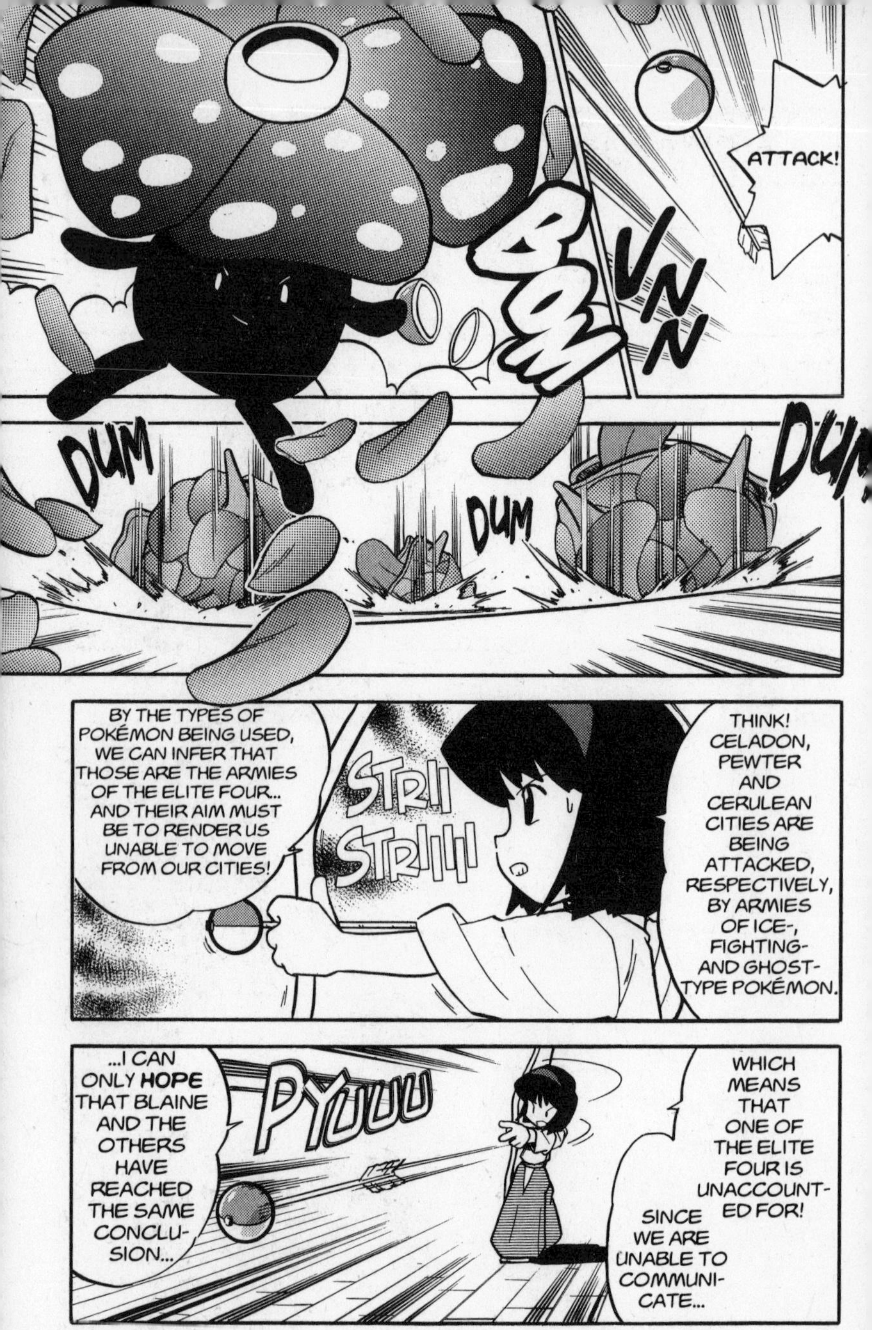
ATTACK!
VNN
BOM
DUM
DUM
DUM
THINK! CELADON, PEWTER AND CERULEAN CITIES ARE BEING ATTACKED, RESPECTIVELY, BY ARMIES OF ICE-, FIGHTING- AND GHOST-TYPE POKÉMON.
STRII STRIIII
BY THE TYPES OF POKÉMON BEING USED, WE CAN INFER THAT THOSE ARE THE ARMIES OF THE ELITE FOUR... AND THEIR AIM MUST BE TO RENDER US UNABLE TO MOVE FROM OUR CITIES!
WHICH MEANS THAT ONE OF THE ELITE FOUR IS UNACCOUNTED FOR!
SINCE WE ARE UNABLE TO COMMUNICATE...
PYUUU
...I CAN ONLY **HOPE** THAT BLAINE AND THE OTHERS HAVE REACHED THE SAME CONCLUSION...

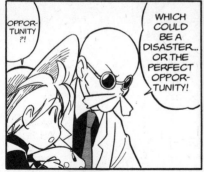

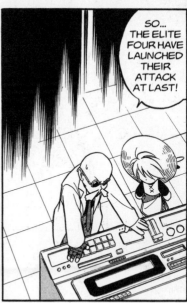

SO... THE ELITE FOUR HAVE LAUNCHED THEIR ATTACK AT LAST!
WHICH COULD BE A DISASTER... OR THE PERFECT OPPORTUNITY!
OPPORTUNITY ?!
THROUGH MY INVESTIGATIONS, I'VE PINPOINTED THE LOCATION OF THE ELITE FOUR HEADQUARTERS—THERE!
FWAP
AN ISLAND ...
CERISE ISLAND
BUT NOT AN ISLAND ON ANY MAP! I'M WAGERING THAT THE ELITE FOUR ARE EXPECTING ME TO GO TO THE AID OF MISTY AND THE OTHERS.
BUT WE CAN GO BEHIND THEIR BACKS AND ATTACK THE ISLAND NOW—YOU AND ME!
WHAT ?!
YOU... AND ME. THE TWO OF US.
TUG TUG
PIKA!

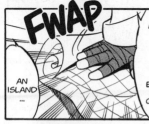

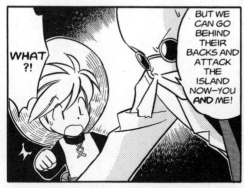

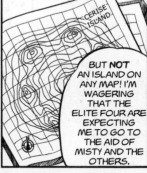

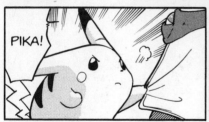

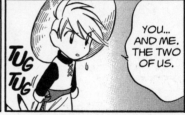

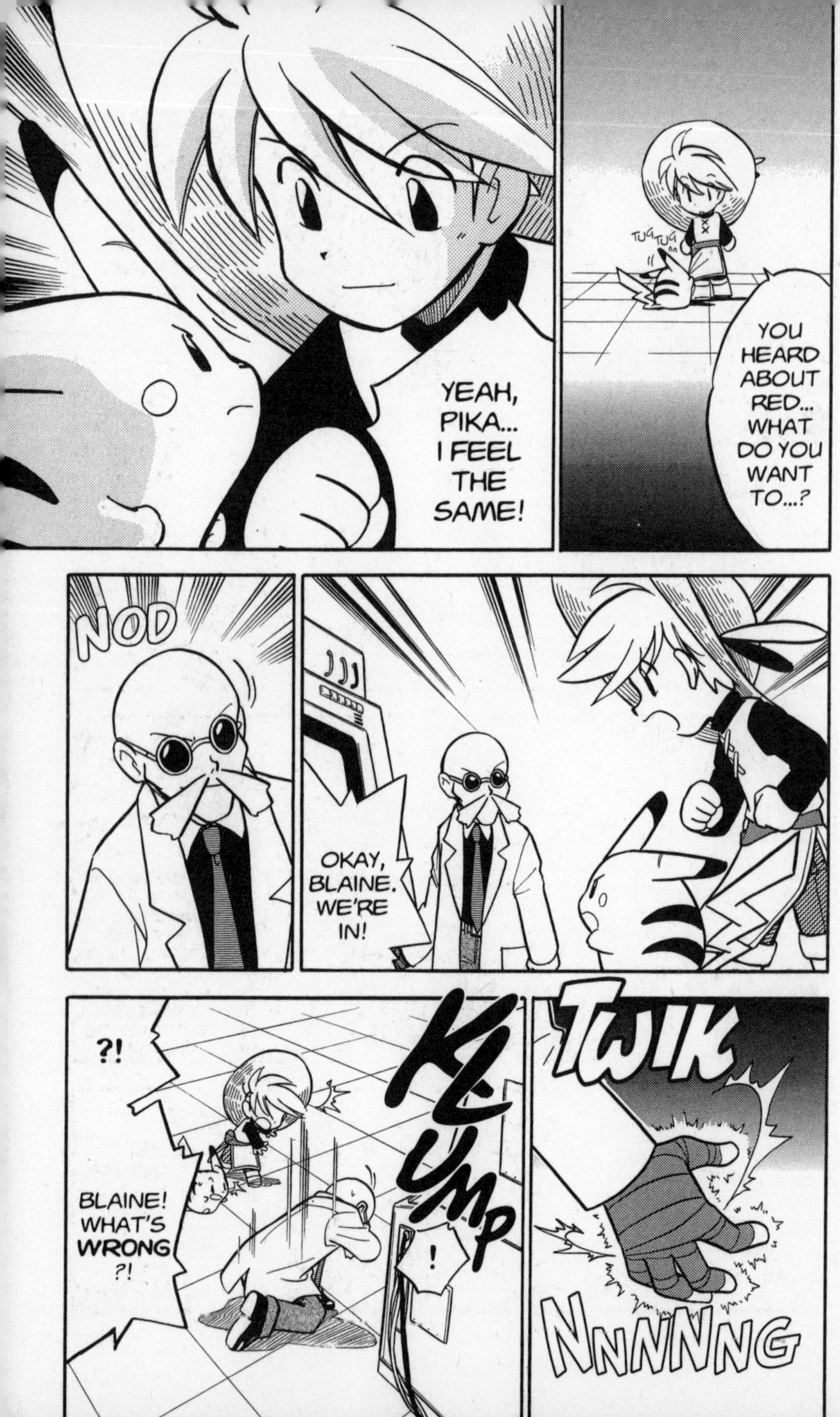
TUG TUG
YOU HEARD ABOUT RED... WHAT DO YOU WANT TO...?
YEAH, PIKA... I FEEL THE SAME!
OKAY, BLAINE. WE'RE IN!
NOD
TWIK
NNNNNG
KLUMP
!
?!
BLAINE! WHAT'S WRONG?!

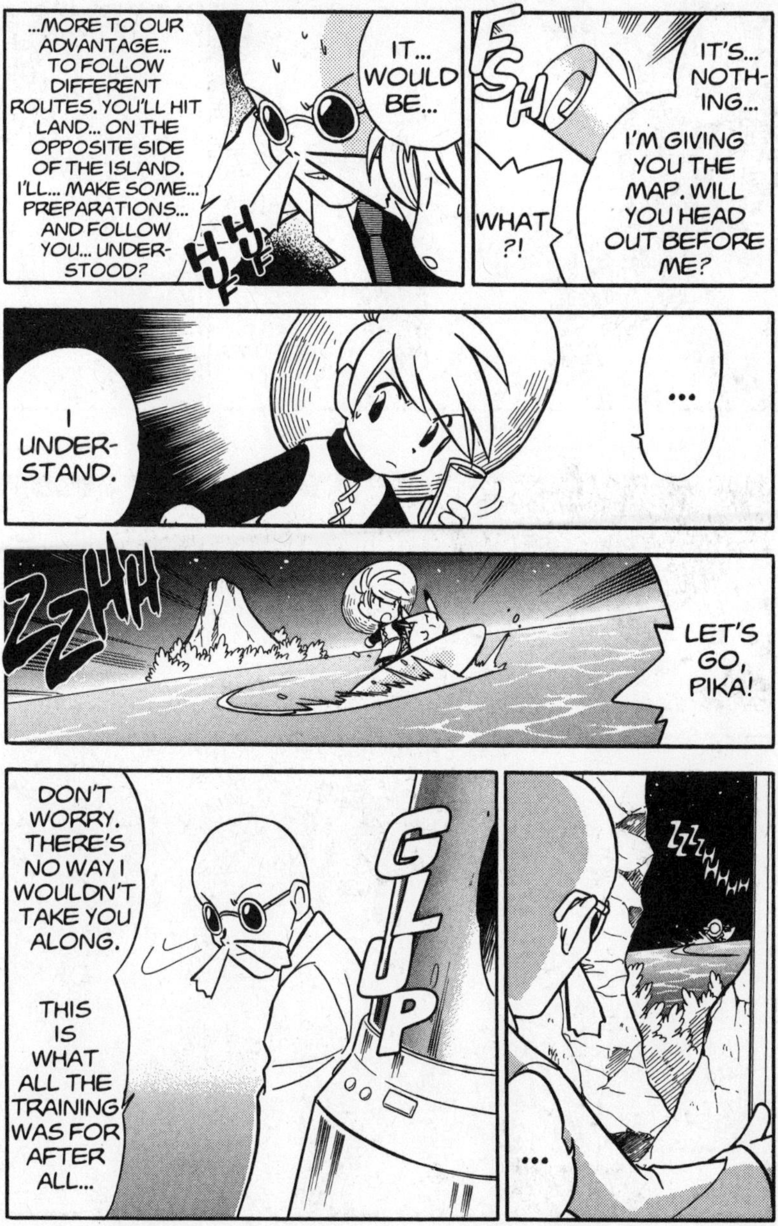
IT'S... NOTHING...
FSHO
I'M GIVING YOU THE MAP. WILL YOU HEAD OUT BEFORE ME?
WHAT?!
IT... WOULD BE...
...MORE TO OUR ADVANTAGE... TO FOLLOW DIFFERENT ROUTES. YOU'LL HIT LAND... ON THE OPPOSITE SIDE OF THE ISLAND. I'LL... MAKE SOME... PREPARATIONS... AND FOLLOW YOU... UNDERSTOOD?
HUFF HUFF
...
I UNDERSTAND.
LET'S GO, PIKA!
ZZHH
ZZZZHHHHH
...
GLUP
DON'T WORRY. THERE'S NO WAY I WOULDN'T TAKE YOU ALONG.
THIS IS WHAT ALL THE TRAINING WAS FOR AFTER ALL...

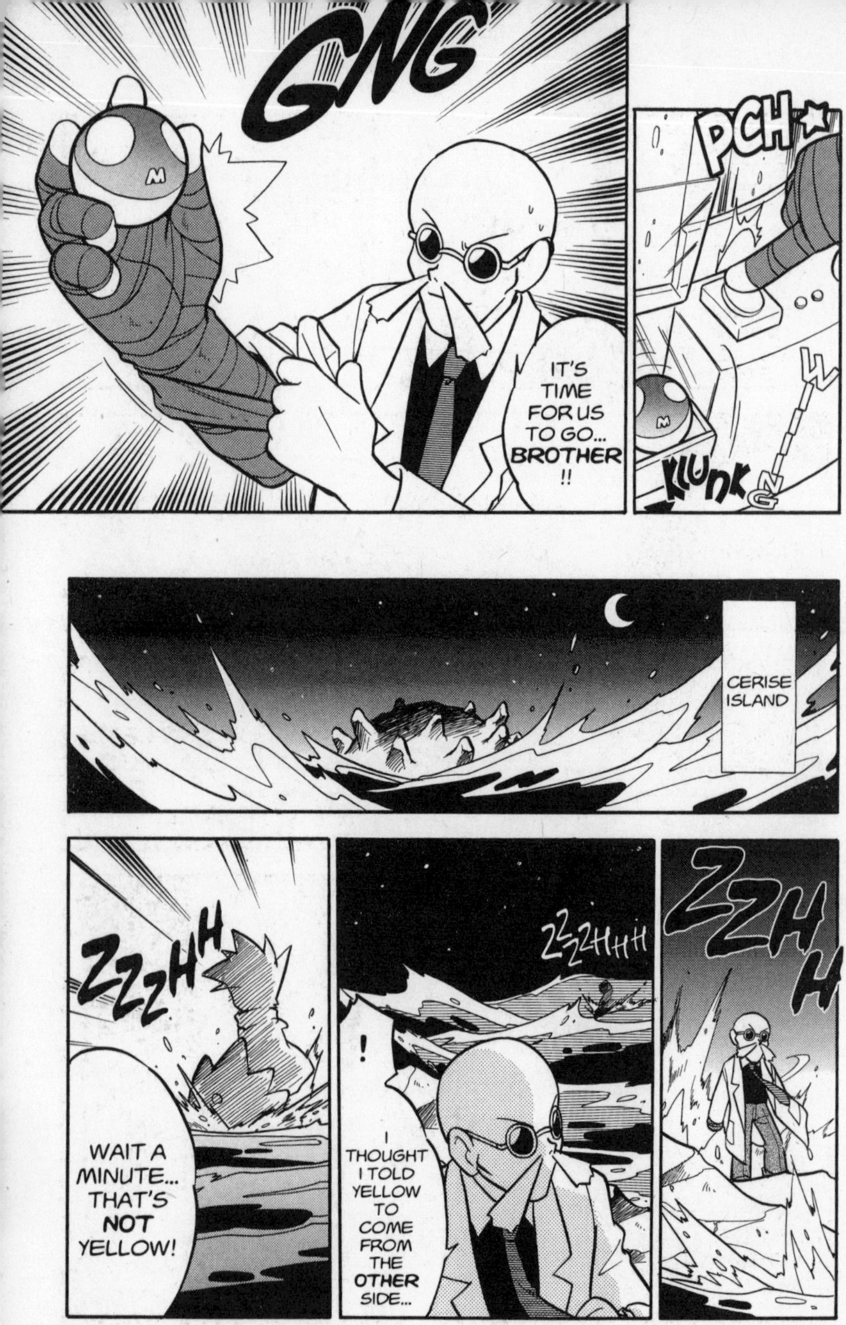
PCH
KLUNK
GNG
GNG
IT'S TIME FOR US TO GO... BROTHER!!
CERISE ISLAND
ZZHHH
ZZZHHHH
!
I THOUGHT I TOLD YELLOW TO COME FROM THE OTHER SIDE...
ZZZHHH
WAIT A MINUTE... THAT'S NOT YELLOW!

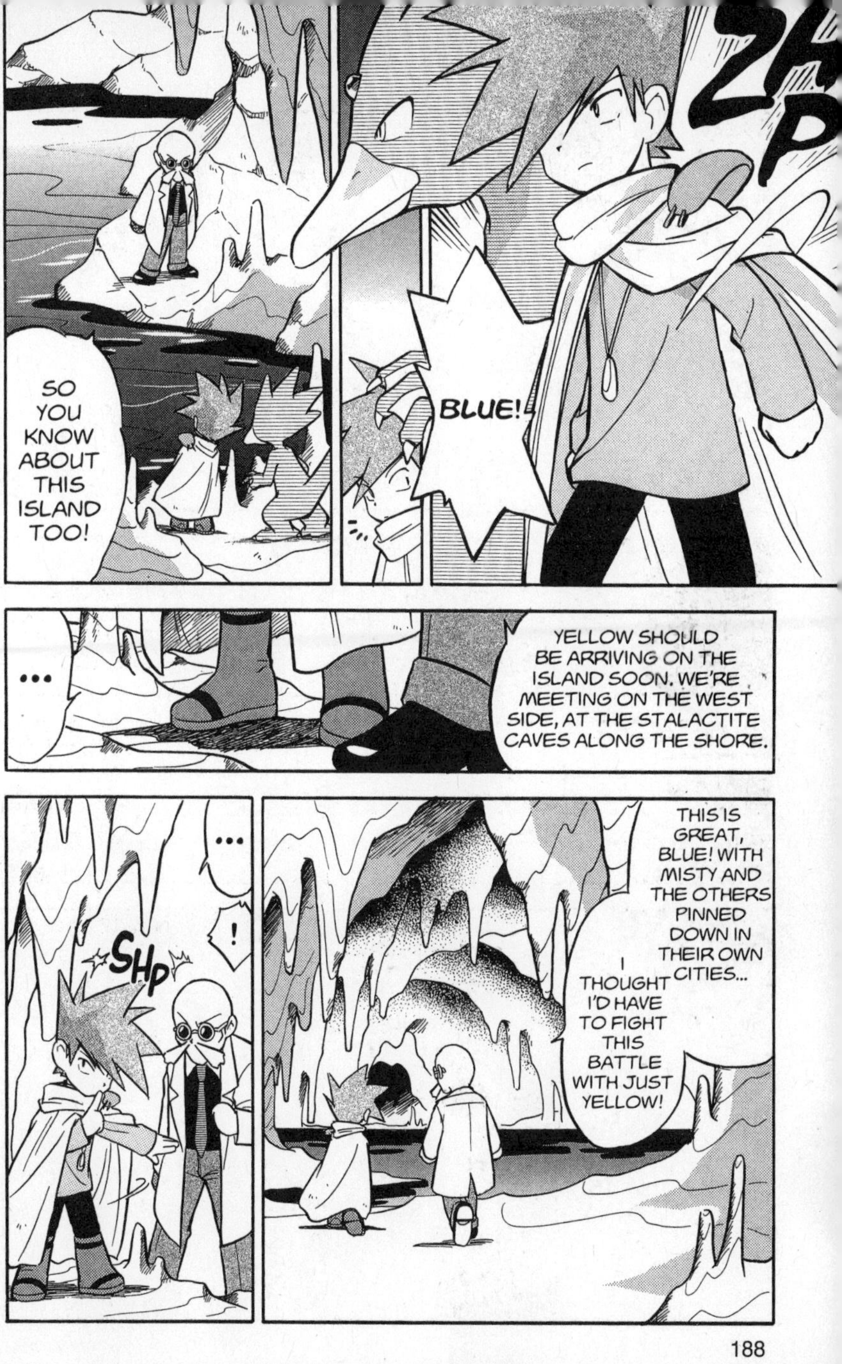
BLUE!
SO YOU KNOW ABOUT THIS ISLAND TOO!
YELLOW SHOULD BE ARRIVING ON THE ISLAND SOON. WE'RE MEETING ON THE WEST SIDE, AT THE STALACTITE CAVES ALONG THE SHORE.
...
THIS IS GREAT, BLUE! WITH MISTY AND THE OTHERS PINNED DOWN IN THEIR OWN CITIES...
I THOUGHT I'D HAVE TO FIGHT THIS BATTLE WITH JUST YELLOW!
...
!
SHP

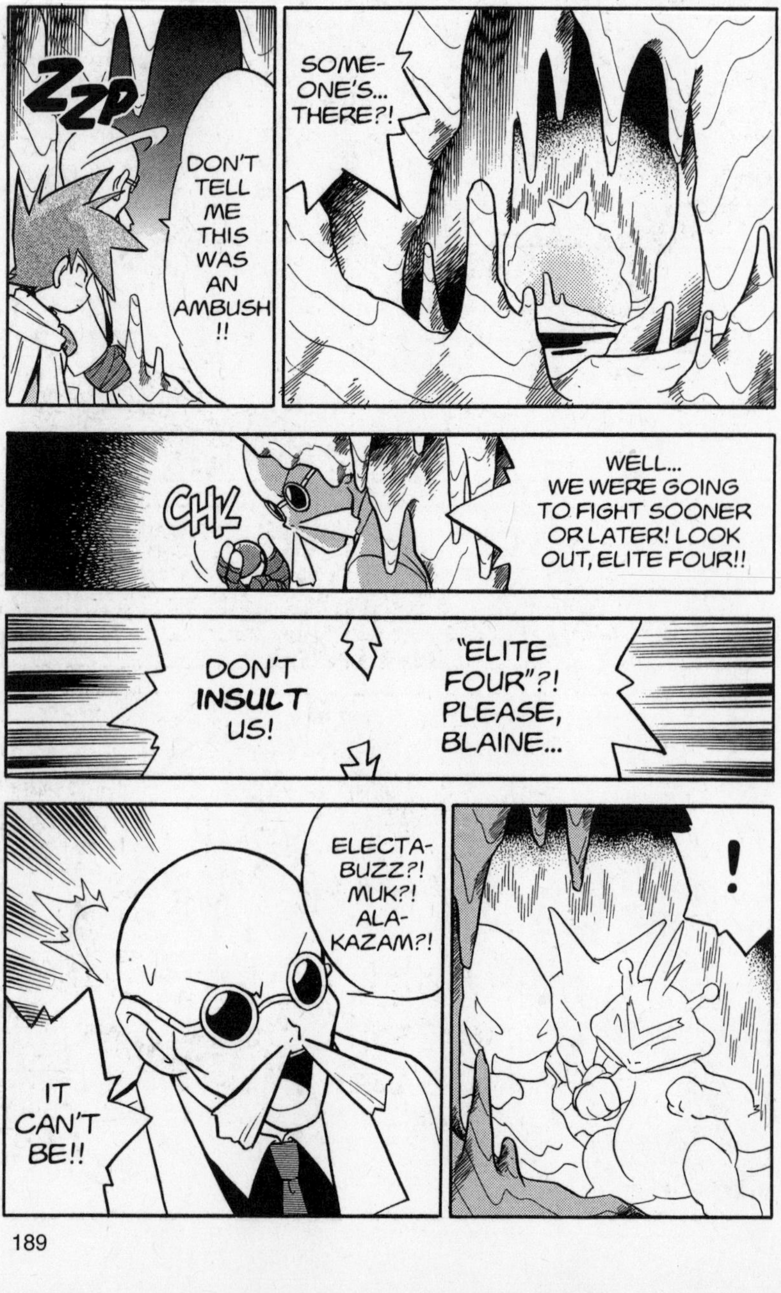
SOME-ONE'S... THERE?!
ZZP
DON'T TELL ME THIS WAS AN AMBUSH !!
WELL... WE WERE GOING TO FIGHT SOONER OR LATER! LOOK OUT, ELITE FOUR!!
CHK
"ELITE FOUR"?! PLEASE, BLAINE...
DON'T **INSULT** US!
!
ELECTA-BUZZ?! MUK?! ALA-KAZAM?!
IT CAN'T BE!!

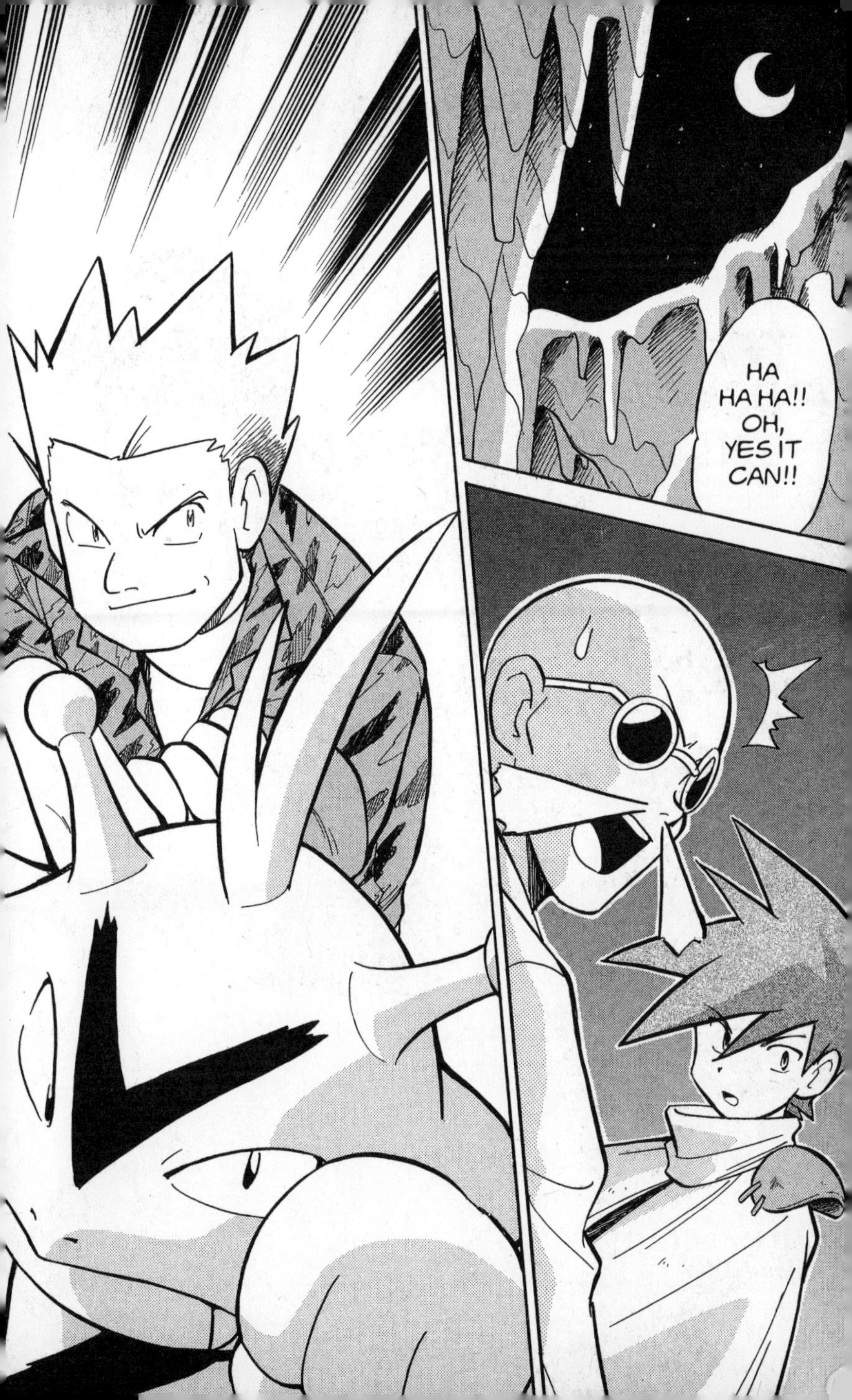
HA HA HA!! OH, YES IT CAN!!

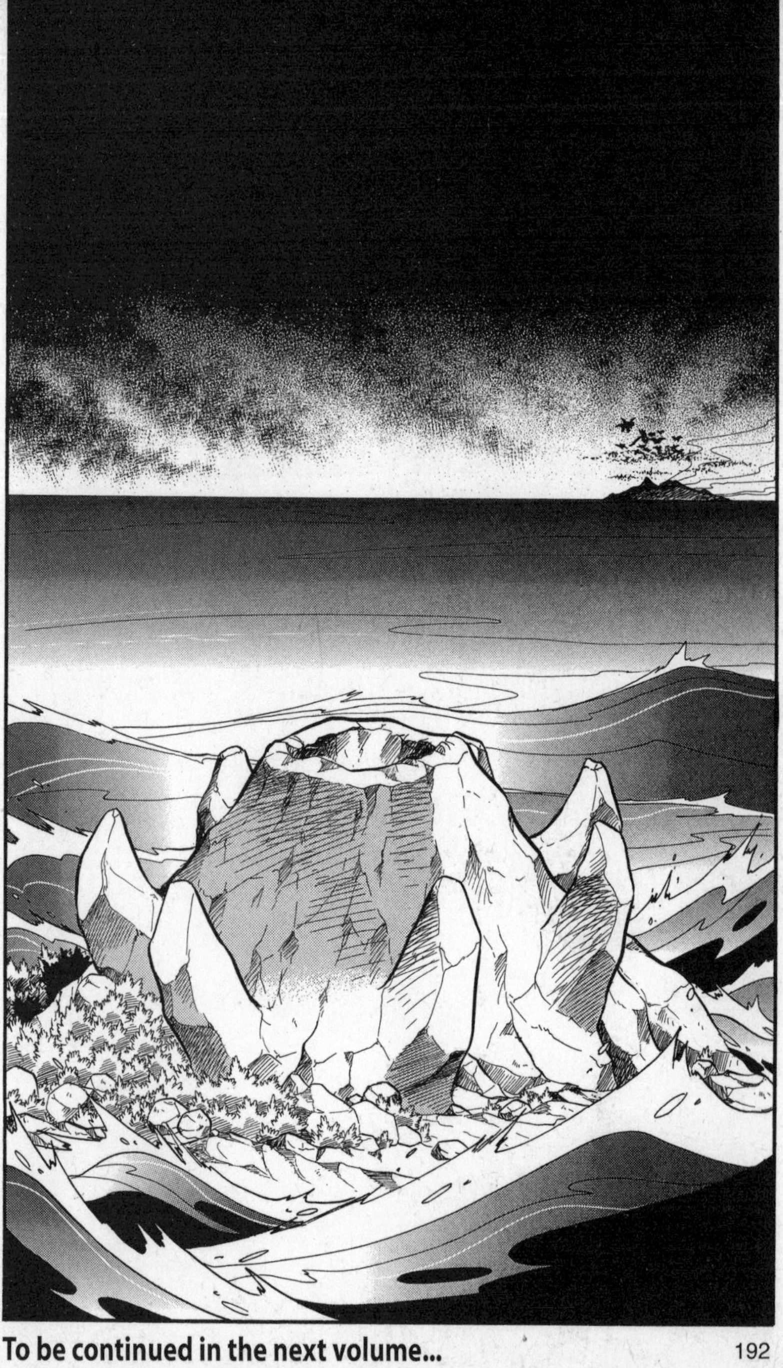

To be continued in the next volume...

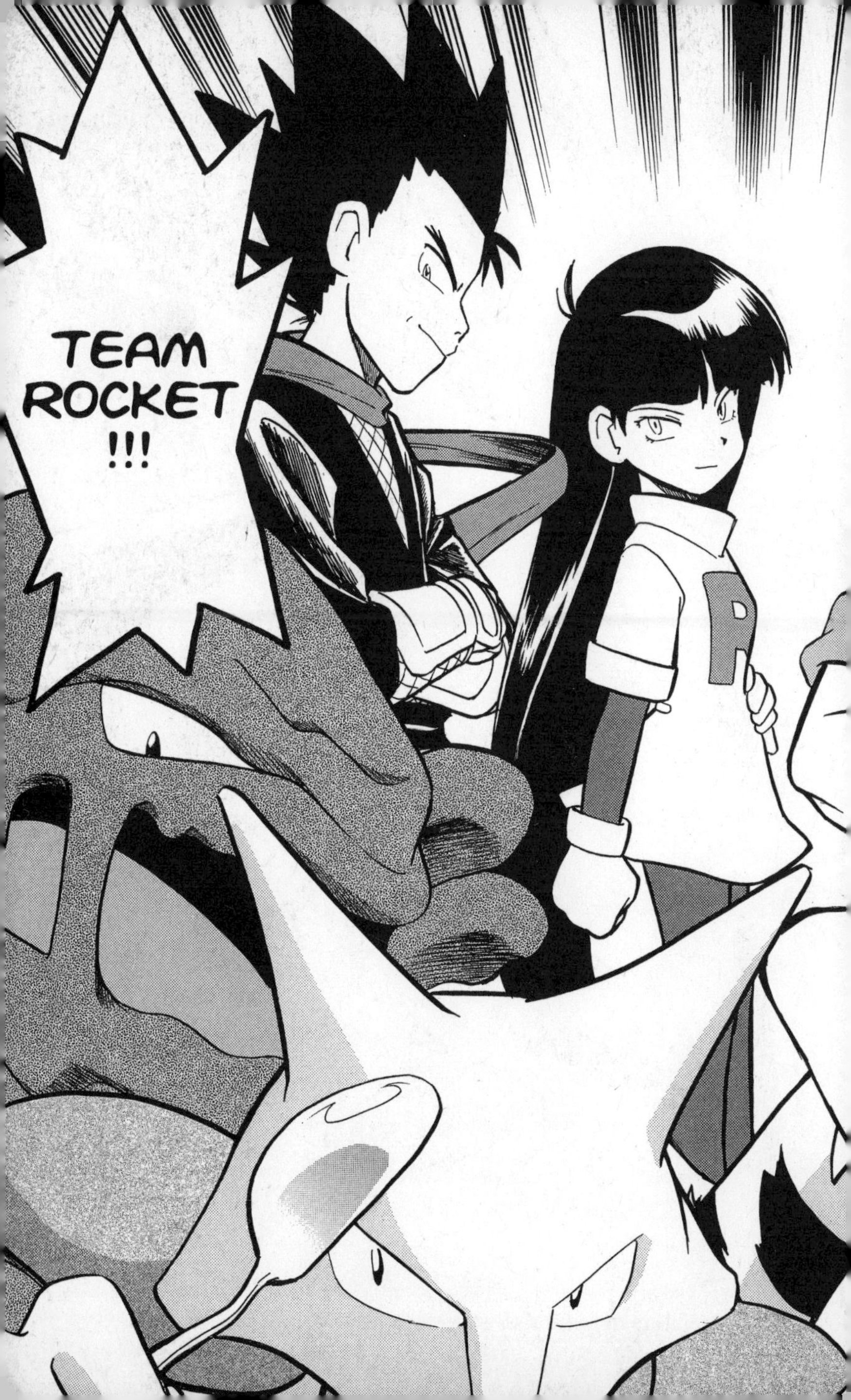
TEAM ROCKET !!!

NEXT VOLUME PREVIEW!

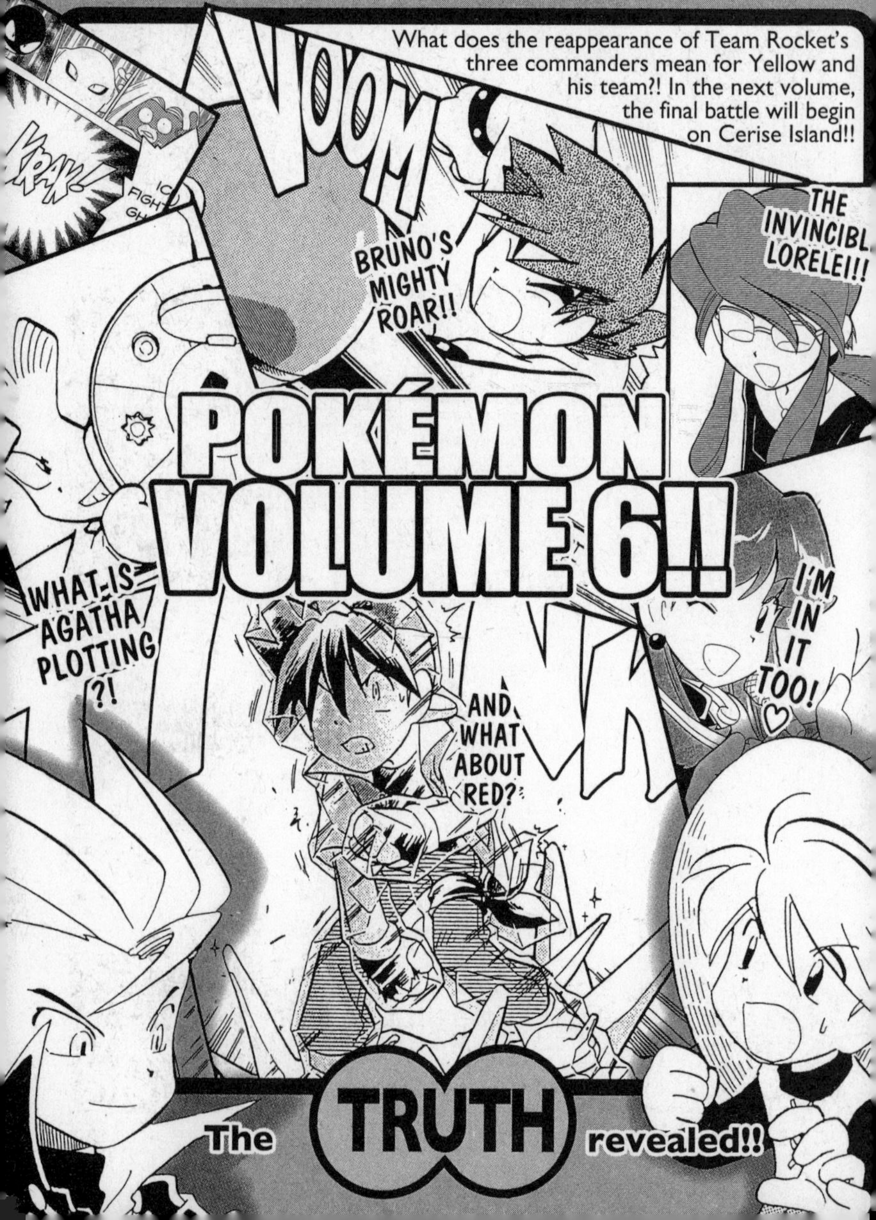
What does the reappearance of Team Rocket's three commanders mean for Yellow and his team?! In the next volume, the final battle will begin on Cerise Island!!
THE INVINCIBL LORELEI!!!
BRUNO'S MIGHTY ROAR!!
VOOM
KRAK!
POKÉMON VOLUME 6!!
I'M IN IT TOO! ♡
AND WHAT ABOUT RED?
WHAT IS AGATHA PLOTTING?!
The TRUTH revealed!!

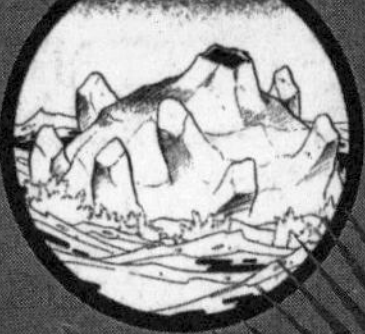

Analysis of Fighting Power

The Elite Four

It is said that every Pokémon used by the Elite Four is of a very unique breed, possessing powers beyond the norm. What are those special powers?

Ice-Type

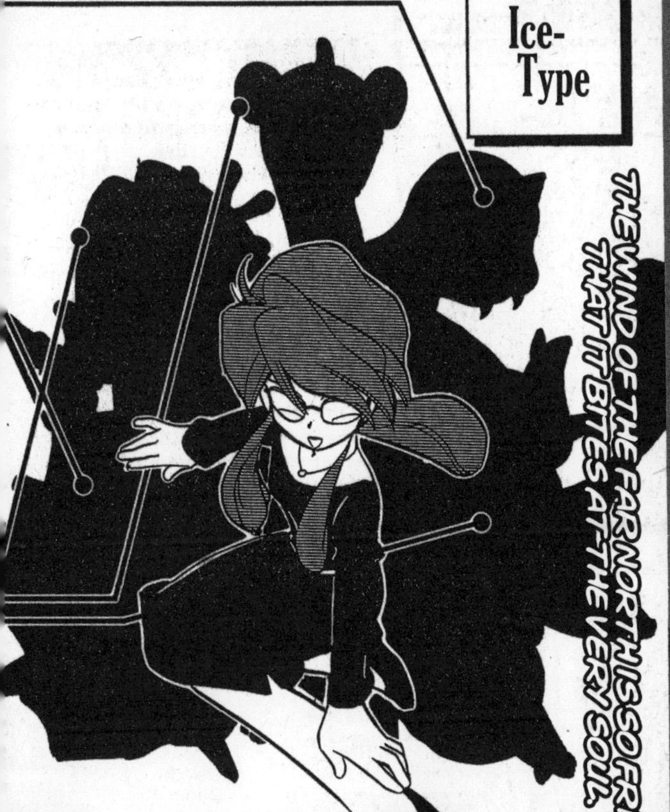

THE WIND OF THE FAR NORTH IS SO FRIGID THAT IT BITES AT THE VERY SOUL.

LORELEI

LORELEI

A PERFECTIONIST, LORELEI CANNOT ACCEPT ANY BLUNDERS IN BATTLE STRATEGY. SHE IS A COLD-BLOODED HUNTER, COOLLY TRACKING PIKA AND YELLOW. SHE ALSO SETS A VARIETY OF TRAPS TO PREVENT ENEMY MOVEMENT.

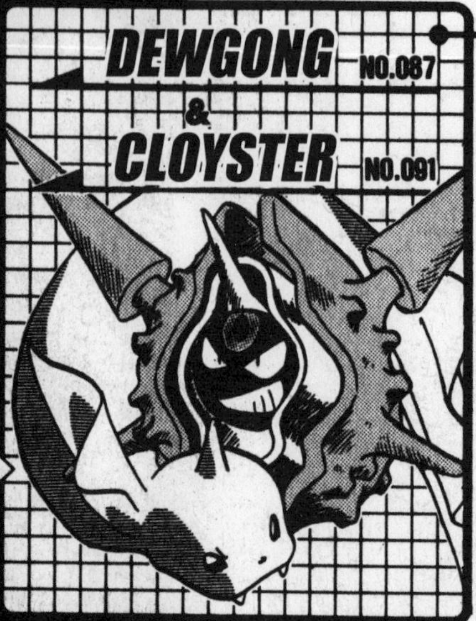
DEWGONG NO.087
&
CLOYSTER NO.091

DEWGONG

Super tracking ability that can be used over land and sea!

A normal Dewgong can zoom through water at eight knots, but Lorelei's Dewgong can maintain such speeds on land as well!

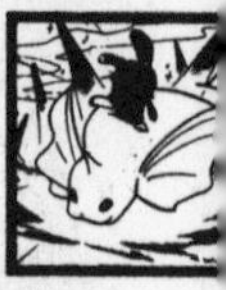

▶ Creates a path of ice to pursue a quarry for as long as necessary.

CLOYSTER

The Ice Missile, weapon of massive destruction

Combining Cloyster's and Dewgong's powers, this attack can only be used by Lorelei.

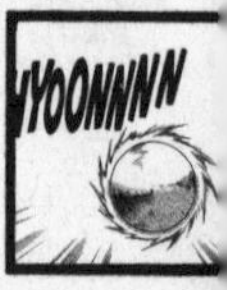
YOONNNN

▶ A devastating missile that slices easily through bedrock.

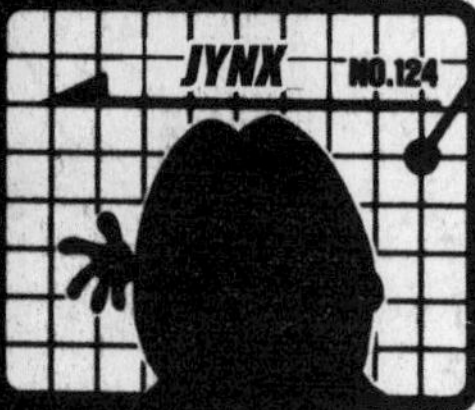
JYNX NO.124

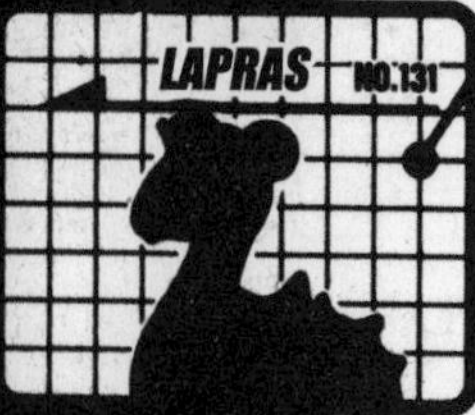
LAPRAS NO.131

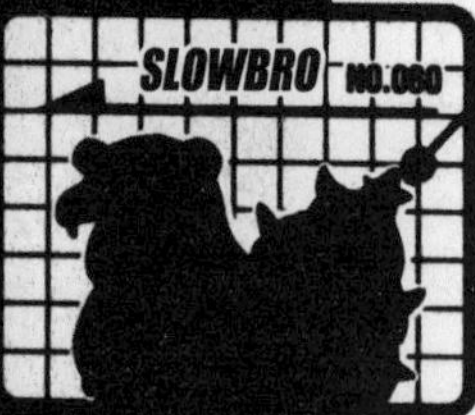
SLOWBRO NO.080

What about the powers of Lorelei's remaining Pokémon?

JYNX
LAPRAS
SLOWBRO

All have yet to appear, but they are sure to be powerful opponents...

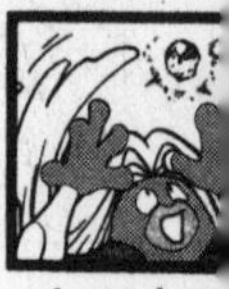

▲Just take a look at this move by Jyr

THE DANGERS OF A WOMAN'S MAKEUP!!

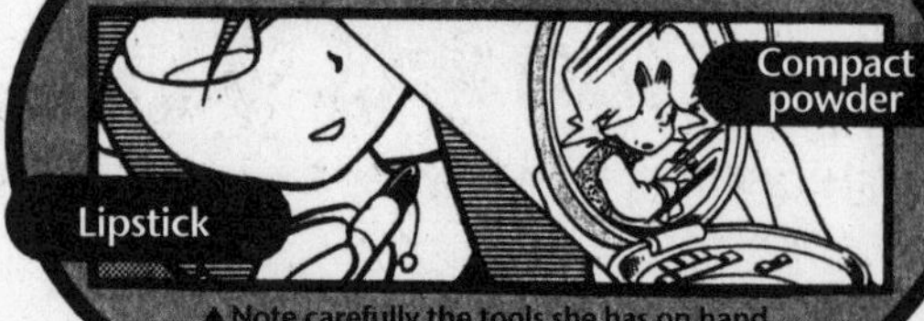
Compact powder
Lipstick

▲Note carefully the tools she has on hand. A compact that becomes a communicator, and apparently Lorelei is known to use her lipstick in some attacks!

CHECK!

Fighting-Type

Analysis of Fighting Power

ALWAYS IN SEARCH OF A WORTHY OPPONENT AND INTENSE BATTLE

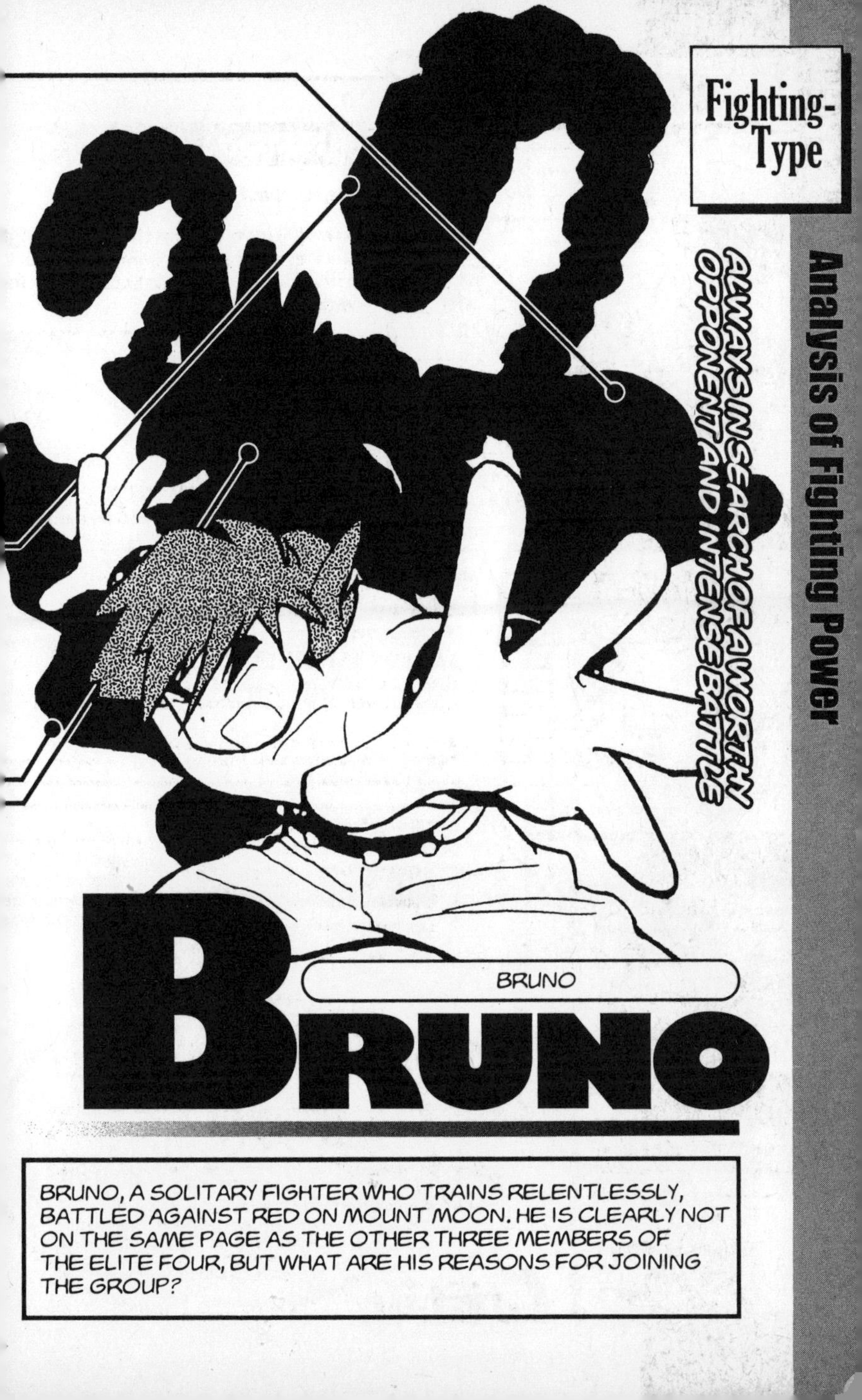

BRUNO

BRUNO

BRUNO, A SOLITARY FIGHTER WHO TRAINS RELENTLESSLY, BATTLED AGAINST RED ON MOUNT MOON. HE IS CLEARLY NOT ON THE SAME PAGE AS THE OTHER THREE MEMBERS OF THE ELITE FOUR, BUT WHAT ARE HIS REASONS FOR JOINING THE GROUP?

BRUNO'S TEAM

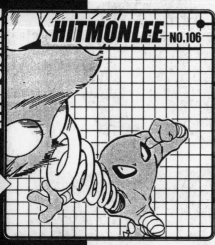

HITMONLEE NO.106

HITMONLEE

Super elastic hands and feet

Bruno's Hitmonlee can change the lengt of its legs and arms. It is impossible to predict which of its four limbs will sprin forth to attack.

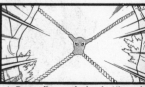

▲ Depending on the battle, Hitmonle limbs can be used for means other than attacking!

ONIX NO.095

ONIX

A giant with the ability to disguise its massive body!

Bruno's Onix is said to have transformational powers as it skulks underground.

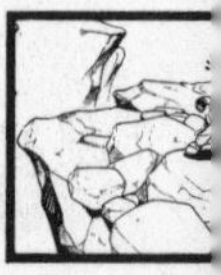

▶ What could this be? Did something strange happen in the battle between Bruno and Red...?!

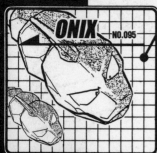

MACHAMP NO.068

HITMONCHAN NO.107

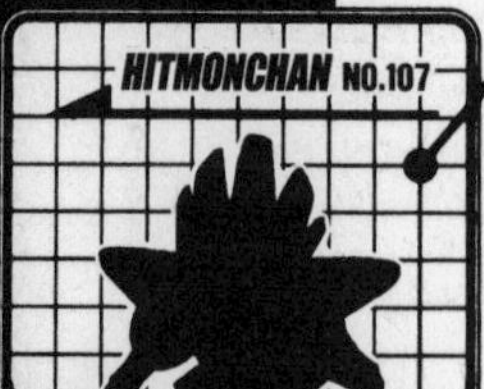

What about the powers of Bruno's remaining Pokémon?

MACHAMP

HITMONCHAN

There are two other Pokémon in Bruno's "Fighting" corps! We all like to discover the powers, but only time will tell!

CHECK!

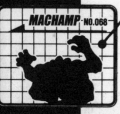

A MODIFIED WEAPON THAT ENABLES PRECISION TIMING!

Poké Ball Nunchuck

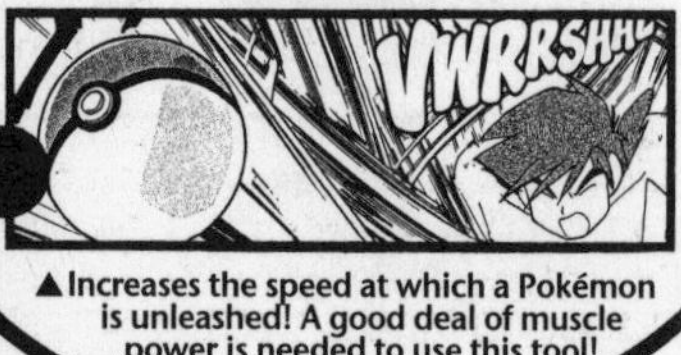

▲ Increases the speed at which a Pokémon is unleashed! A good deal of muscle power is needed to use this tool!

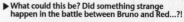

Ghost-Type

Analysis of Fighting Power

AN INVISIBLE ENEMY WHO STRIKES FROM THE SHADOWS

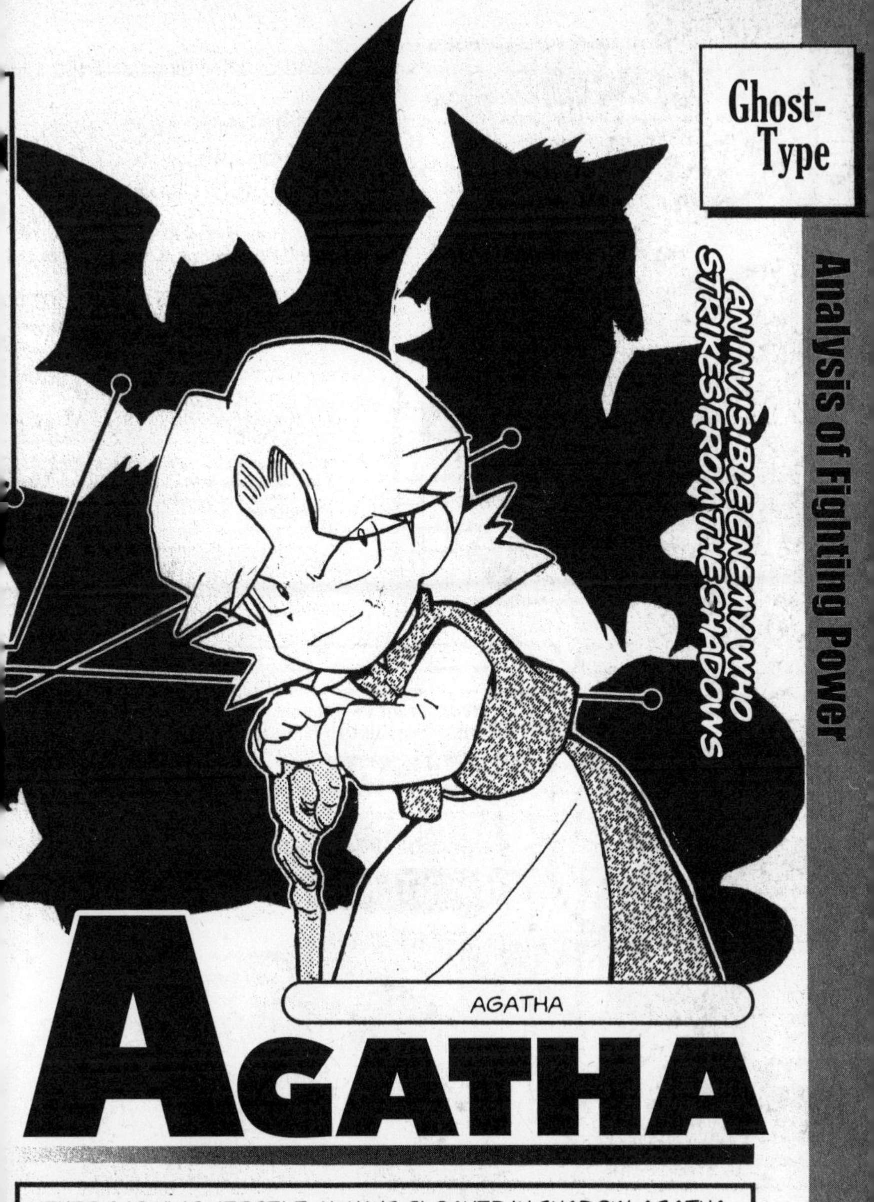

AGATHA

AGATHA

NEVER SHOWING HERSELF, ALWAYS CLOAKED IN SHADOW, AGATHA IS AN OMINOUS FOE WHO COMPLETES ANY MISSION WITH CALCULATED PRECISION! AT HER DISPOSAL IS A TEAM OF GHOSTLY POKÉMON THAT HAVE GAINED DARK POWER FROM LIVING NEAR THE TOXIC RUINS OF AN INDUSTRIAL AREA! EVEN NOW, AGATHA IS IN THE PROCESS OF CONCOCTING SOME DASTARDLY PLAN!!

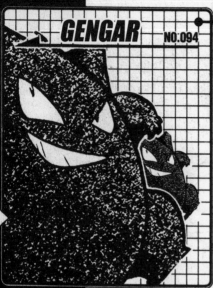

GENGAR NO:094

DEWGONG

The Coffin of Death

Gengar's Hypnosis attack not only puts an opponent to sleep but also traps them in a coffin of black mist. It is a terrifying power that causes torment to both Pokémon and humans alike!

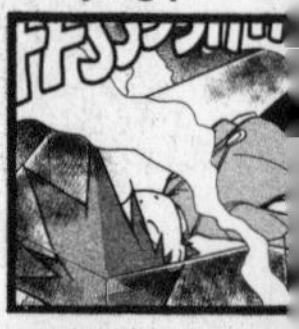

▶ Combined with Dream Eater, this attack is even more terrifying!

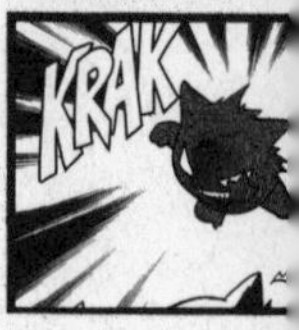

▶ When followed by a Night Shade blast, such a rapid fire of Ghost attacks cannot be withstood!

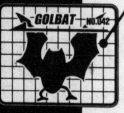

GOLBAT NO.042

What about the powers of Agatha's remaining Pokémon?

GOLBAT

ARBOK

HAUNTER

There are two Poison-type Pokémon that Agatha uses. Is this an ambush?!

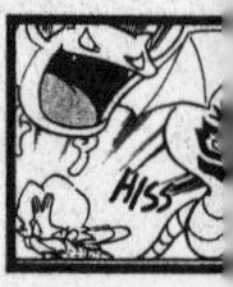

▲ It is only a matter of time before Agatha full power is revealed!!

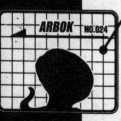

ARBOK NO.024

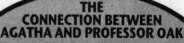

THE CONNECTION BETWEEN AGATHA AND PROFESSOR OAK

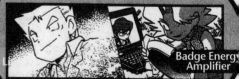

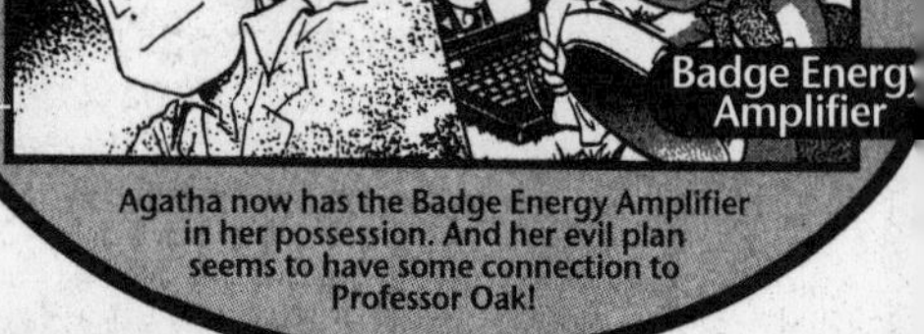

Badge Energy Amplifier

Agatha now has the Badge Energy Amplifier in her possession. And her evil plan seems to have some connection to Professor Oak!

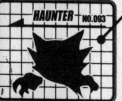

HAUNTER NO.093

CHECK!

Dragon-Type

Analysis of Fighting Power

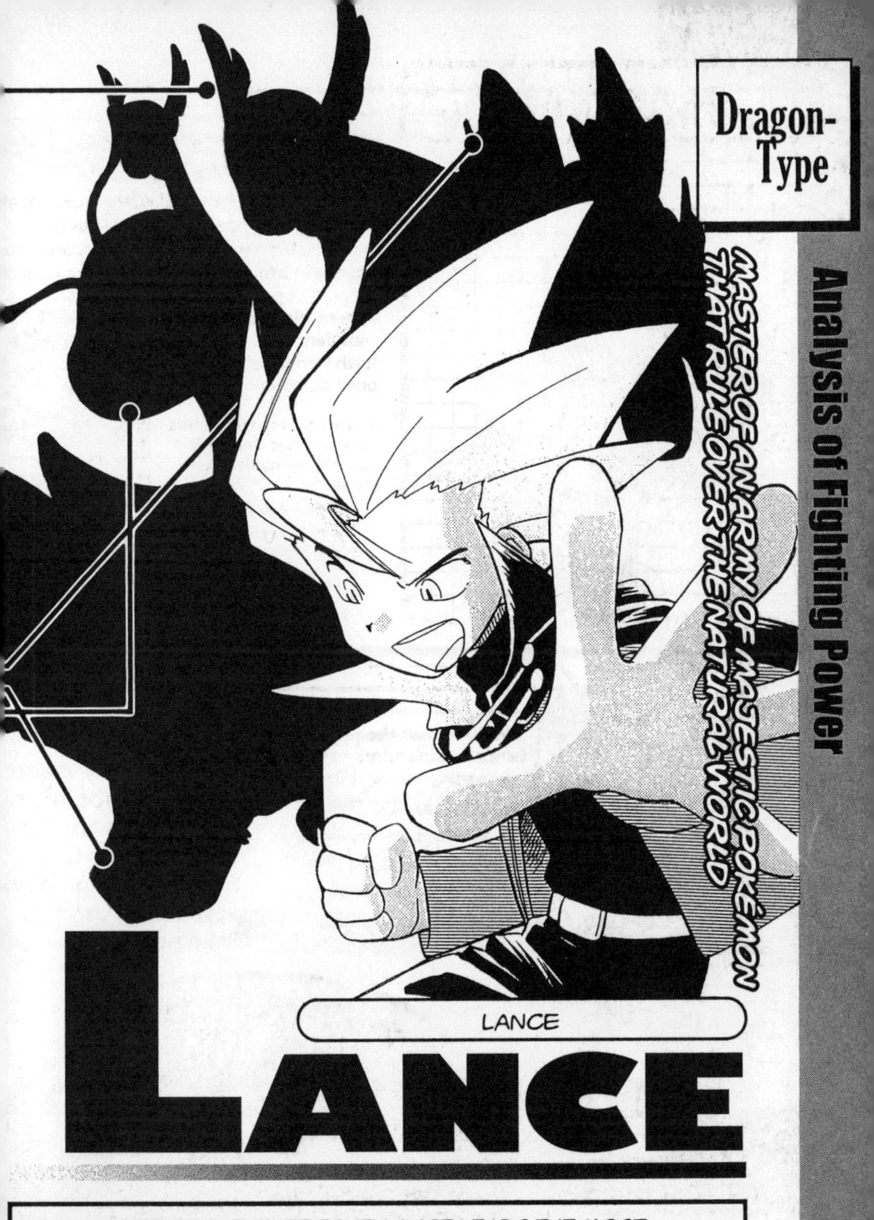
MASTER OF AN ARMY OF MAJESTIC POKÉMON
THAT RULE OVER THE NATURAL WORLD

LANCE

LANCE

COMMANDER OF THE ELITE FOUR, LANCE LEADS THE MOST POWERFUL OF ALL ARMIES—THE DRAGON POKÉMON! HIS ULTIMATE GOAL IS TO CREATE A WORLD WHERE POKÉMON CAN LIVE IN PEACE WITHOUT HUMAN INTERFERENCE. LANCE HAS CRAFTED A PLAN FOR THE ANNIHILATION OF HUMANITY. WHAT TRUTH COULD POSSIBLY HIDE BEHIND SUCH AN EXTREME DECLARATION?

LANCE'S TEAM

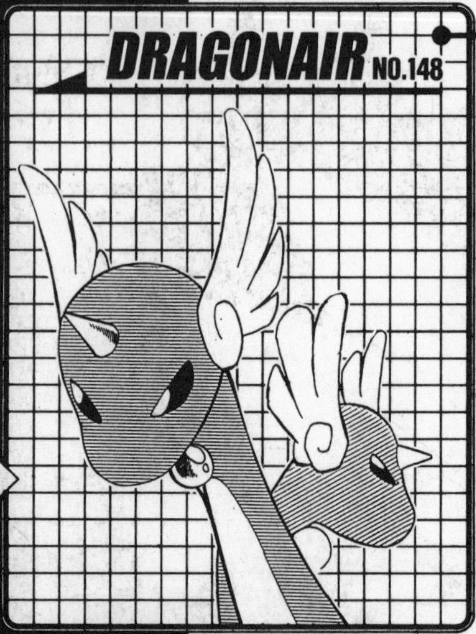
DRAGONAIR NO.148

DRAGONAIR

A weather-manipulating aura that summons thunderclouds.

True, the Dragonair is known for its ability to change weather, but under the command of Lance, this power is off the charts. Lance corners his enemies with thunderstorms and calls forth tornadoes using just one Pokémon!

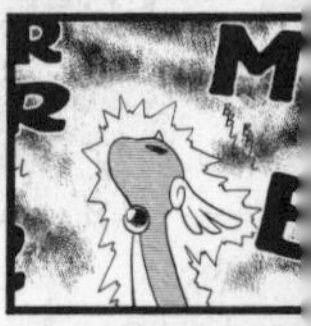
RR
M

▶ When the mysterious aura gathers around Dragonair's horn, the sky suddenly turns overcast!

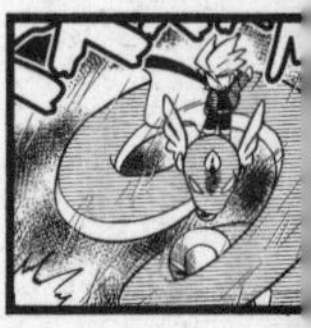

▶ The weather itself becomes a weapon to overwhelm Dragonair's opponents!

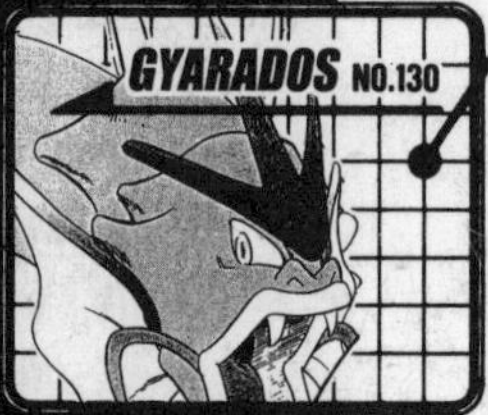
GYARADOS NO.130

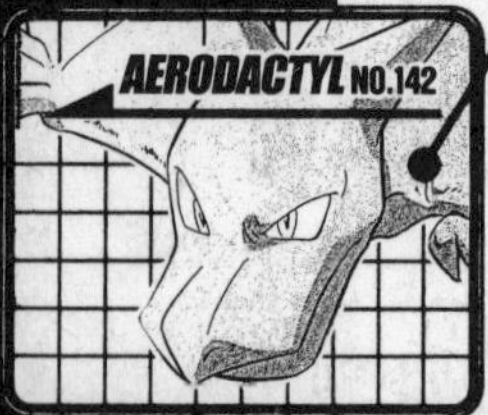
AERODACTYL NO.142

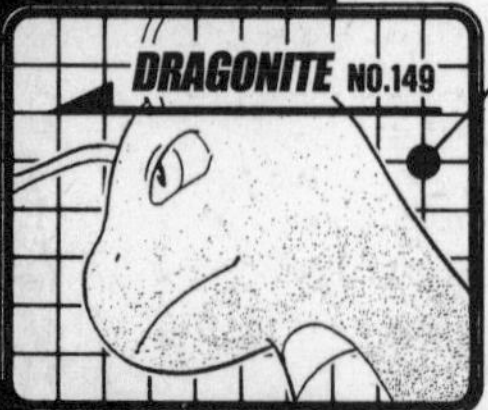
DRAGONITE NO.149

What about the powers of Lance's remaining Pokémon?

- GYARADOS
- AERODACTYL
- DRAGONITE

Although these Pokémon have made an appearance, their power levels are still unknown. Are they capable of combining powers like Lorelei's Pokémon?!

HIS GOAL IS TO ANNIHILATE HUMANITY!!

THE TERRIFYING PLAN

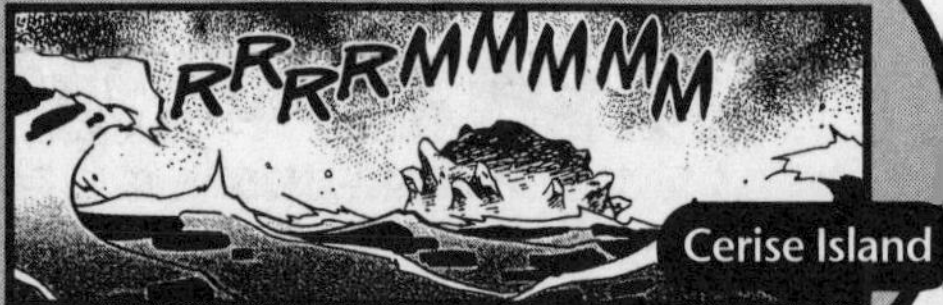
RRRRMMMMM
Cerise Island

▶The solitary island said to be the headquarters of the Elite Four. There seems to be an important reason behind Lance's choice of location...

CHECK!

ADVENTURE ROUTE MAP 5

JOURNEY BY BOAT FROM THE VAST PLAINS OF ROCK MOUNTAIN TO VERMILION CITY. AFTER MASTERING "SURF," TRAVEL ON TO SEAFOAM ISLANDS AND CINNABAR ISLAND. FINALLY, ARRIVE AT THE SITE OF THE BIG BATTLE...

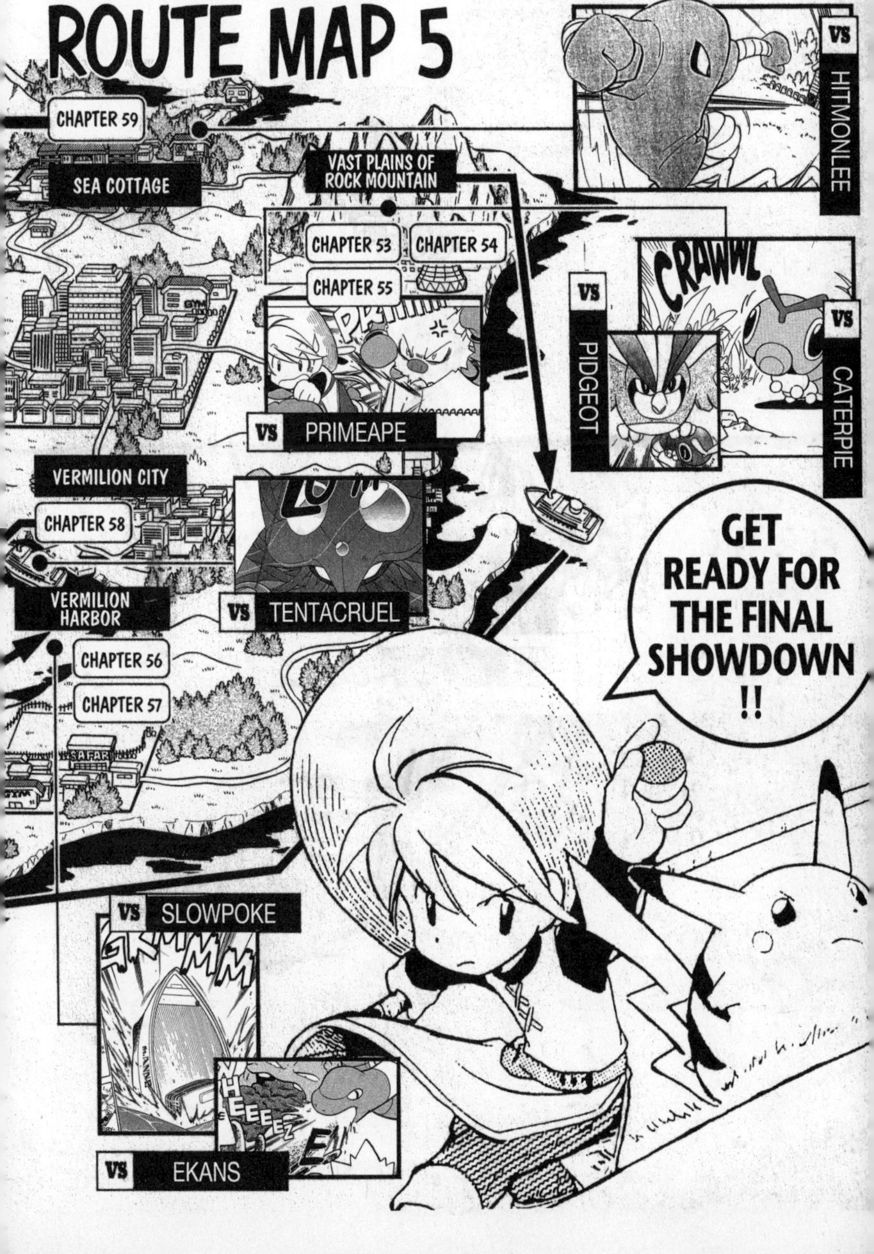

VS HITMONLEE
CHAPTER 59
SEA COTTAGE
VAST PLAINS OF ROCK MOUNTAIN
CHAPTER 53
CHAPTER 54
CHAPTER 55
VS PRIMEAPE
CRAWWL
VS CATERPIE
VS PIDGEOT
GYM
VERMILION CITY
CHAPTER 58
VERMILION HARBOR
VS TENTACRUEL
GET READY FOR THE FINAL SHOWDOWN !!
CHAPTER 56
CHAPTER 57
SAFARI
VS SLOWPOKE
VS EKANS

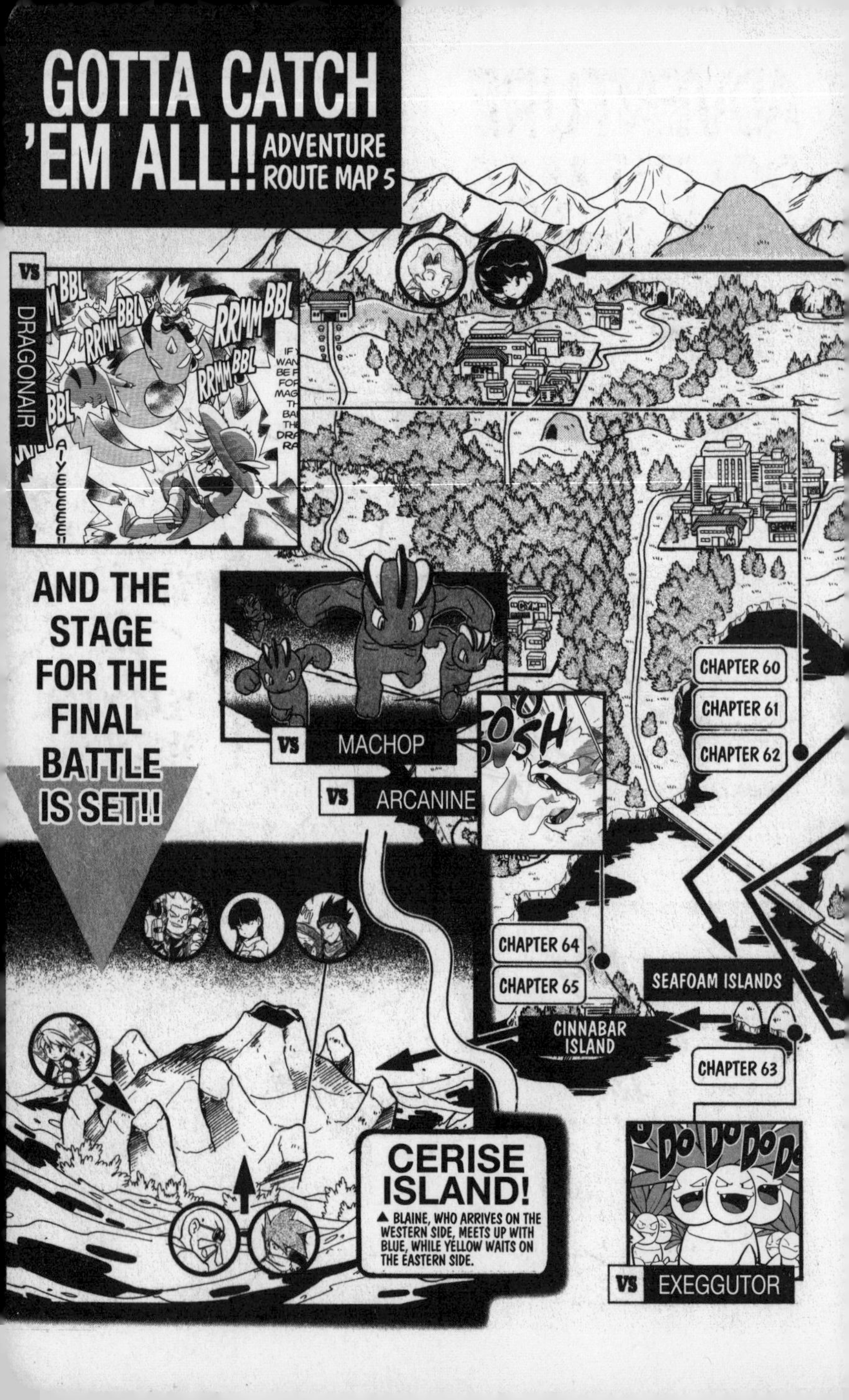
GOTTA CATCH 'EM ALL!! ADVENTURE ROUTE MAP 5
VS DRAGONAIR
BBL
RRMM
BBL
RRMM
BBL
RRMM BBL
BBL
AIYEEEEE!!
AND THE STAGE FOR THE FINAL BATTLE IS SET!!
VS MACHOP
VS ARCANINE
FOOSH
CHAPTER 60
CHAPTER 61
CHAPTER 62
CHAPTER 64
CHAPTER 65
SEAFOAM ISLANDS
CINNABAR ISLAND
CHAPTER 63
DO DO DO DO
VS EXEGGUTOR
CERISE ISLAND!
▲ BLAINE, WHO ARRIVES ON THE WESTERN SIDE, MEETS UP WITH BLUE, WHILE YELLOW WAITS ON THE EASTERN SIDE.

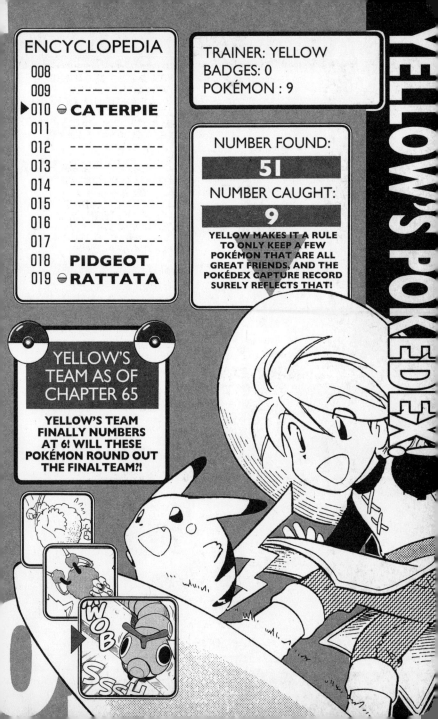

YELLOW'S POKÉDEX!

ENCYCLOPEDIA

008 ------------
009 ------------
▶010 ◓ **CATERPIE**
011 ------------
012 ------------
013 ------------
014 ------------
015 ------------
016 ------------
017 ------------
018 **PIDGEOT**
019 ◓ **RATTATA**

TRAINER: YELLOW
BADGES: 0
POKÉMON : 9

NUMBER FOUND:

51

NUMBER CAUGHT:

9

YELLOW MAKES IT A RULE TO ONLY KEEP A FEW POKÉMON THAT ARE ALL GREAT FRIENDS, AND THE POKÉDEX CAPTURE RECORD SURELY REFLECTS THAT!

YELLOW'S TEAM AS OF CHAPTER 65

YELLOW'S TEAM FINALLY NUMBERS AT 6! WILL THESE POKÉMON ROUND OUT THE FINALTEAM?!

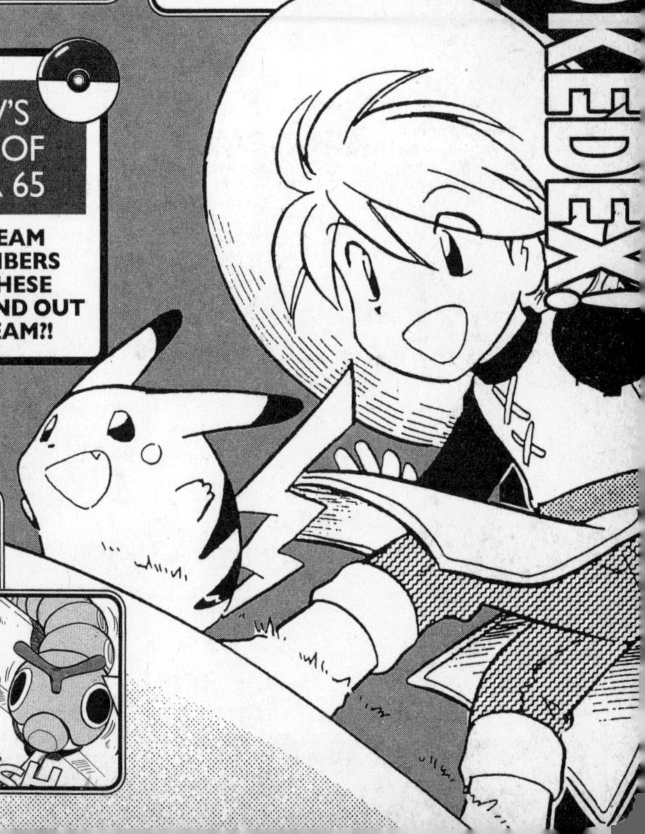

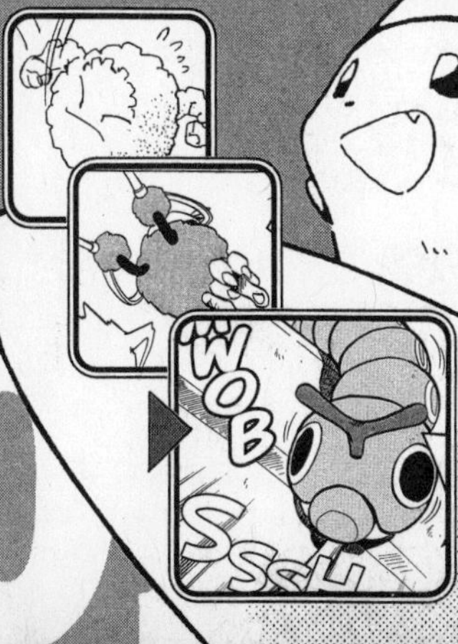
WOB

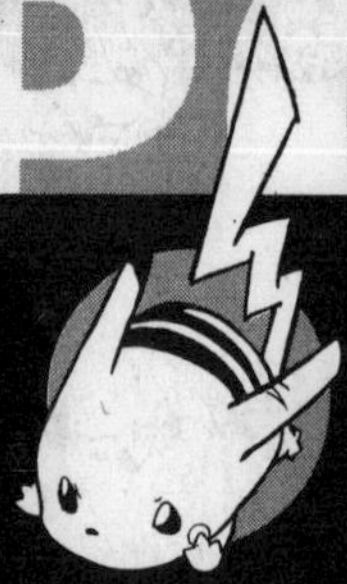

PIKACHU: L58
Type 1 / Electric
Trainer / Red
NO.025

IN THE MIDDLE OF A LIFE-OR-DEATH BATTLE AGAINST LANCE, PIKA MANAGED TO MASTER THE "SURF" MOVE! HAVING CONQUERED THE WATER, PIKA GOES FULL STEAM AHEAD TO REUNITE WITH RED!!

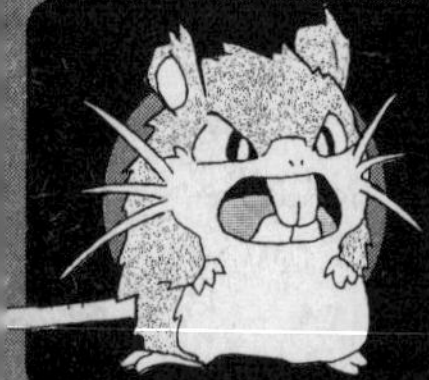

RATICATE: L10
Type 1 / Normal
Trainer / Yellow
NO.020

RATTY WAS THE FIRST TO SHOW YELLOW HOW A POKÉMON'S EVOLUTION OCCURS. THE TEETH OF A RILED-UP RATICATE HAVE THE POWER TO SLICE EVEN A GIANT SHIP IN TWO!!

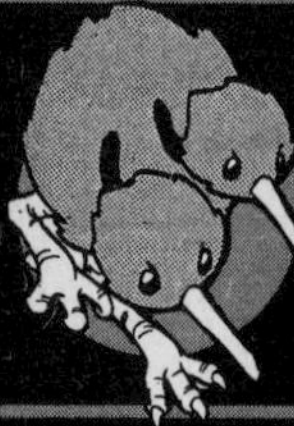

DODUO: L13
Type 1 / Normal
Type 2 / Flying
Trainer / Yellow
NO.084

WITH TRAINING, DODY'S SUPER SPEED HAS BECOME EVEN MORE POWERFUL! A DEFINING MOMENT CAME WHEN DODY USED ITS LEGS AS A SPRING-BOARD AND LAUNCHED PIKA ALL THE WAY TO THE OCEAN!

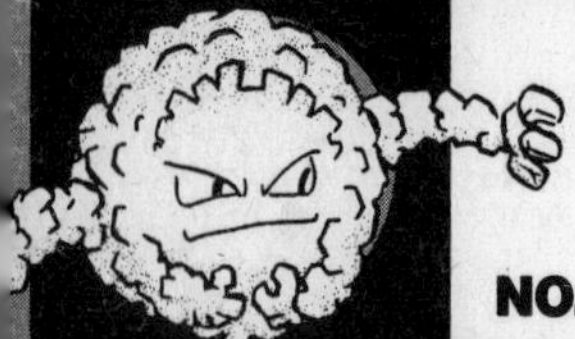

GRAVELER: L35
Type 1 /Normal
Type 2 /Ground
Trainer / Brock
NO.075

GRAVVY THE GRAVELER LIKES TO SHOW OFF ITS STRENGTH! WE CAN ONLY TIP OUR HATS IN ADMIRATION AFTER GRAVVY EFFORTLESSLY HELD THE SHIP S.S. *ANNE* ALOFT…!!

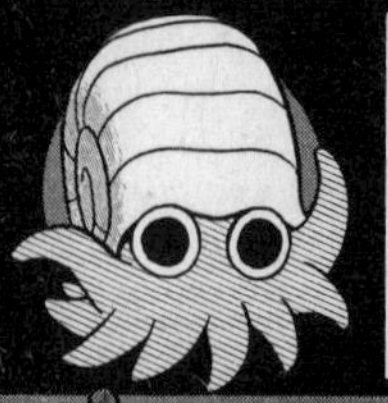

OMANYTE: L38
Type 1 / Rock
Type 2 / Water
Trainer / Misty
NO.138

OMNY, A POKÉMON SPECIALIZING IN UNDER-WATER BATTLES AND FREEZE ATTACKS, HAS BECOME QUITE A DEPENDABLE MEMBER OF YELLOW'S TEAM!!

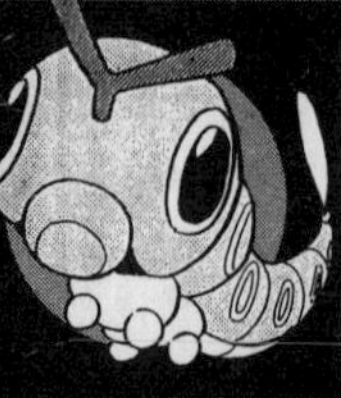

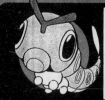

CATERPIE: L11
Type 1 / Bug
Trainer / Yellow
NO.010

SWIMMING RINGS, FISHING STRING, LIFELINES... ALTHOUGH "KITTY" IS STILL LOW LEVEL, THE STURDY STRING THAT IT SPEWS HAS AN INFINITE VARIETY OF USES!!

Message from
Hidenori Kusaka

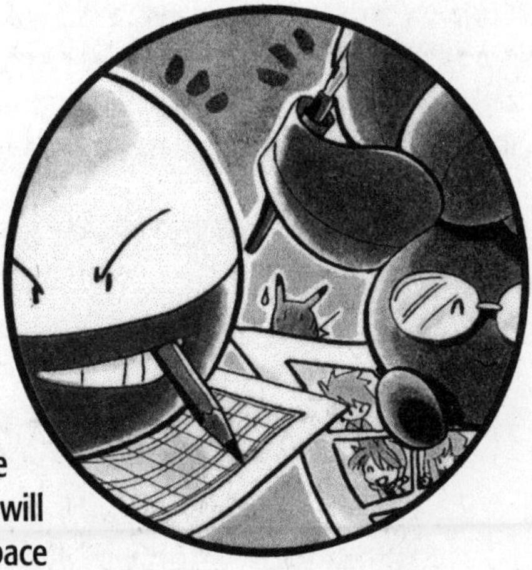

In the ever-expanding world of Pokémon, from Game Boy to Nintendo 64, I'm just bursting with excitement! Pokémon Snap and Stadium have me bouncing around like Pokémon Pinball! The manga will heat up too in order to keep pace with the energy of the new games coming out! So keep rooting for us!!

Message from
MATO

This year ('99) is the third anniversary of the release of Pokémon on Nintendo Game Boy! And since the third-anniversary color is orange, there are limited edition orange Game Boys being sold. And that's why the cover for volume 5 is orange too!!

More Adventures Coming Soon...

Pokémon trainer Red has vanished... Yellow Caballero and Pikachu's search leads them to the mysterious headquarters of the Elite Four on Cerise Island. Who has the baddest Pokémon around...? There's only one way to find out!

And watch out for Team Rocket, Pikachu... *Are they your allies or your enemies now?*

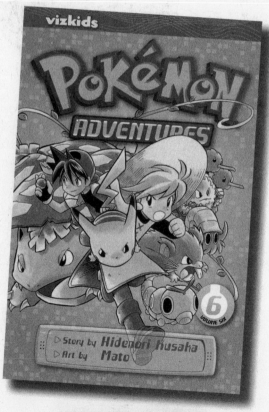

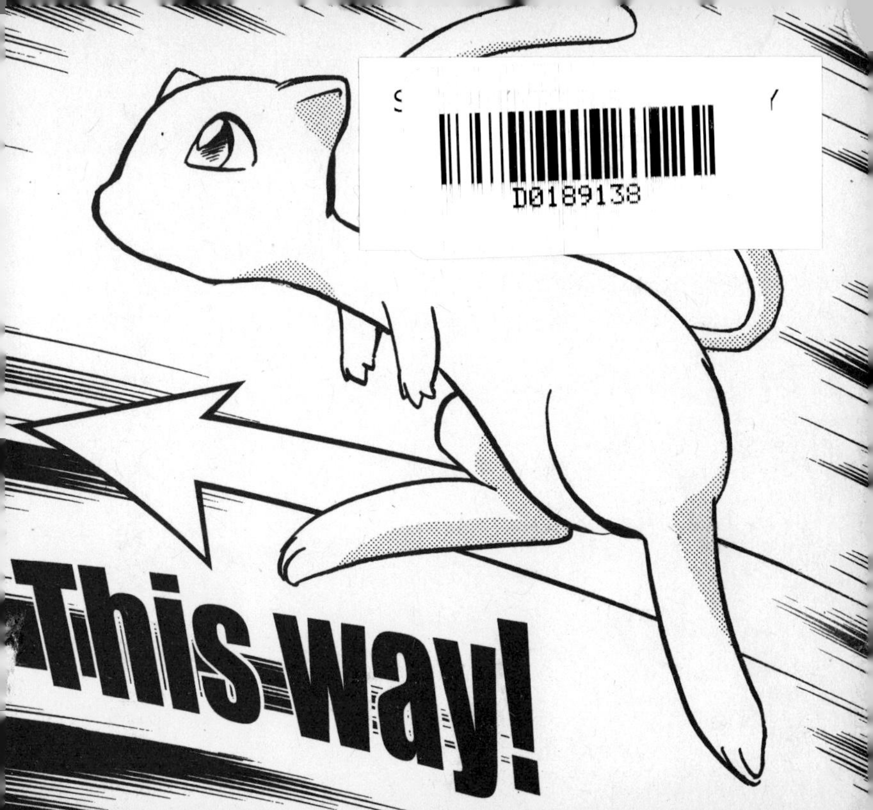
This way!

THIS IS THE END OF THIS GRAPHIC NOVEL!

To properly enjoy this VIZ Media graphic novel, please turn it around and begin reading from right to left.

This book has been printed in the original Japanese format in order to preserve the orientation of the original artwork. Have fun with it!

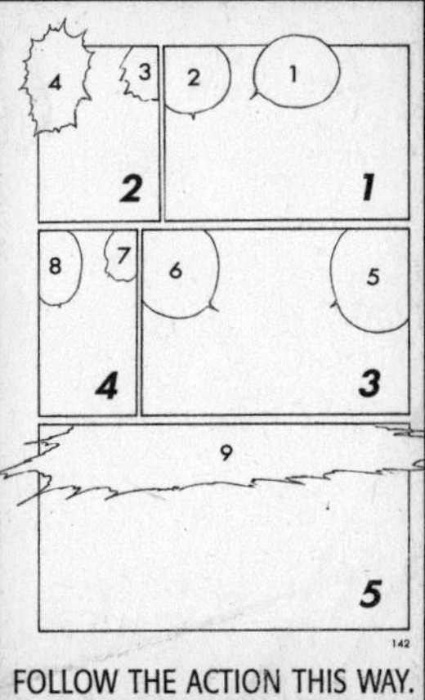
FOLLOW THE ACTION THIS WAY.